MATTER OF TIME

MATTER OF TIME

DANIEL CAINE

Copyright © 2025 Daniel Caine

The moral right of the author has been asserted.

Apart from any fair dealing for the purposes of research or private study, or criticism or review, as permitted under the Copyright, Designs and Patents Act 1988, this publication may only be reproduced, stored or transmitted, in any form or by any means, with the prior permission in writing of the publishers, or in the case of reprographic reproduction in accordance with the terms of licences issued by the Copyright Licensing Agency. Enquiries concerning reproduction outside those terms should be sent to the publishers.

This is a work of fiction. Names, characters, businesses, places, events and incidents are either the products of the author's imagination or used in a fictitious manner. Any resemblance to actual persons, living or dead, or actual events is purely coincidental.

Troubador Publishing Ltd
Unit E2 Airfield Business Park,
Harrison Road, Market Harborough,
Leicestershire LE16 7UL
Tel: 0116 279 2299
Email: books@troubador.co.uk
Web: www.troubador.co.uk

ISBN 978 1 83628 340 9

British Library Cataloguing in Publication Data.
A catalogue record for this book is available from the British Library.

The manufacturer's authorised representative in the EU for product safety is Authorised Rep Compliance Ltd, 71 Lower Baggot Street, Dublin D02 P593 Ireland (www.arccompliance.com).

Printed and bound by CPI Group (UK) Ltd, Croydon, CR0 4YY
Typeset in 11pt Minion Pro by Troubador Publishing Ltd, Leicester, UK

For Den and Layla

1

The Present

The blackout was total, an extreme darkness devoid of even the odd stray photon, a darkness not of this natural world. Relief from the sensory deprivation imposed on those gathered came solely from a sibilant background whisper being punctuated every now and then by the steady controlled delivery of a man's voice that defied every Law of God. No one dared move. No one dared breathe.

The hissing whisper stopped. A momentary silence. Nothingness. And with a terrifying electrical crack of ionising air, a cacophony from hell suddenly distressed the room with the screams and yells of that man, who was surely being burnt alive by some invisible flame. A collective paralysis momentarily prevented any immediate reaction, but within seconds, the darkness was alive with panic, confusion and heart-in-throat pleas for God Himself to help. The switch to the dimmest of lamps was finally located, and a veil of diffuse red light was cast over the scene – the naked man was now writhing in agony on the floor at the feet of the onlookers, while across the far side of the room a woman could be seen darting for the securely locked door.

In the earthlier darkness of silhouettes and shadows in the corridor outside, the woman's trembling hand reached for the phone perched on top of a wooden hallstand, and in her panic, she attempted to punch in a number several times before finally making the right connection.

"*Please…* Pick up!" she pleaded, her distress growing with each unanswered ring. The silence that had descended in the adjacent room now alarmed her more than those screams of agony had. "It's Barbara!" she finally blurted, before the person on the other end of the line had even finished uttering their *Hello*. "You have to come right away… I don't know what to do!"

St Mary's Accident & Emergency Department, located in a new multi-level annexe at the rear of the main hospital building, was quieter than normal. The evening's prolonged heavy rain had kept the usual suspects at home, making for a long tedious shift. But at least one or two beds had been freed up for those genuinely in need of medical attention.

Thirty-two-year-old Dr Nathan Carter was sitting at a desk in a side office gazing intently at the open wallet in his hand, his piercing blue eyes fixed on a small photograph of his parents, his elder brother and himself in a staged pose of happy family smiles held just a second or two longer than any camera shutter should really have allowed. It was obvious which of the siblings had been adopted. Caleb – then nine –

appeared pale, chubby and unkempt, despite obvious last-second attempts to flatten his unruly blond hair; seven-year-old Nathan, on the other hand, presented to the lens with the compliant jet-black hair of his mother, the unblemished tanned skin of his father, and a slighter build that promised athleticism and perhaps an easier passage through life all round. As it turned out, the camera hadn't lied.

"You still here, you crazy bastard? It's already gone nine. Shouldn't you have finished by now?"

The voice from the open doorway redirected Nathan's attention.

"I'd seriously be thinking of getting outta here before the shit hits the fan. It's way too quiet for my liking!"

Nathan closed his wallet and gave a friendly nod, half in agreement and half still preoccupied with his own thoughts. "Hey, Adam. I'm almost done. A patient's just been shown into 3. I thought I'd just check it out before I go."

"*Aaaah*, yes, the little cutie in Cubicle 3." Adam smiled. "I'll admit that I couldn't help but check out *her* chart as I walked past. I'm on it. Get outta here, Nathan. I'll catch you tomorrow."

Adam Faulkner was a hulk of a man whose appearance spoke more of pubs, rugby tackles in Saturday afternoon mud and the long hours spent by his forbears down a mineshaft. His dirty blond hair wasn't really unkempt; it just somehow seemed that way. And no matter how starched and pristine the white coat hanging in his locker appeared to be, when donned, something of his tough working-class upbringing in the northeast of England would always project through. What you saw was what you got. He reminded Nathan in some ways of the person his brother, Caleb, might have grown up to be, had events turned out differently. That's probably why he'd developed an instant affinity for Adam and had come to count him as a trusted friend.

Nathan glanced at the screen of his phone and decided that it really was time to make a move, and with his white clinical coat draped over his arm, he headed for the rear exit of the building.

The ambulance bay and adjacent car park were deserted and free of the usual clutter of police vehicles and mobile response units, and the barrage of heavy water droplets erupting across the surface of pooling rain had now transformed the black expanse of newly laid tarmac into a temporarily obscured mirror to the heavily ominous sky. Nathan paused, holding the door open for a few moments, wondering whether to chance the downpour. But before he had the opportunity to decide on a move, his focus was drawn to the figure of a man covered by a sheet slumped against the outside wall a few metres away.

Nathan yelled for assistance to a nurse back in the corridor and then rushed to the aid of the man, who was completely unresponsive. Within seconds, a team of orderlies and medics had descended on the scene to help heave the rain-drenched naked frame of the well-built man in his early fifties onto a trolley.

"I did warn you that you should've left earlier," came Adam's voice out of the controlled chaos as the trolley trundled its way back through the outer doors and into the fluorescent lighting of A&E. "What the hell!"

Adam had just noticed the large red welt of a burn covering the naked man's entire abdomen and the more disturbing sight of ligature marks to his wrists and ankles.

But before anyone else could react to the observation, one of the medics shouted, "No pulse!"

"Contact the police," Adam barked, unfazed by the escalation as he began to compress the man's chest cavity with ease while still on the move. "They're gonna be needed whether this one makes it or not!"

Nathan allowed the procession to speed ahead, slipping his white coat back on again as he walked. Everything that could be done was being done, and he had already played his part by finding the man just in time. He had to stay to see this one through, though. Since the man had been found in such suspicious circumstances and without any identification, the police would undoubtedly want a statement.

Several kilometres away, a Greater Manchester Police patrol car, windscreen wipers barely keeping pace, turned into a long narrow stretch of tarmac bordered on one side by sections of litter-laden temporary metal fencing that had seemingly been erected and then left forgotten for years. Fifty metres along the access road, the tarmac opened out into a disused car park fronting an abandoned four-hundred-year-old red-brick manor house – the edifice, immune from demolition, having been encroached upon by haphazard development to become almost completely surrounded and hidden from view by unsightly concrete office blocks and commercial warehousing to its rear.

The officer made his way over to join the huddle of security guards and paramedics already on scene.

"What've we got?"

"A first for me," the attending paramedic answered. "Take a look."

The officer shone a torch onto the naked body of a slimly-built-yet-muscular man in his mid-thirties who was lying on the wet tarmac, speaking incoherently and making weak unsuccessful attempts to stand.

"Take it easy, mate. Try to keep still for me."

"Probably an overdose," the second paramedic added, "but take a look at the ligature marks to his wrists and ankles. He's been restrained."

The beam of the officer's torch scanned the length of the man's body, lingering on each of his wrists and ankles, before scanning back to illuminate the torso. There it revealed an extensive burn covering the man's entire abdomen.

"So you saw nothing. No vehicles? No persons acting suspiciously?"

"Absolutely nothing. I was just leaving at the end of my shift... and there he was."

It had been over an hour since the impromptu admission into hospital, and for the past five minutes Nathan had been having the same circular conversation with the investigating detective who'd been called in. The man's eyes were intense, his pupils completely indistinguishable from his dark-brown-almost-black irises, and the fact that he hadn't blinked once throughout their entire interaction only added to the intensity of his unreadable gaze.

"What's his condition? It'd help if we could try and identify him while we're waiting on the security footage."

Nathan knew that the senior detective was already fully aware of the man's condition and was just taking another stab at gaining access. Escaping from Detective Inspector Doug

Pullen's manner of questioning was becoming as difficult as extricating oneself from an endless length of sticky chewing gum being hopelessly transferred from the sole of a shoe to the fingers of the right hand and then frustratingly onto the fingers of the left. The man was visibly ready to pose his next enquiry before the previous answer had even been fully delivered, leaving the constant impression that he wasn't really listening to what was being said. His slicked-back receding brown hair and highly polished shoes gleaming in A&E's lighting spoke of a humourless lifetime's preoccupation with attention to detail and an unswerving devotion to the job. And although his clean-cut appearance outwardly suggested that he was strictly by the book and beyond reproach, a certain slyness about him suggested otherwise. Nathan felt unusually ill at ease with the man and chose his next words carefully.

"Well, he's stable but hasn't regained consciousness yet. The abdominal lesion is being assessed and Neurosurgery will be sending through a report on some scans. As for the cardiac arrest, it's hard to say. ECG looks good. But it wouldn't be appropriate to allow you access just at the moment."

"Any ideas what caused the burn?"

"None whatsoever. It really doesn't look typical. So much so that we're not even sure if it *is* a burn at this stage."

With that, the detective seemed to relent and wandered off to answer an incoming call on his phone with an abrupt, "Yes, DI Pullen…"

Nathan took the opportunity to disengage and immediately made his way up to the Intensive Care Unit located on the second floor to check on the unconscious patient once more. But, on approaching the unit, he could see some sort of commotion in the corridor up ahead.

"What's wrong?"

"He's gone!" a nurse snapped, aghast. "I swear, I was here the whole time. I only turned my back for a few moments to look at the chart, and when I turned around, the bed was empty."

Knowing the condition of the man, Nathan was more than surprised. An alert had gone out, with scores of people searching the corridors in the immediate vicinity, and only moments later, a confounded DI Pullen came running to join the scene, having already called for units to set up a perimeter.

"Damn odd," the detective said as he passed, Nathan's being the only face there that he recognised. "Who was on duty?"

Nathan motioned to the distressed young nurse fearing for her job, and not wanting to engage in another round of interrogation going nowhere, he took the opportunity to make a getaway as Pullen – events now ascertaining him of his jurisdiction – accosted the girl.

Nathan had only made it to the far end of the corridor when he was met by Adam hurriedly making his way towards the seat of the action. If the man had a fault, it was that he was inexorably drawn to life's dramas, like a moth to flames.

"I just heard!" Adam said. "But get this. I overheard that cop talking on the phone. They've found a second naked guy who's been tied up and burnt. Now he's disappeared, too, from the ambulance that was transporting him…"

Pullen's full incredulity, expressed to a colleague on the phone, had been based on sketchy information received that a driver under the influence had collided with the ambulance en route to St Mary's. And in the drug and alcohol-fuelled road rage attack that ensued, the paramedic driving had been dragged out of the cab – it taking both of the vehicle's crew to subdue and control the assailant until the police unit following came to assist. But when they returned to the wagon, the naked man under their care had disappeared.

Following Adam's latest piece of breaking news in the evening's bizarre unfolding events, Nathan was momentarily stuck for a response. "I think I'm gonna take your advice and get outta here," he finally said, turning to leave.

Pullen mulled over the incident on his way back to the station, speculating that both naked men had been involved in some kind of deviant sexual practice gone wrong. Others had to be involved. *How else could they have been found unconscious at locations kilometres from each other?* No sexual interference had been evident on the initial medical examination. But he was certain that blood samples taken would confirm recreational drugs in the system of the subject who'd vanished from ICU. It seemed quite plausible that as the man had come down from his high to find himself in a hospital bed, he had made his escape to avoid questioning – out of sight of an incompetent young nurse not being totally upfront about her negligence. It was frustrating that the hospital's CCTV coverage was confined solely to the main reception areas. The cameras outside had proven fruitless due to the torrential rain throwing a veil over the already shadowy rear of A&E, where the subject had been dumped, and the glare from an illuminating spotlight, reflecting off the unusually heavy water droplets, had only added another layer to obscure the scene.

Pullen was keen to question the drug-crazed driver arrested for attacking the ambulance crew. The detainee was likely a co-conspirator attempting to rescue the man in the back of the ambulance to prevent police from getting involved. And in all the commotion, the particular drug's half-life had seemingly allowed the unconscious man being transported in the back of the wagon to surface from his high and take the opportunity to abscond, too. It all seemed to fit.

Something didn't sit right with Pullen, though – a man perpetually suspicious of even his own thoughts and motives. There were two unsolved sex crimes on his books, along with a disturbing spike in missing young women. And while it would be unusual for a sexual predator to prey on both males and females, he couldn't dismiss the similarities in the cases and had to consider the possibility that the two naked men found were separate victims of an atypical sadistic sex offender already escalating. But that was a scenario he was reluctant to accept, at least for the time being.

2

Thirty minutes after speeding away from St Mary's, Nathan skidded his silver Audi TT to a halt – the layer of loose white stone chips on the driveway of the grandiose house he'd arrived at absorbing his haste without consequence. He grabbed a leather bag from the car's front seat and dashed across to the well-worn stone steps leading up to the imposing double front doors of the beautiful seventeenth-century property he'd visited many times before. This time, he ignored the directive of a rustic wooden sign reading '*The Sanctuary*', skilfully routed out in cursive script, which pointed left to a path running across the frontage of the house. Instead, he rapped on the front door several times and waited impatiently in a harassed stance.

Within seconds, the door opened and the familiar homely face of Barbara, framed by her halo of carefully tussled burgundy shoulder-length hair, greeted him with a strained smile and a demeanour devoid of her usual ebullience.

Nathan spoke on the move. "Where is he? Do you realise

what a predicament this has put me in? I've just had to lie to the police, for *Christ's Sake!*"

Contrary to what he had told the detective, Nathan had, in fact, been well aware of several shadowy figures waiting at the rear of A&E to ensure that the patient had been duly found and quickly attended to as arranged. Stalling for time at the end of his shift and waiting for Barbara's text had been the only way to make an exit right on cue while masking his complicity.

Barbara ushered Nathan hurriedly along to a room at the rear of the property. "I'm sorry I had to call you at work. I just didn't know what else to do."

"Well, like I said, I couldn't have done much for him here. Thank God he made it to the hospital. He might not have survived if he'd gone into cardiac arrest anywhere else. If I'd have known how serious his condition was, there's no way I would've…" Nathan suddenly thought better of recriminations. The woman had been through enough over the last few hours.

"Will you be able to stay the night?" Barbara ventured nervously. "I know you must be tired. I can set up a bed and get you some supper."

Nathan paused momentarily outside the door he had been led to and sighed, unable to prevent a faint *all is forgiven* smile from creeping into his stern expression. After all, in the short time he'd known her, she had become like a mother to him. "Of course I'll stay," he relented, leaning forwards to hug the tearing-up woman. "Just promise me that you'll call an ambulance if there's a next time."

"I promise," Barbara replied with a squeeze. "But you know what he's like with his *protocols*," she complained, with obvious long-standing frustration.

Nathan could only guess at what his unlikely friend had been involved in to have found himself fighting for his life. Theirs was an odd relationship. They had grown close over the last few months, but it was an unequal friendship. Isaac knew everything there was to know about Nathan, whereas Nathan had never been able to penetrate the fog of secrecy in which Isaac existed. Now, in order to provide appropriate medical care in what could be a matter of life or death, both Isaac and Barbara would have to be completely open with him. And those 'protocols of secrecy' and ritualistic 'codes of conduct' that Isaac lived his life by would have to be broken.

On entering the room, Nathan immediately saw a group of people huddled around the bed. The four men and two women were leaning reverently over Isaac and were so focused that they didn't seem to notice as he and Barbara approached. Isaac's eyes were closed and a sheet covered his lower body, leaving the raw burn on his abdomen exposed, and Nathan was relieved that at least no one had attempted to dress the lesion. He knew exactly what had caused it, despite his colleagues in A&E having been too baffled by its presentation to hazard anything more than a vague diagnosis.

"He's in a bad way, Barbara. He needs more than their prayers," Nathan insisted, placing the black leather bag down on the bedside table and opening it. "How the hell did he manage to get out of the hospital anyway?"

Isaac suddenly stirred on hearing voices he could recognise. "*Barbara*," he called out weakly, reaching out his hand wearily as his wife rushed to his side.

Nathan assertively manoeuvred the closest member of the well-meaning huddle aside, the earpieces to his stethoscope already in position.

"Barbara... We did it!" Isaac uttered. *"We made it through!"*

The boy cried inconsolably as he was pushed towards the open back passenger door of the 1990 Ford Sierra. The child was the last thing to pack.

"What's wrong with you? Stop this right away!" his mother half-heartedly scolded.

"To be fair, Jen, it *is* your parents we're visiting. You can hardly blame him," the boy's father interjected, giving an unconcerned smile as he slammed the hatchback of the large family car shut. "Son, stop crying and get in the car. Or Christmas will be cancelled. *Capisce?*"

"John!" the mother snapped – the boy's hair being ruffled by his father heading for the driver's door, keen to get on the road while it was still light. "It's just so unlike him... What's wrong, darling?" she asked, unable to maintain the pretence of being angry with the normally well-behaved child.

"I... don't want... to go," the child sobbed, taking gasps of stunted forced inhalations between his words. "Can't we... just... stay... home?"

With a gentle ushering from a hand in the small of his back, the child was finally positioned in the rear seat. "Be a good boy, Nathan," were Jen Carter's final words on the matter, only wishing that she could've added *like your brother* – Caleb, already having been buckled in, was animatedly pulling faces and laughing at his younger brother's antics.

It had already turned dusk by the time the sapphire blue Ford Sierra cruised out of London heading for Hastings on the southeast coast. They'd made good time and had already turned off the main A21 with only a few kilometres left to travel when young Nathan's worst nightmare began unfolding in a slow-motion replay before his still teary eyes. It was the same vision he'd lived through night after night for weeks without ever finding the words with which to share his fears: the dazzle of rapidly approaching lights heading straight for them; the oncoming truck that had suddenly veered out of control; his mother's scream; the same dizzying sense of spinning and spinning that had terrified him in so many recurrent nightmares, then nothing but silence… until, that is, his eyes and ears began to register a barrage of torchlight and the sound of concerned voices punctuated by the wrenching of crumpled metal being peeled back. The last image burnt into his memory before passing out again was that of his brother, Caleb, being pulled from the wreckage with his skull cleaved open – the wound exposing his brain…

Nathan woke with a sharp inhalation of familiar panic, propping himself up on the mattress set up in Isaac's room. That recurrent childhood nightmare, buried all too shallowly in his psyche, had been triggered by more than just the events of earlier in the evening. The photo Nathan carried around in his wallet had been snapped only a couple of weeks before the accident and was the only tangible reminder of John and Jen Carter and the life he'd had before the unexpected actions of some random truck driver had robbed them of all destiny. No seven-year-old should feel such guilt. But Nathan had been tormented all his life with the despair of not having been able to find the words to tell his parents about his premonition. *If only I could have stopped them getting in the car.* His real guilt, though, lay in the fact that his elder brother, Caleb, had survived the crash.

Nathan took a deep centring breath. "How is he?" he whispered to Barbara, who was sitting across the room in a bedside vigil.

"Sleeping like a baby," she replied, smiling contentedly as she looked over at her husband with obvious relief.

Nathan rolled onto his back and stared at the ceiling, not sharing her sense of calm.

Pullen sat at his desk hitting *PLAY* and *REWIND* on his computer keyboard over and over again. The fifteen-second clip of archived CCTV footage that he was once again mulling over was far from clear. In fact, nothing surrounding the seemingly endless spate of abductions was clear. He hit *PLAY* with another undeterred stab. Of the twelve females reported missing in suspicious circumstances over the last eighteen months, two of them had been found murdered and sexually assaulted. But in the vacuum of evidence surrounding all of the cases, it had proven impossible for him to confirm a definite link between those murders and any of the other abductions. It was even a stretch to make a convincing enough link between each of the two murders themselves. Another stab of the *PLAY* key saw the footage loop around yet again. The body of the first young woman, found eight months ago, had been secreted almost fully clothed in an overgrown bed of bushes being tended to by council workers from the Parks Department, whereas the naked body of the second victim had been found dumped out in the open, some two months later, with horrific signs of abuse. He hit *PLAY* again. The static street-cam view showing the comings and goings around the entrance to the park where the first girl had been found murdered streamed into his visual consciousness for the tenth time, now leaving an indelible reference that his critical mind would continue to process long after the computer had been shut down. The footage he was viewing held the answer, but just as it had done eight months prior, the flickering image repeatedly traversing his screen was refusing to give up its secret.

As he searched doggedly within each frame for a single clue, a collection of youthful girlish smiles, beaming with such promise and ambition, radiated from out of the array of family snapshots Blu Tacked across the whiteboard mounted on the wall behind him. Pullen was old school. He understood *Blu Tack*. You could see it and feel it and instantly knew if it wasn't up to the job. *Bluetooth*, on the other hand, was a mystery he didn't care to solve. And it was to the ire of his old-world sensibilities that computers and the internet were the go-to source for all information these days, despite the waters of the source being knowingly contaminated and muddied. The viral Cut and Paste of inaccuracies – intentional and malicious or unintentional and innocent – had, in his estimation, been the weapon to deal the death blow to history as humankind had once known it. It now lay slowly bleeding out at a crime scene where billions log on daily, Photoshopping the truth, oblivious to what they are both a witness to and complicit in. 'Mis-Information Technology', Pullen called it. Ironically, his job as a detective had been much easier when there was a real paper trail to follow. Information being instantly at his fingertips was pointless if that information was misleading or incomplete, and being sidetracked in any of his single-minded hunts was not an option. He felt the responsibility of not letting down those missing girls and their families. Each photo on the whiteboard in his office reminded him of the daughter he'd never had. Not that he was childless. But a life of selfish dedication to his career had seen bonds long since broken with an estranged daughter somewhere out there in the world. And those bonds could never be repaired.

He hit *PLAY*, convinced that he was onto something. The park entrance was no more than seventy metres away from the office precinct surrounding the old derelict manor house where the younger of the two naked and unconscious men had just been found. It couldn't be a coincidence. There had to be a link. Pullen suddenly stabbed at the *PAUSE* key, the frames freezing on the fleeting image of an unidentified male of about thirty entering the park at a suspiciously late hour. The poor-quality monochrome image still left the face of the individual of interest dressed in jeans and a T-shirt entirely indistinguishable. But Pullen was convinced that he recognised the potential suspect from somewhere. And in that vacuum of information regarding any of the abductions and murders, it was the closest thing he had to a lead.

3

Eight months earlier

"Hey, Wanker!" a man shouted out aggressively, having just been shouldered as he walked along the city centre street.

"Leave it!" his girlfriend pleaded, pulling on her partner's arm, his immovable frame not yielding at first. "He's just off his face. It's not worth it!"

"Piece of shit!" the boyfriend added at the top of his voice, finally relenting, the object of his derision already having traipsed obliviously on a further ten metres, dressed only in jeans and a T-shirt against the cold late-night air.

A group of teenagers waiting at a nearby cabstand laughed and jeered at the spectacle, while the other passers-by in the busy thoroughfare gave the lone figure a wide berth, his fixed staring eyes and mind-altered gait being reason enough for them to divert their paths. Even the near-miss blaring horn of a heavily braking car at the next road junction didn't deter the man.

On and on he walked until the clamour of the city streets gave way to a more suburban silence nestled in a background hum of distant traffic. He made a decisive right and then a left and walked on a further kilometre before arriving at his destination. He hesitated at the park entrance, his demeanour becoming momentarily agitated and troubled. Then he disappeared through the gates, his presence lost in the shadows.

The prolonged static strain made his hands and arms shake. It was never as easy as it's portrayed on the big screen on account of them wanting to live. They kick and squirm, finding superhuman strength, and most of the effort is expended in simply subduing them. Then comes the sweet surrender. But just before that slump, their veins and eyes bulge, turning even the prettiest of faces reddened and ugly. That was part of the appeal. And this one had been particularly pretty. He gazed into her pupils. That's where he could see the life falling away from them in fear and disbelief. She was almost there. Another second. The subtle shadowing created by the dim light being cast by a streetlamp close to the park's entrance made her face now seem even more grotesque, and he fleetingly wondered if he should release the pressure again and rape her one more time – his record was four. He stared deeper into her eyes. The hesitation, though, had left her too far gone, and with the final concerted pressure of both his thumbs, he felt the hyoid bone snap in her throat as he ejaculated… Nathan woke with a start, breathless and perspiring, his hands and arms catatonically clenched and shaking with the flashback strain of remembering.

4

"We might need some help here," Nathan said, trying to control the flailing arms of the ranting drunk he was attending to behind the drawn curtains of the treatment cubicle.

"Sanctuary! Sanctuary! I am Sanctuary!"

The junior nurse assisting fumbled a silver kidney bowl half full of bloodied gauze back onto the instrument table and rushed nervously out through the opening in the drapes to get help.

"You're in danger!" the drunk shouted out, suddenly grabbing onto the lapels of Nathan's white coat before continuing his wide-eyed rant in a more whispered tone. "You need to find Sanctuary. *Sanctuary…*"

Nathan adeptly broke the hold that the mentally disturbed man had on him and took a step backwards as the guy's arms began flailing even more wildly than before.

This was turning out to be more than a drunk who'd slipped on the pavement and cut open his head. Despite the copious amounts of blood that had been running down the man's face on admission, the small scalp wound was superficial enough to barely even require a suture, so it was unlikely that the wild behaviour was due to any kind of brain trauma. More likely, it was a drug-induced psychotic episode kicking in or the alcohol simply exacerbating some pre-existing mental condition. Either way, dealing with a situation like this was the last thing Nathan needed. The disturbing nightmares that'd been plaguing him of late had robbed him of countless nights' sleep, and he'd been praying for a quiet non-eventful shift just so he could get back home to his apartment and finally crash.

Perhaps it was the fatigue that had left his reactions uncharacteristically sluggish, but before he knew what was happening, the man had lunged at him again and grabbed both of his wrists in a tight unbreakable grip.

"It's your fault they died!" he spat with venom, looking directly into Nathan's eyes, a cloud of alcohol-ridden breath enveloping them both.

A chill shot down Nathan's spine.

"You should've stopped them getting into the car! You should've stopped them!"

Nathan froze, rendered impotent and paralysed by those words.

The curtains swished open and two hefty-looking security guards pounced on the drunk. But, on freeing Nathan's wrists, the strong-arm intervention only inspired the man to kick out violently, sending the metal instrument trolley flying.

"You're in danger!" he screamed again, glaring at Nathan throughout the struggle. "You need to find Sanctuary! I am, I am Sanctuary!"

At that moment, Adam strode onto the scene, calmly shaking his head while effortlessly clamping the man's legs against his body with his arm. "We'll get him into a treatment room," he suggested to the straining security guards before reaching for a fresh wad of gauze with his free hand and slapping it firmly over the wound on the man's head. "Damn! I was aiming for his mouth," Adam joked, turning to Nathan with a smile. "I'll take it from here, mate. You OK?"

Nathan nodded but was far from OK. He was shaken by what had just happened, and the belligerent man was still spitting the words "*I am Sanctuary… Sanctuary… Sanctuary*" even as he was being carted away. And while Nathan had been in the job long enough not to give a second thought to what some deranged patient in a drunken state might utter, the sheer insightfulness of those unsettling words had cut through to the raw centre of his psyche. Because, to Nathan's mind, the death of his parents *had* been entirely his fault.

10 Oakdene Lane. Nathan eyed the two-storey white-rendered seventeenth-century property presenting before him as he locked his car. It was certainly not what he had imagined when he'd scrawled down the address earlier that morning. Glancing down at the instructions on the piece of paper, he walked up the stone steps leading to the front door and immediately noticed the wooden sign nailed to a post at the top of the steps directing visitors left across the front of the house and along a path to the far gable end. Around the corner, set towards the back of the main dwelling, ran a long single-storey annexe that appeared to be a converted stable block. But the weathered and sympathetically restored walls and authentic slate of the roofing suggested any remodelling of the building had actually been completed well over a century ago. To the far right-hand side of the annexe's expansive façade was a door bearing yet another rustic sign, identical to the one at the front steps of the main house, announcing in the same skilfully routed script that Nathan had finally arrived at *The Sanctuary*.

A small overhead bell sounded when he entered, as if he had stepped back in time and crossed the threshold of some sleepy little village store. The modest rectangular reception area was sparsely appointed with an overflowing cork notice board affixed to the whitewashed plastered walls and a small equally cluttered desk – obviously chosen for its size rather than its appeal – foreshortening the space.

Standing alone in the chill autumnal air fed by the draught blowing in from under the door, Nathan was left with the feeling that *sanctuary* had not yet been achieved and wasn't necessarily guaranteed.

A few moments passed before the door to his left opened and the nondescript whiteness of the interior was slashed by a blaze of animated colour. In her late forties, the woman's halo of vibrant burgundy hair and kaftan of brilliant oranges, yellows and reds in no way detracted from the dazzling smile that undoubtedly welcomed all-comers as family or long-lost friends.

"Hello. You must be Nathan," she said, elegantly extending a hand that suggested she may be a little older than she looked behind her mask of impeccably applied make-up. "I'm Barbara. Please come in, my lovely," she added, with a hint of West Country homeliness. "Isaac is ready for you."

And with that short exchange of pleasantries, she led Nathan into a charmingly lush deep-red-carpeted interior that didn't disappoint.

Nathan had his reservations about this visit. In fact, as he entered the long corridor that extended the full length of the annexe, he was still considering whether or not it would be too rude to excuse himself and leave. But before he had an opportunity to consider that course of action any further, he was shown into a plush room where a man in his early fifties, casually dressed in jeans and fitted shirt, was seated in one of two armchairs facing each other with a small antique-looking wooden table positioned in between.

The man was seemingly deep in thought with his eyes closed, allowing Nathan a moment to study him. He seemed a complete mismatch with the lady who had just shown him in, his rolled-up sleeves revealing two impressive identical eagle tattoos on the weathered skin of his thick forearms, suggesting past service in the armed forces. Broad in the shoulders and chest and carrying no body fat to speak of, he looked a physically strong and capable man with a full mop of grey-flecked dark hair that still retained much of its natural colour, and his tall powerful stature seemed entirely out of place against the faint floral print of the armchair's upholstery. Nathan was wondering which of life's worries had gouged such deep and permanent furrows in the man's forehead when Isaac suddenly opened his eyes, his features breaking out into a broad welcoming smile, and any sense of a mismatch with Barbara was instantly dispelled.

He stood to greet Nathan with an outstretched hand. "Good to meet you. Isaac McKinnon. I'm so pleased you decided to come."

Nathan had already intimated his scepticism when he'd made the appointment on the phone. It's not that he doubted psychic phenomena in itself. On the contrary, his personal experiences, scientific and medical knowledge, along with a professional interest in Psychology, bore out the reality of such phenomena; he simply doubted the conclusions that people make as a result of observing all things psychic and doubted even more the motives of those who 'speak to the spirits of the departed' to make a quick buck at the expense of the vulnerable. If not for recent dramatic events, and the odd circumstances through which he had come across The Sanctuary's telephone number, it was unlikely that he would have ever visited a place such as this.

"As I mentioned on the phone," Nathan opened politely, putting aside his reservations on being invited to take a seat with a motion of Isaac's hand, "I'm not necessarily a disbeliever in all this, but—"

"Yes, yes, I understand..." Isaac interrupted, even before they had both fully sunk into the cushions of the chairs. His demeanour was suddenly very different. "You have a brother, *yes*...? Elder brother, I feel... but it's like he has the mental age of a child... as if he's mentally disabled in some way... You can understand this?"

"Well, *err*, y-yes," Nathan stammered, completely taken by surprise and trying quickly to shift up a gear in his thought processes.

"An *acquired* brain injury. A car crash, correct?"

Nathan didn't answer. He just stared in shock at the man in front of him, his expression alone serving to answer the question effectively enough.

Isaac's tone became steeped with concern. "You've got to

lose the guilt, Nathan. It wasn't your fault… You were just a kid. Your dad and mum want you to know that… Are you a doctor?" he then added inquisitively, his demeanour having changed yet again. "They've made me aware of that. It's really not surprising, considering… But no amount of doctoring others will fix your own head, Nathan. You've gotta fix that yourself. *Capisce*?"

On hearing that singular Italianism, tears welled in Nathan's eyes. It felt as if Isaac had plunged a hand straight inside his chest cavity and begun a prolonged firm squeeze of his heart, emptying it of blood. The Medium had just uttered the one word that most reminded him of his father. It was the last word his dad had ever spoken to him before getting into the driver's seat of the Ford Sierra that day of the fatal crash.

Isaac offered him a tissue from a box placed out of sight on the lower shelf of the antique table, but Nathan waved it away, choosing instead to breathe through his emotions and grab back his usual self-control.

"I know you said on the phone that you weren't interested in a reading and just wanted information," Isaac explained, "but sometimes those who love us must take whatever opportunity they can to grab our attention. And I, for one, am never going to stand in the way of that."

Nathan paused for a moment to regain his composure as Isaac sat back in silence, allowing him the space he needed. The synapses in the *reason* and *logic* centres of Nathan's brain had already begun to fire off in a protective – all but territorial – response, a reactive flood of neurotransmitters inside the tissues of his brain already swamping his mind with objectivity to quell any thoughts of insurgence. "My parents are dead!" he finally asserted. "I just can't believe that there are spirits in some Afterlife waiting to talk to us!"

"You're making the assumption that, as a Medium, I believe that kind of fairy story too… Which I don't."

Nathan was taken aback by the bluntness of the unexpected comment and hesitated before responding. "I'm confused… You don't believe in an Afterlife?"

Isaac's manner remained forthright and unapologetic. "I'm a man of science. The Sanctuary is a psychic research centre with leading Neuroscientists working alongside us," he continued, an intensity in the delivery now hinting at the complexity and depth of intellect possessed by this otherwise rugged-looking character. "Perhaps it's time we all began engaging in a more sophisticated and meaningful dialogue on the subject of our very life and death… After all," he added, with a measure of irony in his voice, "our fate after death has always been humanity's one burning question. Yet we've consistently chosen to cloud the issue with fairy tales, dogma, and even blatant fear mongering."

Nathan found himself unexpectedly intrigued and challenged by the man sitting in front of him but was beginning to feel that he might well have stumbled upon the right place. Some kind of dialogue was exactly what he'd been seeking, and it was probably fair to say that he was as guilty as anyone of possessing misguided beliefs based on any number of misconceptions, but recent circumstances had forced him to rethink that word *belief*. And he was now desperately in search of answers.

Annie Davenport, arms worriedly crossed in front of her slight frame, braved the chilly morning air and walked to the front gate of her neat semi-detached property and peered both ways down the leaf-littered suburban street for the third time in half an hour. In her slippers and floral print apron, she was a picture of working class. Her blue eyes were as bright as any twenty-year-old's, suggesting some Irish descent in the family line, but the complexion of her face told of a hard life that had made her age well before her time. Annie never had the time or inclination to master make-up, and her long wiry hair, now stripped of its colour, was resigned to its monthly crop in the bathroom with an old pair of utilitarian scissors. Annie's sole concern had only ever been for other people.

Caleb's bed hadn't been slept in again. It's not that she hadn't faced this situation countless times before, to the point that the police were now slow to respond, if not reticent to attend at all. But, more recently, Caleb's expeditions into the great wide world had become both more frequent and prolonged. He was, after all, a thirty-four-year-old man, albeit with the mental capacity of a nine-year-old, and it was almost impossible to maintain the kind of supervision she had extended on first taking over his care following the tragic death of her sister all those years ago. Seeing him exert his independence in itself was a good thing, but the secretiveness that he'd been displaying in more recent times was becoming a real challenge. It was as though he was slowly growing up and finally becoming a teenager.

Never having been able to have children of her own, and being widowed in her early thirties, it had seemed only natural to take both Nathan and Caleb into her home. At the age of eighteen, Nathan had left for medical school, but Caleb had always needed ongoing assistance. Things were different these days, though. She just wanted her sweet, chattering

Caleb back in her life and back in her home but knew in her heart that things were probably never going to be the same again. On more than one occasion, while engaged in similar recent vigils at her front gate, Annie had suffered the annoyance of hearing her front door slamming shut to find herself locked out of her own house. Having sneaked in through the back entrance, Caleb had then seemingly taken cruel pleasure in pretending not to hear as she would try to get his attention by banging on his ground-floor bedroom window.

Annie sighed on remembering and instinctively checked for the key that she now always carried with her in the front pocket of her apron. For the time being, she had no choice but to return inside and wait a little longer.

"You still have me confused, Isaac," Nathan said, sinking back into the armchair of The Sanctuary's reading room. On trawling through web page after web page for a psychic who might be able to shed light on recent events for him, the last thing he'd expected was to come face to face with a Medium who didn't even believe in a *Life after Death*, and the longer the conversation continued, the more confused Nathan was becoming. "If you're telling me that as a Medium you don't believe in a spirit that survives death, then what *do* you believe in?"

Isaac gave a slight smile, recognising a deeper significance behind the question. He had just one opportunity to get through to the young man sitting in front of him, and he had good reason to make sure that he didn't fail. "Trusting our perceptions when it comes to beliefs can be a very dangerous thing," he said, taking a bold step into a minefield of conjecture, hoping that Nathan would follow. "We only have to look at civilisations that believed rainbows to be God, simply because they didn't understand the prism effect of visible light passing through a shower of rain. There's no blame in such misdirected faith or belief. But it does highlight a certain human frailty when belief in a rainbow can be so readily substituted for belief in a Sun or a Spirit or even the mere concept of a Universal Force."

Nathan eyed the man sitting across from him. "So you're saying that things aren't always what they seem…"

"Exactly!"

"That although you were able to provide relevant information about my parents and my history with them, they weren't really there… They were just a figment of your mind?"

"No! That's *not* what I'm saying. Those I communicate with are very much alive, Nathan. That's why your parents presented to me in a way that you would recognise… As a Medium, I'm seeing them as they *were* while simultaneously seeing them as they *are* and as they *will be*."

Nathan sighed with exasperation as the events of the past week flashed through his mind. But at least the direction of the conversation had now turned towards addressing the very reasons for him being there.

"Let me explain it like this," Isaac continued, "Louis de Broglie, one of the Fathers of Quantum Physics, stated over a century ago that *everything which constitutes the Past, Present and Future is given to us en bloc*. He was reviewing the state of scientific knowledge in the wake of the findings of Quantum Mechanics and Relativity. Summarising, he commented that *the events making up our observable reality exist prior to our knowledge of them."* Isaac looked intently at Nathan. "That's just reiterating what humans have been saying for thousands of years. Is it any wonder that millions have claimed to be able to see into the future? To be fair to that esteemed Father of Quantum Physics, *Clairvoyance of the Future* has always been based on scientific fact. It's directly equivalent to our *Memory of the Past!*"

Nathan felt as if he had found himself attending an impromptu lecture from some other era and couldn't help but be strangely captivated by both the subject matter and the orator.

"De Broglie was simply verbalising what mystics have known for thousands of years… In the perpetual *Here* and *Now* of events, your parents are actually still alive at this very moment and tragically crashing their car while simultaneously going out on their first-ever date while teaching you to ride a bike for the very first time. And some aspect of their consciousness is able to reach out and empathise with how you are feeling in this simultaneous *Here* and *Now* of events that you yourself are currently experiencing."

Nathan moved uneasily in his seat. Isaac's relentless stream of words, despite the impassioned delivery, was becoming almost hypnotic, and he almost felt himself drifting away for a moment.

"Your father had no idea that when he got into that car he was about to die. But some level of his consciousness did. Because the scenario of his death was already happening to him… There is no *After*-Life, Nathan. Just simultaneous moments across *many* interconnected lives!"

Nathan baulked. "But that would mean my dad's

consciousness had reached out to me from a past moment in that contact you just made… That's more like time travel!"

"Precisely! His *sub*-consciousness reached out. From across observable reality! The Mind cannot be confined by Space and Time because the Mind is what actually creates and projects out that very illusion of Space and Time… Those ancient mystic teachings are already on the verge of being integrated into Quantum Theory—"

Nathan interrupted with another sigh. "Do you know what kind of ribbing I'd get from my colleagues at work if they knew I was here?"

"Well, you're in good company," Isaac reassured. "Sir Winston Churchill, Abraham Lincoln, Queen Victoria, Air Chief Marshall Lord Dowding, who commanded the RAF in the Battle of Britain…" Isaac began reeling off a Who's Who of history's luminaries in a well-versed tone. "Charles Richet, who pioneered the medical research on Anaphylaxis. And physicist Sir William Crookes, without whom we'd have no modern telecommunications or insight into the quantum world…" Despite his best efforts, Isaac had slipped into one of the unstoppable enthusiastic rants he'd been trying so hard to avoid. "…Prime Ministers, Nathan. Queens, Lords and Knights of the Realm. Professors and pioneers of modern science moving in society's highest circles. All were staunch believers. Those sober minds had been privy to astonishing demonstrations of Physical phenomena that had left them with no doubts as to its authenticity. What conspiracy, I ask you, could have led to today's wholesale cover-up of such demonstrable truth?"

"*Physical* phenomena?" Nathan asked, his interest having been instantly piqued by the odd phrase. "What do you mean by *Physical*?"

Isaac hesitated, catching himself and realising that his enthusiasm had led him to utter one too many words. "That's for another time," Isaac said, redirecting, certain that there would be another time. "Perhaps instead you should tell me what brought you here today. You said that you needed some information, but I sense you have more on your mind than just idle philosophical questions."

Nathan had been left in no doubt as to how knowledgeable and passionate this man was when it came to his work, and the plea to his intellect over the last few minutes had at least started to dispel any concerns of Isaac being just another charlatan fortune teller selling quick-fix dreams to the vulnerable. If what he had just been told was true, there was more to consider than he could ever have guessed.

Nathan paused and, against his better judgement, decided to seize the moment. "I need to share something," he finally blurted.

"Experiences you've been having?"

"*Yeah.*"

"That's the usual reason people turn up on our doorstep. Feel free to be open. This place is called The Sanctuary for a reason."

On hearing Isaac utter the name of *The Sanctuary*, Nathan's thoughts lingered on his recent interaction with the drunk in A&E and the bizarre flashbacks he'd been suffering from that had led him to this place. And he still had cause to wonder if *sanctuary* would ever truly be possible.

5

The shadows that haunted the rear of the old abandoned Hall were pervaded by even darker shadows – figures that loitered while other dark figures busied themselves at the boarded-up windows. But not to break in. They had already accomplished that hours before. Their work, for the time being, was done. The boards were now being carefully replaced, as had been done countless times before, so as not to bring any undue attention from the night security that patrolled the surrounding precinct of office buildings. Not that the shadowy figures were afraid of attention from security. They were afraid of nothing. Contempt was all they had, and in the event of being spotted, contingencies were already in place that would see any overly curious security guard disappear with such efficiency that any police investigation would be futile. Their stealth was based solely on necessity. Orders had been given, and those orders were to be followed.

The old Hall had a chequered past. Built in the late 1500s, it had originally been owned by the influential Mosley family.

Only the building's historical significance had saved it from the bulldozers. But demolition might have been better than the indignity it had been subjected to in recent times by the spitefulness of those scuppered developers with friends in high places. Where landed gentry had once cantered, hundreds of cars were now parked and the foundations of even more soulless office buildings were being excavated. Being gutted and turned into an eatery and function rooms for a period in the 1970s might have been the greatest defilement. Since then, it had lain abandoned with little interest in it except for those shadowy interlopers that had been making frequent night-time visits. The security firm that held the tender to patrol the precinct were already being infiltrated, and soon there would be full control and unhindered access to the Hall. But, for the time being, the mains electricity had been successfully accessed and the metering bypassed. And with the final board now secured back in place at the window, the group of shaven-headed young men swarmed off like storm troopers into the night.

The muted thudding bass of dance music could be felt resounding through the lush carpeted upper floors of the Carousel Club. Downstairs was already heaving with the minions, but upstairs – where only VIP guests were permitted – had a much more exclusive air. In the main corridor, two girls, tongues writhing, kissed passionately up against the wall while a guy dressed in Armani openly snorted a line cut on a small table next to them. Even the boisterous procession striding along past the threesome reeked with excesses of money and outwardly might have been taken for the entourage of some champion prize fighter. A local kid made good. But as the shaven-headed muscle at the front of the pack rapped on the door he'd stopped at, the group made way for a wholly unexpected figure to emerge as the centre of all the attention.

A black leather crop held in a velvet-gloved hand extended silently from out of the doorway and whipped at the man's left pectoral with an audible sting. The man gasped then giggled like a little boy before bumbling into the room.

"Have fun, Caleb. Do what the lady says."

The group responded with loud whoops and laughter as the door was slammed shut.

6

A cheer went up as yet another cork popped. Hugh and Marjorie Wells certainly knew how to entertain their guests at their frequent parties. Cocaine was the drug of choice for the gathered intelligentsia and it was tolerated without a thought. Marjorie, though, much preferred the simple buzz of champagne, while Hugh stoically resisted all such temptations.

"They've only got themselves to blame, those impetuous American cousins of ours. It's just plain bad business."

The talk amongst a coterie of besuited men lounging in a cloud of cigar smoke over in the corner of the room was of the developing, if not yet looming, financial crisis on Wall Street.

"Financial madness, more like. Lemmings over a cliff. Word has it on the floor that London will be hit hard," another of the fat cats responded. "Blatant fraud and corruption, if you ask me. Trust me. It'll all come home to roost as soon as the main players have positioned themselves safely."

The gramophone blared out the latest *flapper* dance craze as a svelte Marjorie approached in all her alluring elegance in an attempt to bring the party atmosphere across to the stuffy corner. With her raven black hair, cropped short in a bob just beneath her ears, and her hypnotising green eyes, she had the kind of sex appeal that could bring kings and the most powerful and influential of men to their knees. Women might have despised her, if not for them being under her spell, too.

"*Whine*, gentleman," Marjorie offered, holding out a tray of charged crystal, smiling outwardly at her guests and inwardly to herself at the cleverness of her cryptic jibe.

"Say, Marjorie, if things get bad and you need to sell the old place…" one of the group ventured, looking around as if assessing the property.

"Spoken like a true realtor," Marjorie responded pointedly. "I'll be certain to call, knowing I'd be assured of a less than reasonable price."

All of the group but one guffawed. Henry Mathieson's bristling silence and shunning aversion of his eyes more than hinted at his contempt.

Marjorie forced an even wider smile. "But you know, gentlemen, in a week or two, all this talk of financial crashes will have blown over. So, in the meantime, how about having some fun!" With that, she set the drinks tray down on a table and grabbed the two nearest men by the hand and dragged them up from their chairs.

Twenty-nine-year-old Marjorie had reason to be upbeat and relaxed. For her, *Les Années Folles – The Crazy Years* of the roaring twenties – need never end. The year of 1929 had been a particularly good one for her so far, and in just a few months time, when the clocks would finally come to strike midnight on New Year's Eve, the 1920s would, to her mind, only be giving way to yet another decade of fun and frivolity. Established through generations of trade and commerce, hers was old money that kept her relatively immune to any and all financial uncertainties. The house that she loved so much, along with a sizeable cash inheritance and property portfolio, had been passed down from her father, Charles Cavendish; her grandfather Spencer and her great-grandfather before that, with the family fortune only increasing with the endeavours of each successive generation. She, however, being an only child and the young socialite she was, had chosen a life of leisure punctuated with overseas travel, and since she had married Hugh, a university research scientist, out of lust rather than for his prospects, the zenith of the Cavendish family wealth had more than likely been reached.

"So what are you working on these days, Wells?" a former colleague asked.

Hugh's eyes were fixed on whatever part of the room Marjorie had flitted to next. "Quantum Mechanics," he answered, finally making eye contact. "It's the future, you know. You really should think about getting on board."

"There's a lot of nonsense in the field if you ask me. I just can't fathom it. Nor, it seems, can any of the proponents, for that *Matter*." The man laughed pretentiously to himself, while Hugh remained expressionless and unamused. "Sorry for the terrible pun, old chap," the man continued apologetically. "No, I think I'll just plod along in my—"

"Please, do excuse me," Hugh suddenly said with a perplexed look, cutting the rather inane conversation short and heading over to a new, somewhat out of place, arrival he'd spotted, already being welcomed by his wife.

At thirty-four, Hugh was still as physically fit as he was when he'd entered university as an undergraduate and prided himself that he could still clock a respectable 4 minutes 20 seconds over a mile of cinder track. With boyish good looks, he was slimly built with a well-developed musculature and a physique that had proven aesthetic enough to turn the head of the very eligible, very sought-after, and exceptionally beautiful Marjorie Cavendish. Aesthetics were everything to Marjorie.

"Sir Oliver! I… I… This is so unexpected," Hugh stammered, having become uncharacteristically tongue-tied on finally coming face to face with the very man he'd been trying to gain an audience with for months. He had written to the legendary Sir Oliver Lodge on countless occasions, despite never receiving so much as a stock courtesy letter in reply. But his dogged persistence in sending through an extract of a paper outlining the groundbreaking research he was engaged in seemed to have had the desired effect. That Lodge had responded by tracking him down at his home was more than unexpected.

"We need to talk, my boy, but it seems this isn't the time or the place," Sir Oliver replied, glancing uncomfortably around the room. "It's just that I was passing and… Well, I really should have called ahead."

It's not every day that a pre-eminent physicist, whose research and countless discoveries had contributed to creating much of the world as we know it, walks in uninvited in the middle of a party. And knowing that there would be any number of enjoyable soirées already penned in by

Marjorie for the near future, Hugh didn't hesitate. "Not at all, Sir Oliver. Please come this way."

Hugh led the elderly gentleman towards the rear of the house. At six foot four, the sprightly seventy-eight-year-old still presented as a formidable man. Even the way he tapped at the floor with his cane only every second or third step gave the distinct impression that it was just being carried for show. In a garish striped jacket, bow tie and donning a boater, he looked like he had just come from an afternoon's punting at Oxford and seemed a far more colourful character than Hugh had ever imagined.

On exiting through the back door of the beautiful seventeenth-century property, they followed a path to The Sanctuary – an old stable block that had been converted into a large single-storey annexe during Marjorie's grandfather's tenure. Hugh invited Lodge into the Library, intrigued as to how this titan of the modern scientific world had even managed to get hold of his home address. They had fleetingly met at a conference a couple of years before, and Hugh wasn't totally unknown in his field. However, it was unlikely that Lodge would have remembered him.

"We shan't be disturbed here, Sir Oliver."

Hugh was not entirely correct in that assumption. A skulking Henry Mathieson had followed them out of the main house and was listening at the door.

"Can I offer you a drink?"

Lodge just glared back at Hugh in response. "Do you know what *fire* you are playing with, Wells?" he suddenly blurted, dispensing with all pleasantries now that he assumed they were alone.

The young scientist was thrown by Lodge's opening

remark. This was not how he had envisaged such a meeting would begin.

The list of Lodge's achievements was spectacular. The motor vehicles Hugh's guests had arrived in that evening ran courtesy of the Lodge Spark Plug. He even held a patent on the loudspeaker in the gramophone that fuelled the escalating party over in the main house. And having first broadcast a radio signal a full year ahead of Marconi, the Courts had eventually ruled Sir Oliver as the *true* father of Radiotechnology in a settlement lucrative enough that Lodge was content for the Italian to keep the undue public acclaim. But it was his talk in the 1880s of Space and Time being considered as *one Spacetime entity*, decades ahead of Albert Einstein usurping the phrase, that had impressed Hugh the most. The fact that Einstein's subsequent work seemed to disprove Lodge's long-held belief in an Ether – *a Zero Point Substrate that permeates the Cosmos* – didn't sway Hugh. It might take several decades and an explosion of those new so-called 'particle accelerators' around the globe before a *Zero Point Field* – an unseen reservoir of energy from which all Matter spontaneously arises – would be accepted again. But Hugh was convinced that eventually Lodge's lofty belief in a *cosmic source of energy so great as to be unimaginable to the human mind* would be proven.

Hugh's interest in Sir Oliver, however, wasn't entirely due to those stellar scientific credentials. The Knight of the Realm had famously turned his back on his career to research what he considered to be the new frontier appearing on the horizon of his beloved science of Physics. That new frontier was *psychic* phenomena.

Lodge sat forwards, resting on his cane. "I've observed some incredible things in my time, and I've witnessed some horrifying things, too. What you're suggesting, Wells, is possibly the most alarming."

"But, Sir Oliver, surely, you of all people…"

Lodge was well aware of the whispered talk of experimental séances at The Sanctuary, still having many contacts around the country that moved in such circles. So when the unsolicited extract from Hugh's research paper found its way onto his desk, he had instantly made the connection and felt compelled to intervene as a matter of urgency.

"Don't get me wrong," Lodge insisted. "The science is sound. I myself have witnessed a two-hundred-pound man with his wrists and ankles tightly bound to a chair dematerialise from the séance room and reappear in the corridor outside of the securely locked room, under the strictest of control conditions. What do you think inspired me to jeopardise the esteem and respect I'd garnered over a lifetime and devote myself in obscurity to this research instead?"

It was well known that Lodge had been shunned by the establishment for his beliefs. Something that the maverick in Hugh admired hugely, because only the greatest of men would ever be willing to fall so publicly on their sword in the name of truth.

"A few decades from now," Lodge ventured, "physicists will be routinely researching such phenomena as the quantum teleportation of Matter in their laboratories. I can guarantee it. It's all there in the mathematics. But as far as a person independently reappearing in a functioning way in the Future or Past…"

Hugh stood his ground. "Convention is correct, Sir Oliver, in stating that traversing physically through Spacetime in a past and future direction is impossible due to convention. But *convention* only applies if you are mistakenly accepting that our reality in Spacetime is some kind of Absolute Reality. Which it isn't… by the very theories we're now adopting."

As a physicist at the cutting edge of known science, Hugh was well aware of what convention said. Relativity implies that a person would have to travel at the speed of light and expend infinite amounts of energy, while gaining infinite mass in the process, to travel significantly into the future relative to the rest of the Universe or would alternatively have to spend time in an intense gravitational field that would kill them. Travelling to the past was said to be fraught with even more impossibility due to the conventions of Thermodynamic Law – left to its own devices, *order* in the universe always tends towards *disorder* as time passes, so travelling backwards against the flow of time would impossibly involve *disorder* tending to *order*. Hugh had little time for convention, though. *Why leave things to their own devices if the inconceivably colossal amounts of universal energy hidden in quantum states could be accessed?*

"It must be remembered that in the Trance states of the Mind we step out of Spacetime completely," Hugh continued to counter. "Our *thoughts* cannot be bound to Earth by gravity. Nor can they be deflected by electromagnetic fields. Such scientific rules and conventions simply don't apply to mental consciousness. And it is at this mental level, in the altered state of Trance, that the quantum make-up of our bodies – the *physical* manifestation in its most basic form – becomes open to manipulation!"

Hugh was beyond excited at finally having someone to talk to about his work, and Lodge, despite his misgivings, found himself drawn in by the enthused young scientist's line of argument.

"As you yourself originally speculated, Sir Oliver, the quantum make-up of our entire physical Reality, including that of the human body, consists of particles that are both spontaneously created and annihilated, to and fro, from that colossal cosmic source you've termed a Zero Point Substrate," Hugh implored. "The dematerialisations you have observed in séances simply involve controlling the illusion of physicality so that particle annihilation occurs, en masse, back to the source, temporarily leaving only pure consciousness. A pure consciousness devoid of physical mass and dimension that can relocate, untethered, across both Space and Time. And in that Trance state, all bets are off on what is considered 'possible'... Providing, of course, we're always balancing and conserving energy across alternate frames of reference. That's why—"

"Again, Wells," Lodge interrupted, "I repeat, the science is sound. Sir William and I spent many hours discussing in detail what we had witnessed."

Hugh realised immediately that Lodge was referring to the old man's deceased friend, the legendary Sir William Crookes, whose work had single-handedly prised open the lid of the quantum world by inventing the tools for its research.

"The evidence we gathered was incontrovertible. In the countless séances we attended, full materialisations of deceased individuals we could attest to would appear in front of our very eyes in the form of light bodies. They were attached to the Trance Medium by an umbilical cord of energy, in much the same way as you describe in your paper."

Hugh smiled to himself on hearing those words. That a legendary figure such as Lodge had read his work and been inspired to travel the country to track him down could only mean he was truly on to something and that his theories were correct.

"Lucid communication was even possible with those so-called spirit manifestations. Voices seemingly generated from out of thin air. Quite astounding. But as far as a living person being able to materialise in another timeframe while attaining enough physical density to function independently... Well, you could be killed trying. Or you could be responsible for killing others. Think about that!"

Sir Oliver suddenly began to look his age as fatigue set in with the late hour and philosophical bantering he'd been engaged in. He paused for a moment. "You remind me too much of myself when I was your age, Wells. We need to talk more. But, for now, I must press on. Would you be kind enough to call my driver." And with that the audience was over.

Sir Oliver left the premises directly from The Sanctuary while Hugh returned to the main house, his senses tingling with excitement, possibility and even more certainty in his beliefs following the impromptu meeting.

Hugh scanned the room. In his absence, the dark cloud of Henry Mathieson had thankfully left, and the party atmosphere had already descended into one of the usual debaucheries. He saw Marjorie over by the staircase giggling in the embrace of a young handsome guy he only vaguely recognised and watched on as she seductively took the eager young man's hand and led him upstairs.

At that moment, a very attractive lingerie-clad young woman, laughing uncontrollably, threw herself into Hugh's arms, placing a reefer to his lips. He inhaled deeply. It had been a while. Keeping his system clean had been an inconvenient yet essential experimental control in his research as a Trance Medium. Tonight, though, he had something to celebrate and resolved that he was going to make up for all those months of self-imposed abstinence.

7

"It's hard to put into words," Nathan began, sinking deeper into the armchair.

"Try," urged Isaac. "I can guarantee that you won't surprise me."

Nathan took a shallow nervous breath. "I'm a doctor. I'm trained to be objective. But last week, I…" He paused, shaking his head in disbelief at what he was about to say before thinking better of it and deciding to start on a different tack. "I've been worried about my health, recently," he resolved.

Isaac sat forwards in his chair, his brow furrowing even more heavily than normal with obvious concern. "In what way?"

"I've been having some kind of seizures."

"*Epilepsy?*"

"Absence Status Epilepticus is the closest diagnosis I can come up with. Or at least that's what I'd put on the shortlist if a patient presented to me in A&E with those kinds of symptoms. I've been fazing out for a while, but…"

"But what?" Isaac urged again, now sitting back with a less concerned look about him.

Nathan reached for words again in an attempt to verbalise his predicament for the first time to anyone.

"It's OK, Nathan," Isaac reassured. "Remember that this is a safe place. Just relax."

"The episodes have been getting worse," he admitted. "I've been blacking out completely."

"And, for some reason, you no longer think it's epileptic in nature?"

Nathan shook his head. "I've been coming around in different locations than I lost consciousness in, with absolutely no recollection of what I've done in between!" He felt the colour draining from his face. "A few weeks ago, I even zoned out in my apartment and came around in a public park at midnight!" Obvious distress was creeping into his voice. "And I've been having these disturbing flashbacks. As if..." He stopped himself from surrendering his darkest fears and gave a deep sigh.

"Relax, Nathan. Just relax."

"It's worrying me, though, Isaac. I must've walked five or six kilometres in a completely oblivious state," he reiterated, wondering if he was making any sense, his thoughts becoming more and more confused as he opened up. "I really should come clean at work... I'd think I was going crazy, but it... it just..."

"Relax. It's OK. Just remember that you're safe here. Relax... Relax," Isaac reassured again, his voice becoming softer and softer.

Nathan felt himself beginning to slip helplessly and disconnectedly into a distant half-world of slowing time. He fought to remain present, but his visual focus was becoming fixed, and any vestige of peripheral vision was already lost to his senses. His speech finally petered out to a disjointed garble. "I... I don't know... it... it just doesn't seem en... entirely med... ical... I've... I..." The axes of *Space* and *Time* began stretching away to infinity. "I..."

From somewhere inside of himself, Nathan watched in slow motion as Isaac's lips moved and mouthed such familiar shapes. But only silence ensued. He stared back blankly at Isaac, transfixed, empty of thought and incapable of response, as a soundless chain of somehow *visible* words that had issued from Isaac's mouth flowed slowly yet inexorably towards him. He had no defence. The linear sequence of soundless sounds was upon him and penetrated his subconscious mind without resistance, and once inside, the complex chain of frequency patterns – losing all integrity and structure – disintegrated, leaving countless partial fragments circulating randomly around each other. Then, in an instant, the ball of churning confusion evaporated completely, leaving only the faint residue of *meaning* in what Isaac was saying.

"Relax, Nathan. Just relax and breathe. You're safe. Just relax."

Nathan surrendered ....
....
....
....
.... *BLUE* ....
....
....
....
...... *SUSPENDED IN LUMINOUS ELECTRIC BLUE* .....

. . . .
. . . .
. . . .
. . . .
. . . .

If *silence* has no place for sound, *BLUE* had no place for *silence*; if *stillness* has no place for motion, *BLUE* had no place for *stillness*; if *eternity* has no place for an ending, *BLUE* had no place for *eternity*; if absolute *purity* has no place for faults, *BLUE* had no place for absolute *purity*. Thought did not exist. Existence was *BLUE*.

Nathan's re-entry was instant and disturbing. There was no gentle relaxed afterglow. He was buffeted and thrown violently. Confusion tore at him as his physical reasoning brain tried to kick in again by computing concepts such as direction, magnitude, location and time: *BLUE* had not possessed a height or weight; *BLUE* had not possessed a place or span. He stole a long, constricted inhalation. Awareness returned. The suspension of blue void that had been lack of self had vanished, and he sat in his chair unable to move.

It took some time for his respiration to normalise, and he was too scared to close his eyes, not even daring to blink in case he slipped away again.

"…Take a sip, nice and easy," instructed Isaac, holding a glass of water to Nathan's lips. "Just breathe normally. You're safe. There's nothing to worry about."

"What the hell just happened!" Nathan finally managed.

"Trance, Nathan. I could see you slipping for a good ten or fifteen seconds before you went. You're a natural. Very impressive, I have to say."

Nathan looked perplexed.

"I can guarantee that the blackouts you've been having are not due to any kind of pathology. Trust me; this explains all of your experiences of late. You've been slipping gradually towards deeper and deeper altered states… Well, that's not strictly true from a continuum perspective…" he added, in more of his incomprehensible enthusiasm, "but that's not important, right now." Having had to remain perfectly quiet throughout, Isaac now allowed himself the luxury of ranting with unbridled exhilaration on seeing that his young charge was fully back to his senses. "It's no coincidence that it happened to you *here* of all places, Nathan. Do you know how exciting this is?" Isaac was grinning broadly. "Such an intense *blue*."

Nathan was left stunned by Isaac's words. There seemed no end to this man's insight. Questions upon questions were now colliding within the maelstrom of his mind, each collision spawning transient answers that were immediately annihilated by their own contradictions. "Are you telling me that you could see the *blue* and everything that was happening to me!"

"In a way, Nathan. In a way," Isaac answered, a little evasively, before redirecting. "Let me show you something!"

Isaac hurried over to a writing bureau on the other side of the room and rummaged through a drawer, and on retrieving a scruffy-looking A4 notebook, ragged with use, he strode back over to Nathan, flicking through the leaves as he walked. "Take a look for yourself."

Nathan scanned the open page of what appeared to be a handwritten journal of some description. It was overflowing with scrawling writing, presumably penned by Isaac himself.

The header of the entry being offered to him was dated 4th October, just seven days prior, and crammed in the centre of the page was a single line of prophetic words: *Nathan. Doctor. St Mary's Hospital. Trance. Blue. 11th October.* The words predicted the day of their meeting. Clearly, Isaac had been expecting him.

Isaac watched the video clip on the phone that Nathan had handed him. Judging by the sound of the audio and from the way the image was jumping around the screen, the impromptu recording had been captured by a giggling and vivacious young woman dancing tipsily around the lounge room of Nathan's inner-city apartment. The footage showed all the trappings of an enjoyable evening in progress as the girl zoomed in on the remains of dinner on uncleared plates before panning across to two extravagant bottles of Bollinger – one empty and the second opened, with glasses already charged.

"Hey, take your shirt off and sing me a song," she dared, finally steadying the viewfinder on Nathan, who was sitting over on the couch. "We can YouTube it!"

Alex Stanton was a girl who liked to party hard outside of her practice of Corporate Law. She was a lot of fun, filthy rich but hardly marriage material. Nathan did find her worryingly irresistible, though, and she had become a constant fixture in his life of late.

Alex danced the camera expectantly towards Nathan, zooming in too closely on his face.

"Not a hope!" he laughed, motioning defensively with his hand, doing his best to avoid the encroaching focal length of the lens.

"*Aww*, you're no fun," she pouted. "Well, how about just taking the shirt off?"

Isaac raised his eyebrows with a smile and gave Nathan a sideways glance.

"It's not what you might think," Nathan responded. "Take a look at my eyes."

Isaac focused again on the screen, and over the next few seconds of footage, an all-too-familiar change in Nathan's demeanour became evident. While the girl began swinging the phone wildly side to side in a new dance around the room, Nathan's voice could still be heard uttering something beneath the blaring audio of her playful, chirping Latin rhythms.

"You OK?" Alex asked, lowering the phone on finally noticing the odd change in behaviour. "Nathan."

Nathan didn't answer, and for the next few moments the static view of the apartment's polished rosewood floorboards was accompanied only by silence interspersed every now and then by muffled dialogue from the Smartphone's speaker. "We're flying blind... thirty minutes southeast of Melbourne... To be honest, if we get much lower than this, I..."

"Nathan!" Alex demanded for a second time, sounding a little uncomfortable. "Stop fooling around."

"*One o'clock!*" his voice asserted, still making no sense whatsoever. "I shouldn't have let them fly..."

Alex remained silent and tentatively raised the phone until the screen was again centred on Nathan, now sitting with his eyes closed. "Nathan?" she ventured quietly.

"I'm scared... Out of control... We're coming down! No! No...!"

It was obvious to Isaac, watching the footage, that Nathan had slipped into a deep Trance state and was completely unaware of his actions. Despite him fully expecting Nathan to show a real propensity for Trance, he hadn't been prepared for the extent of the unharnessed potential that he was watching.

A moment's silence in the recording followed in which Nathan seemed to calm down and regain composure from his distressed state. "Someone's just come close," he continued in a whispered tone. "Very close! I can see him…"

"What does he look like?" Alex finally prompted, the hint of a giggle surfacing in her voice again. Experience told her that walking a friend through the occasional bad trip by humouring them was often the easiest and safest course of action. She really hadn't taken Nathan for the type and was frankly a little disappointed he hadn't chosen to share. The footage, she'd decided, was going to be good blackmail material the next time she wanted some outrageously expensive shoes.

"Beard. Weather-beaten face," Nathan answered, matter-of-factly. "He's the pilot – *I DON'T KNOW WHERE I AM!*"

Alex suddenly felt ill at ease again. With the last utterance, it was as though someone had just taken over Nathan's persona. Even his well-spoken southern accent had become momentarily unrecognisable.

"I can see Venus from the air and a lighthouse in the distance," he ranted nonsensically, "and a long straight beach with a small islet just offshore…" A second or two of hesitation signalled that he was troubled over something. "No, no, it's a *straight* beach…" he finally asserted, as if correcting himself by re-emphasising the word *straight*. "There's debris washed up on the shore…" Suddenly Nathan began to hyperventilate with uncontrolled emotion. "I can see them face down in the sand… My God! What have I done… My beautiful girls… I've killed them! I've killed them!"

"Stop it! Stop it! Stop it now!" Alex screamed, distressed by what she was witnessing. This was like no drug-induced state she'd ever seen, and there was now no funny side.

"What's wrong?" came Nathan's voice through the speaker, sounding confused yet otherwise back to his normal self.

"What's wrong? You're what's wrong!" Alex said, with a tremble in her voice.

A blur of tumbling frames, followed by a darkened screen, indicated that Nathan's phone had been thrown forcibly onto the couch where he was sitting.

"Alex! Where are you going? Alex…!"

Nathan reached across and pressed the pause button. "I haven't heard from her since. That was over a week ago."

Isaac didn't respond immediately. He'd undoubtedly just witnessed Nathan communicating with a deceased pilot – at the precise moment of his death – struggling with the horror of killing two women in an air crash. Isaac knew of few Mediums alive possessing such ability, and his estimation of Nathan's untapped potential had just grown immeasurably.

"Then I came across this, yesterday," Nathan said, eagerly taking back his phone and scrolling through to find a news item he'd downloaded. "I just took a stab and searched for any air crashes near Melbourne, thinking it might've been an incident from the past."

Isaac scanned the screen. The news report from the day before was headed by a photograph of a bearded middle-aged man standing proudly next to a light aircraft parked in front of a hangar.

"That's the guy I saw, Isaac! I swear that's him!"

The columns of text below the image described the ongoing Search and Rescue attempts to locate the man's aircraft along the route of its logged flight plan, the plane having gone missing at some point in the last twenty-four hours. *Grave fears are held for the pilot, his wife and his daughter who were passengers in the aircraft*, were the final words of the journalistic piece.

"You do realise, Nathan, this means that you were communicating with a dead pilot a whole week before his aircraft had even taken off on its last-ever flight?"

Nathan knew that Isaac was right. While Alex was recording that time-stamped video communication with the dead, the individuals concerned would still have been going about their normal daily lives, unaware that a stranger, somewhere on the other side of the world, was locked in a struggle with the emotions surrounding their tragic deaths – deaths that had not yet occurred but were soon going to make headline news.

"That's what's been freaking me out, Isaac. I need to know what the hell's happening to me in these blackouts..." He couldn't contain himself any longer. "I've been having flashbacks of torturing and killing, for Christ's Sake!" he blurted, the impromptu confession leaving a hanging silence in the air that nothing could fill.

A chill shot down Isaac's spine on hearing the unexpected and shocking admission, and he was momentarily thrown. Over many decades, several of his predecessors had prophesied that *a Medium of extraordinary ability will one day emerge, heralding an auspicious period in The Sanctuary's history.* And when Nathan had walked in that day, Isaac had been sure that those prophecies had finally found a resolution. But there had been many pretenders over the decades, and some had even been intent on the destruction of The Sanctuary and all it stood for. It suddenly struck Isaac that there was nothing in his scribbled-down prediction of their imminent and much-anticipated meeting that suggested it would necessarily be a positive encounter. Nathan could be just another one of those pretenders.

A wall of doubt and suspicion now separated the pair, and Isaac had more reason than most not to trust everyone that entered his world. "Tell me what made you come *here* of all places? Why The Sanctuary?" he asked bluntly, rapidly redirecting the conversation 180 degrees, all semblance of cordiality having vanished.

Nathan took a breath, half embarrassed and half relieved at finally having confessed his deepest fears. Isaac's now guarded attitude towards him was certainly off-putting, but it came as no surprise given what he'd just admitted to.

"I'm here because of a drunk!" Nathan answered with equal bluntness, now having nothing to lose.

"A drunk?"

"The other night, I was accosted by a drunk in A&E. He had mental health issues for sure and just kept on repeating that I was in danger and needed to find *sanctuary*."

Isaac's brow furrowed.

"I wouldn't normally have thought twice about it, but he started going on that it was my fault my parents had died and that I should've stopped them getting into the car. It was as if he was inside my mind." Nathan shook his head to himself.

"He had to be restrained in the end but kept on shouting the word *Sanctuary, Sanctuary* over and over again at me. So when I was looking for someone to—"

"You saw the name *The Sanctuary* and decided it was serendipity?" Isaac interrupted.

"Pretty much."

Isaac gave Nathan a long hard look. He knew all too well that the criminally insane and mentally disturbed often exhibit uncanny psychic abilities – they could truly get inside your head. The sometimes-cryptic nature of psychic communication was also familiar to him. Deciphering messages from other realms was sometimes more akin to a game of Charades than anything else. Nathan's entire story, he decided, just wasn't the sort of thing some interloper bent on causing trouble would present with, and after taking a moment to hold Nathan's gaze and search his eyes and soul for any trace of malicious intent, Isaac chose to trust his gut.

"Leave this with me, Nathan. I'd certainly like to invite you back at some point to take you through a series of psychic tests to explore your potential," Isaac offered, his demeanour softening and becoming amiable once again. "With your permission, there are some people I would like to speak to about this. In fact, you should meet them. Maybe you could join us for an evening we've got planned this coming week."

Nathan nodded his agreement, and with that, Isaac simply stood and reached out his hand, indicating that the consultation was at an end.

The rat padded heavily across the cold stone floor along its usual track, quite at home in the filth and grime. It flared and twitched its nostrils two or three times in the dim half-light of the room as it paused for a second to lock onto the odour of fresh meat before its nocturnal scurrying ended at the mound of human flesh in the corner of the room. Warily checking that the carcass wasn't about to move, it clambered onto the naked skin and then made its way cautiously up to the roughly sutured sickle-shaped incision line of clotted blood that extended some twenty centimetres across the shaven scalp, from the midline of the forehead to just in front of the left ear. There the rat began feasting ravenously while two of the other girls chained to the walls slept as best they could where they lay.

"Jess! Jess!" the youngest managed from out of a weak, terrified sob on waking. "It's back!"

Jessica Mahr roused immediately and being the closest to the feeding rodent screamed and kicked out with her legs, the clanking of her chains forcing the rat to flee, for the time being, at least.

She pushed herself back to the wall, wrapping her arms around herself in a futile attempt to find some warmth. "It's OK, Maddie. It's OK," she reassured her young cellmate. "I'll stay awake now."

Another vigil over the motionless body of the young girl lying close by in the corner of the room began. Jessica prayed that the girl was unconscious but was starting to worry that she might be dead. In truth, the girl's paralysis and catatonic stare into the shadows belied the fact that, within, a fully conscious soul lay silently screaming.

8

The evening world news streamed through, its relentless digital feed spilling inexorably over sovereign border after sovereign border, washing away the arbitrary lines of time drawn across the surface of the globe. And with a slide of paper across his desk and a turn of his head towards a single locked-off camera, the Australian anchor began his live report on Search and Rescue's efforts to recover bodies from the wreckage of the missing light aircraft that had just been found southeast of Melbourne.

In following the breaking news from the other side of the world, Nathan hadn't been able to drag himself away from his computer for over two days. He'd barely slept on account of the half-day time difference, with search efforts having to resume at an Antipodean dawn at odds with the need to close his eyes and drift away to find some refuge from his own mind. An obsessive compulsion kept him fixed to the screen for hour after hour watching the news feed. But at last the aircraft had been found.

"Air Traffic Control logs suggest that the plane took off at 12.30 pm from a small airfield just outside of Melbourne," the report continued, "but never arrived at its easterly destination on the New South Wales coast…"

"*Thirty minutes flying time… southeast of Melbourne… One o'clock!*" The words spoken by Nathan's own voice in Alex's video recording echoed through his being as the report unfolded – if the pilot had taken off at 12.30 pm, then the crash would have occurred at precisely *one o'clock*.

The anchor's expression remained suitably grim. "Search and Rescue's efforts were initially frustrated by the pilot having flown on a course different than initially planned, the wreckage having been finally located 300 kilometres west of the initial search area. We now cross to Ed McCormick on location at Venus Bay."

"Thanks, Peter…"

"*I can see Venus…*" Nathan was stunned. The apparent nonsense he'd uttered to Alex suddenly made sense, and despite the tragedy behind the details, he was feeling strangely euphoric as resolution after resolution assaulted his senses.

"…Yes, a tragic outcome to what was supposed to have been an enjoyable family trip interstate," the reporter began. "The bodies of the pilot, his wife and twenty-five-year-old daughter have now been recovered after washing up on the beach some fifteen kilometres from where I'm standing," he continued, motioning over his shoulder with wooden professional sympathy, allowing viewers a glimpse of the endless stretch of sun-drenched golden sand he had chosen as his backdrop.

"Police and investigators are on scene. However, reports over the last few days of dense fog shrouding this twenty-kilometre stretch of inaccessible beach do suggest that the pilot may well have become disorientated and, flying too low, crashed into the Bass Strait at speed, just off shore between Arch Rock and the nearby lighthouse..."

"...*there's a lighthouse in the distance... and a long straight beach... and a small islet just offshore... No, no, it's a 'straight' beach.*" Nathan stared at the aerial footage of the *Strait*'s coastline being broadcast, showing the eroded offshore islet and lighthouse that he'd described to Alex in Trance. Every word he'd uttered in the recording had just been echoed by the reporter standing on that stretch of secluded beach across the other side of the world. Nathan now knew he truly had communicated with that dead pilot an entire week *before* the man had even boarded his plane to taxi out on its final fateful journey.

9

Heavy black drapes hung in front of a door halfway down The Sanctuary's corridor. Nathan remembered noticing them when he'd first been shown into Isaac's reading room earlier that week but hadn't given it a second thought. Now he found himself standing directly in front of the drapes after having been asked to remove his shoes, belt and watch by a wiry bald-headed man of about fifty who was attending to his duties with a blank expressionless focus. Nathan raised his arms parallel to the floor as instructed and was subjected to a frisk search worthy of even the most diligent of airport security officers. But it seemed that he wasn't being singled out. Further down the corridor, a young female also waiting to enter the séance room was being searched just as thoroughly by an equally expressionless middle-aged woman whose diligence even extended as far as probing and examining a bandage on the girl's wrist in the course of the search.

Nathan's phone was finally checked to be off by the

humourless man before the device was placed along with his watch inside his shoes on a rack against the wall.

"Prevents any confusion afterwards," the man explained impersonally with a brusque nod, giving Nathan the all-clear to enter the room.

As he brushed past the drapes and walked in through the open doorway, he was struck by a macabre sense of theatre inside. The spacious room, with original polished floorboards and mahogany-panelled walls, was lit by a scattering of dim wall lights and one central unshaded bulb hanging from an ornate plaster ceiling rose. Pairs of the same heavy black drapes as hung outside dropped to the floor in front of each of the windows. A gap in one pair revealed that the panes of glass had been boarded up on the inside with single sheets of snugly fitted plywood, and even the narrowest of seams between the boards and the window frames had been fastidiously gaffer taped over. The offending gap was noticed by a man walking around the room checking the drapes, and they were pulled securely shut, leaving Nathan perplexed at the seemingly excessive efforts at blackout on such a moonless and overcast night.

Three people chatting in subdued tones were already seated in a ring of twenty identical upholstered metal-framed chairs. The circle was completed, however, by a sturdy-looking antique wooden chair that wouldn't have looked out of place in the throne room of a medieval castle. Nathan eyed the curiosity, assuming that it would be for Isaac's use, and couldn't help but be intrigued by the words *A DIOCESE FOR TRUTH* carved ornately across its backrest. The two chairs either side had 'Reserved' labels placed on them, and the one on the right had been pulled out of the arrangement to allow access into the circle for seating purposes, the ring of chairs being otherwise so tightly placed as to prevent anyone from squeezing through.

Nathan scanned the remaining group of about ten not-yet-seated individuals looking on from the perimeter. Their attention was on Isaac, who was standing in the centre of the circle while being searched by two others as Barbara supervised. Another was examining Isaac's chair, checking it over thoroughly as if it was a magician's stage prop. Tipping the chair to examine underneath, the man inadvertently revealed four scorch marks marring the luxuriantly polished floorboards, and Nathan noticed that the marks lined up perfectly with the base of each chair leg. The defacement was completed by the words 'I AM, I AM' having been gouged deeply into the flooring just in front of the chair in what appeared to be some ritualistic cryptic proclamation.

A shiver shot down Nathan's spine at the sight, and the words of the drunk who'd accosted him in A&E assaulted his being again – *I am, I am Sanctuary!* It just could not be a coincidence. And remembering the drunk's chilling insistence regarding some unspecified danger he was supposed to be in, Nathan scanned the faces of those present once more. He felt uneasy but couldn't see anyone that even remotely looked threatening amongst the group of benign-looking individuals scattered around the room. With a sharp intake of breath, he shook off the paranoia that had been thrust upon him by the crazed patient, still unable to resist the troubled man's vitriol from capturing his mind at times. If nothing else, it was now clear that he was where he was supposed to be. The Sanctuary undoubtedly held the answers he was seeking.

Nathan turned his attention back to the centre of the ring of seats where the man checking the sturdy antique chair had finally deemed all of the joints to be solid and secure. And he watched Isaac painstakingly reposition the chair himself so that each of the legs was back in place, precisely over their marks.

Barbara, her supervision of Isaac's body search complete, immediately hurried over to Nathan on noticing his arrival. She seemed a little more flustered than the last time they had met but still offered a smile and a hug from over the backs of the seats.

"The body searches are just precautionary," she opened, obviously well versed in having to explain the protocol. "Everyone here is most definitely trusted, but it would be terribly impolite just to search newcomers like yourself without subjecting everyone else to the same procedures," she quickly added. "You've read through the *dos* and *don'ts*? It's all common sense, really."

Nathan nodded his understanding, holding up the leaflet he'd been handed in the corridor earlier but thought it all a little over the top. He couldn't imagine what could warrant the security measures he and everyone else had just been subjected to.

Barbara's rolling itinerary allowed no time for Nathan to speak. "Let me introduce you," she continued, before raising her voice ever so slightly to gain the attention of the room and reeling off a list of names for Nathan's benefit that was impossible to remember in just one pass. "Oh, yes, and that was Mike and Doreen on the door," she concluded with a smile, before hurrying over to attend to Isaac, leaving those gathered staring silently at the newcomer.

"She gets a little anxious beforehand," a female voice apologised. "Pleased to meet you, Nathan."

Nathan had been saved from a socially awkward moment by a tall, attractive blonde in her late thirties who was the only one to step forwards and acknowledge his presence. Even in her stockinged feet, the woman had the poise of a fashion model, with long elegant calves in no need of the heels she'd left outside in the corridor. A certain smart officiousness about her two-piece power dressing and designer glasses, however, did suggest that she had used her brains rather than her looks to power her way through life.

"Anne-Marie?" Nathan ventured, trying to remember her from the list of names.

"Anne-Marie Burns," she countered, with a lingering handshake and a glance of hazel eyes from over her frames.

Nathan smiled politely, still locked in her gently tightening grip, having no choice but to maintain eye contact with her. Everything about her appearance was youthful and faultless. Only her self-assuredness gave away her true age. But before the flirtatious introduction could proceed any further, he was saved from yet another socially awkward moment when Isaac summoned him over.

"*We'll talk later*," Anne-Marie mouthed.

He nodded with a smile before making his way around to Isaac through the opening in the circle.

"Perhaps you'd care to check these and then secure me to the chair. Wrists first, and then ankles," Isaac invited from his seated position.

Nathan was surprised to be handed a set of four heavy-duty propylene security ties – the kind used by law enforcement in lieu of handcuffs.

"Give them a good tug and when you're happy..."

"Is all this necessary?"

"All will become clear. But just make sure that's tight... No, tighter... No, much tighter."

Nathan pulled on the ties just short of compromising the circulation to Isaac's hands and feet. The man was now, undeniably, tethered to the chair with no chance of escape.

"I take it you saw the news reports about the aircraft?" Isaac asked, adjusting his position in the chair to get as comfortable as possible.

Nathan hadn't expected the question and answered with just a nod.

"Come and see me again in a few days. We have a lot to discuss," Isaac suggested, before closing his eyes to indicate that Nathan's job was done.

Mike and Doreen had by now also entered the room and were themselves being frisked. Barbara locked the door behind them and pocketed the key before motioning for everyone to enter the circle and take a seat, her right hand hovering over the panel of light switches by the door.

Nathan headed for a chair directly opposite Isaac to ensure the best possible view, and as the others swarmed in, Anne-Marie darted across to sit next to him, immediately grabbing his left hand in what seemed to be another of her entirely over-familiar gestures. A second or two later, though, the man who'd taken a seat to his right grabbed his other hand, mirroring everyone else that had now taken their places in the circle of chairs, leaving Nathan feeling unaccustomedly awkward at his assumption.

Anne-Marie leant over towards him. *"Hope you're not scared of things that go bump in the night!"* she teasingly whispered, leaving Nathan wondering what he'd let himself in for by accepting Isaac's invitation to the séance.

Mike took the reserved sign off his seat and sat down next to Isaac and flicked on a small lamp at his feet. He nodded to Barbara over at the door, who duly extinguished the lights, leaving the room bathed in the lamp's diffuse red glow. The circle was finally completed by Barbara rushing over and pulling her chair back into tight alignment as she sat down.

"Welcome to our Circle, everyone… A Diocese for Truth," Barbara opened with a proud smile, now palpably relaxing.

The carved words on the back of Isaac's séance chair, Nathan realised, were nothing more than a simple proclamation of the séance Circle's name.

"Well, if everyone's comfortable, we'll begin. As Circle Leader, I must remind you that we insist on absolute silence unless you're invited to talk," she instructed. "And under no circumstance must anyone break the Circle. If some kind of emergency arises for you, let me know immediately and either Mike or I will attend to the matter. But you must remain seated. And if we do proceed into full blackout, it is essential that everybody keeps hold of the person's hand next to them. If for some reason the person next to you lets go without permission, even for a second, you must immediately make that known. Then we can name and shame them!"

The group laughed in response.

"Well, ladies and gentlemen. Sit back and enjoy."

Full blackout? The drapes, the boarded-up windows and Anne-Marie's teasing comment now all made sense. Certainly, a lot of effort had been put into the evening's arrangements to make a statement that everything here was above board. But as Nathan looked across at Isaac tied theatrically to the chair, he couldn't help but be reminded of a Las Vegas show he'd once caught to kill time on a forced stopover. The illusionist's slick exaggerated moves in a black sequinned one-piece and Cuban heels had all been too much to stomach, but the sheer scale of the illusions had impressed. Nathan was as certain as he could be, though, that a Vegas crowd would be howling for blood if at the climax of every disappearing act the venue was plunged into darkness while stagehands leisurely wheeled a Monster Truck off into the wings, allowing time for a pretty assistant to stroll on and strike a sparkling leotard *"Ta-daaa! It's disappeared!"* pose, just as the lights flicked back on. His expectations for Isaac's demonstration were waning.

Nothing happened for an inordinate amount of time, and Nathan fought squirming in his seat. Pareidolia played havoc with his visual senses as Isaac's features seemed to change constantly and morph into countless male and female faces. For a split second, he swore he even saw his father's face in the low-light conditions playing cruel optical tricks on his mind.

Isaac had remained uncannily motionless throughout, but his breathing had now become deeper and even a little laboured. Then, with a single cough to clear his throat, he began to speak. The timbre of his voice was easily recognisable, though the words were laced with a very well-spoken English accent. "Good evening, friends."

"Good evening!" responded everyone except Nathan, the regulars knowing their cues on whether to speak or not.

Nathan baulked.

"We have a newcomer this evening?"

"Yes, Hugh," Barbara answered.

Hugh? Nathan thought. *This character has a name?* He feared the sense of theatre was about to descend into Act One of some lame farce. Hearing Isaac put on an accent while purporting to be some ethereal visitor called *Hugh* was just about as ridiculous as he could have imagined. At the conclusion of their first meeting, Isaac had assured him that there were explanations for what he'd been experiencing in those involuntary altered states he'd been slipping into, hence the invitation. But this show of theatrics seemed unlike anything that had been caught on video by Alex. He couldn't believe that he'd allowed himself to be taken in.

"Hmm, but I sense his doubts," Isaac relayed. "To question is noble; to doubt is… not! Perhaps I could get you to agree, my friend?"

Barbara nodded across at Nathan, and Anne-Marie squeezed his hand at the same time, both encouraging him to respond.

Nathan felt put on the spot and certainly wasn't about to be intimidated by Isaac or any of his alter egos. "So you *doubt* my sincerity, Hugh?" he countered, before fully appreciating the overt rudeness inherent in his retort. After all, he needn't have accepted the invitation to the demonstration. And the footer on the leaflet handed to him earlier had clearly invited any person feeling unable to enter into the spirit of the occasion or not able to abide by the stated rules to take their leave before the doors were shut.

Isaac, however, laughed loudly on Hugh's behalf. "Well said, my friend. I think we are going to get along just fine."

"You are talkative tonight, Hugh. If you're comfortable, perhaps the Circle can relax?" Barbara interjected, redirecting the proceedings, being accustomed to Hugh's tendency to probe newcomers.

"Of course. Please."

The man seated to Nathan's right followed the cue and let go of his hand, taking the opportunity to get more comfortable in his chair, as did the rest of the Circle. Nathan's other hand, though, remained firmly in Anne-Marie's grasp for a few seconds longer than was necessary, and he eventually had to take the initiative himself. Over the next few minutes or so, he listened while 'Hugh' spoke amiably to various members of the group with whom he had obviously interacted before, and Nathan had to admit that the persona was highly amusing, catching himself laughing a few times. As time passed, the initial absurdity of the entire scenario even began to wane somewhat as Isaac sank deeper into character. Much of the talk was about the earthly life the man was supposed to have led in the 1920s – nothing that couldn't have been googled or gleaned from a history book. And Hugh, in turn, asked many questions of the group about the state of the world now.

"Am I repeating myself?"

"*No, Hugh. No. No,*" the members of the group replied from around the Circle.

"You must understand that when I return to a normal state in my own time, I can't remember what has been said, like *you* would remember our conversations. I forget much. But those fragments that I do remember drop into my mind as when trying to grasp a fading dream upon waking. I have to trust that some of my wonderings and contemplations throughout my day are, in fact, those incredible things my friends in this room have told me about regarding the time you live in. Only occasionally am I sufficiently lucid that my recall allows me to maintain full confidence in our work. In this way, though, I am slowly able to build a picture of *there, here*."

"You're doing well, Hugh," Barbara encouraged again.

"*Yes. Yes. You really are,*" several of the group reiterated.

Nathan remained silent, intrigued at how utterly gullible those gathered obviously were.

"It is so important to remember, my friends, that our human subconscious unfolds into the conscious through insight. And when that unfolding is retained within the conscious mind, we gain a degree of enlightenment. That collective enlightenment includes scientific discovery. The unseen can be seen. The elusive dark matter of the cosmos becomes no longer dark and all manner of phenomena is exposed… But Consciousness is not a mere *Observer* of nature's laws in action; it is the *Creator* of those very laws."

Nathan's ears pricked at Hugh's last comment; it sounding suspiciously like something Isaac himself would have said. But before it could be elaborated on, the flow of words was interrupted as Isaac's breathing suddenly deepened again. A noticeable chill seemed to have descended across the room, and Barbara reacted with a glance across at Mike, who was already looking at her and nodding in agreement.

"Everyone join hands," instructed Barbara, with a slight urgency in her voice. "And under no circumstances let go until you are told… Mike, if you would, please."

Mike leant forwards to switch off the red lamp with his free hand, but before he'd quite reached down far enough, something appeared to distract him in his peripheral vision, causing him to hesitate for a moment. Nathan followed

Mike's gaze across the room to his right, where the wrought iron brush, shovel and fire poker hanging in the fire tool set near the fireplace seemed to be moving eerily of their own accord. Nathan had just about enough time to convince himself that it was another optical trick of the low-light conditions when the sobering realisation hit that he could actually hear the faintest creaking of metal against metal as the implements swung side to side in their stand. But before his paralysed intellect could recover and formulate any acceptable conclusion, a photo frame sitting on top of the mantelpiece suddenly skated off the wooden mantel and flew through the air, just missing the heads of those in its line of trajectory, before crashing to the ground in the centre of the Circle. Gasps could be heard all around just as Mike finally flicked the red lamp off. The effect was instantly disturbing to the soul. This was more than simply being plunged into darkness. The blackout was so complete that Light could no longer be said to exist. The rods in Nathan's retinas strained to accommodate but were asphyxiated by the vacuum of photons, and the only parameters remaining of the physical Reality that had existed only seconds before were now the warmth of the hands he held, the feeling of his clothing's fabric against his skin, and a forced appreciation of gravity as his drowning awareness flailed and grasped for a safe island in the sense of his own weight pushing him down into the chair. Within seconds, even the floor beneath his feet seemed to have ceased to exist – he was suspended in an unearthly darkness. The sound of a faint electrical crackling in the atmosphere in the centre of the Circle brought Nathan's attention back to the here and now of the room. And out of the rising potential of expectancy, a powerful flash of horizontal fluorescent blue lightning suddenly cracked across the room just above head height.

Everyone jumped in unison and the room was filled with more short gasps and a simultaneous chorus of "*Whoa!*" and "*No way!*" before nervous giggles took hold around the Circle. Everyone's grip was suddenly tighter in the blackness.

"It's OK, everybody," Barbara reassured, raising her voice slightly. "No matter how many times you see that, it always makes you jump. It's just the energy building. You will have smelt the odour." A musty sulphurous smell hung in the atmosphere, a sure sign to Barbara that some phenomenon was about to occur. "That's ectoplasm," she added, for the benefit of those in the group who might not have experienced it before. "It's thought to be a substrate halfway between Matter and Energy. A kind of precursor, if you like, that builds and exudes from the Physical Medium in Trance states. It's thought to be sensitive to the higher energy frequencies in white light. That's why we need the complete blackout and the precaution of the red lamp."

Nathan's heart was unexpectedly racing. His critical sense of what was real and unreal was under threat. He'd carefully surveyed the room beforehand. The door was locked. He'd secured Isaac to the chair himself, and the ring of chairs was utterly impregnable. No one could have broken it without several people knowing. It would simply have been impossible to introduce some kind of electrical equipment into the centre of the Circle, especially something capable of generating the kind of charge needed to ionise the air across the whole width of the room. Nathan's need for reason and logic launched an attack with a volley of words such as *Vegas*, *Monster Truck* and *Pretty Magician's Assistant*. Every nerve fibre and synapse of his body urged him to break the circle, jump the chairs, and switch on the light to expose the trickery being perpetrated. But something stopped him, and it was more than just the social conventions of peer group pressure. He desperately needed to know if there truly was some answer in all this to explain what he'd been suffering through lately.

Nathan's sense of Reality, though, was to be warped beyond all stretches of the imagination when a well-circumscribed swirl of light could suddenly be seen spiralling upwards a couple of feet into the air from an area of the floor close to where Isaac was sitting. Within a second or two, it collapsed back into the darkness, only to reappear moments later in exactly the same spot. There it lingered, wafting gently from side to side like a candle's flame in a gentle breeze.

"Oh My God!" one of the group exclaimed breathlessly.

The others, including Nathan, were left speechless. As surely as some high-tech holographic equipment had been fired up in the centre of the room, a bluish white mirage burgeoned upwards into the air, forming a semitransparent outline of a light body. The head, shoulders, torso and limbs were readily discernible in the materialisation, and a faint umbilical cord of light could be seen extending backwards to Isaac.

Unbeknown to Nathan, while the regulars in the Circle had witnessed many kinds of astounding phenomena in their regular visits, never had such a clear physical materialisation appeared before them.

"We can see you!" Barbara exclaimed, trying to control her excitement. "Is that you, Hugh? Are you still able to communicate?"

With that, the body of light turned and drifted across the floor in Nathan's direction. He was transfixed but could still feel Anne-Marie gripping his hand tighter and tighter, perhaps regretting her teasing quip of earlier.

Amidst the body of light approaching him, Nathan could see a face starting to emerge. And as the features became more distinct, the lips could be seen mouthing out words. The air then suddenly resounded with the unmistakeable sound of his father's voice.

"*Take care of Caleb, Nate…*"

A chill ran down Nathan's spine. The now recognisable light manifestation standing directly in front of him had just uttered the ultimate confirmation of his father's presence. *Nate* was his dad's nickname for him – John Carter being the only person ever to call him by that name.

10

Adam swigged on a beer, sitting on the edge of the coffee table in Nathan's apartment.

"You need to take some time off, mate," he suggested, mulling over his friend's predicament. "Look, I'm supposed to be starting a fortnight's leave in a couple of days. Just kicking back at the farmhouse. I had nothing planned other than gutting the kitchen. Why don't you head down there? I'll cover for you."

Set in the idyllic rural plains of Cheshire, just south of the city, Adam had been planning to renovate the secluded two-hundred-year-old farmhouse since buying it as a weekend retreat. But, despite the best of intentions, he'd always found something more recreational to do on his infrequent visits, usually culminating in a few hours at the nearby pub. The farmhouse was comfortable in its quaint old-world appeal, and Nathan was as sure as he could be that the property would still largely be as it was when Adam had first taken him there to view it eighteen months prior. Still, with everything that had been going on, some time away in seclusion with space to clear his head could only help.

"That's kind of you, but I really can't ask you to give up your vacation. I—"

"Already done!" Adam insisted, cutting Nathan off. "I'll take care of everything. The Kombi's parked in the shed. Feel free to use it while you're there. I wouldn't want you getting mud all over that beautiful sports car of yours!"

Nathan finished his beer knowing better than to argue. Generosity was something Adam offered freely, adamantly preferring that people dispense with social pleasantries at the risk of them feeling in any way indebted by a kind offer. It was one of countless unwritten social protocols sprouting from the dirt and grime of a northern upbringing that Adam's working-class sensibilities were still rooted in, and Nathan had learnt that those protocols were best navigated rather than fathomed. He himself had been torn from his own roots in the outskirts of middle-class London, where a '*no, thank you*' was simply a '*no, thank you*' and not necessarily a *faux pas* that might incite indignation. Despite growing up fighting the "*Faggot*" taunts over his well-spoken southern accent throughout his high school days, and quickly gaining acceptance through a few effective retaliatory punches, he'd never fully come to understand the pervading underclass psyche of those he'd been thrown amongst. He had learnt to respect them, though. Beneath it all, there was a raw honesty and strength of character that could always be relied upon if trouble showed its face.

"So you don't think I'm losing it?" Nathan summed up, in response to the impromptu mental health assessment he'd just undergone over the last hour, albeit carried out on the couch of his apartment. Self-diagnosis, even for a doctor, would be futile. Psychotics have no way of knowing that they are psychotic. And Adam – as well as being the person you'd want around when multiple terrorist bombs explode during the aftermath of a thirty-car pileup – had specialised in Psych earlier in his career before working his way through to Specialist Registrar in A&E. A role much more suited to him.

"I'm not saying that you don't need to speak to someone," Adam replied, "but no more than anyone else does. Me included. I watch far too much porn by some people's standards," he added, only half joking. "I see no evidence of pathology in that head of yours. Your hang-ups about Caleb's condition are just that… *hang-ups*. And entirely understandable ones. The traumatised seven-year-old inside of you has invented a story, and if he can only change the ending of that story by preventing Mummy and Daddy getting into that car, all will be well again. You've just got to find a way of letting go of that childhood fantasy."

Nathan listened to Adam's neat summation regarding the premonition of the car crash that he'd just confided while keeping his own thoughts to himself.

"As for the flashbacks, it's easy to forget how gruesome the job can be. Think of how many cadavers you've dissected, morgues you've visited and post-mortems you've attended. Not to mention the deaths you've witnessed and crazies you've had to stitch back together in your time as a medic. Sure, we could run some tests for those epileptic-type episodes, but my sense is that you're simply overworked. Back-to-back ten-hour shifts in A&E get to everyone eventually. You don't want to invite questions on record about your suitability to practise, without good reason."

Nathan nodded thoughtfully. "And the séance?"

"I was hoping you wouldn't ask."

Nathan held eye contact with his friend until he had no choice but to answer.

Adam gave a sigh, resigning himself to the conversation. "It's all bullshit, mate. The experience you had can easily be explained through the most basic of our psychological roots." Adam's tone more than hinted at his disdain for psychic Mediums. "The literature's full of papers citing the ancient rituals of primitive cultural groups. More often than not, they involve tribal elders administering hallucinogenic drugs such as Mescaline or Psilocybin. But there are any number of ways of manipulating an individual or group into an altered state of hysteria." Adam was a pragmatist to the core and had no time for fanciful beliefs and had even less tolerance for those who would prey on such misguided believers. "For all our outward sophistication, the primitive parts of the human brain are there to be tapped into. And there's no end of so-called therapists and gurus these days doing just that. Dangerous New Age quacks, if you ask me. Snake-oil shamans with no business playing around with suggestible minds grateful for the extortionate bill!" Adam took a breath. "Look. I wasn't there. But a few theatrics, a subliminal suggestion heightened by expectation, and throw in a touch of sensory deprivation… It doesn't take much."

"But surely a group of twenty people can't be wrong," Nathan said, torn between his own logical thought processes and by what he'd witnessed at the séance. "All of us witnessed the same thing!"

Adam remained unimpressed. "Shared experiences are proof of nothing!" he replied bluntly. "You know that. The

Asch Conformity Experiments show us that individuals in an experimental group, some of them unknowingly fed entirely different information to the others, will start to agree with everyone else about what was seen, heard or felt when placed in a discussion group afterwards."

Nathan let slip an unconvinced look, which only prompted his friend-turned-counsellor to drive home his point.

"At first, the targeted individuals are observably confused, but within a few minutes of listening to the others, they start to voice agreement with the majority view. Question them a few days later and their minds can be entirely convinced of a shared experience they'd only ever been told about." Adam shrugged. "It's called the 'black sheep effect' for good reason. Humans tend to be hardwired to ensure we fit in with the group. Those that aren't wired that way either find themselves shunned and alienated or end up using that very knowledge to become cult leaders, conmen or dictators."

Adam's scepticism wasn't entirely unexpected. Neither was his dismissal of that childhood premonition of the fatal car crash. So Nathan thought better of sharing the news report mentioning the aircraft wreckage found in the location predicted, as well as the footage of himself in communication with that deceased pilot – all that would have been impossible to explain away with the conventional medical line. Nor had he been totally upfront about the full sickening details of the flashbacks. He needed a friend on side, and admitting to thoughts of callously raping and murdering while ranting unconsciously about dead people might well have pushed even the naturally seditious Adam to contact the authorities regarding his suitability for registration.

Despite the necessary subterfuge putting limits on Adam's diagnosis, Nathan was relieved that there seemed nothing obvious to a trained eye that would summarily label him as insane. But that only led to more questions than answers. It had been unfortunate that, after the séance, Isaac had claimed to have felt fatigued and had been ushered out to the main house by Barbara, preventing anyone from questioning him. That had been highly frustrating. *Disbelief* had not yet been *suspended*. In fact, the séance had been so fantastical that rather than convince him of its authenticity, his scepticism – born out of ingrained objectivity – had only been given free rein to concoct any number of scenarios to reaffirm the sharp boundaries of the concrete reality he'd enjoyed for over thirty years. And each one of those scenarios necessarily involved charlatanism on Isaac's part, which was something that Nathan, equally, just did not want to believe.

He was torn. Thanks to Adam's offer, though, at least he could get away, clear his head and try to make some sense of everything. Whatever demons were lurking in the dark recesses of his mind, he knew that he would soon have to face them.

11

AXIS Technologies wasn't hard to find in the neatly landscaped labyrinth of the blue-chip industrial park on the outskirts of town. While the company logo didn't have the instantly recognisable branding of the surrounding multinationals, the research company's sprawling facility competed in every other respect. Its four storeys of black-tinted mirrored glass would have stretched the greater part of half a city block, presenting a reflected vista that suggested those outside had no business seeing in.

Nathan pulled up to the entrance and was met by an efficient and courteous security guard who checked the list of names on his tablet before raising the barrier and abruptly announcing the arrival into his headset. The tightness of the outwardly benign security, though, became evident the moment Nathan stepped out of his car in the underground car park and was confronted by a second security guard intent on escorting him every step of the way to his destination. If only Nathan had known that the barrier guard's tap on the tablet's screen had already alerted an operations room on the ground floor with access to details of his passport, driver's licence, bank accounts, tax history and every posted photo and comment he'd ever been included in on social media. Privacy Laws and trivial matters such as jurisdiction were of little consequence this side of the barrier. Facial Recognition databases had already been cross-referenced for any dubious associations, and the "Clear" was being reaffirmed into the second security guard's earpiece before Nathan had even shut his car door.

They exited the elevator on the fourth floor, the interior of the building being just as sterile and characterless as Nathan had imagined. Other than the two security guards, there hadn't been any sign of human endeavour behind the entire façade of that black-tinted mirrored wall of glass he'd managed to breach.

Barely a few strides down the corridor, Nathan's escort stopped at an unremarkable door labelled *Neuropsychological Research* and stabbed at the security intercom button. "Dr Carter for Dr Burns."

A moment later, the door opened to a gushing Anne-Marie. "Nathan, so glad you could make it. Please come in."

She held out her hand in one of her lingering handshakes, leaving Nathan yet again having to take the initiative in withdrawing his own hand to end the greeting. He turned around to acknowledge the security guard before crossing the threshold. But the man had already gone.

Anne-Marie had extended the invitation to AXIS on the night of the séance – the Circle having dissolved quickly after the demonstration, leaving Nathan and her talking alone for over an hour. She was obviously trusted, since Mike, who'd earlier been in charge of searching people at the door, hadn't questioned their lingering in The Sanctuary while he packed up and collected the fragments of glass from the broken picture frame that had flung itself into the Circle during the séance. The man of few words seemed to take even the simplest of janitorial duties very seriously, his obsessive-compulsive *'a place for everything and everything in its place'* attitude being more than evident as he worried himself over the inch-perfect positioning of the chairs he'd been stacking over in the corner of the séance room while Nathan and Anne-Marie had chatted. But the man obviously had issues. When Nathan had earlier knelt down in nothing more than a polite gesture to help him pick up the fragments of shattered glass, Mike's bristling reaction had been so surprisingly hostile at an outsider having the audacity to intervene in his duties that Nathan had been left with no other choice than to back off as one would from a dog baring its teeth over a cherished bone. Frankly, he'd been relieved when Mike had finally left.

Over the hour that he'd chatted with Anne-Marie in the séance room, Nathan had been struck by how intelligent she was. But she was hard to get a handle on. Three times during the course of that evening, he'd been convinced that she was blatantly flirting with him, only to be left feeling a touch embarrassed at the apparent misread. She had certainly been nothing but cordial since, and during their conversation did provide some intriguing information about The Sanctuary. Isaac and Barbara didn't own it – the property being managed by a Trust, with them as its live-in caretakers. Nathan had been wondering what stroke of good fortune had landed the unassuming couple, with obvious working-class ties, such a spectacular property. Most Premier League soccer players would have coveted it. He had also realised that Anne-Marie was one of the Neuroscientists that Isaac mentioned he was working with – the very reason she'd been permitted to sit in the séance circle. The protocols in place for the demonstrations, it seemed, involved more than just body searches, and since Anne-Marie's scientific research was relevant to the many questions he still had, he hadn't hesitated in accepting her invitation to AXIS.

"Welcome to my lair, Nathan," Anne-Marie said with a smile as she closed the outer laboratory door behind him. "I guarantee you'll find this interesting."

12

A gentle caress served to smear the rivulet of tears across the girl's cheek. Hers was a quiet, breathless sob, despite the horrifying predicament she now found herself in. Sitting bound and gagged at the end of the bed, she was already under full control. This was going to take hours. And, as yet, the girl had no idea of the unending torturous pain she was going to endure. Nothing in her short life, no conceivable experience, could have possibly prepared her for the depravity that was going to be meted out on her. Each agonising sensation, each excruciating indignity suffered, would bind them through eternity. She belonged to him. The now moist caress of his fingertips continued across both nipples of her naked breasts. She was physically perfect, and that perfection had to be marred. It was too much to take. The fingers momentarily squeezed and pulled mercilessly at the flesh of her breast, causing the girl to give a muffled gasp through the gag. It was time.

*

Hugh Wells flicked through the corners of the inch-thick pile of papers he'd collected together and slid them into a large envelope. The documents were all accounted for and in the correct order. He then reached for the four separate lengths of tightly coiled rope on the table and added them to the contents. The gravity of his actions was not lost to him as the flame of his sterling silver cigarette lighter sparked into life to light the wick of the red sealing wax he held over the closed flap. Drop by drop, the molten wax bled onto the paper, congealing just enough on cooling for him to press in The Sanctuary's seal. He opened the Library's safe and placed the envelope inside. The seal would not be broken for the better part of a century – not until the one named Isaac was chosen. *The Guardian with eagle tattoos*. That Hugh could trust in the succession of The Sanctuary's Circle Leaders and Mediums over the coming decades was something he didn't doubt, because he knew for certain that Isaac, eighty-five years in the future, had already taken possession of the items inside the envelope.

13

On walking through the door of the Neuropsychological Research office at AXIS Technologies, Nathan had expected to be entering a cramped space where he would sit across from his new acquaintance at a desk while they sipped coffee and talked research. Instead, he was being shown through a series of vast interconnected sterile white rooms equipped with an excess of the most expensive diagnostic equipment imaginable. During the guided tour, further signs of human life did finally become apparent in the guise of several young researchers in casual attire who would nod distractedly from behind their computer monitors as Nathan walked past their workstations scattered around the lab.

"Jesus, Anne-Marie. You've even got a PET scanner as well as MRI," Nathan said incredulously, eyeing the signage on one of numerous electronically locked doors that emphatically read 'AUTHORISED ACCESS ONLY'.

"Magnetoencephalography, too," she answered, a little too matter-of-factly. "You never know when they might come in handy," she added with a smile.

Nathan was sickened at the thought of even one of the £500,000 pieces of equipment lying idle, especially considering the endless waiting lists he had to deal with due to the hospital system's constant funding problems. Even with the addition of the new wing, St Mary's wasn't equipped so well.

Ironically, when they finally reached the furthest end of the lab, Anne-Marie did lead him into a surprisingly cramped office space where they sat at a desk across from each other, and only moments later, a member of the team – a girl in her mid-twenties with fresh-faced good looks – entered carrying two takeaway coffees balanced on a tray.

"Soy decaf, extra hot?" the girl offered with a pleasant smile.

Nathan didn't quite have the chance to register that he hadn't actually put in an order for his preferred choice of beverage – courtesy of Security's frighteningly interconnected database – before the girl clumsily tipped the tray, sending the drinks tumbling towards his lap. He caught one mid-flight, but the other bounced onto his thigh expressing a splurge of coffee-coloured froth onto his jeans through the cup's sealed plastic top.

"Stupid girl! What the hell's wrong with you?" Anne-Marie spat. "Just get out of my sight!"

The sudden venom and stinging contempt displayed took Nathan by surprise. "Really, there's no harm," he countered calmly to both Anne-Marie and the profusely apologising girl, who was by now blushing and already retreating from the room.

"She's totally useless. I'm terribly sorry, Nathan."

From a box on the desktop, Anne-Marie grabbed a wad

of tissues far in excess of what was needed to blot the small stain and hurried around the desk to aid Nathan, who had been left awkwardly holding both cups. "It'd be easier to get the damn coffee myself," she complained, kneeling down beside him and gently blotting the coffee from the denim fabric covering his thigh. The undue attention continued for second after silent second, her intentions only becoming clearer with each unnecessary lingering dab.

"You mentioned that you'd tested Isaac here in the lab." Nathan motioned a coffee cup towards her and took a sip of his, signalling that the inappropriate interaction should come to an end. This time, he was not left guessing as to her intentions. The woman was incorrigible, and he now resolved to keep a professional distance from her. Perhaps his initial lingering look at the pretty assistant who'd delivered the coffee had triggered the reaction, or maybe she'd felt unnecessarily envious of the girl's youth. Either way, it all pointed to an unsettling unpredictability regarding all of Anne-Marie's actions.

"Yes, yes. Isaac's been very generous with his time," she replied, standing and returning to her desk and discarding the tissues. If she'd been left in any way embarrassed by the emphatic redirection, the woman certainly wasn't showing it. "I've run countless brain scans while he's been in Trance states," she continued with unabashed cordiality as she sat down again. "But it's proven extremely difficult for him to perform on cue in a laboratory setting and next to impossible to set up the necessary equipment in The Sanctuary itself."

Nathan frowned. He couldn't believe what Anne-Marie, a leading scientist, had just said, and the interaction of the last few moments was instantly relegated to the back of his mind.

"As a researcher, aren't you suspicious if Isaac can't reproduce what he does outside of a blacked-out environment that he himself controls?"

Anne-Marie smiled, understanding the inference in the question. "Certainly, the blackout conditions do open up the arena to abuse from charlatans, but Isaac's failure to reproduce Physical phenomena in the lab isn't at all suspicious, considering that he's hooked up so unnaturally to a battery of machines and sensors."

Her counter left Nathan pondering over that word yet again. "I keep hearing that term *Physical*," he said, determined to get some clearer answers. "The searches I've done lead me to believe that it has something to do with the visible and audible nature of Isaac's supposed Mediumship?"

Anne-Marie leant forwards on her desk, relishing the opportunity to share what she knew. "*Physical* refers to the tangible nature of the phenomena brought in by the Physical Medium. It actually affects the surrounding physical environment and so is verifiable by more than one independent observer." She paused momentarily on gauging Nathan's unenlightened expression, realising that she might have to back up even further in her explanation. "You see, the majority of Mediums work by receiving clairvoyant images… visual thoughts, if you like. Some even hear messages through their auditory centres, while others talk of simply having a *feeling* or a *knowing*. But regardless of how the information happens to be received, ultimately, it has to be verbally relayed to a particular recipient who must then confirm the psychic message for the benefit of all the other observers in the room."

"So you're saying that, other than the recipient of

the message, no one else present is really in a position to corroborate what has occurred?"

"That's right. The clairvoyant experience, in that scenario, is the Medium's alone, whereas in Physical Mediumship, the opposite is true. It involves invoking energies that actually manifest in a very real sense so that everyone present in the room experiences it. But generally speaking, the Physical Medium is zoned out in a Trance state, not necessarily having any recollection of anything that's happened." Anne-Marie leant back in her chair. "There's any number of documented phenomena," she added, motioning behind him towards a large metal filing cabinet in the corner of the room.

Nathan glanced over his shoulder at the deep drawers, wondering if the cabinet's contents held the answers to his questions. "What kind of phenomena?"

"Percussions. Raps. Audible sounds emanating from objects such as tables or structural surfaces like walls."

"Surely that sort of thing can be simply explained by thermal expansion of timber?"

Anne-Marie refrained from rolling her eyes, being all too used to such inane comments. She was a highly qualified scientist working at the absolute limits of human understanding and was endeavouring to unify Neuropsychological Theories with a Quantum Mechanical approach. The pent-up frustration she often felt at people offering elementary school explanations for her intensely complex work was more than evident in a jaded reply that had plainly been rendered monotone through repetition. "Comparative analysis of the associated sound waves in thermal expansion and raps shows attack and decay patterns that bear no resemblance to each other," she responded dryly. "More importantly, Nathan, there is an intelligent pattern associated with the percussive sounds, with several raps occurring in perfectly even and measured succession in response to a question… People have even used such percussions as a means of communication with what they assume to be The Beyond."

"Like a Ouija Board?"

"Similar. One rap for Yes, two raps for No. There's always going to be people joking around and pretending. Such hoaxers and fraudsters long since destroyed all hope that quantum science would ever involve itself in investigating the very thing they should be investigating as a matter of priority. But there's no doubt that the phenomena *can* occur for real under stringent experimental control conditions. Individuals capable of invoking true Physical phenomena are exceedingly rare and tend to hide themselves away, demonstrating only to a small select group. Fraudsters and hoaxers don't fit into that cohort. The real conjecture should be over where the intelligent interaction is coming from and what the ramifications of that might be."

"It all sounds straight out of a horror movie."

"Hollywood has a lot to answer for," Anne-Marie agreed. "So-called Poltergeist activity is very much misunderstood. Both Levitation and Telekinetic influence on objects are about as basal and raw as Percussions on the scale of Physical phenomena, despite their seemingly dramatic presentation. Light Manifestations and Direct Voice of the deceased, or otherwise, being both seen and heard is where it starts to get interesting… Like the appearance of your father at the séance."

Nathan refrained from reacting to the mention of that

manifestation. Witnessing his deceased father standing in front of him and hearing his voice communicating had been the most confronting experience of his life. In truth, it had shaken the foundations of his world and even forced him to question the very definition of life, death and physicality itself. His already troubled mind had enough to contend with, and if he was to get to grips with those disturbing flashbacks and blackouts that he'd been experiencing, he needed to remain focused. He needed to know if those vivid flashback memories of killing and raping were his own or someone else's; he needed to know if that experience with the dead pilot had inspired some delusional episode given undue credence through a mere passing coincidence, and he needed to know if Isaac had somehow perpetrated an elaborate scam on him and everyone else through trickery and illusion in the darkness of the séance.

"All that still doesn't explain why full blackout conditions are necessary for Isaac's work?"

Anne-Marie was emphatic in her reply. "We can be sure that the array of phenomena Isaac generates has a quantum basis. And since Light itself can behave as a subatomic quantum particle, we cannot exclude the observers of the phenomena themselves from our analysis... After all, Light – the quantum messenger – is the most basic mediator between our environment and our experience of that perceived environment. But our perceptions can't even be sure where a subatomic particle of light is at any one instant in time."

"Heisenberg's Uncertainty Principle and Schrödinger's work?" Nathan interjected, remembering his scant recollection of basic high school physics.

Anne-Marie nodded. "It cuts to the very fabric of our

illusory physical Reality. Subatomic particles make up that physical Reality, and the state of a particle can be hard to pin down as far as its speed and location. It can only ever be said to have a probability of existing *somewhere* until it's observed, and on being observed, all the other possibilities of its location collapse in the process… Our solid Reality really does seem to flicker with illusion, Nathan. Even the surfaces we touch are far more than 99.99999% empty space at an atomic level. So what is it we are feeling? There is no solid matter to speak of for an observer to perceive. Even our experimental observation of light at a point in the future can affect whether that light acted as a particle or a wave in the past." She shook her head in awe, despite her years of study in the field. "Scientists in all fields have to develop protocols to distance themselves as observers in their own experiments, at the risk of them influencing the results by the very act of that observation. The stakes are just greater for quantum researchers… In the experimental séance room, we surmount the same kind of issues with sensory deprivation in extreme blackout conditions. In the total absence of Light, the observers in a séance are effectively *distanced* from the action and must rely entirely on any light being generated by the Mediums themselves. The blackouts also serve to temporarily wipe the sensory slate of the observer clean and remove the inertia of their expectations from the experiment. We tend to see what we expect to see, and overcoming that allows incredible things such as apports to occur." Anne-Marie took a sip of her coffee. "I still believe that an apport is the best chance we have of capturing some useful data."

"An apport?" Nathan's blank expression was painfully easy to read.

"I'm sorry. I keep forgetting that you're new to all this," Anne-Marie apologised. "An apport is an object that appears out of thin air. It almost always has relevance to someone sitting in the séance – sentimental usually. Like a ring or a bracelet. Or sometimes an object from inside one of the sitter's homes kilometres away might miraculously appear in the centre of the Circle. Even pieces of antique jewellery, lost for years, have been known to materialise... Incredible, I know. But seeing is believing."

Nathan was left speechless. He was in a state-of-the-art laboratory talking quantum physics with a leading scientist, and the woman had just suggested that Isaac's array of phenomena included causing objects to materialise out of thin air.

"Now would be a good time to close your mouth," Anne-Marie teased. "We accept that an entire Cosmos can appear instantly in a Big Bang, yet dismiss the idea that a tiny object can do the same. So it's not such a crazy idea, even in conventional scientific terms. After all, we know that infinite amounts of Matter are constantly being created and annihilated out of, and into, the Universe's Zero Point Field in every instant. Compared to that unseen reservoir of potential, the physical reality of the observable Universe represents a minute speck at the very tip of an iceberg in energy terms... We know that those randomly created subatomic particles coalesce and organise into structures that ultimately form our entire intricately interconnected Cosmos. So, in the grand scheme of things, a wedding ring dropping out of the air during a séance shouldn't be that astounding."

The argument was compelling, albeit staggering. "And all this is backed up by science?"

"Every bit. I worked at CERN. But they would never publicly admit that their particle accelerators are on the way to confirming what human experience has been documenting for thousands of years," Anne-Marie responded, with a wry expression. "Interestingly, there's a belief that in the 1800s, Radio and Television technology actually spawned from Sir Oliver Lodge's and Sir William Crookes' initial efforts to reproduce both the 'direct voices from thin air' and the 'manifestations of light bodies' that they had witnessed at countless séances. They were mistakenly convinced that the newly discovered electromagnetic energy of the time was involved as a carrier wave for the 'spirit' manifestations. '*A voice from thin air*' would certainly be a good way to describe today's radio broadcasts. And people manifesting as '*light bodies*' dance across our TV screens every time we switch them on... Not a bad result on Lodge and Crookes' part, wouldn't you agree?"

Nathan was both astonished and riveted by the suggestion. If Anne-Marie's assertion was grounded in truth, then humanity's more recent history would have to be rewritten. His brain was in overload, perhaps even more so than on the morning of his first meeting with Isaac just over a week ago. Still, he couldn't have asked for more from his visit to AXIS.

The next hour passed very quickly, with Anne-Marie being open enough about her work to talk Nathan through a series of scans of Isaac's brain before closing the laptop at the conclusion of the radiographic slideshow. "Might be interesting to hook you up," she then suggested from out of left field.

"To what end?"

"Well, Isaac seems to feel you have some potential."
"As a Medium?"
"As a *Physical* Medium, by all counts."
"Why on earth…?"
"A propensity for Trance, innate clairvoyance, indistinct boundaries between Past, Present and Future!"

She was clearly referring to what Isaac had told her about the death of the pilot.

"Tell me," she continued, "do you ever recall objects flying around in your presence when you were younger?"

If Anne-Marie's intention had been to probe the underbelly of his psyche to search for any repressed vulnerabilities, she couldn't have done a better job. "That's all just crazy talk," he said, with a forced indifference. "I think Isaac's just getting a little carried away with himself," he added, taking the opportunity to glance at his watch, in a blatant demonstration that it was time for him to leave.

Following another unavoidable lingering handshake across the desk, Nathan thanked her for her time and stood to leave. But just as he reached the office door and turned around to smile a final goodbye, he found himself face to face with Anne-Marie, who had followed him over and taken the opportunity to cross every boundary of personal space imaginable.

Nathan remained expressionless as Anne-Marie moved even closer. Frankly, he'd had enough of her games and thought it best to make it clear that he wasn't interested in her. He was about to regret maintaining his steel, though, when her attempts at seduction escalated into placing her hands on his chest and leaning in to tempt his tightly closed lips with sensual mouthing kisses. Nathan was certain that at any second his lack of reaction would force her to back off, leaving him the victor in this power play. But Anne-Marie's hands persisted by sliding down his torso and around his back, her fingers edging under his T-shirt.

Nathan was the first to break. "Anne-Marie, I—" Before he'd fully verbalised his protest, she'd already thrust both hands upwards, her fingernails digging into the musculature of his back.

Nathan pushed her away, causing her long manicured nails to scratch painfully across his skin. Catching her by both wrists, he held her against the wall.

Anne-Marie was breathless and smiled brazenly as she struggled against him.

"I'm sorry, Nathan. Please don't think badly of me. You can't blame a woman for trying, can you?" she continued demurely, holding his gaze for a few seconds before relaxing in surrender. "I'll let Security know that you're on the way down."

Nathan released his grip on her hands, thinking better of engaging any further. He left without a word, striding through the lab to the main exit.

"*Nathan!*"

Nathan kept walking, refusing to look back.

"*Nathan, please!*"

On hearing the second call of his name, he relented and turned around, not wanting to be the centre of some embarrassing scene. But there was no one there. Anne-Marie was still in her office with the door closed.

"Can I help you?" one of the research assistants sitting at a nearby workstation offered, noticing his hesitation.

Nathan looked confusedly around the sterile characterless

surrounds before shaking his head with a strained smile. "No," he admitted to himself out loud. He was starting to believe that he may be beyond help.

14

Nathan's heart was pounding.

"Dumb-arse fuck!"

The youth pushed Caleb hard in the chest with both hands, sending the bumbling thirteen-year-old reeling clumsily backwards onto the ground.

"*Stop them*," Caleb whimpered amidst the cruel laughter all around.

But Nathan could do nothing. He was being held by his wrists by two other youths on either side of him, while a third had him in a tight headlock from behind.

Caleb and Nathan had been boyishly chasing each other up and down and along the steep rampart-like riverbanks for over an hour, their breathless laughter brought to an abrupt end on realising that they had been menacingly surrounded. Not only were they outnumbered, their tormentors were older. Caleb's size had seen him targeted as fair game, at first, but when the adolescent pack had realised that one of their prey was "slow", the opportunity for some real fun had been too much to resist.

The leader of the group hocked up a ball of saliva and green mucus and spat it in Caleb's face as he lay submissively on the ground, causing the overgrown youngster's face to contort in a soundless display of tears.

Nathan struggled against his tormentors, only to feel the head and wristlocks tighten. "Leave him alone!" he attempted, with a constricted high-pitched voice that hadn't yet broken.

"*Leave him alone. Leave him alone,*" the main instigator mockingly squeaked to the amusement of the others standing around. "Your girlfriend wants us to leave you alone," he teased, standing over Caleb. "OK, lads," he shouted to his cohorts, "let's clean him up and leave him alone."

The youth reached for the fly of his jeans and unzipped, prompting the others to follow his lead, and Caleb squirmed as four of the gang urinated on his face and chest to more raucous laughter all around.

Nathan was scared. He had never experienced such a feeling of vulnerability in his powerlessness to protect his brother. Those restraining him were at least three years older and far too strong. But even more disturbing for Nathan was an all-consuming desire welling inside him that he'd never encountered before – this was the moment in which his childhood would end. He wanted to lash out. He wanted to harm. He wanted to kill. And struggling against those inescapable restraints only heightened a surge of emotion that surpassed anything he had previously recognised as anger.

An odour began to develop in the air.

"*Eww!* The little fucker's farted."

The kid holding the headlock released his grip and

covered his nose, misconstruing the tell-tale smell of ectoplasm building – Nathan himself being oblivious to the odour.

"*Shat* himself, more like," the eldest kid jibed, zipping himself up. "Filthy li'l bastard. Best chuck him in with the piss where he belongs."

Nathan's wrists were released, and he was pushed headlong into the pool of urine surrounding his traumatised brother while the teenage gang looked on, laughing to each other at having exerted their prowess before finally sauntering off.

He touched his brother's drenched face reassuringly to calm him, but instead of lying there quietly and letting their attackers leave, Nathan immediately got to his feet. He was seething, glaring intently at the eldest kid as he walked away, wishing him dead. His solar plexus pulsated with an ever-increasing amplitude of rage barely contained inside his being. Then something erupted within, an invisible shockwave of energy exploding from him, propagating outwards towards the youth… *How calm he suddenly felt…* The impact was as powerful as if a charging bull had slammed into the teenager's back and the wind was forced out of his chest cavity with an audible rush, leaving no air left with which to scream… *How tranquil…* By the time the boy's body had left the ground, two of his ribs were already broken… *Serenity…* Sailing off the top of the bank into midair, the boy hung spectacularly before crashing heavily down onto the steep incline of the riverbank with a sickening *crack* as he tumbled down the rest of the slope onto the lower flood bank level below… *Dissipation…* There the boy lay unconscious with his fractured left femur bent sickeningly out at ninety degrees to his body while the other kids at the top of the bank looked on in stunned silence – one of them vomiting at the sight.

Nathan stared blankly for a moment, content to exist in that domain of slowing Time, his anger and frustration having exploded from within, en masse, quantum-like, projecting itself across Space. But he couldn't hold back the inevitable shift as reality began accelerating rapidly to real time again. Nathan grabbed Caleb's hand and dragged him away in the opposite direction, making for the safety of the banks across the nearby bridge a short distance downstream. There he hid with Caleb in the undergrowth until he was sure that no one was following, his young mind in turmoil at what evil had possessed him. He'd wished the boy dead, and on seeing the motionless body lying at the bottom of the bank, he had no reason to believe that his wish had not been granted by whatever malignant force had just visited him. He was scared of the consequences of being found out but was even more scared of the guilt he felt – the guilt he felt over not feeling entirely bad about what had just happened. The euphoric release of energy he'd just experienced, irrespective of the devastating outcome, had made him feel ecstatic beyond anything he had ever felt before.

Certain that no one had noticed their escape, Nathan helped his still-whimpering brother to his feet and they hurried off home, the quicksands of his subconscious already claiming the memory of the event in an attempt to bury the uncomfortable truth. He swore to himself that he would never find himself so helpless again.

15

"Maybe you could talk to him," Annie suggested. "He'll listen to you."

Sitting at a table in his aunt's lounge room, Nathan sipped on the last dregs of coffee from a mug he remembered drinking from as a child. There was something comforting about the fact that nothing ever changed here. Even down to the unfinished daily newspaper crossword lying strewn across the couch that Annie would get back to as soon as he had left. Other than Caleb playing up, this day really did seem as reliably the same as any other.

Wearing her usual slippers and apron, Annie was sitting at the head of the table, with her chair angled slightly to face her nephew. He had always tried his best to visit her and Caleb at least once a week, but with his workload at the hospital over the last few months, he just hadn't been able to make it as often as either of them would have liked.

"I hate to say it, Annie, but maybe it's time to think of other options."

"No!" his aunt snapped. "I can cope. He's probably just being influenced by someone at the facility. He's growing up a little, that's all."

Caleb spent four days a week, between the hours of nine and three, attending an adult day care facility, and as it provided him with the only real contact he had with the outside world, some influence from that quarter was the most likely cause of Caleb's more recent misbehaviour.

"We've got to be realistic. He'll never be able to look after himself fully, and if he's going to keep wandering off... Frankly, it's dangerous. I just don't have the space or the time. I wish I did. And you're not always going to be able to take care of him yourself."

Annie teared up at the prospect of losing Caleb to a long-term residential care facility.

"Look," Nathan relented, reaching over to place a hand lovingly on his aunt's shoulder, unable to bear seeing her so upset, "we'll work something out. I promise. I'll talk to him."

Relieved that he was going to sort everything out like he always did, Annie gathered up the mugs and headed off to the kitchen to brew another batch while Nathan headed for Caleb's room. It certainly seemed strange that his brother hadn't rushed out to say hello. Those constricting bear hugs that visitors usually had to brace themselves for were something Nathan looked forward to, and he had to agree with Annie that the house really did have a lifeless air about it without Caleb's usual incessant happy chattering.

"Hey, buddy," Nathan shouted out as he reached Caleb's door.

"*Fuck off!*" came the totally surprising response from inside the room.

Annie's concerns suddenly made sense, and Nathan had instantly been brought up to speed. The expletive did seem to be devoid of any real venom, though. Caleb's boyishness was still evident in his delivery, in much the same way a toddler might swear without really knowing what it meant.

Nathan pushed open the door and entered. "Hey…" he repeated, not prepared for what he would find inside.

Caleb was standing by his bed, bare-chested and barefooted, wearing nothing but his jeans, and Nathan was left momentarily speechless as he caught sight of the multiple whiplash marks all over the front, back and sides of his body, several being so severe as to have scabbed over. A fresh tattoo now also adorned Caleb's left pectoral: '*Motherfucker*', it announced across a black-inked scroll. Most shocking of all was the array of seriously disturbing hardcore pornographic magazines spread across the bed, each cover photo depicting naked girls gagged and strung up in various helpless poses that left nothing to the imagination. The centrefold of one open magazine revealed an image of agony across the contorted face of a girl, similarly bound into submission, having needles pierced through her nipples and breasts by a group of masked men.

"Where the hell did you get *these*!" Nathan blurted to himself, making for the magazines and hastily collecting them together. The thought that Annie might have stumbled upon the scene horrified him. He couldn't believe how Caleb had changed so much in just a few short weeks.

"They're mine!" Caleb protested, feigning tears, as if a set of comics had just been confiscated from him for failing to tidy his room.

Nathan paused, his mind spinning with anger. He could

be forgiven for not knowing how to react. For Annie's sake, he could only think to remove Caleb from the house immediately until he could work out what was going on and plan a course of action.

Nathan needed to keep calm and took a deep breath before addressing his brother, refocusing on the fact that this was no adult mind he was reasoning with. Now wasn't the time for an interrogation, either, at the risk of Annie overhearing. "That's a great tattoo, buddy. OK if I take a photo?" he asked quietly.

Nathan snapped away on his phone, taking the opportunity to capture a 360-degree record of the injuries as evidence while Caleb smiled proudly, if not a little smugly, at the attention he was getting.

As he scanned around Caleb's body, Nathan noticed bruising to his brother's lower back and a faint bruise developing in the cubital fossa of his right arm, as if he'd recently had blood taken. That just didn't make sense. Annie would never take Caleb for a medical appointment without running it past him first. The shocking possibility that those responsible for the tattoo had also plied Caleb with illicit intravenous drugs reignited Nathan's anger, and it was all he could do not to explode.

"I'll just take care of these for the time being," he suggested, waving the magazines in the air with a forced brotherly smile. "C'mon. Get dressed. We're going for a drive."

Nathan tossed Caleb a shirt from the end of the bed and grabbed a sports bag from the corner of the room. He threw the magazines into the bottom of the bag before raiding the closet and drawers for whatever he could get his hands on.

"*What the fuck!*" Nathan eyed the full-face leather zip

mask that he'd inadvertently grabbed from amongst a pile of Caleb's underwear. Finding the headgear elevated the situation to beyond disturbing. Someone was obviously intent on corrupting his brother's mind in the sickest of ways, leaving Nathan seething as he threw the mask into the bag before hastily zipping it up.

Annie looked bemused as she walked from the kitchen holding the two fresh mugs of coffee.

"Caleb and I thought we might have that chat now," Nathan called out while rushing Caleb bodily through the hallway to the front door, not taking any chances.

"But—"

"Sorry, Annie. I'll call you later," Nathan said, as he firmly shut the front door behind him.

It was untenable for Caleb to stay at Nathan's apartment for even a night. He could escape from there just as easily as he had from Annie's place. But that was the least of Nathan's concerns. He was well aware that the local police had grown tired of Caleb's disappearing antics. Tattoos weren't illegal and the authorities were unlikely to be sympathetic to pleas of assault by persons unknown concerning the whipping Caleb had suffered, especially considering the nature of the obscene material found in his brother's possession. Not that he could show that to the police at the risk of Caleb being taken in for questioning. God knows what else was secreted around his bedroom. If Nathan was going to discover who'd been influencing his brother so negatively in recent times, he needed to find somewhere safe for Caleb to stay while he investigated.

Nathan had no choice but to call in a favour. An old friend, David Hearsham, was the director of a privately run residential drug rehabilitation centre, a half hour's drive north of the city. It was the only place he could think of for the time being. The centre was accustomed to dealing with the worst of the worst of drug offenders, many having appalling histories of abuse and violent crime. As such, the constantly monitored facility prided itself on being as secure as a jail while still maintaining the outward ambience of a share house. The highly trained specialist staff achieved their success through kindness mixed with firm uncompromising discipline, and Nathan knew that on initial admission the patients were isolated from the other residents while being assessed. At least his brother would be safe and secure there while he tried to find out what was going on – if only he could persuade his friend to allow it.

"This is beyond highly irregular, Nathan. It's not the money and it's not that we don't have a place. There are legalities and procedure to consider. The very act of locking Caleb in a room might effectively make us guilty of false imprisonment in the eyes of the Law. I'd have to run it by the company's legal department."

"I fully appreciate that, David," Nathan pleaded. "I've just got nowhere else to turn. It's my brother we're talking about. You know how vulnerable he is. If he disappears again, maybe next time he'll be killed. I just don't know what we're dealing with. Someone's abusing and taking advantage of him. I'm as sure as I can be that he's already been plied with drugs of some description. As I explained, the police are just not going to be interested… It's for his own safety. Please!"

The director of the rehab centre looked uneasily at Nathan before glancing through the glass door of his office at Caleb sitting benignly outside in the corridor. Hearsham let out an exasperated sigh. "Two nights! That's it!"

"I owe you."

"You owe me nothing. We're even."

Nathan had carefully removed the obscene magazines and leather mask from Caleb's sports bag and left them in the trunk of his car before entering the rehab centre. Now, having pulled into the underground car park of his apartment complex, he had to decide what to do with them. His first thought was to dispose of the items deep inside the refuse skips in the common area, at the risk of some serious potential embarrassment if they were found in his possession; on the other hand, they were tangible evidence that at some point might be useful to police should he find out who had been corrupting Caleb's vulnerable mind. After a moment's thought, he gathered them all together to take inside. But as he lifted the graphic pile off the interior matting of the Audi's trunk, Nathan noticed a business card drop out from in between them: 'Toxic Ink – Tattoo Studio', the card announced.

"Bastards!" Nathan fumed. Only the lowest of scum would have taken it upon themselves to ink someone so vulnerable.

Caleb collected business cards the same way that he collected chocolate bars and cigarette lighters from the checkout counters of supermarkets. His hands were quicker than the eye, and his outwardly mature appearance presented a constant challenge in explaining his light-fingeredness to sceptical store managers. He'd amassed thousands of business cards over the years, but some he treasured more than others. Annie had always needed to be careful as to which ones she secretly discarded to keep things manageable. At least the unfortunate obsessive-compulsive trait had now landed Nathan with a clue.

En route to Toxic Ink, Nathan decided to swing by the care facility that his brother attended several days a week. The staff agreed entirely that Caleb's behaviour had been changing recently but were naturally defensive at any suggestion that their facility was in any way at fault. And on surveying the range of disabilities endured by the individuals engaged in therapeutic pursuits around the room – not to mention the kind and patient encouragement being displayed by the carers – it was hard to disbelieve. The day manager did seem relieved, though, when Nathan mentioned that Caleb wouldn't be attending for a while. They'd had their fair share of disruptions with him going AWOL from the premises on several occasions, too.

Mulling over his fruitless enquiries, Nathan had just about made it to the exit of the building when he heard an "*Excuse me!*" from behind him. Turning, he saw one of the carers from a few moments earlier rushing to catch up with him.

"I'm sorry, I just couldn't help but overhear. You're Caleb's brother?"

Nathan answered with a nod.

"It's probably nothing," the prim middle-aged woman

tentatively offered, "but on a couple of those occasions when he went missing, I'm sure I noticed the same man hanging around outside in the car park. I did report it to the police the second time they were called, but they didn't really seem that interested. I thought I'd just mention it."

"Do you remember what he looked like? Did Caleb seem to know him?"

"Early thirties, shaved head and some kind of tattoo running up the left side of his neck. A snake, I think. He was wearing a black leather bomber jacket, if I remember correctly. There was just something about him... He made me feel really uneasy." The woman was visibly troubled at the thought. "I can't say that I ever saw him with Caleb," she continued, "but on both those occasions, your brother would get very excited, almost uncontrollably so, for about ten minutes before he went missing. He kept looking outside through the windows, as if he was waiting for someone. I should've said something sooner, I suppose."

"Not at all," Nathan reassured. "The work you do can't be easy. Thanks for letting me know."

Plenty of people have tattoos, Nathan thought to himself as he parked up in front of the emblazoned plate-glass frontage of Toxic Ink, crammed narrowly in a strip mall between a Chinese takeaway and a vacant shop with a half-peeled-off 'To Let' sign adorning its window. His own right shoulder was testament to that – the black and grey wolf a reminder of the wild drunken night of his eighteenth birthday. Even countless numbers of grandmothers and grandfathers sport ink, these days, he told himself. There wasn't any reason to suspect a link between the man that the care assistant had seen and the establishment he was just about to enter. But the word *tattoo* had certainly been chasing him all day.

Entering the shop, Nathan sized up the indie-looking tattoo artist in his late twenties lazing at a makeshift reception table, and it was several moments before the guy looked up from his phone through a shock of black hair covering half of his face to greet Nathan with a relaxed nod.

"Dude."

"I'm looking for Benji," Nathan enquired casually, *Benji* being the name tagged onto the business card.

The young guy, pierced and inked within an inch of his life, eyed Nathan's appearance: expensive, designer, yet decidedly high street. Not the typical client that sought out his services, so he thought it safer to remain incognito. "Who's lookin'?" he asked, with an attitude that ironically identified himself.

"Friend of mine had some work done and I wanted something similar." Nathan handed Benji a printed photo of Caleb's pectoral tattoo, the cropped image chosen carefully so as to avoid displaying any signs of the whiplash marks.

On glancing at the image, Benji's relaxed posture stiffened slightly, and Nathan wasn't slow in registering the micromovements.

"Don't look like Benji's work," the artist responded, feigning disinterest and handing the photo back.

"This says different!" Nathan insisted, angrily flashing the business card. The guy's recalcitrance, butting against the now sure knowledge that he'd been somehow involved in hurting his brother, made him seethe enough to want to strike out and inflict some pain, too.

"You a cop?" Benji asked.

"No."

"Then *fuck off* outta here!"

Nathan wasn't even close to being intimidated. The years of martial arts training that had seen him safely through his youth, following the incident on the riverbanks, allowed him to stand his ground. "Did you do this?" he persisted, waving the image in Benji's face. "He's disabled, you piece of shit!"

"The retard seemed happy *enou—*"

Benji was sent hurtling off his chair with a swift involuntary reflex left, and Nathan was across the table and on him before he'd hit the floor.

"*Dude! Dude!*"

Benji's bluster was spent, wincing and covering up as Nathan pinned him down next to the overturned chair.

"Who brought him here?" Nathan threatened, his fist cocked for another blow.

"Look, man, I didn't even get paid!"

Nathan tightened his grip. "Who?" he screamed again.

"OK! OK!"

Nathan waited for a response, the spent adrenalin spike giving rise to an uneasiness in the situation he now found himself in. But it wasn't the time to let the man pinned beneath him sense his regret over his temporary loss of control. He seemed ready to talk.

"There was five of them, including the *retar...*" Benji thought better of what he was about to say. "...the disabled guy, I mean," he quickly corrected. "They were off their faces... They told me what they wanted, and when I'd finished, they pinned me up against the wall and held the tattoo gun to my face, asking if the work had been *on the house*." Benji seemed to realise the irony of his current predicament in being pinned down yet again. "I'm not gonna argue with a group of skinheads, man."

"One of them have a snake tattoo on his neck?"

Benji hesitated with a nervous look, unsure of how much the man on top of him actually knew. Lying probably wasn't the safest option.

"You know him, don't you?" Nathan seethed, this time for effect.

"I've seen him around. Look, I don't want to get involved…"

"You're already involved! Where have you seen him? Give me a name!"

Nathan gripped the neck of the guy's T-shirt and jolted his head against the floorboards in more of a threatening gesture than anything else. He'd started to feel sorry for the guy and didn't know how much longer he could keep up the pretence, especially as it was becoming clear that Benji had been a victim, too. He needed information, though, and whatever tactics he was using seemed to be working.

"The dude fights cage. Goes by the name Bedlam. He hangs out at Brophy's Gym down the road. I swear that was the first time I'd spoken to him. He scares me shitless, man."

"And the others?"

"The Ashton… The Ashton Arms… They hang at the Ashton Arms!"

Nathan released his grip and exited in silence. He now had a solid lead.

Slamming the car door shut, he reached for the Audi's ignition button with a trembling hand. The enormity of what had just happened began to hit hard. He would never have thought himself capable of such uncontrolled violence on a stranger. *What's happening to me?* He had to make a swift getaway. The last thing he needed was Benji taking down his licence plate. If he'd had any idea of what was going to eventuate, he would have chosen somewhere less visible to park when he'd first arrived. The engine growled into life, and with a short screech of tyres, he was gone.

When Nathan had put enough distance between himself and the tattoo studio, he pulled over to the side of the road, got out of the car and leant against the roof. He thought that he might vomit. If he was capable of losing control to such a degree, what else was he capable of? In truth, his anger had given way to euphoria the second that his fist had smashed into Benji's face. For the second time in his life, he'd displayed a level of violence that had shocked him – and for a fleeting moment, he had enjoyed it. The possibility that he had actually committed those atrocious murderous acts during his blackouts again swept through his mindstream, setting off a second wave of nausea.

Nathan shook the thoughts from his head. He needed to keep focused for Caleb's sake. At least he now had an answer, in part, as to who was harming and influencing his brother. He just didn't know why, and what he had learnt only inspired another more pressing question. *What the hell am I going to do about it?*

Nathan was brought back to the moment with an incoming message on his phone. It was from Isaac, inviting him over to The Sanctuary to take the series of tests meant to explore his psyche. He glanced at the time – 3 pm. It had only been six hours since he'd been sipping on a mug of coffee over at Annie's place. In the intervening time, he had kidnapped his newly sadomasochistic brother, falsely imprisoned him in a drug rehabilitation centre and beaten up a tattoo artist to extract information about a gang of thugs who engaged in illegal cage fighting. The invite was timely. He needed to plan his next move. And he would at last have an opportunity to question Isaac directly about the séance.

Nathan got back in his car and hit the ignition. Oddly, he found himself eager to return to The Sanctuary. As if he was going home.

16

"You look like shit," Isaac said, sitting down in the armchair of The Sanctuary's reading room.

Nathan had failed to notice the rip in the sleeve of his shirt and the dust marks on his pants that he'd picked up from the floor at Toxic Ink.

"Everything OK?"

"Long story," Nathan answered dryly, patting down both trouser legs as he too took a seat. "I'm fine."

Isaac was left unconvinced by the response but chose to navigate around whatever was troubling Nathan. "Anne-Marie told me that you visited her at the lab."

Nathan hesitated before answering, surprised at the degree of communication Isaac and Anne-Marie apparently had. They were obviously closer than he'd assumed, enjoying a relationship that extended beyond the bounds of just researcher and test subject. Isaac's matter-of-fact tone suggested that he knew nothing of what had happened at the end of their meeting. Still, Nathan chose to opt for a neutral response, just in case. "Yeah, it certainly was interesting," he answered, while feigning to brush off yet more remnants of dust from his pants.

"Being a Neuroscientist, she obviously has her own way of seeing things," Isaac continued, registering the unease in Nathan's body language. "We certainly don't agree on everything. But having all the answers is usually a sure sign that you know next to nothing. Especially in this field!"

Isaac looked across, reading the mood of his young visitor, and decided that there had perhaps been enough small talk. "It was good to see that they found the victims of the plane crash," he said, engaging Nathan's attention more fully.

"I get the feeling that you had something to do with that. They certainly seemed to switch the search area to the exact location quickly enough."

Isaac gave a tight-lipped smile. "You just have to know how to approach the authorities with this kind of thing," he admitted. "Call them up and say that you're a psychic with important information and you're probably going to have the phone slammed down on you or find yourself being questioned as some kind of suspect. Fortunately, I've made a few contacts within police forces over the years through the success in cases I've worked on. It helps sometimes." Isaac paused for a moment. "Do you want to talk about the séance the other night?"

Nathan's was a *need* rather than a *want*. "It's been constantly on my mind."

"I'm sorry that we had to leave so quickly. Barbara would normally see to it that you were OK and had the proper support in a situation like that, but Anne-Marie kindly offered to take care of you in our absence. I really wasn't feeling too well on coming out of Trance. It happens sometimes in séances."

Nathan finally understood why Anne-Marie had lingered with him for so long in the séance room after the demonstration had finished, albeit with a now obvious ulterior motive.

"I was told that your father materialised. I hope you weren't too freaked out?"

"To be honest, I still don't know what to think… I mean no offence by that," he quickly added, not wanting to seem disrespectful, despite the doubts he still had. He'd found himself uncomfortably invested in Isaac's authenticity. Those abilities, if proven credible, could hold the answers to the vile flashback assaults on his psyche. If proven otherwise, then an unravelling of his sanity would be the only other possible explanation.

"No offence taken."

"I saw my dad in the light. I heard his voice. And the relevance of the words spoken just couldn't have been known by you or anyone else in the room." Nathan's tone revealed the ongoing battle with the critical and reasoning faculties of his brain. "Objectivity tells me one thing, but what I've been witnessing recently tells me the complete opposite. I feel like my whole world's been turned upside down these past few days."

"Objectivity is far from Absolute," Isaac responded. "In fact, it's just about the most relative commodity the human intellect has to deal with." He looked Nathan squarely in the eyes. "You're a natural Physical Medium, Nathan. Trust me; it's no coincidence that you feel that your world is being challenged. There are changes occurring within you. You can try and fight the inevitable, but you'll just be setting yourself up for a difficult time. From now on, every belief, value and assumption that you've ever held is going to be challenged far more than anything you've experienced so far. Believe me. If you were to take my advice, I'd simply let go of what you've come to know and surrender to what is unfolding within you, no matter how challenging that may prove to be."

Nathan held Isaac's gaze for a few seconds. "Anne-Marie asked if I'd experienced objects moving about around me. I take it that was your idea to ask?"

"We've talked at length about you. But, frankly, I don't need to question your history. I can guarantee you've had such experiences. Perhaps on more occasions than you even realise."

Nathan didn't need any reminding – the disturbing childhood memory of that day on the riverbank had been repressed and forgotten until the cascading events of the last few days had forced it to surface. It had just been easier to believe that it never happened. But if ever there was proof of what Isaac was telling him, maybe that incident alone provided it. He momentarily teetered on the knife-edge fulcrum of belief and disbelief before the gravity of logic and reason pulled him back yet again.

"The thought that there could be some violent malevolent spirit possessing me is terrifying," Nathan said uneasily, mulling over both the childhood memory of those events on the riverbank and his more recent disturbing flashbacks.

Isaac frowned. "The idea of *evil* malevolent spirits and *good* benevolent spirits is nothing but a throwback to the scare tactics of a medieval Church intent on keeping a tight control of the masses," he attempted to reassure. "The only true malevolent spirits to worry about are those individuals in *this* world who live a life intent on causing harm to others."

"So you don't believe in such a thing as Evil, either?"

"I can't think of a better definition of Evil, Nathan, than 'the inappropriate expression of *self* to the detriment of other sentient beings'. There is no Devil or Satan other than that which dwells within our living breathing selves. But that's not to say that those evil inflated egos can't exert devastating actions at a distance on a psychic level."

Nathan was yet to realise that his formal tutoring as a Physical Medium under Isaac's guidance had just begun.

"You first need to make the distinction between your Mediumship and the phenomena itself," Isaac continued. "It's quite possible to generate Physical phenomena in *this* world without necessarily communicating with a consciousness dwelling in some other Time, Reality or Dimension."

Nathan was left uneasy at Isaac's words. "That's even more worrying than the thought of some malicious spirit possessing me."

"It certainly is!" Isaac agreed. "No one should take this phenomenon lightly. In the wrong hands, its potentials are devastating."

The pair fell silent for a moment, and it seemed the perfect opportunity for Nathan to raise the questions he'd been waiting to ask Isaac since the evening of the séance. But he had to choose his words carefully at the risk of blatantly accusing the man of being a scamming charlatan. "I'm still confused over something," he began circumspectly.

"On the day we first met, you said that you reject the idea of an Afterlife. Yet you held a séance in which the spirit of my deceased father apparently showed himself in a physical manifestation and communicated. And I've listened to your thoughts on bridging Time in the *here* and *now*. But it seems such a—"

"There is no illusion or trickery, Nathan," Isaac spat angrily, his expression suddenly turning grave and his being seething in a way that Nathan hadn't encountered before. "And I can tell you that the Spirits of the dead are very real. But they only exist if the living allow them to."

Nathan was thrown by the overbearing authority in Isaac's voice, and it instantly felt as though the Medium's sheer presence was pinning him to the chair's backrest, almost stopping him from breathing.

"You'll come to understand that so-called Spirits are nothing but powerful expressions of remnant ego with such *need* and *craving* that, even after death, the anger, remorse and regrets of their previous lives still pollute the fabric of this Cosmos we share."

The crushing pressure on Nathan's chest intensified, and he immediately felt himself becoming distant and disconnected from his surroundings. The words assaulting his senses circulated in a confusion of swirling fragments that obstructed all thought processes and left him struggling to maintain consciousness.

"Those pollutants of ego need a *You* so that their *I* can still exist in this world," Isaac's vitriol continued, "because without a *You* they have no *I*… Reject them and they simply vanish into the ether as the self-perpetuating illusions they are."

Nathan's slip into Trance accelerated as those words,

spitting out at him in a rapid-fire staccato attack, became totally lost to his senses.

Isaac waited for a moment to let Nathan stabilise in the altered state he'd just forcibly induced. He then lowered his voice to a soft subliminal whisper and continued. "When the time is right, Nathan, you will realise that the imprinted craving and need of remnant ego hangs in the surrounding ether as a potential, and it only takes a sensitive individual like yourself to turn their attention to it, and that potential can finally be realised in a flood of contact and information. Physical manifestation is just the full limit of that potential being expressed. Don't underestimate the healing you extended to the pilot at the moment of his death by simply acknowledging his pain. You helped his being find peace by helping him break contact with this world. So it's time to put all thoughts of those flashbacks of raping and killing out of your mind… Completely out of your mind. Those disturbing thoughts are not your own. When you wake, you will have no direct memory of them. Let them return to a mere potential in the ether. Nor will you remember the words I have been speaking to you since sitting down here today. Now relax, Nathan… Just relax…"

Isaac sat back in his chair in silence and waited for a few minutes, watching over his oblivious student. The series of tests that he'd intended to complete could wait for the moment. The Shock and Awe induction technique he'd just utilised was unconventional, but Nathan's dishevelled appearance, obvious fatigue and troubled demeanour on arriving had signalled the opportunity for a breakthrough in his protégé's awakening – a gentle shove in the right direction while temporarily in a vulnerable state. And Isaac hadn't hesitated to grab the opportune moment to protect Nathan's troubled mind.

Nathan stirred on slowly coming around. "I... I'm sorry... I..." He had absolutely no conscious recollection of anything that had occurred over those past few minutes.

"That's OK. Are you sure you don't want to tell me what's been going on?" Isaac asked, nodding towards the torn shirt sleeve, cleverly picking up the conversation they'd been having when Nathan first arrived. "There's no need to face things alone. You're amongst friends here."

Nathan looked confusedly around the room, aware of something but unable to grasp onto the fleeting edit points in the proceedings. "...My brother, Caleb, is in some sort of trouble," he continued, as if the last few minutes hadn't happened. "I'm just trying to figure out how to deal with it. That's all."

"Being an only child myself, I can't imagine what it's like to be worried over a brother. The only brothers I ever had were in my unit in the Army, and..." Isaac stopped midsentence, becoming momentarily pensive and distant, as if something haunted his own psyche. "Well, I suppose there are times when a man's just gotta stand up and do what he's gotta do... whatever the consequences might be," he finally counselled, keen to move the conversation along to allow Nathan's subconscious to claim those impromptu hypnotic suggestions. "How about we get into those tests I mentioned. The results should be interesting."

Nathan sat forwards and adjusted his position in the chair in readiness, trying to shake off the cloudiness in his head. But he couldn't shake off the feeling that he'd forgotten something important.

*

Nathan was familiar enough with The Sanctuary by now to let himself out. The series of tests had been interesting, and Isaac had promised to get Anne-Marie to run a statistical analysis on them as soon as was feasible. For all Isaac's apparent enthusiasm in the initial results, Nathan had just been grateful to be spending some time back in the calming and energising surrounds of The Sanctuary. He still didn't know what he was going to do about Caleb, but the afternoon had certainly left him more relaxed and in a clearer state of mind.

Nathan stepped into the small reception area and closed the door to the main corridor behind him, taking a moment to glance around. It was hard to believe that it had only been a little under two weeks since he'd stood there waiting for his appointment on the morning of his first visit to The Sanctuary. So much had happened. With a shake of his head, he turned and reached for the main outer door, resigning himself to stepping out into the harsh realities of the world beyond the serenity of what had become a true sanctuary. As he grabbed onto the door handle, though, he hesitated, thinking he'd remembered what it was that he'd irritatingly forgotten. *The séance… He had meant to question Isaac about the events.* Nathan wondered if he should go back inside and confront Isaac but thought better of it and instead opted to leave. But before he had a chance to pull on the wrought metal handle, the door was flung open by someone entering – the hefty body of timber striking him squarely on his left temple.

"*Gomen nasai…* I'm so sorry," came a concerned female voice.

Nathan's left eye temporarily failed to focus as he nursed his head, but a perfectly functioning right eye found him peering at the same young Eurasian girl who had dropped the coffee cup on him at AXIS.

"Have I done something to offend you… In a past life, perhaps?" he weakly joked from out of the mild concussion. "…Nathan," he added with a smile, by way of introduction.

Half hidden behind a teetering pile of books balanced on top of a cardboard document box she was dropping off, the girl blushed again on recognising Nathan and awkwardly reached out a hand. "Mia. Mia Kerr," she responded, in a well-spoken cosmopolitan accent laced with the slightest trace of Japanese, just as the heftiest of the antique-looking books – the words *Quantum Mechanics* embossed archaically along its spine – toppled to the floor and landed heavily on his foot.

Nathan swore out loud in pain but still had the presence of mind to reach over and steady the pile, relieving the girl of the precarious load. Limping over to the reception desk, he set the box down and turned to give her a long hard look. "You know," he opened, "some people believe that it's no coincidence when we accidently bump into a stranger. They even suggest that, when that happens, we should seize the opportunity to talk to the person and find out what we're supposed to learn from them." Nathan grinned, holding his head and gingerly placing some weight back on his bruised foot. "Under the circumstances, Mia, what are your thoughts on that…?"

17

Sounds of mindless drunken laughter being amplified in the night air echoed back and forth along the deserted inner-city street. The man and woman staggered along holding each other up – the woman regularly falling to her knees with a cackle, the guy having to pick her up and bodily manhandle her along. She was dressed to party and had every intention of doing just that.

They turned into a narrow cobbled side street to be met by the inevitable odour of urine, and halfway along the shadowy cleft slicing between the outwardly grim towering Victorian buildings, the guy fumbled for his keys and opened a door that had not been at all evident from the street. Once inside, the flicking-on of lights surprisingly revealed the polished boards of the most expensively appointed, high-end warehouse conversion imaginable.

"*Cooool!*" the girl howled, looking around approvingly before staggering into another fit of giddy laughter.

"Well, just look at you," Bedlam uttered to himself, circling her, without the slightest trace of the inebriation he'd been faking. His spiralling gaze rose slowly up the length of the pretty twenty-six-year-old brunette's shapely stilettoed legs to take in her pert behind, barely covered by an ultra-short miniskirt, then on to her exposed flat stomach, courtesy of the suggestive skimpy bra top she'd chosen to wear. The time of year was the last thing going to stop her from flaunting what she'd got on her Friday night out.

Bedlam reached down for the bottle of vodka on the table beside him and unscrewed the top. "Here's that drink I promised you, darlin'." And grabbing the girl's shoulder-length hair by the roots and tipping her head backwards, he poured the liquor into her mouth from the open bottle, sending most of the drink spilling down her chin and neck as she spluttered and struggled to swallow.

Bedlam released his grip, and the brunette managed a couple of gasps of air after she'd gulped down the last of the contents forced into her mouth. She gave a quieter, more apprehensive giggle, her degree of intoxication leaving her unsure as to her new friend's demeanour. They'd been having such fun at the Carousel Club. A slight tug at her back signalled the clasp of her top being unfastened and she watched in expectant silence as it fell to the floor. The guy's T-shirt flew across the room, and a slight smile returned to her face as she tried to turn to get an eyeful of that muscular physique she'd been admiring for the last few hours. But powerful hands grabbed at her naked breasts aggressively from behind in an immobilising bear hug.

"Aaaagh! That hurts. I don't like it!"

Bedlam squeezed harder and twisted her flesh mercilessly.

"Aaaagh!"

Tears began streaming down her face. The girl now knew she was in trouble but was paralysed with alcohol and fear.

"Shut the fuck up, bitch!"

A heavy slap to the right side of her head sent her to the ground as he released his hold. But, within seconds, he was on her again, pouring more vodka into her mouth. This time, his grip on her hair didn't let up, Bedlam forcing her to her feet, his free hand tearing at the zip of her skirt while they were on the move. The skirt fell away before they'd made it into the adjoining room. He threw her face down to the floor and began tying her hands behind her back and strapping leather buckles to each of her ankles, her legs held in a vice-like grip against his torso. Finally, a ball gag was forced into her mouth and tightly secured.

Bedlam stood and silently viewed his handiwork, admiring the streams of mascara-streaked tears latticing the now macabre and grotesque-looking face that had appeared so pretty a few moments before. "That's more like it, darlin'," he whispered calmly, grabbing her under both arms and pulling her to her feet again.

With an effortless push, the girl found herself sitting at the bottom of a bed facing a barrage of video cameras on tripod stands set at different heights and angles that she hadn't noticed on being thrown into the room. And at the risk of being hit again, she didn't dare struggle as Bedlam pushed her knees apart and tethered her ankles to the bottom of the bed. The gag reduced her weak, fatigued cries to a barely audible whimper – until the doorbell rang and she realised that there was going to be company. No one would have been able to hear her, though, as she screamed and writhed where she had been forced to sit. Bedlam pulled on a black leather mask to hide his identity then set the cameras rolling and checked the viewfinders before strolling out of the room to greet his guests. More mascara flowed as the girl realised she could now do nothing but accept her fate – Camera One's tight focus, Bedlam's favourite, capturing the unfolding story frame by frame in the close-up expressions of her face.

A procession of masked men poured noisily into the room, whooping at the sight before them. Instantly, she was surrounded and they began to grab at her naked body.

"Alex! Alex! Alex!" one of them shouted excitedly from behind his mask, clapping his hands like a child.

Alex froze, momentarily oblivious to the attention being forced upon her as the horror of recognising the voice and mannerisms of Nathan's disabled brother hit hard. And as panic flooded back with the stinging sensation of a slap to her face and the tearing at her breasts, the nauseating thought that Nathan might also be behind one of the masks made her retch uncontrollably. Her eyes widened with even more horror as she caught sight of the masked Bedlam calmly wheeling over a trolley covered in countless metal implements of torture. After a second or two of deciding, he grabbed a pair of nipple clamps and a handful of six-centimetre-long thick-gauged silver needles, which he handed to Caleb.

18

"How the hell could he have escaped?" Nathan asked into the speaker of his phone.

David Hearsham at the rehab centre was just as embarrassed as he was annoyed at himself for being drawn into his friend's problems. An uncomfortable moment's silence followed as the previous evening's security footage replayed in his mind. "It seems your brother simply walked out of the back entrance behind a staff member who went to put the rubbish out," Hearsham admitted, his real humiliation lying in the fact that it had taken so long for his staff to realise Caleb was missing.

Nathan took a deep controlled breath. "Thanks for letting me know, David," he finally said, breaking the still-hanging silence over the line. "I understand what a predicament this has put you in. It's me that should apologise. I'll be in touch."

"Dog escaped from the yard?" Mia asked, guessing at the scenario from Nathan's side of the phone conversation while gently pushing the half-finished serving of honey and almond granola away from her – the only offering on the café's breakfast menu that had appealed.

Nathan looked across quizzically at his new acquaintance, momentarily distracted from his concern over Caleb by her peculiar question. Mia was waiting for an answer, resting her chin on delicate feminine hands all but hidden from view inside the loose sleeves of the fashionably oversized slinky knit she was wearing, the garment only serving to emphasise her petite frame. The girl's expertly razored shoulder-length black hair was as straight and compliant as his own, and the mere hint of make-up she was wearing only highlighted how naturally pretty she was. Nathan had to force himself to break his gaze, it only taking a couple of seconds for him to realise the premise behind the girl's odd assumption that he owned a dog. *How the hell could he have escaped?*

"No, no, Mia. It's a little difficult to explain," he finally answered. "I'm so sorry to do this to you, but I'm going to have to leave."

Nathan had no idea what he was going to do about Caleb, but he could at least call Annie and see if his brother had headed there – a prospect that only presented a problem in itself. His aunt was under the impression that Caleb was staying with him for a couple of days, and contacting her would only mean having to perpetuate the lie even further to prevent her from worrying.

Mia girlishly pouted her disappointment at having to cut the breakfast date short, the mannerism serving to confirm her early upbringing in Japan. Over breakfast, Nathan had learnt that her English father and Japanese mother had settled in Australia when she was only nine years old. And after graduating from university there, and following a stint in the United States, she'd ended up joining her recently widowed father back in the UK before being offered the position working under Anne-Marie at AXIS.

"Maybe I could tag along," Mia suggested, nonchalantly gazing past Nathan's shoulder out of the café window. "I could help you find whoever it is you're looking for… I am a researcher. I like a good mystery," she added, making full eye contact again.

"It's very kind of you to offer," an inwardly torn Nathan replied with a smile. He definitely didn't want to discourage Mia's obvious wish to spend more time with him, but following the breakfast date, his intention had been to visit the fight gym Bedlam trained at. That situation was volatile, at best. The skirmish with Benji had put him on notice to control his emotions and think his way through the problem. And now he had the added worry of Caleb's whereabouts. "Thanks, but I have to sort this out on my own," Nathan said, excusing himself and reaching for his wallet.

"I really think you should reconsider, under the circumstances," Mia persisted.

"Under what circumstances?"

"Well, isn't that your silver Audi being towed away?" she calmly said, indicating with a point of a finger.

Nathan turned just in time to see his car being dragged off at a forty-five-degree angle from the morning *Clearway* zone he'd failed to notice on parking across the road from the café. He rolled his eyes and sighed, comically deflating himself until his forehead rested flat on the table where he began to gently bang his head over and over against the table's edge. This was the last thing he needed.

"*Kawaisou!*" Mia giggled, slipping naturally into her

native tongue, sharing Nathan's pain. "You poor thing!" She reached for her car keys from inside her bag. "I'll drive you."

Nathan had priorities other than having to retrieve his car. The pick-up location plastered across the side of the tow truck was miles away, and he knew from past experience that the retrieval procedures were made purposely inconvenient as an added deterrent, having once been given the runaround for over three hours at an impound yard. He'd just have to take the overnight storage charge on the chin and hire a car. Mia tagging along would only make things difficult, especially considering the identity and bizarre events surrounding the escapee she had taken an interest in.

"Thanks again, Mia, but I really do need to take care of this on my own. It would be great if you could drop me at my apartment, though. There's a car rental place nearby, and I can—"

"Mine's the red Fiat Panda. Take it!" Mia insisted, dangling her keys in front of him, accepting that the breakfast date was definitely at an end. "I really don't need it for a couple of days. Drop me off at home on your way. We can have dinner at my place tomorrow night when you bring it back."

Nathan smiled his acceptance, impressed with her persistence.

"After all," Mia said, "some people believe that there's no such thing as *coincidence* in the misfortunes that we encounter... Under the circumstances, what are your thoughts on that?" she teased, echoing Nathan's own words from the previous afternoon.

19

"Asphyxiation on her own vomit," the medical examiner answered coldly. "More than likely unconscious at the time. Post-mortem levels suggest that her blood alcohol would have been through the roof."

"And the mutilation?" Pullen asked.

"The pattern is ordered with the multiple puncture wounds very evenly spaced. There was nothing frenzied about this. They took their time. The superficial burns are from hot wax, while the others are more like brandings with a hot metal implement. And the petechial haemorrhaging and bruising around the base of both breasts are definitely indicative of the blood supply being severely restricted for prolonged periods with rope tourniquets. It's a common BDSM practice. The breast tissue becomes starved of blood and the resulting pain is intense."

"And that's supposed to be sexually arousing?"

"For the perpetrator, certainly. But for some consenting women, too, believe it or not. The simultaneous stimulation of pain receptors and erogenous tissue is said to send those that way inclined into cascades of intense multiple orgasms."

"Anything to suggest she didn't consent?"

"It's impossible to differentiate. The nature of such sex play is violent in its very nature. Her wrists were tied. Her ankles, too. Abrasions at the angles of the mouth suggest she was gagged, which obviously would have contributed to the cause of death."

"Semen?"

"Not a trace. There's severe tearing anally and vaginally similar to what we'd see in a gang rape. But the subculture I'm referring to will often engage in group sex practices with the woman ostensibly consenting to play out a rape fantasy… Sex play gone wrong or the random victim of a psychopath pulling the strings of one or more associates. That's your call, Doug."

Pullen hadn't even considered the possibility of consensual sex when he'd first been shown the horrendously mutilated corpse. The body had been found by a group of early-morning joggers on the tow path of an exposed stretch of disused canal that cut unnoticed beneath the roads and backstreets of the city centre. The perpetrators had seemingly been disturbed in the act of disposing of the victim, evidenced by the weighted body they'd intended hurling into the murky waters, never to be seen again. The girl's trashy appearance and the circumstances of her demise might have initially suggested hooker. But in his time as a cop, Pullen had compared enough post-mortem slab photographs with tearfully offered graduation snaps held in trembling hands not to assume anything anymore.

Scanning the body, he let his highly trained mind slip

into rewind mode: her deathly pallor gradually became suffused with the warmth of life-giving blood once more; the mascara runs and lipstick smudges retreated away until they were again perfectly applied to what were the prettiest eyes and lips imaginable, and the brunette hair was now just as the last carefully aimed spray had left it. The woman stood from the slab, ignorant to Pullen's gaze, rising from the dead with healed wounds, her nakedness revealing a vision of feminine perfection – a lean, toned body that undoubtedly practised yoga and pounded cardio equipment at the gym for hours. She leant down and began to dress, slipping on predictably sexy daytime lingerie before zipping on a figure-hugging skirt and buttoning up a crisp pastel-coloured blouse. The phantom getting ready for her day was oblivious to the fate she would have avoided simply by choosing a different bar to frequent the night before. Pullen pressed the *STOP* button in his mind and stared at the freeze-frame. This was no hooker or trashy nightclub tragic. Pullen's intuition told him that she was a professional woman. Lawyer, perhaps. Granted, one that might like to indulge herself a little too much in the more hedonistic pleasures of life but of a social status that gave Pullen real cause for concern. He was now certain there'd been nothing consensual in whatever chilling fate had befallen her.

Another rush of opiate coursed through the veins of a pretty young girl, leaving her insensible to the procedure. The main femoral artery supplying blood to her left leg had already been blunt dissected out and ligated, and all that remained to do was saw through the bone at the top of the femur, a few centimetres below the hip joint. Others would dispose of the limb, just as they had disposed of the girl's right leg days before.

The girl's calf was long and slender, her thigh slim yet shapely. She'd moved well in heels. Perhaps a little too well. It had been her body writhing sensually to the rhythm of the music across the dance floor that had first brought attention to herself. Still adorned by its sparkling stilettoed party shoe, the limb was now being held aloft in bloodied hands and viewed with appreciation. The surgical butcher pressed a cheek sensuously against the inner thigh to take in the soft cooling skin, then licked up its length while eyeing the two stumps the girl had been left with – the rough suturing having closed the latest surgical wound.

20

Nathan collapsed exhaustedly onto the gym matting set up in his apartment, sucking in oxygen as the heavy bag suspended from the ceiling beam continued to swing from side to side with his efforts. Those recent long hours at work had certainly taken the edge off his fitness, but his fight training in full contact karate that had seen him through his years of high school and university, he decided, was still evident somewhere in muscle memory. Sitting up with a single rapid contraction of his abdominals and getting to his feet, he pulled off the gloves and undid the wraps, using them to wipe the sweat from his neck and forehead before throwing them into the laundry basket and heading for the bathroom.

Nathan stared at himself in the mirror. He recognised the face but not necessarily the person anymore. Maybe Isaac had been right in his prediction that every assumption, value and belief that he'd ever held was about to collapse like a house of cards. He sensed it himself. But who would be left staring back at him in the mirror then?

Thoughts of Mia passed through his mind. The timing of their meeting could not have been worse. He was still coming to terms with Alex walking out on him and now the drama surrounding Caleb was constantly playing on his mind. There was definitely something irresistible about the girl, though. The oversized stuffed toy she had buckled into the rear seat of the Fiat – a black and white panda bear that had stared inanely at him in the rear-view mirror all the way home – was completely at odds with the voluminous academic texts and complex treatises on the chemical composition of neurotransmitters that were haphazardly piled up next to it on the back seat. After dropping Mia off at her flat, he had already realised that he was hooked. The light floral scent hanging in the car's interior had made him think that the vehicle quite possibly ran on a tank of pure perfume. And, despite the initial embarrassment of being seen getting into such a car, once on the road, he could have happily driven for hours inhaling those traces of Mia. That she was lost between cultures only added to her appeal. When she spoke English, she seemed bold, edgy and devil-may-care, but when she slipped into Japanese, she was girlish, coy and even a little overly apologetic. The complexity intrigued him.

Nathan took one last look at himself in the bathroom mirror before flicking on the electric clipper he was holding in his hand. Placing it to his scalp, he cut an irreversible swathe through his thick black hair. To rescue the brother he loved from those skinhead thugs, he had no other choice but to become one of them.

Nathan parked up a good distance away from Brophy's gym, not wishing to repeat his mistake of parking directly in front of Toxic Ink. It also wasn't likely that many *wannabe* cage fighters would turn up in an old Fiat Panda with a stuffed toy in the back seat. Even fewer would be seen glancing in the rear-view mirror to check their appearance before exiting the car. At least he now looked the part. The gym was his only potential lead, and he could only hope that if he hung around long enough Bedlam would show his face. He needed to know if his brother was safe. He needed answers.

Brophy's wasn't what Nathan had imagined. The premises were clean, spacious and incredibly well equipped, and seemed to attract patrons from all walks of life, like any other gym. If anything untoward was going on there, it would be the perfect front. Nathan chose to settle into some bag work close to two rings – one surrounded by ropes with boot scuff marks across its square canvas, the other surrounded by an octagonal metal cage with more ominous stains to its flooring. A group of skinheads stood ringside watching a fighter sparring with two oversized opponents in the boxing ring. The stocky solid-framed man bobbed and weaved, forever moving forwards, his fists inflicting lightning stings through the defence of both his opponents. The display left Nathan feeling decidedly amateurish in his efforts and in awe at what would happen if the man actually chose to open up on the formidable-looking training partners.

"How's it going, Champ?"

Nathan stopped mid-punch and turned to be confronted by both the late middle-aged paunch of a long-since retired heavyweight and the man's fist suddenly heading towards his face. In shock, Nathan instinctively reacted with a swift yet unnecessary rising block – the man's feigned strike hanging harmlessly in mid-air.

"Jodan Uke," Brophy commented, displaying his knowledge across a number of fight styles, having exposed Nathan's *go-to* move when put on the spot. "Figured you weren't a boxer," Brophy grinned. "You need a lot of work." He nodded towards the swinging bag. "But there's enough speed there. Balls, too."

The realisation that he himself had been unwittingly under scrutiny while attempting to carry out his own covert surveillance put Nathan ill at ease. It highlighted how completely out of his depth he was. All he could do was bluff his way through until he found some thread of information that would lead him to his brother.

Nathan recognised the man from the glory-days photos of mouthguard victory smiles and raised gloves that hung around the gym. "I'm looking to fight," he responded coolly, seizing the opportunity. "Heard this was the place."

Brophy raised his eyebrows. "What did you hear?"

"That Bedlam fights outta here."

The reference wasn't lost on Brophy. Bedlam only fought illegal bouts that didn't end even when a defeated opponent lay unconscious on the blood-soaked canvas. Those sickening post-knockout blows were what kept the punters coming back for more, fuelling the lucrative gladiatorial gatherings.

"You're not in the same league, boy. I'd forget what you've heard," Brophy suggested derisively, turning to walk away.

Nathan saw the best opportunity yet to gather information about Caleb's whereabouts retreating. "I can get better…" Nathan snapped, in an attempt to get the man's attention again.

Brophy turned back around just in time to catch sight of Nathan connecting with the hefty bag in a textbook spinning kick that sent it flying sideways beyond an angle of forty-five degrees, the clanking supporting chains drawing attention even from ringside.

There was always some testosterone-fuelled hothead that fancied their chances. The purse for those that survived even a few fights was substantial. But Brophy knew that Bedlam's reputation was making it harder to find willing opponents. Some of the fodder he had fed Bedlam never fought again after the bout, and one or two of them never walked again, either. He weighed up the possibilities. Such an unfortunate mismatch in a warm-up fight before the main event might prove an entertaining way to stir up the bloodlust of the punters. And in the unlikely event that the kid did end up being good enough to survive for a win, he could always feed him to Bedlam in a later bout.

Brophy looked hard at Nathan. "Come with me, boy," he commanded.

Nathan grabbed the bag to dampen its violent pendulum swing and followed Brophy over to the ring area, suppressing his nerves.

"I'd like you to meet Charlie," he said, pulling down on the middle ropes, inviting Nathan to climb in.

The action in the ring ceased immediately with Brophy's gesture. Both of the training partners climbed out, leaving an unblinking Charlie standing waiting, as if menacingly pre-empting the bell for the next round of some upcoming bout that was still playing out in his head.

"Kyokushin… Kwon Do, if you like," Brophy suggested with a shrug, bearing in mind the styles he'd observed in Nathan's technique. "It's all the same to Charlie."

Nathan froze. This wasn't what he'd had in mind. Blurting

out that he wanted to fight had been meant as a verbal bluff to engage Brophy in further conversation and prevent him from walking off. It certainly wasn't meant as a challenge. But if he was going to retain the gym owner's attention, taking up that challenge and stepping into the ring was about the only option he now had. He'd taken enough solid blows to the head and body in his martial arts training over the years not to be completely fazed, but the gloved anvil fists attached to the end of Charlie's thick arms were like nothing he'd ever faced before. Giving a decent account of himself without getting too hurt before succumbing was about as good as he could hope for. If he did end up getting hurt, he figured it was the least he could do for his brother. He was also well aware that there were other members of the public working out around the gym, and he thought it worth a punt that Brophy wouldn't allow a complete bloodbath to ensue right in front of the eyes of his paying customers.

Nathan climbed in and circled the battle-hardened fighter in a wide sweep of the ring, thinking it best to keep a distance. He knew it would be suicidal to go on the offensive and so readied himself to be reactive to whatever Charlie threw at him – an eventuality that only took seconds. With lightning speed, the fighter had traversed the distance between them and swung a wide arcing right hook to Nathan's head. Nathan's reactions, though, didn't let him down as the scuffed leather of the training glove brushed past his nose. Muscle memory kicked in, and he involuntarily opened up in a rapid combination of punches to the fighter's exposed head that sent the man reeling and covering up against the ropes. That's where Nathan's killer instinct failed him and he backed away, only to see a white towel come flying into the ring.

Amidst the sound of his pounding heart and the rasp of oxygen-debt air being sucked into his lungs, it took Nathan a second to register the laughter coming from all corners of the ring. He looked around in confusion, only to return his gaze to Charlie, who was still against the ropes, feigning defeat, and peeking from behind his gloves with the broadest of mouthguard grins.

Brophy wasn't laughing. "Like I said. You've got balls."

Nathan immediately realised that the invite into the ring had been as much a test of his mettle as that fake punch Brophy had delivered towards his face earlier.

"You were a tenth of a second from a wheelchair, boy. Just remember that," Brophy said, as Charlie grunted a derisory scoff through his nostrils and turned to face his sparring partners re-entering the ring through the ropes. Brophy took another long and hard look at Nathan. "When you've finished up, meet me over at the Ashton. We'll talk," he decided.

Unlike Brophy's, the Ashton Arms was every bit what Nathan had imagined. The vapour mix of bleach and vomit floating on a background stench of stale beer and cigarettes that met him on entering was probably its most endearing feature; its most worrying was the poster in the entranceway inviting all-comers to the ultra-right-wing British Party's weekly meetings. Nathan knew that the group were 'proudly fascist' through the occasional news report that surfaced about them when some peaceful demonstration would be hijacked and whipped up into a full-scale city centre riot. The global phenomenon in recent times of extreme right-wing Nazisympathising politics re-emerging and gaining popular support, especially in Europe, was all too evident at the Ashton Arms – the picture that tattooist Benji had first begun to paint was certainly taking shape.

Sitting in a far corner of the bar, holding court, Brophy waved Nathan over. Surrounded by his captains, lieutenants and an outer ring of lower-ranked henchmen, it was obvious that he was much more than just a gym owner and organiser of illegal fights.

As he approached, Nathan registered the absurdity of the situation he now found himself in. *A physician, pretending to be a street fighter, looking to pick a fight with a group of neo-Nazi skinheads.* He had to force the thought out of his mind at the risk of losing his nerve and putting himself in even more danger as he waded deeper and deeper into the unknown. He just needed one clue as to Caleb's whereabouts so he could get out of there.

Nathan picked his way through the surly ranks until he reached the inner sanctum of chairs, feeling sick to his stomach with a nervousness his expression fought to conceal. But he couldn't help almost outing himself when an athletic-looking guy sitting next to Brophy turned around in his seat, revealing the head of a striking cobra emblazoned up the left side of his neck. He was finally face to face with Bedlam.

Everything about the man seemed at odds with those he chose to associate with. He was impeccably groomed and smartly dressed in designer jeans and T-shirt, and his impressive muscular physique was the only sign that he was a fighter. He probably only weighed in at 85 kilos. The smooth skin of his face was blemish-free, and his hands bore no hint of the cruel punishment they had meted out.

Even the severely short light blond hue of regrowth and sharp lines of his cheekbones would easily have allowed him to pass as some smouldering ex-member of a now defunct boy band rather than the thug he actually was. His general demeanour was unnervingly calm behind those intelligent unblinking eyes. That there was another side to him was clear, and Nathan was relieved that the fighter appeared to show no interest in him whatsoever.

Nathan stood for some time like a summoned busboy while Brophy continued his conversation with those at the table.

"This is Paulie," Brophy finally barked, looking at Nathan and motioning to the man sitting to his right.

Paulie was over fifty, squat, with slicked-back thinning hair. And, unlike Bedlam, he looked like he'd taken every punch ever thrown at him full in the face. The man didn't so much as raise his eyes as Brophy spoke, his deadpan expression fixed on the beer mat he was continually turning around between his fingers.

"He'll take care of everything," Brophy continued. "Do what he says, boy. No lip. No questions. You train how and when he says. He doesn't look much, but he taught Bedlam here everything he knows."

Bedlam gave Nathan a sideways glance.

"Paulie speaks for me, boy. What Paulie says goes. Got it?"

Nathan nodded.

"Get your arse over to the gym at 5 am tomorrow," Brophy concluded dismissively before turning away to resume his conversation as if the interaction had simply never taken place.

Nathan hadn't needed to say a single word, which was a relief. Saying nothing and just nodding did seem to be the safest option given the circumstances. On entering the pub, he had been hoping to find out more about Bedlam's connection to Caleb and glean something as to his brother's whereabouts. But at least he now had an *in*, and while he didn't relish the thought of returning, the chances of making contact with Bedlam at the training session seemed good.

He turned to weave his way back to the relative safety of the bar, only to find his path suddenly blocked by a heavy boot being slammed onto an empty chair. The recalcitrant skinhead barring his way nonchalantly continued to run his tongue along the paper's edge of a roll-up, as if he had no clue that anyone was there. Nathan had no idea how he was supposed to react to such a challenge and glanced over his shoulder at Brophy to check if he was being watched again. It was Bedlam, though, that seemed to be taking an interest as he leant over and whispered into Brophy's ear while nodding obviously in Nathan's direction. The fighter, it seemed, hadn't been that oblivious to Nathan's presence, knowing better than to discount any new kid on the block that made an appearance.

Brophy suddenly called to Nathan with a brash "Wait!"

Nathan turned around.

"It's your lucky day, boy. I've just been reminded of an opening in a bout this evening, on account of some light-fingered *fucker* having those fingers removed with a hacksaw blade!"

The corner of the pub erupted in laughter, indicating that Brophy wasn't in any way joking.

"Meet Paulie at the Carousel Club tonight at ten."

The skinhead blocking Nathan's path suddenly thought better of his actions and slowly removed his leg while saving face by blowing a cloud of smoke from his first drag in Nathan's direction.

Nathan nodded and walked off, only to catch Brophy asking, "*Will Caleb be at the fight tonight?*" Bedlam's reply became frustratingly lost in another sudden crescendo of laughter from a group across the other side of the bar.

Nathan made his escape from the pub, knowing that he now had no choice but to head for the Carousel Club as ordered.

21

DS Fitzpatrick consoled the old woman who had collapsed into his arms, while Pullen remained professionally stoic and unreadable as the wails and desperate sobs diminished to a chilling distant echo as she was led away from the mortuary's examination room and out into the corridor. Pullen looked again at the surgically excised arm lying on the slab. There was usually more for a loved one to identify, but Jessica Mahr's grandmother had instantly recognised the tattoo on the underside of the delicate wrist. *Carpe Diem*, it read. Unfortunately for Jessica, there were no more days, hours or minutes left to seize.

The distraught woman had been resolute about seeing the remains for herself rather than being presented with a photo for identification purposes – Pullen having chosen to spare her the gruesome news that all four dismembered limbs had now been recovered from the site of the refuse tip. The search teams needed more time. But despite the ongoing intensive search, it now seemed less and less likely that the head and torso would be found at the location.

22

Nathan surveyed the heaving crowd. A raised hexagonal fight cage all but filled the upstairs converted function room of the Carousel Club with just enough space for five rows of tiered seating along the back wall where Brophy and his VIP guests were seated. The remainder of the makeshift arena was standing room only, with the jeering mob pushed right up to the mesh of the cage – those at the front suffering the whiplash spatter of sweat and blood from blows delivered only inches from their faces. A collective groan from the crowd signalled a failed roundhouse kick to the ribs that had just been smothered by the perfectly timed lunge of an amorphous burly fighter who was far from being a poster boy for the blood sport. But, despite his bulk, the man had been light enough on his feet to have caught the leg mid-kick while sending his ripped opponent hopping awkwardly backwards in a desperate attempt to keep his balance before being slammed into the side of the cage and onto the floor. The leaner fighter writhed to free himself from between the cage wall and the crushing brawn, only to find the side of his bloodied face being pushed mercilessly against the mesh. "*Die, you fucker! Die!*" screamed a spectator closest to the action, repeatedly striking at the fighter's head with the flat of his hand through the safety of the chain link, inspiring the crowd all around the octagonal cage to follow suit in pounding on the walls and chanting for the man's blood.

Despite the vile spectacle, Nathan's attention remained fixed on the tiered platform of chairs on the far wall. If Brophy was expecting Caleb at the fight, the seating area would be the best place to look. His brother didn't like crowds and would burst into tears if someone even raised their voice, so it was inconceivable that he would be amongst the mosh pit of depravity beating on the cage. Why Bedlam had named himself after an asylum for the insane now made complete sense, and it was disturbing to think that the rabid jeering mob were free to walk the streets once the event was over, especially considering he would regularly medicate patients fit for a psychiatric ward that were far less aggressive and more in control of their behaviour. Nathan had no intention of fighting in the planned bout, knowing he was already in far deeper than was safe. He just wanted to find Caleb and get out of there, which wasn't going to be easy. Brophy's henchmen were everywhere, making sure only invited guests made it in.

Brophy looked every bit the lord of all he surveyed. Even the smouldering viciousness dressed in Armani satellited around him – each surrounded by their own constellation of uneasy-looking minders – seemed to accept their place in the natural order of things. But the rest of the gathered VIP audience seemed a very unlikely-looking group to be assembled at an illegal fight night where a fatality was potentially on the cards before the evening was out. They could easily have been taken for a busload of middle-aged doctors or lawyers shipped in from a weekend conference.

Brophy kept his eyes keenly on the fight while he side-talked to one elderly, nervy and particularly bookish-looking man in a dark grey suit who was sitting next to him in the top tier of seats. The man seemed the most out of place of all, having no apparent interest in the fight as he sat anxiously on the edge of his seat looking as though he just wanted to get out of the place.

Another collective groan, followed by a crescendo of manic screaming and chanting, saw the leaner fighter inside the cage viciously strike the temple of his adversary with an elbow he'd managed to free as the pair had fallen back down to the canvas again in a deadlocked grapple. The unexpected blow momentarily stunned the heavyweight and allowed the underdog turned aggressor to kick himself free and get to his feet. Within a second, the fighter's heel was stamping repeatedly onto his opponent's throat and jaw and face, and the savage rapid-fire blows to the man's head from lightning fists that followed were made all the more sickening to watch due to the defenceless fighter on the canvas being able to do nothing but hold his throat with both hands as he fought to breathe amidst the onslaught. And throughout, not one person ringside was inspired to make a move to intervene.

"This way," came a voice in Nathan's ear.

The unison screams of the crowd that accompanied each savage blow were all Nathan could hear as he turned to follow, with the ultimate fate of the defeated man being denied him by Paulie's terse instruction. Nathan had hoped that once inside the venue he would be able to disappear into the crowd until he located Caleb, and hadn't counted on being spotted so quickly. Now he'd been left with no choice but to comply, and the degree of danger that he was placing himself in had just escalated. The sports bag he'd carried in with him contained a pair of training gloves, a mouthguard, a towel and little else – enough, he'd figured, to convince those on the door that he was expected. Other than that, he was suspiciously ill-equipped.

Paulie led Nathan into a long and fairly narrow adjoining room full of edgy fighters. One of them was already on his feet warming up for the next imminent bout while his surly-looking opponent eyed him off, unperturbed, from across the room before also getting to his feet and gesturing a couple of lazy side-to-side stretches of his neck. The remainder of the silently brooding gladiators were seated in various degrees of undress on two long benches pushed up against the facing walls, and the only talk in the buzzing atmosphere of the room was from amongst the huddles of surrounding sidekicks and hangers-on.

"Dead man walking!" a voice shouted, causing everyone in the room to look around and weigh up the newcomer. A jeer went up, mainly from the hangers-on in a display of second-hand courage, while the grinning toothless hulk sitting on the bench immediately to the right made a derisory comment aimed at Nathan that sent those fighters within earshot into fits of mocking laughter. It took Nathan a second to realise that the voice of the initial instigator had belonged to Bedlam, who was standing at the far end of the locker room. Wearing jeans, a shirt and black leather jacket, it was obvious that, on this particular fight night, Bedlam wasn't headlining the evening's bill.

Nathan was guided through a wave of rapidly subsiding heckling coming from either side of him until he reached the empty section at the far end of the bench.

"You'll be fighting him," Paulie offered in his usual monotone, still dispensing with all need for eye contact.

Nathan took his allotted seat and glanced over to where the expressively devoid trainer had motioned. On the bench directly opposite was a young fighter in his early twenties who was sitting in a slumped backwards lean against the wall with his eyes averted to the floor. The youth looked terrified yet somehow resigned to his fate, giving Nathan the impression that the guy belonged in this place about as much as he did.

"You've got about half an hour," Paulie grunted, reaching for Nathan's sports bag for no other reason than to place it on the shelf above his head.

Nathan's uneasiness and fear of being found out caused him to tense up and tug the bag possessively back towards himself in a reflex reaction.

Standing only a couple of steps away, Bedlam noticed the unexpected stand-off over the bag and chose to intervene. "What've you got in there? Gold-plated protector for your… *balls*?" he concluded sarcastically, the star fighter having obviously been unimpressed by Brophy voicing his opinion about Nathan's display of courage at the gym earlier in the day.

Nathan was immediately surprised at just how well-spoken Bedlam was. The man was obviously educated, even university educated, and it was hard to conceive how such an intelligent person could have become so intimately involved with the dregs of humanity that Brophy ruled over.

Realising that he was only drawing suspicion towards himself, Nathan instantly let go of the handles and allowed Paulie to do his job, but it was too late to prevent Bedlam from stepping forwards to confront him.

The off-duty fighter knelt down directly in front of Nathan until they were practically nose to nose. "Something about you I don't like," he quietly intimated, an underlying menace in his tone, his eyes staring unblinkingly into Nathan's as if he was probing for an answer. He turned his head, indicating towards the young fighter Nathan was supposed to do battle with. "See that sorry fucker," he continued, turning back to confront Nathan's gaze. "You'd be doing him a favour if you put him out of his misery tonight. His brother owes a debt he can't pay. So he fights. Otherwise, his brother and younger sister will come to a very unhappy end… Especially his sister," he added with a smile.

Nathan stared back without displaying even the slightest reaction, forcing himself to control the loathing welling inside.

"Everyone's got a reason why they're here," Bedlam hissed, losing the smile. "I'm just not sure what yours is."

The confrontation was brought to a fortunate and abrupt end when one of the henchmen called to Bedlam from the door of the locker room. "Boss wants you."

Bedlam gave Nathan one last glare, suggesting unfinished business, before quickly standing and walking off, just as a team of four men carried in the viciously beaten heavyweight from the previous bout that had now ended. Followed by three of his own minions, Bedlam forcibly pushed his way through with a total disregard for the casualty, who looked as if he could be near to death. As a doctor, Nathan was torn. The unconscious man needed urgent attention, and any medical aid in this place was definitely going to be of a deregistered backstreet kind. He couldn't do anything without attracting even more suspicion to himself. In any case, it was unlikely that anyone present would be keen for an emergency call to be placed for paramedics. He just couldn't get involved. The distraction, though, had provided him with a chance to make a tactical escape. Everyone in the locker room was focused on the condition of the defeated fighter being manhandled into the room – everyone except for the reluctant young fighter sitting opposite him. Nathan furtively eyed the metal release bar of the fire door just a few feet away and then looked back at the youth, who was now staring directly at him, having realised his would-be opponent's intentions. Nathan hesitated, unsure as to the young man's allegiances, despite what had been intimated about his predicament. But when he gave the slightest nod in response and averted his eyes back down to the floor, Nathan seized his opportunity.

He slipped away unnoticed into the fire escape stairwell and took the steps three at a time, frustrated that he hadn't been able to rescue his brother. The situation had turned out to be far more dangerous than he'd ever imagined, but at least he'd got out of there with his life, and he would now be able to think of a better plan, knowing who and what he was dealing with. He was under no illusion that if his attempts at deception had been discovered, his bloodied body would have been dragged out of the club, never to be seen again.

Crashing through the ground-floor fire door and sprinting along the service corridor he'd found himself in, Nathan made for the safety of the exit sign at the far end. But the sound of heavy footsteps descending the staircase that joined the corridor up ahead put a stop to his, so far, flawless escape. He had no reason to be loitering where he was, so he retreated back to the staff toilets he'd just passed, hoping to slip inside unnoticed. Pushing on the door, he found they were locked, leaving him dangerously exposed to whoever was approaching – Caleb stepped out into full view, both brothers freezing as they caught sight of each other.

Caleb was the first to react. He bolted for the exit and disappeared outside with such swiftness that Nathan's brain was left momentarily struggling to relay any sensory connection within his visual cortex that would allow his motor centres to respond. Finally giving chase, he reached the exit just in time to see his brother clearing the tall brick wall of a grubby yard area cluttered with refuse skips. Nathan scaled the obstacle in a single leap before heaving himself over the top. It had been over twenty years since the pair had engaged in such brotherly pursuits in the playgrounds of their youth, but there was going to be no giggling laughter at the end of this chase.

Nathan dropped down onto original cobblestones in an alleyway lit only by the rear lighting and security lamps of the adjacent buildings. The alley was clear in both directions, with no clue to suggest which way Caleb had gone, so after catching his breath for a second, he made for the main street he could see at the end of the passage. It was the only real option. If Caleb had gone the other way, he would surely have still been in sight. But Nathan had only made it a few steps before the rear wooden gate to a neighbouring property slammed into him with the force of a freight train, sending him flying. He collided with the opposite wall, his scalp glancing off a metal stud fixed into the brickwork before he crashed to the ground. Landing heavily on his back, he was still shaking the cloudiness from his head when he saw his brother in the half-light walking slowly towards him. A wave of rapidly burgeoning paralysis swept over his body, while a breath-denying crushing sensation against his chest pinned him to the ground. The grip he was under only intensified as Caleb came closer and knelt down over him.

"Don't come looking again, Nathan," Caleb seethed, his voice that of a very capable adult male threatening to exert superior physical prowess. His words were crisp and clear, and his demeanour showed no signs of the bumbling manchild Nathan had expected to rescue. "Now it's my turn to have what you've enjoyed all these years, you bastard!" His venom instantly spilled into derisory laughter as he spoke. "And I have to say, brother, I really like your taste in women!" he said, tilting his head back and spitting in Nathan's face.

Nathan struggled to breathe, the constant sensation of pressure on his chest now as intense as an aerial G-force pull. Confusion gripped his mind. The blow to his head must have left him concussed – nothing about what he was seeing and hearing made sense. He was losing consciousness and fought to keep a focus on his brother's face. But it was hopeless. All faded to dark.

13

The transaction was almost complete. The money would be correct. There was no need to count the £20,000 in notes inside the sealed envelope because the consequences of short-changing Brophy were known to be so unspeakable. The wads of cash would have been painstakingly checked again and again by the elderly bookish-looking man in the dark grey suit whom Bedlam had personally escorted from the tiered VIP seating of the fight arena.

Bedlam took the envelope without saying a word, indicating that he was happy with the fulfilment of the transaction, and signalled to an underling with a slight nod of his head. The silent OK was relayed, and only moments later a man entered from an adjoining room carrying in a girl who was gagged and wearing only lingerie. The pale blue of the lacy half-cup bra and G-string flattered her skin of porcelain perfection, causing the elderly client's breathing to become shallower and more rapid in anticipation. The girl was placed down on the floor on her back, her tears streaming backwards down over her temples and disappearing into the silky honey blonde hair pushed alluringly behind her ears.

Bedlam smiled as he opened the door leading to the main corridor. "Enjoy!" he suggested as the music from downstairs momentarily blared into the room before the door was slammed shut, leaving the girl alone with the elderly client.

The old man gazed across the girl's young body as she trembled helplessly in fear, and approaching tentatively, he knelt down to stroke her hair. "It's OK. It's OK," he reassured. "I'll be gentle," he added, with the kindliness of a mild-mannered grandfather.

It was then that he noticed the silver necklace adorning her décolletage, each of the seven letters hanging from the chain like charms, girlishly spelling out her name.

Arthritic fingers slipped under the chain presenting each of the letters to his eager eyes. "Jessica," he exhaled, before letting it drop gently back onto her skin and proceeding to slip the bra straps slowly off both of her shoulders.

Jessica Mahr squirmed, unable to fight back, the stumps of her four recently amputated limbs aiming phantom strikes and kicks against the sickening assault.

24

Sitting on the edge of the mattress, Nathan gripped the metal framework of the bed as the local anaesthetic needle tunnelled painfully into his scalp over and over again on either side of the wound. The thought did cross his mind that he might suggest any future patients dispense with the step, concluding that even the thickest gauge suture needle in the hands of a blacksmith would be less uncomfortable than the anaesthetic needle's piercing assault. Not that Adam was anything but gentle, despite his size.

"Thought you were supposed to be taking it easy!" Adam said, tugging the edges of the wound together with the silk. The last two hours of the graveyard shift he had just endured had dragged interminably, and while he'd been secretly praying for some emergency to crop up to pass the time, the last thing he'd expected was for a friend to turn up as the casualty. "What's going on, mate? You look like you've just stepped off a prison bus."

Nathan caught sight of his reflection in the mirror of the

treatment room he'd been ushered into. Adam was right. His attempts to blend in with those skinhead thugs had worked a little too well, the suturing to his scalp and the congealed blood on his neck and sweatshirt only adding to the picture. "I had a change of plan," Nathan responded wryly, remembering Adam's offer to cover shifts for him but not – thanks to Isaac's subliminal intervention – the exact reason why. The stress he'd been under concerning his missing brother had consumed him to the exclusion of all else. "I guess I'll be taking a rain check on that stay at the farmhouse."

"C'mon," Adam persisted, sincerely concerned for his friend. "How did this happen? And don't bother feeding me any *I tripped and fell* bullshit."

Nathan figured that he owed his friend at least some of the truth. "I got into a fight with Caleb," he admitted, not strictly lying.

"Caleb?" Adam was shocked. He knew Caleb to be a gentle chattering giant. "I know that you mentioned his behaviour was changing, but I would never have guessed that you and he would…" Adam, for once, was lost for words. "Anything I can do?"

"Find him," Nathan suggested bluntly, as thoughts of what he would say to Annie momentarily drifted through his mind.

"You mean he's gone missing again?"

"This time for good, I think."

"What!"

Nathan thought twice before sharing any more of the events that had landed him in A&E. In the alleyway behind the Carousel Club, he'd plainly heard Caleb talking to him without the slightest trace of disability. And while reason dictated that such a warped perception had to have been caused by the blow to his head, he just couldn't help but dwell on that first glimpse he'd caught of him in the corridor inside the club. Normally bumbling and lacking all semblance of coordination, Caleb had bolted with such speed and agility that it'd taken Nathan a second to recognise the fleeing man as his brother. Nor could he dismiss the fact that Caleb had effortlessly vaulted the back wall of the club in making his escape. Even his physique had drastically changed. He now appeared markedly leaner and more muscular – something that, in hindsight, was already becoming evident the morning Nathan had crashed into Caleb's bedroom and seen him standing by his bed wearing just his jeans. Concussion couldn't account for all that. The inexplicable changes in his brother had already been evident *before* Caleb had attacked him in the alleyway.

Nathan finally opted to ask Adam for his professional opinion. "In patients with Caleb's degree of brain damage, have you ever heard of cases where there's been apparent spontaneous recovery so many years later?"

Adam raised his eyebrows, naturally surprised by the question. "Are you suggesting that Caleb's recovering?"

Nathan evaded the question with a noncommittal shrug.

"Well, there's obviously a lot of research these days into Neuroplasticity... Stimulating the development of new neural pathways to compensate for those lost in acquired brain injury is definitely the future. But I can't say that I've heard of it occurring spontaneously twenty-five years post-injury without any clinical intervention." Adam paused for a moment, sensitive to the fact that it was Nathan's own brother he was commenting on while not wanting to encourage any false hopes. "Let's face it, fifty years ago, the idea of Neuroplasticity itself would have been laughed at by this wonderful profession of ours. So who knows with an organ like the brain… but I wouldn't be holding out too much hope for Caleb's condition improving," he added, turning around in his seat and reaching over to grab a hypodermic syringe still in its sterile packaging. "Tetanus shot," he stated, his thoughts returning to the job at hand. "You're about due, anyway. I'll save you the indignity of having to drop your pants in front of the nurses. Though I'm sure they'd love to get an eyeful," he joked, without the slightest trace of a smile on his face. "We'll keep an eye on you here overnight. You know the drill concerning the knock you've had, so make sure you're not alone after you get home. Doctors aren't immune to bleeds!"

Nathan was as guilty as any medic, at times, in ignoring the advice he himself would give to a patient, but he'd witnessed enough cases of life-threatening bleeds to the brain following far less trauma than he'd just suffered to be naturally cautious. And having lived with the aftermath of acquired brain injury, it was something that he, of all people, didn't take for granted. It was just so ironic that it had been Caleb inflicting such a wound on him.

"Rest up. Maybe Annie or someone could look after you for a couple of days?" Adam suggested, before wrapping things up in the treatment room.

Nathan nodded and smiled, surprising himself when Mia immediately came to mind.

Later the following morning, after he was discharged, Nathan swung by his apartment to clean up and change clothes before heading off to Mia's place. All in all, physically, he was feeling none the worse for his encounter with Caleb. Emotionally speaking, it was a different matter. Caleb's show of viciousness had disturbed him. The person he'd thought of as a blood brother his whole life now may as well be a stranger. He'd never really given a second thought to Caleb's prior family background before being adopted by his parents, but now it played on his mind. Who knew what unknown dormant tendencies and predispositions lay within the unfolding DNA of his adopted brother's genes?

It was late afternoon by the time Nathan was ready to set off for Mia's place, and she'd sounded more than happy on the phone at the prospect of his return with the car a little earlier than expected. He turned the key in the ignition of the Fiat Panda, pulled out of the car park of his apartment building and took a right onto the main road, having no reason to be anything but oblivious to the vehicle that had been parked across the street for hours and that now slowly pulled away from the kerb and began to follow.

Mia opened the front door of her modest two-bedroom flat to see a set of keys dangling in front of her eyes, and despite expecting Nathan to arrive any moment, it took her a full two seconds to recognise him as the bearer.

"*A-re!*" she finally exclaimed in a breathy rising tone.

By the look on Mia's face, Nathan took '*A-re!*' to be a Japanese expression of surprise. He was correct in his assumption. And the wide-eyed "*Hansamu da naa!*" that followed was without doubt a show of approval – now that he was out of his training clothes and minus the surly grimace he'd earlier had to force into his expression, the shaven-headed look did quite suit him.

Mia noticed the sutures in Nathan's scalp. "What have you done?" she asked, instinctively reaching out with concern to touch the still-raw injured area.

Nathan immediately flinched and pulled back slightly, only too aware of the girl's propensity to cause him pain, albeit unintentionally. And having the same realisation, Mia stopped herself just in time. "Sorry!" she said, offering a comical face.

"I'm fine. I just slipped and fell during fight training at the gym."

Mia didn't reply, and for a seemingly endless moment they both just stared at each other in silence. Then, moving in close, she pushed the front door shut and reached up to place her hands delicately behind Nathan's neck and pulled him in to an inevitable kiss.

In the open-plan kitchen of Mia's apartment, a pan simmered unattended and a paring knife now lay redundant next to a pile of unpeeled vegetables on a board of Tasmanian blackwood. Over in the corner, the TV she'd been half watching while preparing dinner continued to flicker unnoticed, the sound barely more than a background garble. The image of an attractive young brunette's Facebook smile flashed onto the screen in the late-afternoon news bulletin. Twenty-six-year-old Alex Stanton's mutilated body had now been identified through missing person reports, and police were appealing for any information surrounding her murder.

*

"Do you remember the first time we met?" Mia asked, curled up next to Nathan on the couch, enjoying an after-dinner glass of wine.

Nathan raised an eyebrow, the cascade of events he'd been caught up in over the last week running through his mind in a fast-forward replay. His visit to AXIS now seemed like a distant memory. "Well, let me think. It being all of three days ago, I'll admit my recollection's a little shaky, but didn't you drop a cup of coffee on me?"

Mia slapped Nathan's chest with a surprisingly forceful sting. "Actually, we first met *five* days ago! I can't believe you don't remember. You obviously have no feelings for me," she suggested in a mock dramatic tone before moving closer and leaning her head contentedly on his chest.

"Five days?"

"Yes. At the séance."

Nathan immediately sat up, inadvertently taking Mia with him. "You were at the séance?" He just couldn't believe that she hadn't mentioned the fact over breakfast at the café and began mentally scanning all of the faces he could remember around the Circle in The Sanctuary's séance room, only to draw a blank.

"You looked straight at me… When we were being searched."

Nathan suddenly pictured the girl wearing a bandage on her wrist in the corridor outside of the séance room. "That was you?"

"I even smiled at you while Mike and Doreen were patting us down, but you ignored me. So cruel… I truly question our future together."

Nathan smiled at Mia's suggestive teasing. In truth, the

idea of a relationship, wherever that may lead, appealed. But he'd been surprised at how quickly this girl had grabbed his attention in the split seconds it had taken her to spill a cup of coffee on him and slam a door into his face. Breakfast at the café had only lasted all of forty minutes before he'd had to leave. They'd barely had a chance to engage in a proper conversation in the time they'd spent together. Yet some deeper connection existing between them was obvious.

"Actually," Mia admitted, "I did intend sitting next to you in the Circle, but Anne-Marie barrelled past, elbowing me in the chest as we made for the chairs. That woman! She obviously has the hots for you."

Anne-Marie's competitive dash for the chairs at the commencement of the séance that evening suddenly made sense to Nathan, and bearing in mind the events that followed at AXIS, he thought it wise to change the subject. Mia's animosity towards her boss was obvious.

"What's your interest in Isaac's work?" he asked, redirecting, and keen to learn what had led Mia to attend the séance.

"It's Anne-Marie's interest, really. I'm just her *fetch me, carry me*. I seem to spend half of my time getting the coffees and delivering those damn boxes to The Sanctuary. Not what I expected when I took the post."

Mia was being deliberately self-deprecating. She held a Doctorate in Neuroscience and had every right to feel sidelined. Her own research was at the frontiers of brain function, and she was only too aware that Anne-Marie's dismissive attitude towards her belied a certain clandestine interest in her work. She hated the professional and personal politics but had landed a position that paid well and provided her with a platform to continue her work – albeit carried out through clenched teeth and a half-bitten-through lip. "I've only sat in the Circle a handful of times," she continued. "It's very intriguing. I spend all my time trying to work out how Isaac does it."

"So you think he's a fraud?"

Mia hesitated. "The jury's out. I know enough about the workings of the human psyche and the nature of consciousness to be able to accept much of the phenomena. From a purely scientific perspective, witnessing an object floating through the air certainly doesn't faze me like it would some."

Nathan felt a certain relief at hearing that particular fact.

"Obviously seeing something like the light manifestation of your father and hearing his voice coming out of thin air is impressive and hard to dismiss. But I wonder if at other times Isaac doesn't have a back-up plan."

"In case no phenomena occurred in a demonstration, you mean?"

"Well, it must be tempting. The pressure to perform must be immense. After all, Physical Mediums need a Circle of people to carry out their work. I'm certain interest and enthusiasm would quickly fade without constant spectacular phenomena occurring to keep them coming back all the time. The odd illusion here and there would take the pressure off, surely."

"You sound like an apologetic sceptic. Safe on the fence," Nathan suggested with a smile.

"Not at all," Mia asserted, placing her wine glass down. "Just because an illusionist is able to recreate the illusion of certain phenomena with trickery, it doesn't necessarily follow that the phenomenon being recreated can't occur for real. That's where a sceptic's reasoning falls down. I'm just trying to keep an open mind. Though Isaac did himself no favours with the scandal a few years ago."

"Scandal?" Nathan was shocked. He knew nothing of any scandal involving Isaac.

"Oh, you didn't know?" Mia seemed genuinely sorry that she'd been the one to mention it. She disliked gossip but had assumed Nathan was closer to Isaac than was the case. "It's no secret, I suppose," she said, feeling compelled to continue. "Isaac was invited onto a TV show to promote an upcoming book about his work as a Medium in some of the murder cases he'd worked on with police. He was savaged, by all accounts. The illusionist James Neilson had apparently been invited on by the producers to act as Devil's Advocate without Isaac being informed. It all ended up being a messy personal attack on Isaac. Turns out he was dishonourably discharged from the Army when he was younger, and there was some dirt they'd dug up about accusations of sexual assault on a woman."

"Sexual assault!"

"No charges were ever laid," Mia added quickly. "I don't know much about the details, but it was enough to cast doubt on his integrity, at the time." She gave a noncommittal shrug. "The rest of the interview involved Neilson playing secret camera footage of several fraudulent psychics he'd exposed. Nothing to do with Isaac, and nothing to do with Physical Mediumship, but it was enough to destroy his reputation by association. The book was pulled by the publishers straight after."

Nathan processed what Mia had just told him. Whatever accusations had been levelled, he was open to there being an explanation and would reserve judgement until he'd heard Isaac's side. The tactic of digging up unsubstantiated dirt to ambush someone so publicly was distasteful enough in itself to suggest to Nathan who the real fraud was. He'd seen some of James Neilson's sceptical diatribes on TV and had often been struck by the irony of a professional trickster – practised in the art of deception, and making a living by double and even triple bluffing the unsuspecting – having the temerity to ask the public to 'trust' him in his hard-line stance renouncing Mediums and psychics. The venom with which he tenaciously pursued his personal witch hunts did hint at issues other than mere philosophical ones.

"I find it hard to believe Isaac's capable of sexual assault," Nathan said, "and if his character was in that much doubt, why would a high-calibre scientific researcher such as Anne-Marie take so much interest in him and his Circle at The Sanctuary?"

"History," came Mia's immediate reply. "A Circle has been held there for well over a century. Isaac's just the latest in a long line of Physical Mediums in an almost unbroken chain stretching back over 150 years," she explained. "Anne-Marie places a lot of significance in that. I guess she thinks that something with that kind of history behind it must have some authenticity worth investigating... Each new Medium over that century and a half has apparently been identified and chosen through psychic means. It's then been a matter of locating that person, somehow persuading them to join the Circle, and then grooming them to take over. Uncanny, really. It's no wonder she has an interest in researching the phenomena."

Nathan listened, intrigued.

"You've got to bear in mind that most of those people you met at the séance are highly qualified and respected professionals. There are also some extremely powerful and influential government and business figures amongst them. They are very impressive people, and some of them drive over a hundred miles to attend the séances. That alone is enough for me to question my own doubts, at times."

"You said an *almost* unbroken chain? Does that mean there have been times when no séances have been held at all?"

"I heard something about there being a period in the 1930s and again in the 1980s. Other than that, I'm pretty sure it's been continual."

There was a moment's silence between them before Mia took the initiative to change the mood with a smouldering look. She stood seductively and slowly straddled Nathan's lap. "But I didn't get you here to talk about Isaac's Circle and Anne-Marie," she whispered, leaning over towards Nathan's lips.

Nathan responded, instantly forgetting every thought and worry of the last few days. But when Mia leant back and grabbed the hem of his T-shirt and began to peel it off over his head, he suddenly froze, remembering the deep claw marks to his back. Any woman would be unlikely to believe the truth of how he'd received them. So he decided that it was probably best to claim he'd suffered them along with the laceration to his scalp during the fight training at the gym.

Mia had failed to read his hesitation, though. She was taking her time to gaze admiringly over Nathan's body, her fingers traversing his chest and then running sensually over the black and grey wolf tattoo emblazoned on his shoulder and upper arm. "*Mmm*, I like," she murmured, placing both of her hands back on his chest and leaning forwards once more towards his mouth. "Oh!" she suddenly exclaimed, teasing him by sitting up for a second, as if remembering something important. "Did you find who you were looking for today?"

"No!" Nathan answered emphatically, immediately pulling her back towards his lips, the initiative now with him, her body submitting willingly to his embrace. Ironically, his answer had been the truth.

25

Their bodies merged as one. A picture of female and male perfection entwined in ecstasy. Irrepressible physical strength under the spell of sensuality. Potent femininity willingly surrendering to an irresistible force. Lovers in the throes of ecstatic abandon, neither knowing where she ends or he begins. Everything that a man and woman should be. The card was still warm to the touch and was held reverently by its edges, its image one of flesh tones against such vibrant shades of scarlet reds and azure blues possessing depths of colour rarely seen in this world. *THE LOVERS*. The seventh card of the Tarot's Major Arcana.

A small key turned in the lock to open the glass-topped display cabinet situated in The Sanctuary's Library, and the apport was carefully placed face up on the green felt lining for safekeeping. Its materialisation was memorialised by a small label handwritten in an elegant cursive script recording the provenance and bearing the date:

THE LOVERS. Apported Tarot Card, Inaugural Séance, 4th November 1863. Sitting Medium, Spencer Cavendish.

After pausing for a moment to look at the solitary card in the otherwise empty display cabinet, Spencer Cavendish closed and locked the lid once again. He wondered what other treasures might materialise in the future. The apport of the Tarot card – despite it being from a less than otherworldly source – had been a better start than he could ever have hoped for in the Circle's inaugural Physical séance. But he now realised the need to guard against accusations of fraud. The seventy-eight-card boxed Tarot deck, which had been lying within anyone's reach on one of the Library's shelves, was missing one card. And that errant card now lay on display inside the cabinet. Allegations of trickery or sleight of hand to explain away such phenomena as a card apporting from inside a sealed box in the Library and materialising into the centre of the séance room next door would be hard to defend without the strictest of protocols being put in place.

Spencer's mind was already turning over and formulating a mental list: *Ropes to bind me to the chair while in Trance, body searches of all Circle members entering the séance room* and *locking the séance-room door once everyone was inside* would all be necessary from now on. Allowing the wholesale denial of the truth concerning what those present had just witnessed was not an option. That truth held too much importance. It would revolutionise humankind's understanding of the Cosmos and transform the way people lived their lives.

Spencer picked up the boxed set of remaining Tarot

cards and eyed them thoughtfully. One other protocol, he decided, would be necessary. The securest safe that money could buy would be acquired for the Library, inside of which the deck would now always be kept. With the sealed deck secured within a safe inside the locked Library – while he was tied to the séance chair in the locked séance room – even the most sceptical of detractors would be silenced if another of the cards ever apported into the centre of the Circle again during one of the séances.

26

"You have to trust me," Isaac insisted, grabbing either side of Nathan's shoulders in an attempt to shake him out of the downward spiral into which he was descending. "You are not a killer!" The subliminal attempt to block out those vile assaults on Nathan's psyche had been derailed.

The Sanctuary was the first place Nathan had thought to head for when he'd heard the devastating news about Alex on returning home that morning after leaving Mia's place. Alex was dead. Murdered. And, according to the news reports filtering through, it had been an unspeakably violent and sickening attack – as violent and sickening as his own memories of killing. The nightmarish flashbacks that had polluted his mind were now flooding back with even more vividness, haunting his bloodshot and unblinking eyes with what he might have done.

"Listen to me, Nathan! The Void of the awakening mind can be a frightening place unless you remain fearless. All manner of memories will force themselves upon you in that realm of interconnected unconsciousness. But, as real as they seem, they are not necessarily your own. That's why it's crucial to remain on your guard at all times and maintain control with a concerted mental effort. Trust me!"

Despite the reassurances of both Isaac and Adam concerning his state of mind, Nathan was struggling to remain convinced. The last time he'd seen Alex alive, she'd been running out of his apartment frightened and disturbed by the unconscious rantings of the blackout he'd suffered. And now she was dead. *Did I follow Alex and kill her?* The thought consumed him. Even the scant details of the murder that were emerging bore a frightening similarity to his flashback memories of sadistic rape and torture.

"But what if you're wrong?" Nathan finally responded with a snap. "What if I kill someone else?" His thoughts turned to Mia. "How can I take that risk?"

The breaking news of Alex Stanton's murder was now being linked by the media to both the recent string of unsolved abductions and the rape and murder of another young woman in a public park a couple of months prior – an incident that had passed across news editorial desks barely noticed at the time, on a hectic day of city centre bomb scares and airport strikes. As if the news of Alex's death hadn't been enough, the slaying of the other woman had taken place in the same public park Nathan had found himself in on the night of that murder, leaving him seriously questioning his innocence, as well as his sanity.

"I'll definitely have been caught on CCTV somewhere near the park. I've gotta hand myself in!"

Nathan's fears weren't groundless. Detectives scouring Alex's phone records would put his name at the top of a list of known associates they'd want to interview as part of their investigation, and it would only be a matter of time before footage placing him in the vicinity of the other crime scene surfaced, too.

"You can't hand yourself in," Isaac commanded. "Mediums like us can be railroaded by the authorities into charges of murder for being guilty of nothing more than *sensing* the details of a crime." He looked intently at Nathan, his pleas coming from the benefit of experience. "Look at me! You are not a killer. Trust me, even if you feel you can't trust yourself."

Isaac's words washed ineffectually over Nathan. The thought that he might be capable of killing in a psychopathic rage was terrifying enough, but that he might have vented his insanity on someone he loved was just too much to bear. Despite realising that their relationship would likely go nowhere, in truth, he'd fallen for Alex the moment they'd met at a party thrown by Adam the year before. Now he could only stare inconsolably into space, fixated on the memory of first laying eyes on her, willing himself - in that moment - to avoid talking to her before fate's gravity locked on and set them up for collision…

Alex's flirtatious laughter infected the entire atmosphere of the room. The sheer femininity in her every move and gesture entranced all of the men present at the gathering, each being entirely convinced that she was the most physically beautiful woman they'd ever seen. Her overt sexuality, on the other hand, only served to infuriate the women. Though it was her spirit - challenging anyone who caught her glance to dare and live life recklessly in the moment without a thought for tomorrow – that was the real issue.

Nathan, too, found himself losing all focus in the overly polite party conversation he was engaged in. But that was because he was convinced that the girl in question kept glancing over at him. So it had nothing to do with luck when their eyes finally did meet from across the room and Alex began her slow and resolute sashay over to where he was standing. And her intention of rescuing him from the dull group of strait-laced hospital administrators he'd been stuck talking to became all too clear when – before even introducing herself – she leant in and audibly whispered into his ear.

"If I'm *M*, will you be *S*?" she asked with a pout before sensually running her tongue up the side of his neck.

Nathan laughed aloud at the perverse sadomasochistic suggestion uttered by the shameless stranger and turned to address the gobsmacked partygoers within earshot. "Please excuse my sister," he said apologetically. "She gets like this when Mum and Dad are away!"

Alex responded with her own appreciative burst of laughter and led Nathan away with a link of his arm.

Over the next thirty minutes of chatting, it became obvious that the girl had a razor-sharp intellect and that her tendency for outrageousness was more likely born out of a need for constant stimulation than it being any kind of façade or defence mechanism. They really seemed to be hitting it off and Nathan gladly accepted when Alex unexpectedly clinked their empty bottles together mid-conversation and offered to go to the kitchen to get them both another beer. Five minutes later, though, she reappeared from out of the kitchen laughing wildly in the arms of some guy who'd only just arrived at the party with a friend of someone's friend. And ten minutes after that, the pair were seen leaving together, much to the amusement of Adam and the disgust, and relief, of most of the women present.

"I see that you met Alex... Nothing but heartache with that one," Adam jibed, noticing his friend's deflated demeanour. "She's as much trouble as she is fun! She can't be tamed!" he added, drunkenly restraining Nathan in a headlock while painfully pummelling knuckles into his scalp like an overgrown school kid.

Nathan tried unsuccessfully to push the encounter with Alex to the back of his mind over the next few days and was surprised when she called him, having tracked down his number through Adam. He was even more surprised when she invited him out for those belated drinks they'd intended sharing at the party. It seemed odd. But the girl *was* odd. And their no-strings-attached relationship began.

Whatever it was they had between them worked for a time, and he did become the one constant in her life over those next few months. But Nathan was at a point in his life where he was ready to settle down, while Alex only ever seemed ready to party. Any sense of real commitment always seemed lacking from her. So when she'd slammed out of his apartment that fateful night, he'd decided enough was probably enough and resolved to let things slide. And when she'd failed to contact him in return, he'd been sure of his decision. Until he learnt of her fate...

"I can only help so far, Nathan," Isaac finally counselled, "but ultimately this is something that you have to work through yourself. We've all been there. It's just that you're having to come to terms with the full scope of your ability in a matter of weeks rather than it unfolding gradually over many years. That must be hard to cope with. But every awakening mind at some point experiences the terror of its own insanity – because that insanity belongs to us all. It's those very fears of yours that tell me you *are* sane!"

Isaac felt for Nathan. Some ten years prior, when he'd first found himself at The Sanctuary, having to come to terms with his own abilities had left him thinking he was going out of his mind, too. And, of all people, Isaac knew all too well about being unjustly accused of things he hadn't done.

The guttural banter and outbursts of laughter from across the rims of beer glasses readily identified the pasty young warriors out on the town as squaddies, despite them having followed remote directives from above to dress in civvies 'in consideration of personal security'. They had to be squaddies. There'd be no other reason for the lively conversation in the corner of the inner-city pub to be awash with *Fucks* from the banks of the Clyde, *Fucks* from the banks of the Mersey and *Fucks* from the banks of the Tyne. The rusting gantries of closed shipyards and docks had once been the visible gallows on which the aspirations of the lower working-class youth from those parts had hung. And even though the estuarine skylines were being cleared to make way for picture-perfect housing, artful yet architecturally plonked bridges and sparsely patronised multi-million-dollar exhibition centres, the banks on which they stood were still haunted by the sound of steel on steel and the siren clamour of end-of-shift exoduses. Joining the Army was often the only option for the displaced indigents who couldn't afford those picture-perfect houses.

With the raucous chants of *Scull! Scull!* and the simultaneous slam of glasses on tables, it was time to move on. Another pub, a club, and then their attention would turn to tits and arse. A strip show more than likely, on account of them being so pissed by then that even the most virulent of the local skanks would think twice.

As the boys streamed out of the pub's narrow entrance hall into the night, the sight of a group of scantily clad girls passing by was cause for some hopeful whistles and inane filthy remarks. On any other evening, the attention might have been enough to enamour them to the girls and make the collective high-heeled strut slow to a desperate and equally hopeful teasing linger. A forceful shove to the back of one of the high-spirited lads, though, was to put an end to that possibility.

"Fucking squaddies!" was the last thing heard before the premeditated attack from the group of skins that'd followed them out of the bar ensued. In an instant, the pavement was alive with twenty young men swinging, kicking and flailing for their lives. The boys from the barracks were predictably outnumbered, but 15km predawn TAB drills carrying 25kg of kit would always give them the edge if they could only just hold their own for the first twenty seconds of concerted onslaught. The locals would typically run out of steam by then, having fully intended running off anyway before the cops – never far away on a Saturday night – arrived to mop up the aftermath.

Isaac, being the most heavily built in his unit at six foot

two, always had to contend with multiple assailants from the outset. But this particular recreational hit mob had underestimated the young private in assuming that *three* were going to be enough. The squaddies were giving a good account of themselves and Isaac had already seen off more than his fair share when his last opponent – now devoid of support – thought better of his presence and scurried off, tripping over himself as he went. Isaac turned to assess the waning battle, only to see his closest friend lying defenceless in the road while two of the gang frenziedly kicked at his head and body. Isaac's pumped frame tore across the pavement to save his mate, just as the first responding patrol car rounded the corner at speed. But in the flash of action witnessed by the officer through the edge of his windscreen, the only thing that could be attested to was Isaac's fist connecting with the face of another youth who then fell backwards, striking his head on the edge of the kerb. And by the time the patrol car had screeched to a halt on the main strip, the sound of the other converging sirens had seen everyone else at the scene scatter, dragging away their casualties, leaving Isaac standing guiltily over an unconscious male who was critically injured and bleeding from the back of his skull.

Mist rolled eerily over the steep banks from the river's surface and carpeted the flood plain in a low hang. The meadowland had the air of a graveyard without graves, and the occasional snapping twig from unseen nocturnal scurrying in the undergrowth all around threatened and harried the darkest depths of the imagination as awareness slowly began to return. Any faint light from the distant row of houses on the estate backing onto the vestige tract of land that clung to the river's suburban meanderings was lost as soon as the dazed man traipsed still mindlessly on across the footbridge. Even the isolated centuries-old pub nestled at the bottom of the steps leading down from the far riverbank offered only a meagre glimmer cast from its dimly spotlighted signage – the pub having closed its doors hours before. The late-night desperates in the back seats of vehicles had also long since deserted the leafy canopied seclusion of the pub's cinder car park, and the only companion left to the senses was a distant orange halo glow filtering through the treeline from the motorway up ahead on the unlit narrow access lane, hedged either side by dense barbed scrub, along which the man now found himself slowly walking. He had no idea as to his whereabouts and didn't know what had possessed him to slip out into the night alone and obliviously hike what must have been several kilometres from the comfort of his home. The return to full awareness, though, brought with it a sense of vulnerability in the surrounding darkness. Each of his steps on the gravel underfoot now seemed to echo back at him from behind, and with a sudden chill down his spine, he became sure that someone was following. His pace quickened with his heartbeat. But the echo steps quickened, too. In sudden terror, he exploded into a sprint equal to the pounding in his chest. He covered the next 200 metres of track in a peripheral blur of shadowy gnarled undergrowth but began tiring and sucking for air. The orange glow of safety at the end of the lane ahead was almost within reach, and he gritted against the burn in his lungs.

Seconds later, he burst out onto the tarmac of the roundabout intersection situated beneath the motorway overpass and was blinded by the sweeping headlights of a passing car heading for the on-ramp. With a check over his shoulder, he bent over in exhaustion, unable to run a step further. He stared back at the opening to the dark laneway he had just escaped from. All was quiet and still, except for his own painful laboured gasps for air against the fading sound of high-speed tread on asphalt as the passing car accelerated away. It was then that thirty-five-year-old Isaac McKinnon first heard a voice whispering inside his head. *Sanctuary, Sanctuary, Sanctuary* was all it kept repeating. He truly thought he must be going insane. He just didn't yet know what forces were calling to him. Nor did he realise that his presence in the laneway had just disturbed a serial killer before they'd had a chance to slice open the throat of another victim that had been dragged unconscious into the undergrowth.

27

10th September 1905, The Sanctuary

Pristine razor-sharp double-edged blades, plunged deeply into the chest cavity, glinted with reflected light. The ornamental hilts crowning the blinding steel were as elaborate as any sword ever fashioned, and their beauty and intricacy of design drew attention away from the inevitable consequence of use – the expanding scarlet pool on the marble floor being fed from a fatally wounded heart. A central blade had been thrust vertically downwards just below the sternum, while the second and third pierced the heart at angles of forty-five degrees either side. The *THREE OF SWORDS*. The third card in the Tarot's suit of Conflict and the second from the deck to have ever apported.

Charles Cavendish hurriedly opened the Library's safe and reached inside for the sealed box of cards. It had been forty years since *THE LOVERS* had materialised in a séance held by his father back in 1863. Charles had been just an infant at the time, but he knew the provenance all too well, his father having instructed and groomed him since childhood to take over the Circle at The Sanctuary when the time was right. The story of *THE LOVERS* card apporting in the first-ever séance held was legend. Now history was repeating itself.

Cavendish broke the wax seal and opened the box to reveal the deck of cards nestled innocuously enough inside. The full enormity of what had happened in the séance just held began to hit, and the mere sight of the deck caused him to pause momentarily. He could clearly remember the occasion of his very first séance as The Sanctuary's sitting Medium at the incredibly young age of twenty-one. And every month since, he'd wondered if *this* séance would be the one. Compared to his father, whose mediumistic abilities had generated an embarrassment of riches in the apport and phenomena stakes over the years, his own tenure had been more of a simple embarrassment. That he had some ability as a Physical Medium was unquestioned; that he had a degree of ability equal to the established Circle's initial expectations was the issue, considering his father's investment in him. These days, only the most loyal of Circle members still attended the séances, and Charles knew that even their waning loyalty belonged to The Sanctuary, to the memory of his father, and to a time long past. If it hadn't been for the occasional guest Medium invited in to hold séances, the Circle at The Sanctuary would have folded many years before.

Charles stared at the deck he was holding, his fixed gaze bridging every one of those forty years – the boxed set of cards having been sealed and locked away in the safe untouched, ever since. The moment of truth had finally arrived, and the slow deliberate count began as he dealt the cards face up onto the large oak table that occupied the centre of the Library.

"*One... Two... Three...*" those gathered around the table called out in unison.

The excitement of the Circle members at having witnessed the apport during the séance was still palpable.

"*Twenty-two... Twenty-three... Twenty-four...*"

The count for Charles was more or less a formality. He was already certain that a second Tarot card out of the seventy-eight-card deck would be missing.

"*Seventy-four... Seventy-five... SEVENTY-SIX!*"

Everyone cheered, bursting into laughter and congratulatory applause at confirming the absence of the *THREE OF SWORDS* from the face-up spread. The card had undisputedly apported from inside the sealed box within the safe of the locked Library and materialised on the floor of the locked séance room. But Charles was too preoccupied with his own thoughts to share the group's excitement and could only offer a strained smile to everyone in return. He had now seen for himself what was possible and was already starting to formulate the next bold step. What had been unattainable to him was now a new reality of his own making. The possibilities were far beyond anything his father, Spencer, had tried to allude to throughout all that incessant instruction in his formative years. Physical phenomena, he now realised, opened a portal into the source of ultimate universal power for those who could control it – not that Charles had been oblivious to his father's teachings, despite never seeming able to manifest apports himself. He was certainly a gifted clairvoyant and had spent years mulling over whether some link existed between physical phenomena and clairvoyance that would finally allow him to find a way to manifest an object in a séance. Some of his father's apports had particularly intrigued him since childhood, and the fact that 'information' from the future could be clairvoyantly relayed to the past had always left Charles wondering if apports, too, could materialise in and out of the séance room across Time. Those Tarot cards twice apporting into the séance room from the Library next door had proven that they could materialise across Space in any one moment, so a bridge across Time might also be a possibility. Now he could test his theory. Two further séances would have to be arranged as soon as possible, he decided. If all went to plan, those séances would transform the way humanity viewed its place in the universe, and the global accolades would be his alone. His status amongst the landed intelligentsia – and doubters – in which he circulated would be elevated beyond imagination. But to win such a social coup, with all its limitless power and leverage, he knew that he would need the endorsement of the likes of Oliver Lodge and the French scientist Charles Richet, who were globally recognised as having a keen scientific interest in psychic phenomena. It was just a matter of persuading them to be involved in the experiment.

As the applause petered away, there was only one last thing to do. Handling the card with the reverence it was due, Charles Cavendish, as appointed Guardian of all the apported objects, turned the key in the lock of the display cabinet and lifted the lid. Amongst the eclectic array of objects that had materialised over the decades, the *THREE OF SWORDS*, for the time being, was carefully placed face up on the green felt lining next to *THE LOVERS* – the shared message of the two images side by side, at a glance, seeming to predict such a devastating fate. Those next two séances to be held, Charles was now certain, would come to be celebrated as the greatest experiment ever attempted in the history of humankind. And that is precisely how he intended to promote the venture to Lodge and Richet.

Incessant peals of high-pitched giggling in recent times had coloured the otherwise stuffy atmosphere of the Library. The starched, winged-collar reserve of forty-one-year-old Charles Cavendish had been found to have a weakness. And that weakness was young Marjorie, who was unlike any child he had ever encountered.

"Daddy, Daddy! Can I play with the Princess's jewels?"

Marjorie was hard to ignore, but Cavendish was so engrossed in his thoughts that he only half heard her pleas. He stared at the image of the *THREE OF SWORDS* that had been placed in the display cabinet next to *THE LOVERS* following the séance of a few days earlier.

"Daddy! The *jewels*!" Marjorie pleaded.

"Yes, yes, Marjorie," Cavendish finally answered, knowing better than to ignore Marjorie for too long, at the risk of her pleas escalating to a tantrum shriek.

"I can show you, but you cannot touch." He let a smile slip on seeing his daughter's face beaming angelically back at him, and he lifted her up so as she could gaze down through the glass top of the locked display table.

"Am I a princess, Daddy?"

"Most definitely," Cavendish answered proudly with a smile.

"Then why can't I touch them?" Marjorie retorted

curtly, her green eyes boring an indignant stare into him, demanding a convincing answer.

Cavendish lacked the basic wherewithal to deal with such feminine wiles, especially from a five-year-old, and his normally razor-sharp mind had no response.

Marjorie pouted, processing the power she'd just wielded, something as yet ungraspable deep within telling her to bide her time for just a few more years.

The little girl's sulk turned to bubbling excitement as the jewels came into her view through the cabinet's glass top. "They're so pretty!" she squealed, marvelling at the treasures and reaching longingly out to them.

"I have something important to do now, Marjorie," Cavendish said after a few moments, putting his daughter back down. "Run along," he ushered. "I'll be with you shortly."

A reluctant Marjorie headed for the door.

Charles unlocked the cabinet. The objects of Marjorie's desire kept inside did not belong to any fairy-tale princess. In fact, for the most part, no one knew who they belonged to. He scanned the contents. The array of apported objects collected over the four decades since séances had been held at The Sanctuary was eclectic, to say the least, each item being identified by a small label beside it giving information as to the date it had materialised, the name of the sitting Medium and any relevant evidential provenance associated with it regarding its link, if any, to a recipient's deceased loved one. The larger pieces included a three-string pearl necklace and a sparkling jewelled tiara – hence Marjorie's insistence that the entire collection belonged to a princess. Several rings of varying sizes and styles were also laid out in a horizontal row at the bottom of the display. But many other entirely unassuming pieces were exhibited: a small thimble reportedly once belonging to a deceased seamstress related to a member of the Circle; a gold fob chain minus its watch; a clay pipe stem and a single chipping of mineral ore to name just a few.

Other than the Tarot cards that had kept materialising, the most incredible inclusion, in Cavendish's estimation, had been a tiny piece of paper, now contained in a small envelope, that had apported in his father's tenure. It bore an obscure ink-written communication penned in handwriting so minute that without a magnifying glass it was almost impossible to read. Yet no nib existed that could have accomplished such an intricate feat. Presumably, some warping of the physical matter had occurred in the apport process. Charles eyed the envelope inside the cabinet. As to whose otherworldly hand had written the cryptic apocalyptic message had fired his imagination ever since he was a child. It prophesied the final demise of the Circle '*after the Last Guardian across Time identifies himself*', claiming that The Sanctuary would be '*reduced to rubble and dust*'. More ominously, it added the grave warning that '*whoever so remains at The Sanctuary after the Last Guardian becomes known shall perish at the hands of a new bloodline*'.

That Cavendish could be so certain of the prophecy lay in its other predictive caveats, including one stating '*the ship of titanic proportions will strike ice*' – something that had sounded as cryptic as the rest of the message until a consortium of businessmen had recently approached him with a fanciful investment offer to get on board with an ambitious project to build the world's largest and fastest 'unsinkable' passenger liner. The mere suggestion of the ship's intended name had been enough to warn Cavendish off from parting with his money. How he could try to avert a future catastrophe in the making hung heavily on his mind, and he could only hope that the planned project sank before the ship did.

Under the circumstances, Cavendish could also be quite certain that one day *'the Wall in Berlin will fall'* – whatever the Wall in Berlin happened to turn out to be – so sealing The Sanctuary's fate sometime thereafter.

Charles reached inside the cabinet and removed the two Tarot cards from display. Apports had been known to dematerialise spontaneously hours, days or even years after they had materialised, so it had long been supposed that the physical structure of apported matter might retain some atomic instability as compared to normal matter. It seemed only logical, therefore, to take advantage of any such potential instability and include the cards in the imminent experiment he was meticulously planning, in which an array of cards apported away in one séance would rematerialise a few days later in a second séance – in the future – proving his theory. With the distinguished Professor Oliver Lodge having now accepted the invitation to attend the next two experimental séances to be held at The Sanctuary, nothing could be left to chance.

Charles knelt at the safe door and unlocked it, and feeling inside the front edge of the safe's roof, he located a small hidden lever. With a tell-tale click, the metal drawer compartment in the safe's false base disengaged and he carefully placed the two Tarot cards, along with his notes and plans for the upcoming séances, into the hidden drawer for safekeeping and away from prying eyes. No one but he and his father, Spencer, before him knew of the safe's hidden compartment – no one, that is, except for a young inquisitive Marjorie, who was now watching her father from outside a slightly ajar Library door.

1914, The Sanctuary

Saint or *Sinner*? *Friend* or *Foe*? The fixed hypnotic stare gave nothing away. A hint of a smile at the corners of the shaven-headed man's mouth seemed to encourage and even tempt, yet something in the expression of those eyes – those deep oriental pools of ancient Eastern wisdom – seemed to warn against daring to take even one more step. It was pointless giving any thought as to what his motives or intentions really were. For, in truth, he had no interest in anyone's fate either way. He would still be smiling the same perpetual smile if he was directing you on the path to Heaven or ushering you on the road to Hell. His was a Mind that contained all Minds. *Live and die by your own thoughts and actions* was his mantra – a mantra that could only be heard by those who had learnt to listen through having been foolish enough in the past to assume he'd be there to help. *THE MAGICIAN*. The third card to apport. A conduit for both the forces of creation and destruction. A portal to the scintillating maelstrom of primordial subatomic possibility. A door to the source of all potentials and realities.

Charles held the Tarot card by its edges. The image of *THE MAGICIAN* mocked him with that knowing smile. On walking into the séance room to check on a report of rainwater leaking in through a cracked window pane, he had almost stepped on the card, which just so happened to be lying on the floor in the centre of the room. A chill ran down his spine. He had aborted the planned second experimental séance nine years prior back in 1905 – a séance in which the Tarot cards apported away in the first séance would have rematerialised. The card in his hand now, however, implied that what he'd unleashed across time in that reckless experiment had still yet to wreak the full extent of its havoc, notwithstanding the fact that the first séance *had* proven to be the greatest experiment ever undertaken. All of the cards had indeed disappeared in front of everyone's eyes. It was now clear that there would be more cards to apport. A prospect that left Charles stricken. The experiment was running its course across time regardless, and the repercussions of his meddling with reality could not be known. The cards, having no target séance to materialise in, were instead rematerialising into The Sanctuary over decades, so any further apports would likely occur in future tenures. At fifty-one years of age, Charles didn't know how much longer he would be able to keep up his mediumistic work at The Sanctuary. Finding a successor was soon going to be necessary, and that successor must never know about the experiment. Enough damage had been done to the fabric of reality. Hiding the first three apported cards to prevent any knowledge of their existence in future generations was imperative. He had nearly died in the experiment, and it had taken months to recover from the burns. The horrors of future war and genocide he had glimpsed in his trance state in that first experimental séance had scarred his consciousness. There were some visions that could just not be unseen, and he couldn't be certain that the changes to reality he had unwittingly instigated nine years prior weren't in some way involved with those horrors. More worrying still, the daily news was touting an imminent breakout of war in Europe, undoubtedly signalling the first of "two Great Wars" long predicted by the sitting Mediums at The Sanctuary. No one must ever know of the experiment nor try and recreate it. Any future cards to materialise in other tenures must come to be seen as mere curios. And since apports had been known to vanish spontaneously, as mercurially as they had materialised in the first place, he could, for the time being, secrete *THE MAGICIAN* away along with *THE LOVERS* and *THREE OF SWORDS* without questions being asked. The dilemmas for Charles were as endless as Time itself. He would have just settled for destroying the apports if not for being unsure of the consequences across Time of such an action. Hiding the cards and removing any reference regarding them in the Library's archival material was the only safe thing to do. Over the decades to come, any memory of the items would fade and all knowledge of them would die with him – all knowledge, except for that now held by a young fourteen-year-old Marjorie, who was again inquisitively watching her father from outside a slightly ajar Library door.

28

18th November 1929, The Sanctuary

"*Cronos*," Lodge offered cryptically while sitting forwards in his chair, carefully examining the apported card. "Very appropriate under the circumstances," he added, squinting through his monocle, captivated by the exquisite detail in the miniature masterpiece.

Lodge may as well have been staring at a portrait of himself. Absent were the vibrant hues colouring the cards of *THE LOVERS*, the *THREE OF SWORDS* and *THE MAGICIAN* that he'd been shown earlier. Instead, he was marvelling at masterful strokes of grey and black that revealed the lone figure of an old grey-bearded man in a cowled robe holding a scythe in one hand and carrying a lantern in the other.

"*Cronos*?" Hugh remarked quizzically, with the air of a schoolboy taking afternoon tea with his headmaster. Any kudos he'd gained in their first meeting on the night of the debauched party, to his mind, had been irretrievably lost over the course of the disappointing séance just held. The Circle, with Sir Oliver as the esteemed guest, had sat for well over an hour with absolutely no phenomena being generated – the latest Tarot card to have apported only materialising seconds before Hugh had come out of his Trance state. Not that it was unheard-of for no phenomena to occur in a séance. Nor could the materialisation of a single apport be considered anything but an astounding success. Some recent short tenures had produced none. But Hugh was a high achiever who lived by a different set of rules. To his way of thinking, anything less than multiple spectacular paranormal displays in his séances was considered abject failure, and he'd desperately wanted to impress Sir Oliver.

"Son of Uranus, father of Zeus..." Lodge continued, oblivious to Hugh's embarrassment. "Cronos was one of the Titans in Greek Mythology," he explained. "The god of Time who ultimately could not accept his own immutable laws."

Ascribed with such a meaning, Hugh had to agree that the image on the card did aptly describe the scientific work he had been involving himself in.

Lodge placed *THE HERMIT*, the twelfth card in the Major Arcana, onto the table in front of him before sitting back in his chair, ecstatic at having witnessed its materialisation into the séance room and intrigued to learn that the cards had been presenting over several decades.

Not being the most typical of Mediums, Hugh's interest in the Tarot was limited. He knew enough, however, to be amused that many of the latest trends in the new field of Psychology were based upon the centuries-old divinatory system. It was common knowledge in the circles that Hugh moved in that pioneering psychologist Carl Jung, the one-time protégé of Sigmund Freud, had been exposed to the more esoteric side of human experience from a very early age, with Jung's mother having been diagnosed as clinically insane on account of her claims she could communicate with the dead. Any Tarot reader with even the most basic understanding would recognise that Jung's work on *Archetypes* simply rehashed, in a clinically acceptable way, shades of the centuries-old folklore he would have been exposed to as a child. Even his controversial notions of *Synchronicity* and the *Collective Unconscious* were concepts that had been known and utilised by mystics and clairvoyants for millennia.

"So tell me more about the Void," Sir Oliver prompted, eager to hear more of the young man's work. Following their first meeting, Lodge had spent many hours mulling over what had been discussed. His only motive, at the outset, had been concern over the real potential for catastrophe in the work he had learnt Hugh was involved in – catastrophe not just for the young scientist himself but one that could affect the very history and future of humanity. But Lodge had become torn. Their meeting had infected his ageing mind with the youth he'd lost, and the electrifying possibility that he could finally find answers to a lifetime of his own research had left any sense of caution the casualty. In all his days as a physicist and scientific researcher, he had never encountered a Medium with both the necessary ability and scientific prowess to describe lucidly what was being experienced in experimental Trance states, and that presented a unique opportunity. After all, the *Void* – that Zero Point Substrate of Cosmic proportions – was a concept that he himself had proposed many decades before.

Hugh took a moment to collect his thoughts, with Lodge's

apparent continued interest in his work having buoyed his spirits. "The Void is a precursor," he began, continuing the discussion from where he'd left off prior to the séance. "A creative matrix of potential Space, Time and Matter. And being non-attached to it, in the altered state of Trance, our mind can navigate that matrix with ease. Undoubtedly, that's the mechanism by which clairvoyants mentally view both the *Past* and *Future*. My aim, however, as a Physical Medium, is to actually dematerialise from one coordinate of the Void and rematerialise in another."

"But surely you couldn't just pick and choose where and when?" Lodge commented, with an incredulous look. "And what of Causality?" he quickly added. "I still fail to see how you can be so cavalier at the prospect of manipulating the events of the past."

"With all due respect, Sir Oliver, perhaps we need to think of the events of the past in less concrete terms."

Lodge threw a sober look.

"*Entropy*, not Causality, is the determining factor in traversing time," Hugh asserted. "In each instant that passes, Spacetime and Matter, our observable Reality, has entropy – a bubble of total Reality possessing a certain fingerprint of chaos and order... I think of it as having an irregular yet specific 'shape' that it has adopted at any one instant through the sum of the various pulls on its Space, Time and Matter components. And the 'shape' of that bubble of Reality changes considerably as it morphs with those varying states of chaos and order, creation and annihilation, growth and decay that arises from out of the cosmic Zero Point Substrate you have postulated. It's this continual 'morphing' in our consciousness that we perceive as passing Time."

A bubble of Spacetime-Matter was easy for Sir Oliver to visualise. After all, while Einstein had become famous in recent times for popularising the term *Spacetime*, Lodge himself had been amongst the first minds ever to think of Space and Time being locked together as one entity, a continuum, with the components being inseparable from each other, in much the same way as the dimensions of *length*, *breadth* and *height* forming a three-dimensional cube are an inseparable continuum. At the end of his lectures, Lodge would often challenge the undergraduates he was teaching to remove the dimension of height from any three-dimensional object in their rooms and to bring the resulting object along to the next lecture. No one ever succeeded… and Lodge had made his point concerning continuums.

"Space and Matter are so obviously inseparable, Sir Oliver," Hugh continued. "Matter cannot exist without a Space to exist in. They are both part of the continuum. There are already whisperings amongst some researchers that Space might be some dark unseeable substrate rather than being *empty*, and Matter is simply some kind of tightly knotted region of whatever 'Space' actually is. Either way, Space and Matter *are* inseparable. So considering Matter as part of the Spacetime continuum is just common sense. And since Time is known to be entirely malleable and relative to an observer's conscious perception, then Matter in *Space*, too, is malleable relative to an observer's conscious perception. That's just another way of stating the *Relativity* that we accept. The perceiving Mind and Consciousness become the operative missing links in our quantum understanding, no matter who denies it! Matter is just the most tangible physicalisation of perceived Reality within Consciousness."

Lodge was left wide-eyed and speechless, the inevitable conclusion piercing his intellect like a bullet. *If Space and Time are one inseparable entity, and Space and Matter are one inseparable entity, then it follows that Time and physical Matter must also be one inseparable entity.* And if the mental construct of Time within the Mind is locked together with – and inseparable from – Matter, then Matter becomes equally an illusory mental construct that can be manipulated by the Mind. The scientific establishment's arguments against Matter travelling across Time were based on a myopic view of their own findings. Observable Reality had been laid bare by Hugh's words back in their first-ever meeting at The Sanctuary: *"… 'convention' only applies if you are mistakenly accepting that our reality in Spacetime is some kind of Absolute Reality. Which it isn't… by the very theories we're now adopting."* His explanations had summarily rendered the solid Matter making up the natural world and cosmos just as illusory as the mental perception of passing Time itself: *"… thoughts cannot be bound to Earth by gravity. Nor can they be deflected by electromagnetic fields. Such scientific rules and conventions simply don't apply to mental consciousness. And it is at this mental level, in the altered state of Trance, that the quantum make-up of our bodies – the physical manifestation in its most basic form – becomes open to manipulation… A pure consciousness devoid of physical mass and dimension that can relocate, untethered, across both Space and Time. And in that Trance state, all bets are off on what is considered possible…"*

Lodge squeezed the armrests of his chair in an involuntary gesture of reassurance. He was electrified by the possibilities, but the unease surrounding his initial fears came flooding back with the realisation that Hugh was closer to his goals than he could have ever guessed.

"I implore you to think this through fully," Lodge said. "In dismissing Causality, any attempt at meddling with the past in a slip through Time might well not result in someone killing their grandparent, so preventing their own birth, but what if they were to murder or inadvertently kill someone else?" he challenged.

Hugh paused, summoning all the gravity he could. "Then, Sir Oliver, you and I, in this very moment, would be none the wiser for it. And I'm sure that particular scenario has played out more often than anyone would care to think," was his ominous reply.

Lodge sat forwards in his chair again. "What aren't you telling me, Hugh?"

Hugh didn't answer but instead redirected, gambling that any moral dilemmas would always take second place to Lodge's scientifically enquiring mind. Those persistent letters of introduction had not been in vain, after all. "Sir Oliver, the séance just held was somewhat of a dress rehearsal. I would like to invite you to act in an official capacity as an independent scientific observer in the greatest experiment ever to be attempted in the history of humankind. One of The Sanctuary's future Mediums, named Isaac McKinnon, will hold a simultaneous experimental séance eighty-five years from now, in which he and I *will* traverse the Void of Spacetime-Matter. Everything is in place. It's planned for tomorrow. I trust you will remain at The Sanctuary as our guest until then?"

Lodge didn't reply and just stared at Hugh with apprehension, having been given a very similar invitation from Charles Cavendish in this very location twenty-five years before.

"Oh, and Sir Oliver," Hugh added, with the utmost courtesy in his voice, "perhaps I could ask you, for the time being, not to mention the other cards you have seen to anyone here at The Sanctuary. My wife, you and I are the only ones who know of their existence, and I must guard them carefully under the circumstances. They are critical to the experiment's success."

29

"*Nathan!*"

Nathan resisted looking over his shoulder. The girl's voice he'd first heard calling out to him on his rapid exit from AXIS was by now assaulting his auditory senses relentlessly. But there was never anyone there.

"*Help me!*"

He read through the formal letter of resignation he'd just typed up in his study. It was hard to believe it had come to this. But at the point that the voices in his head were incessant enough to find himself cupping his hands tightly over his ears to no avail, he knew it was time to act. He signed the letter in a flurry of ink and neatly folded the paper before sliding it into an envelope. His career was over.

Everything he could think of had been attended to. A full stop had been put to every line of narrative in his life, right down to finalising the apartment's utilities and cancelling a dental check-up. There had been so much to organise in such a short time, he just knew that something had to have been overlooked. All that was left to do now, after handing in his notice, was to head straight for the police station.

"*Nathan! Nathan!*"

He picked up the handwritten letter he'd spent hours penning to Mia. The words still seemed pitiful. His phone's message bank was now full with distraught pleas to contact her, and each time it had killed him not to answer the insistently ringing phone. But he knew it was the only way to keep her safe.

"*NATHAN!*"

The words were no longer inside his head. The intensity of the shout cutting through the air forced Nathan to turn around in a reflex response just as the unmistakeable sound of glass on wood skated past his ears from the other side of the room – the heavy cut crystal vase decelerated as it left the shelf on the far wall. The vase hung spectacularly in mid-air before gravity once again intruded into the reality of his perceptions and it began a rapid acceleration to real time again, crashing down onto the floorboards.

All was eerily silent for a moment, but the atmosphere remained charged with the threat of what would happen next. And with a terrifying crack of ionising blue lightning through the air, a swirl of light emerged out of nowhere and morphed into the translucent outline of a girl. He had no time to react or make sense of what he was seeing before the body of light shot towards him and collided with his being, the explosive impact shattering his entire sense of self into a quantum cloud of potential. A Nothingness. A Void. Nathan had been flung into an empty eternity of Trance.

Awareness began to kick in again with sporadic disconnected

and confused thought. The surrounds of his apartment were no longer evident. Instead, he now found himself in a void of blinding *WHITE*. A silence beyond silence. A nothingness in which there existed no form, no shape, no dimension, no mass, no perspective, no outlines or borders that could be perceived. He had absolutely no parameters for his stirring awareness to lock onto – except for the passing of Time. Then out of the nothingness came a singularity of sound. A sound that suddenly seemed to have location at a point directly behind him. A sound that rapidly burgeoned to a cacophony and forced his attention in its direction.

"Hey, darlin'," a friendly voice shouted above the pumping bass line of music. "Allow me."

Nathan's discarnate being was instantly swamped with a complete visual of Bedlam reaching past a girl and pressing a wad of cash into a barman's palm, just as the girl herself was about to hand over a single fifty to pay for her drinks. The 360 degrees of white void had vanished and been replaced by the scene in a bar. A bar that Nathan suddenly recognised all too well. "Alex…? Alex!" he instinctively called out on realising who the girl standing next to Bedlam was. But she was oblivious to Nathan's presence. In his discarnate state, the ability to see, hear and speak were being expressed in mere thought forms of pure consciousness – dream-like – within the framework of the presenting scene. But the scene was no illusion.

He had met Alex at the Barfly a few times. It was her law firm's watering hole and the place where everyone in the office was expected to meet up after work on Fridays. Alex could play office politics as well as anyone and had always been careful to keep her social life and workplace friendships very separate. The tedious after-work obligation, though, always provided an opportunity for a few stiff drinks before her night began in earnest, wherever that may take her.

Nathan watched Alex turn and smile admiringly at the physique of the man.

"Send me over three bottles of Blue Label," Bedlam instructed, leaning over the bar to be heard. "Keep the change."

The barman's eyes widened in astonished appreciation at what would easily have amounted to a £100 tip.

"Celebration?" Alex shouted over the music, realising that the timing of his approach to the bar had been no coincidence.

Bedlam smiled, ignoring her question, his eyes focused on his own reflection in the mirrors behind the bar. "I'll be over at the Carousel Club later. Perhaps I'll see you there?"

"Perhaps," Alex replied teasingly.

With another smile aimed at his own reflection, Bedlam walked off.

Alex's gaze remained fixed on the man's wide shoulders and powerful back that tapered down in a perfect V-shape. Her plans for later in the evening were now decided upon, and grabbing the round of drinks bought for her, she returned to her table already thinking of how she'd excuse herself from her colleagues' inevitable invites on to bars and clubs afterwards.

Nathan felt confusion swamping his thoughts... *Alex had crossed paths with Bedlam before her murder...* The confusion turned to terrifying realisation as his attention shifted across the crowded room over to a booth where Bedlam was now sitting and laughing raucously with a group of men. A hand could be seen reaching out eagerly towards the fighter, as if pleading for something. In response, Bedlam reached over for his jacket and from the inside pocket pulled out a business card that he placed in a grasping hand keen for the prized possession to be returned… *Caleb?* Nathan focused in closer. His brother was holding one of Alex's business cards that he'd helped himself to from out of her handbag months before to add to his collection – only for Alex to wave away any need for apologies, at the time: "Work pays for them. I've got hundreds," she'd added with a smile. Bedlam's presence at the Barfly was no coincidence. Alex had been targeted. And the company address on the card had made her easy to find – and to follow.

The sickening truth suddenly hit Nathan. Caleb's taunt – *I really like your taste in women* – flashed into his thought field and sent him reeling. "NO…! Alex! NO!" he screamed into the Void.

Vertigo hit! The shock of discovering that both Bedlam and Caleb had been involved in Alex's rape and murder had suddenly pushed Nathan's awareness to the brink of some hidden precipice of consciousness. And teetering precariously on that invisible edge, he could do nothing but surrender helplessly again to the forces of the gravity he'd been free of. The very substrate of the Void he had been existing in started to crumble.

The earthward plunge began. He now felt miniscule – a minute particle plummeting through a night sky generated from dream-like visions. The descent seemed endless, and the rarefied air of the vast upper atmosphere had his lungs straining to inflate. Every molecule in the cells of his body vibrated en masse in waves of electrical activity. He had never had such a sense of being alive as his state of pure consciousness physicalised in that descent back to his own Here and Now. Far below loomed a pure black sea surrounded by a thin blue rim and a white cornea that curved away to form the distant horizon of the world to which he fell, and he could do nothing but plummet towards it through the airless surround. *The asphyxia broke.* He could at last suck hard on oxygen from the now rushing air and instantly felt himself accelerate downwards again to a phenomenal speed. All around him, the horizon was becoming lost in that rapidly approaching expanse of blackness, and he braced for collision... *Impact!* But he felt nothing. He pierced through the surface of his own pupil with ease, and the drag of the still body of water beneath stripped him instantly of all momentum... *motionless... suspended in an amniotic silence...* A silence punctuated only by the distant rhythmic beating sound of his own heart.

Searing pain signalled his full return to consciousness as he writhed on the floor of his study. Nathan ripped open his shirt, the contact of the fabric against his skin being unbearable, and looking down he was confronted by the red welt of a burn across his abdomen. The realisation of what had just happened hit hard – the light body he'd witnessed earlier had been generated by his own physical mediumship; the translucent figure of the girl shooting across the room towards him had been the manifestation's ectoplasmic energy rushing rapidly back inside of him. In that instant, he knew everything that Isaac had told him was true, but any relief he felt at now being sure of his innocence was lost in that revelation as to who had murdered Alex. And knowing that his own brother had been involved in the crime filled him with an anger he couldn't contain. "*Bastard!*" he screamed, the word petering out to inconsolable sobs in his helplessness at not having been able to protect Alex. He wanted to tear the heart out of Caleb's chest. He wanted to subject him to the same pain that Alex had endured. But even getting close to him again would be fraught with danger.

Nathan's mind was now spinning with more questions than answers. *How had Caleb transformed into the killer he now was? And what was his connection with Bedlam?* Alex's rape and murder had to involve more than just a warped display of sibling rivalry as punishment for all those years lost to Caleb in suffering through his disability. None of it made any sense. He did know for sure that conventional police procedure would not uncover the truth, and his own knowledge of the details concerning Alex's murder – facts that hadn't been released to the public – would now only make any questioning by police even more difficult. It was only a matter of time before they would want to speak to him. According to Alex, her being in a steady relationship for once had been the main topic of salacious gossip around the water fountains at the law firm's offices. Someone there was bound to name him to police in the course of the investigation. He could only hope that his damning presence at the park weeks ago would not come to the attention of detectives before he had cleared his name and found justice for Alex.

Nathan looked down at the burn across his abdomen. It crossed his mind to call Isaac, but he then thought better of it. If Isaac learnt of the physical harm that he'd just suffered, he might be excluded from The Sanctuary all together for his own safety, and although he had found the answers he'd been seeking, there was still more that he needed to know. Not least the identity of that girl who'd been calling to him and why she needed help.

The dilemmas of his dire predicament aside, Nathan now had only one overwhelming need. He had to see Mia. He couldn't lose her. And without wasting another second, he reached for both his letter of resignation and the farewell note he'd written and tore them to pieces. He then grabbed for his car keys and headed off to her apartment.

30

Several weeks later – The Present

Nathan sat in a side office of the A&E department, gazing intently at the open wallet containing the photo of his family. With Caleb's disappearance and his involvement in the murder of Alex, it truly was the only tangible reminder of his life before the car crash. The distress in Barbara's voice over the phone still echoed with him as he looked at the image of his mother, father and elder brother – *Please... You have to come right away... I don't know what to do!*

He'd had no choice but to instruct Barbara to bring Isaac to the rear of the hospital's A&E. She'd point-blank refused to call an ambulance, despite the apparent seriousness of Isaac's condition. Nathan could tell she was torn, but Isaac's pre-séance instructions, based on protocols that had been unbroken for over a century, had to be honoured. It was madness. No life was worth risking over some protocol of secrecy. Barbara's other concern was more understandable.

From what he could make out, Isaac had been burnt by ectoplasm in some kind of aberrant energy transfer during a séance, and Nathan himself had only recently experienced first-hand how dangerous that could be. Along with those phenomenal electrical ionising cracks through the air in the séance room, it wasn't hard to understand how the energies involved, if misdirected, might cause serious physical harm and destruction. Isaac had previously mentioned that Physical Mediums had been seriously injured and even killed in the past on being disturbed in their altered states of Trance by people who were unfamiliar with the condition, so Barbara's fears that a well-meaning ambulance crew or doctor might only precipitate a life-threatening turn for the worse simply by applying conventional first aid were understandable. She couldn't very well explain the medical dilemma to arriving paramedics making critical decisions on a clinical history that was out of the ordinary, to say the least.

All in all, he had to agree with Barbara that he should be the first to examine Isaac medically. Thankfully, due to the torrential rain, A&E was unusually quiet, and if they brought him to the rear, Nathan figured that he could steal him into a private treatment room to assess the injury and decide what to do from there.

"You still here, you crazy bastard? It's already gone nine…" Adam's voice brought Nathan back into the moment. "I'd seriously be thinking of getting outta here before the shit hits the fan…"

"Hey, Adam. I'm just about done," Nathan answered. "A patient's just been shown into 3. I thought I'd just check it out before I go."

Nathan still had to stall for a little more time. Barbara had said that she'd send a text through to his phone when they'd arrived at the rear of the hospital. And he had no choice but to hide his complicity, even from his friend. Attending to a patient outside of proper admission procedures would get him hauled in front of a disciplinary board, not to mention being sacked on the spot.

Adam smiled at the thought of the patient in cubicle 3, whose good looks had stopped him in his tracks as he'd walked past, his white clinical coat alone having been sufficient to mask his true motives in entering the cubicle with the pretence of flicking through the girl's – as yet – blank chart. Adam looked straight at his friend and colleague. "I'm on it. Get outta here, Nathan. I'll catch you tomorrow."

Adam disappeared along the corridor, just as the message from Barbara flashed onto the screen of his phone, and draping his clinical coat over his arm, he made for the rear exit. There was hardly anyone around, and he was sure that if Isaac was able to walk well enough, he could easily get him to the safety of one of the vacant treatment rooms without drawing attention.

Peering through the darkness into the downpour of rain, he could see no one, at first. But his gaze then locked onto a small group of people retreating into the gloom and the figure of Isaac lying against the outside wall a few metres away, covered in what seemed to be a sheet. This was definitely not the scenario Nathan had expected to be dealing with, but seeing the outline of Isaac's slumped form beneath the sheet immediately spurred him into action without any regard for the consequences. He yelled for assistance to a lone nurse walking by in the corridor behind him before rushing over. Isaac was completely unresponsive, and Nathan just couldn't conceive how the strict adherence to their protocols could have led Barbara and the other Circle members to have delivered the man in such a condition.

Thankfully, within seconds, Adam and a team of orderlies and medics were on the scene. Isaac wasn't safe yet. But at least he now had a fighting chance.

DI Pullen walked out of the interview room confident that the driver who'd attacked the paramedics in the ambulance knew nothing. Pullen had a sixth sense for the guilt and innocence of those persons he had cause to interview. But the way in which the man had spontaneously lost control of his bladder when the questioning had escalated from 'traffic violations and assault charges while under the influence' to accusations of involvement in sadistic torture and murder was a sure sign in itself that he was just a miscreant out on the town who'd got high on any number of psychosis-invoking drugs and temporarily lost his mind. Any perceived connection with those two naked men that had disappeared from both St Mary's and the ambulance was just coincidental.

Pullen knew that it would be highly irregular for a sadistic sex offender to target both men and women as victims. However, the still-unsolved case of Alex Stanton's murder bore too many similarities with the circumstances surrounding the case of the two unconscious males just found – similarities that were impossible to ignore. All three had been found naked in public places and within a few kilometres of each other; all three had been restrained by their wrists and ankles, and all three had burn marks to their torsos. There was now one other intriguing similarity to add to the list. A connection so significant that Pullen was still pondering his next move. The interrogation of the driver who'd attacked the paramedics hadn't been in vain. On reviewing the CCTV footage from the park opposite the old derelict Hall again, to check if the driver matched the subject loitering on the night of that murder, he had finally realised who the male figure in the grainy flickering image actually was – the young doctor who had found the naked man at the rear of A&E had also been routinely questioned at the time of the murder of Alex Stanton, his number having been found in the contacts list of the victim's phone, along with any number of lewd and suggestive text messages she had sent to him. And, suspiciously, this new person of interest had not numbered amongst the group of concerned friends and colleagues that had reported Stanton missing at the time of her disappearance. It had been the significant regrowth of hair that had thrown him – when routinely questioned over his relationship with the victim, Alex Stanton, at his apartment, the young man's head had been completely shaven.

Dr Nathan Carter was now Pullen's prime suspect.

31

Marjorie sat on the edge of the bed and dabbed Hugh's forehead with a damp cloth. He had been in and out of consciousness for hours since the disastrous séance. But calling for medical assistance was impossible, despite the burn covering his abdomen looking as though it needed immediate attention. Secrecy was paramount. The Witchcraft Act might well have been a historic relic born out of times when innocents were burnt alive for simply boiling up a pain-relieving infusion of willow leaves to yield nothing more than a natural form of the aspirin now kept in apothecary chests around the world, but the authorities had still continued to enforce the Act to great effect through the mere *threat* of imprisonment. A visit from the police would be the least of her problems, though. Attracting unwanted attention from religious conservatives, even in these otherwise promiscuous and liberal times of the 1920s, was fraught with danger. Throwing bricks through windows and setting fire to the houses of those accused of 'sorcery' – while the so accused were asleep inside – was a common way of exercising their staunch Christian values, and The Sanctuary had only been spared such a fate over the years due to her family's clandestine approach and the careful vetting of those invited into their séances.

Finally stirring, Hugh opened his eyes, and after taking a second or two to realise where he was, he greeted his gravely concerned wife with nothing more than a blunt question. "Did Isaac materialise?" he asked with urgency, wincing in pain, the slightest movement of his diaphragm as he spoke being enough to aggravate the burn. He looked down, studying his exposed abdomen. "When did *this* happen?" he asked, more to himself than to Marjorie, assessing the burn with a quizzical look.

Marjorie ran her fingers through Hugh's hair. "This can't go on. I can't bear to see you like this." Her face drained of colour, recalling what she had witnessed just a few hours earlier.

"Tell me what happened," Hugh demanded, gritting through the pain, eager to know the full details of the events of the experiment across Time from the observers' perspective. "Did you see Isaac? Did he materialise? What did Sir Oliver have to say?"

"Hugh! Don't you understand? I thought you were going to die!"

"But I didn't."

Hugh forced an unconcerned smile, mindful of his wife's countless pleas for caution that he'd refused to heed since embarking on his research. Never having been one for sentimentality, he was keen to cut straight to a debrief.

Marjorie was used to her husband's innate lack of

appreciation for other people's emotions. That came with the territory of him possessing such a scientific mind. Like most people so afflicted, it wasn't that he didn't care; he just lacked some empathetic connection that would allow his highly developed thought processes to engage fully with the simple human act of *feeling*. Frankly, it was a trait that Marjorie had both recognised and found appealing from the moment they'd first met, on Hugh being chosen as the most unlikely Physical Medium ever to have sat in the Circle at The Sanctuary. The adventurous Marjorie had always thought of love for just one person as a social inconvenience she could do without. Until she'd found the perfect partner in crime on meeting Hugh. She'd enjoyed the best of both worlds throughout their unconventional – some would say scandalous – marriage. The last few hours, though, had profoundly changed all of that. Facing the prospect of the man she loved dying in her arms had ignited emotions inside her that she hadn't known she'd possessed.

"Did you see Isaac?" Hugh persisted.

Marjorie finally relented and answered in exasperation. "Yes, Hugh! We saw him!"

Hugh laughed wildly, now oblivious to all pain, hauling himself up against the bedhead. It was one thing for him to have his own recollection of events, but that recall might just have been a dream-like fantasy generated by his psyche if not independently supported by those observers in the Circle.

"How long?" Hugh demanded. "How long did he hold the manifestation for?" Hugh knew that his ability to judge passing time was the first casualty of the senses in Trance states.

"A couple of minutes, at least."

"Only a couple of minutes?"

Marjorie was surprised that Hugh seemed both disappointed and troubled by her answer.

"Did he completely physicalise?" he asked, with the same abruptness that he might use to address a junior research assistant at his laboratory. "I need to know precise details," he insisted.

"Yes, he physicalised!" Marjorie confirmed. "At first, he appeared in the centre of the Circle as a light body, like a conventional séance manifestation. Then, just as you'd predicted, his luminosity simply kept decreasing as he became denser and denser, until we couldn't see him any longer in the blackout. He communicated throughout and did manage to follow all the protocols to confirm his physical presence… But then something went wrong." Marjorie's voice began to falter. "He started to scream in agony as he reverted to a light body again, and in a flash the manifestation spontaneously collapsed. It was horrific, Hugh. Like he was burning alive inside some invisible flame. Everyone was so shaken. Not least Sir Oliver."

Hugh glanced at the burn on his own abdomen again before doggedly pressing Marjorie for more information. He was eager to share with her his own experience but was unable to until she had corroborated the sequence of events as seen by members of the Circle. Time was of the essence. The longer he delayed, the more chance there was of inaccuracies creeping into Marjorie's account, and the more chance that his own recollections would fade like a dream on waking. "And how long before I rematerialised back here?" Hugh pressed with urgency. "It's important. I need to know *exactly* how long."

Marjorie thought for a moment, still unsure of where all this was leading. "Well, after Isaac dematerialised, we continued sitting in blackout for forty minutes or so. We just didn't know what to do and so kept following the instructions you'd given us. We kept calling out your name, assuming that you were in the room but just unable to speak. It was only when we had no choice but to switch the red lamp on that we realised for certain that you weren't there... That would have been at a quarter to nine," Marjorie recounted, thinking through the events. "I looked at the clock when we saw that you weren't anywhere to be seen. Sir Oliver and two others were then allowed out to search the other rooms and the grounds, in case you'd rematerialised somewhere outside of the séance room, and they must have been looking for about thirty minutes or so. After that, all we could think to do was to sit back in the Circle and pray. It would have been twenty-five past ten when you finally returned." Marjorie visibly shuddered. "Your screams were worse than Isaac's, Hugh."

"You prayed? *Ha!*" Hugh exclaimed, oblivious to how his wife had been affected.

Hugh was a devout atheist, and until a few hours ago, Marjorie had been just as devout. But what she'd witnessed had seen her, for the first time in her life, desperately praying over and over along with the others – praying that a God might just exist.

"One hour and forty minutes in total, then?"

"Or thereabouts."

Hugh seemed deep in thought at that answer. The two minutes or so that Isaac had maintained his physicality in the séance room would just not have accounted for Hugh's own recollection of events those nine decades in the future. He must have been unconscious outside of the Hall for longer than he'd realised before rematerialising back to 1929. But where had Isaac been for the greatest part of two hours? *Had he been found by medics? Had he even survived?*

Hugh looked intently at his wife, confident that her recall of events had been accurate. "I was thrown to the Hall, Marjorie. You wouldn't believe what's happened to the place."

Transported in his thoughts, Hugh again pictured the unmistakeable outline of the imposing edifice he'd seen framed in an orange-tinged sky that he just couldn't explain – the ubiquitous sodium glare of street lighting was, for him, still forty years from being an unquestioned feature of the night…

Regaining consciousness under the orange glow, Hugh had found himself lying face down on an unfamiliar hard black surface wet with rain. The pooling water reflected a surrounding vista that was as equally unfamiliar, for he knew that there should be grass and rolling pastures in the Hall's grounds where he lay. Most surprising of all was the sight of countless strange buildings of dubious soulless architecture that surrounded and tormented the Hall. The acres and acres of English countryside it had commanded for centuries were no more.

The distant rising and falling tone of a siren getting louder and louder gradually surfaced from out of a constant background rumble of sound that was disturbing and difficult to place. He simply lacked the vocabulary to describe the alien cacophony of modern-day metropolitan traffic noise rolling over his partially disconnected auditory senses as he tried to force himself back into full consciousness. He tried to stand several times, to no avail, and it was in those futile attempts that he looked down and noticed his nakedness. Hypothermic waves of shivering coursed over his whole body, and he grasped for awareness as his memory of eighty-five years prior began to re-engage. His last recollection, before awaking in this new timeframe, had been sitting in the séance room of The Sanctuary in 1929, having just been tied naked to his chair as protocol had directed. The rest was a blur.

The blaring siren that had been assaulting his senses had at some point stopped. Several men dressed in various unfamiliar uniforms now surrounded him, and he found himself being manhandled onto a stretcher and loaded into the back of what seemed to be an ambulance. Not that he could see much, because the harsh brightness of the vehicle's interior burnt painfully at his retinas. This was not supposed to have happened. The intention had been to physicalise temporarily in the séance room of The Sanctuary across those nine decades of time.

In recognising the outline of the Hall, Hugh realised *where* he was but had no idea of *when*, and he couldn't afford to let anyone attend to him in his delicate state. Any medical intervention, he knew, might kill him. He had no choice but to attempt to calm himself and fully re-enter a Trance state in order to return to his own Time. It was his only chance of survival. And perhaps the only chance that Isaac had, too…

Hugh's thoughts came back to the present, and he began to relay his own account to Marjorie with all the emotion of a military debrief.

Marjorie was filled with apprehension at her husband's mention of seeing the Hall, her immediate thoughts being of the murmurings about a Dark Circle being held there by Henry Mathieson and individuals with less than positive ideals. '*A Diocese of a Lie*' Hugh had called them, and it seemed that his initial fears about Mathieson plagiarising the séance protocols after he'd quit The Sanctuary's Circle had been valid, after all. "The dark séances?" Marjorie asked uneasily.

Hugh nodded solemnly. "We have to stop them, Marjorie. Someone has just succeeded in intruding into mine and Isaac's Trance states. And they're bound to try again."

But Hugh had not shared everything with Marjorie. As the interface between his Mind and physicality had slipped through Time on his return, he'd caught glimpses of a potential future – a future that did not bear thinking about. Hugh knew what those in the Hall's Dark Circle were attempting to do.

32

Nicholas Mosley surveyed the proposed site for the Hall from horseback. His loyalty to Queen Elizabeth now saw him next in line for the office of Lord Mayor of London, with talk of a knighthood in the offing, and he intended wasting no time in bolstering his own personal wealth through the influence he could now exercise, especially in the lucrative arena of foreign trade.

The perimeter of the planned building was circumnavigated in a slow restrained trot while Nicholas, in the saddle, built a detailed picture of every room, corridor and cellar in his mind's eye. He smiled to himself, pleased at what he saw. His return to the North had been a triumphant one. The grandiose Hall, replacing the family residence built by his great-grandfather, would be a declaration as to the power and influence he had gained in his years away. But the Hall was only the beginning of his imaginings. He was intent that the nearby Manor of Manchester that he'd also recently acquired would one day burgeon into a city to challenge

London as a seat of power and wealth. It would then be *his* descendants that would rule the land of England – a legacy that would leave his name indelibly imprinted in history as the Father of a New Order. So much for loyalty to the realm.

The horse circled around on the spot, rearing slightly as if making ready to charge into battle, the powerful animal following his master's shifting directives through the expertly manipulated reins. Mosley focused through the flurry of hooves on a single point on the grassy terrain beneath him that marked the southwest corner of the build. His gaze then traversed the ground in a dead straight line before he set off in pursuit of the line's imagined end somewhere in the distance. After a 150-yard gallop, he pulled hard on the reins and came to an abrupt halt at the lip of the steep bank of a brook that babbled through the tract of land. The chasing posse of loyal armed attendants – escorting a very intimidated master builder masking his nerves – also came to a regimented stop at Mosley's flank. Nicholas looked back to the mirage image of the Hall's southern aspect that, as yet, only he could see.

"Here!" Nicholas pointed, indicating the proposed exit to the tunnel amidst the overgrowth of greenery covering the near bank. There were those that despised the monarchy with its landed gentry, and talk amongst the common people of a once unthinkable uprising was becoming more frequent. The meandering brook hidden at the bottom of the steep bank would act as a suitable escape route in case of attack or siege. Any secretly located hiding holes designed into the Hall might only prove safe for a short time, but the tunnel would connect the cellars to the shallow waterway that emptied into the River Mersey only a few miles' march away, and from there the highways to any part of the country could be accessed and forces gathered.

The master builder nodded his understanding. He'd been chosen on account of his expertise in building perplexingly undetectable priest holes into the fabric of country houses following the Catholic uprisings of the North back in 1567. The Queen's men had sometimes spent days tearing down parts of a suspect manor house without ever finding the priest hidden away inside his seamless work. The builder also never asked questions of those who employed him, especially those with larger than usual pockets who also boasted their own private army. He surveyed the area, trying to picture Mosley's vision. The tunnel would be long and exit further downstream than any insurgent would think to search. It would have to be secretly dug out by Mosley's most loyal men, he decided, well before the Hall's foundations were laid, to minimise any undue attention to its existence.

Across time, a man's hand rested motionless on a sheet of foolscap. The nib of the pen he held in contact with the paper's surface had bled its blue Indian ink in a slowly spreading blot that now marred the once pristine blank page, as if weakness had overcome the man before he could pen his final words.

The absolute silence in the room was broken by a faint sigh of air. A breath. A sign of life. Then came a movement in the hand that was at first so slight and barely discernible that it seemed unable to overcome the frictional inertia of the nib against the fibres of the paper. Another sigh of air. The pen began to move across the page, leaving a wavering blue line in its slow traverse. A letter began to form from the trail of ink... N... The nib stopped, as if the effort had been too much, before the dithering hand found strength and continued on, leaving short stabbing ink marks on the surface of the paper between the letters... I... CHO... LAS... MO... SLEY.

The movement of the hand came to an abrupt stop.

Having finished her work earlier than expected, Mia entered Anne-Marie's office, as instructed earlier in the day, with the intention of picking up more of the document boxes she'd been endlessly shuttling back and forth between AXIS and The Sanctuary – Anne-Marie having gained extraordinary permission from Isaac to borrow some of the Library's antique scientific texts and other papers from The Sanctuary's historical records that documented past séances. Mia didn't mind the drive; it was Anne-Marie's belittling delegation of her as an errand girl that riled her. But, on this occasion at least, it seemed there were none of the particularly heavy leather-bound volumes from the Library's stack to return.

As usual, the sealed boxes were sitting on Anne-Marie's desk ready for collection, but instead of the three boxes mentioned, Mia could see only two in the pile. Glancing around the office to check, she saw what was undoubtedly the third one on top of the large filing cabinet in the corner of the room, and picking it up, she was surprised at its lack of weight. It seemed to be empty. Equally surprising was finding that the filing cabinet had been left unlocked with the top drawer slightly ajar, which was highly unusual. Mia could only think that Anne-Marie had been called away and distracted in the middle of packing the boxes and had forgotten to return to complete the task at hand. Anne-Marie had always seemed unduly protective of whatever was kept in the cabinets – the way that she would slam the drawers shut with the guilt of a teenager up to no good on the occasions she'd been unexpectedly disturbed was by now a tired office joke, and it had often left Mia wondering. On more than one occasion in the lab's weekly meetings called to discuss the direction of each researcher's current work, she had been annoyingly blindsided when Anne-Marie had announced, to everyone assembled, some interesting line of investigation she claimed to have come up with herself that might as well have read straight out of Mia's own experimental notes.

She wasn't one to pry or snoop but had long since lost all respect for the woman, and the opportunity to finally confirm her suspicions of professional plagiarism and in-house spying on the research of her and her colleagues proved just too tempting. "*Screw it!*" she thought. Placing the box down, she glanced towards the door to check that no one was in the immediate vicinity and opened the drawer fully to expose the countless folders crammed inside. She knew that this would be her one and only chance.

The first folder that caught her interest was headed *The Sanctuary*, and she was surprised on glancing inside to see a dossier on Isaac. The folder was filled with court transcripts, copies of police reports and old press articles, and any worries over being caught snooping quickly faded as she became engrossed in an emerging story she was piecing together of an attack by a gang of youths on Isaac and his unit while out on the town when he was only twenty. Despite reacting in the only way he could in the defence of himself and his friends, it seemed that Isaac had ended up paying the price of a military justice system sensitive to the armed forces' public image, after a member of the gang suffered serious injuries by striking his head on a street pavement as he fell. Other reports and documents showed that the allegations of sexual assault levelled against him were even more spurious. Mia was left feeling more than a twinge of guilt about doubting Isaac on reading a yellowing newspaper clipping of a tacky tabloid page-filler headlined 'SLEAZY PSYCHIC SEX SCANDAL', which sensationally told how a rival psychic had vindictively employed an ex-prostitute to cry attempted rape while having a reading with Isaac at The Sanctuary. Not only were charges never laid against Isaac, police instead brought charges against the guilty parties involved for filing a false report – all facts that had never been aired in the TV exposé aimed at ruining Isaac's reputation. Those vague whispered rumours about his past had no basis in truth.

Intrigued at what else she would find, Mia reached for another of the folders: *KARL HOLZER* a label unassumingly read, giving no hint as to what lay inside. Sliding out the thick wad of papers, she was immediately shocked to find herself scanning through a pile of what appeared to be research notes, along with countless photocopied translations from the original German, outlining medical experiments carried out on Jewish prisoners in concentration camps. Mia was chilled to her core. Sickening photographs sporadically illustrated the text with 'before' mugshots of men, women and children – displaying expressions ranging from apprehension to sheer terror – juxtaposed with 'after' images of their contorted, blank and palsied faces of post-surgical oblivion. Close-up frames of the less fortunate ones even showed them lying on dirty floors with exposed regions of brain visible through purposely unclosed surgical wounds. '*The Jew makes a good subject. Their wretchedness lends them to surgical probing without fear of consequence,*' read a section that finally forced Mia to slam the folder shut in utter abhorrence.

Mia had always disliked Anne-Marie, but the fact that the woman was even in possession of such reference material disturbed her more than she thought possible. And as much as she wanted to run immediately from the building and never return, she knew that she had to take the opportunity to see what else Anne-Marie was hiding.

The other variously titled files she flicked open were simply concerned with conventional paranormal experiments and documentation of the various phenomena. One label, though, towards the back of the drawer, particularly grabbed her attention: *The Quantum Energy Template of Physicality*, it read. But just as she was about to reach for the folder, the voices of two of her colleagues walking close to the office door prompted her to suspend the impromptu investigation immediately.

Mia motioned to shut the drawer in response but hesitated for a second. What she had read had made her realise that she was done with Anne-Marie and she was done with AXIS – serving tables would be preferable to continuing on there. Nathan should at least take a look at the contents, she decided. He was the best person to approach Isaac over the revelations. It was unlikely that Isaac would cooperate further with Anne-Marie's research at The Sanctuary if he knew that a dossier was being compiled about him, let alone the appalling nature of the experimental reference material uncovered in the files.

With a glance over her shoulder, Mia grabbed all the

folders of interest she'd stumbled upon and secreted them inside the empty box and then closed the drawer as she'd found it before heading out to her car. She could not have conceived that amongst all the papers was a dossier bearing the name *Nathan Carter*.

33

"I'm here to tell you, it's a beautiful world,
I looked outside the other day, if it was any other way, I wouldn't be quite satisfied.
There'll be floods and there'll be fires and a host of inconceivable situations.
But I'm here to tell you, it's a beautiful world,
In an infant's faintest smile, I recall some far of time but can't imagine what he sees.
Child, there'll be floods and there'll be fires, and a host of undesirable circumstances.
So I'm here to tell you,
There'll be those who'll scheme to tear your dreams apart and crush your heart,
But you'll grow,
Like a flower's imperceptible exposure.
I'm here to tell you, it's a beautiful world."

Nathan's fingers let go of the calligraphy-adorned vellum

he'd just read from, and the sheet of paper floated gently downwards into the ground. Handful after solemn handful of soil thudded down onto Annie's coffin lid, those sounds of such finality bringing tears to his eyes as the lyrics of his aunt's favourite song became buried forever under the accumulating earth. His parents had nurtured him as a very young child and provided for his future through life insurances and monies placed in Trust. But it had been Annie who had stepped up and given her life to raising both him and Caleb. The end had been sudden and unexpected, a neighbour having found her collapsed at home following a heart attack. But, in truth, after learning that Caleb's disappearance was for good, she'd been left feeling alone, unneeded, and had simply lost the will to live. He had tried his best to visit her as often as he could, but her smiles and attempts at conversation had belied a preoccupation with all that had previously been rather than what could be in the future. The loss was devastating. His mum and dad were gone. Annie was gone. And Caleb was dead to him. He had been left with no family, and his sadness was only compounded by the memory of standing in a stunned state of disbelief at the funeral of Alex at this very cemetery only weeks ago.

Nathan lingered in silence at the graveside for a short while after the ceremony, Mia linking his arm, while a small procession of mourners touched his shoulder in sympathy on slowly making their way from the grave.

"It's good that you got to know her before she died," he finally said.

Mia responded by tightening her clutch on Nathan's arm and leaning her head against his shoulder, thankful that she'd had the chance to meet Annie and connect with

Nathan's past in the handful of times she'd been able to visit. She knew how alone Nathan was feeling, and no one was more sensitive to his sadness nor more willing to offer the undivided emotional support he needed. But something was playing on her mind. Since they'd been back together, after her having been suddenly abandoned without any real explanation, it had become obvious that Nathan was keeping something from her – likely connected with those awakening psychic abilities of his that he'd alluded to. An evasiveness at odds with his usual honesty and openness made her feel that he was trying to protect her from some truth. But the truth was all that she wanted. Not that her own lack of openness was lost on her. She'd been wanting to tell Nathan about what she'd discovered amongst the folders procured from AXIS, the contents having continued to disturb her since laying eyes on them. It had just never seemed the right time to bring it up, at the risk of adding to whatever it was he was already worried about. And now he had Annie's death to deal with. She would have to pick her time carefully in broaching the subject but knew she couldn't hold off much longer.

After saying a last goodbye, Nathan and Mia made their way slowly back through the gravestones in a thoughtful silence, oblivious to the black sedan parked inconspicuously on the cemetery's Remembrance Boulevard. Still linking arms, they walked over to Isaac and Barbara, who were waiting for them by the kerb.

Nathan sighed with relief, finally able to relax on seeing faces that he recognised. "Just the reception to get through, now. I really don't know half of these people. And the rest of them I haven't seen since I was a kid."

Isaac smiled his understanding. "Why don't you drop

into The Sanctuary for an hour or so, afterwards. We'd love to have you both over. It's practically on your way."

Nathan had been granted two weeks' compassionate leave, and he and Mia were finally heading down to Adam's farmhouse for a few days of relaxation. The Audi was already packed with his luggage, and they'd intended swinging by Mia's place straight after the funeral reception to drop off her car and pick up her bags before heading off. So he was just about to decline Isaac's kind offer when he noticed Mia already nodding her acceptance on behalf of them both. He smiled for the first time in days. "Well, I guess we'll see you later!" he said, shaking Isaac's hand and accepting a motherly hug from Barbara.

All the while, the shutter of a camera whirred continuously from the driver's seat of the black sedan as the attached telephoto lens captured yet more images to add to the collage of shots already compiled over the last few days. It would have taken a keener eye than that possessed by Detective Sergeant John Fitzpatrick, though, to notice the figure of Caleb shadowing Nathan and Mia at a distance as they walked amongst the headstones. The detective had good enough reason to have his complete attention through the viewfinder focused solely on the murder suspect Nathan Carter, now under surveillance.

34

The damp stagnant space smelt as if it was rotting from the inside, and Nathan's gasping attempts to suck in the thick air that pervaded the stifling darkness only served to allow the foul stench to pollute what little saliva still moistened the mucosal lining of his mouth and tongue.

He clambered along on his stomach, knowing that survival depended on keeping moving. On and on and on he crawled, the effort burning inside his lungs, his core, across his chest and through the tendons and ligaments and musculature of every limb. Gritting his teeth, he propelled himself along with one painfully cramping hand while dragging a dead weight with the other. *Was he crawling away from danger or towards it?* There was no way of knowing. He was simply possessed of a desperate need that kept him moving. On his next clawing reach, his hand suddenly felt a different texture on the floor of the confined space. It was grittier and stonier and he definitely sensed that he was now moving on a shallow upwards incline. The skin of his fingers was being grazed and cut on the edges of buried rubble and what felt like broken half-bricks, and the pain with each grasp of earth was now weakening him and slowing him down. He manoeuvred himself awkwardly onto his back, hauling the dead weight on top of him, the jagged edges and corners ripping at the skin of his back as he slid along the ever-increasing gradient. Holding his breath and straining with the sheer effort, he finally found purchase on the rubble and pushed harder with his legs towards what he hoped was safety. A cool waft of air teased his face. And, with a final thrust, he broke out into the open…

Nathan inhaled one forced rasping breath after another, eyes wide in a terrified stare.

"It's OK, Nathan. It's OK, it's OK."

Mia cradled his head and stroked his hair.

"I'll get you some water," Barbara offered.

"Did you recognise where you were?" Isaac immediately asked with one of his usual frowns before Nathan's breathing had even normalised.

"Isaac!" Barbara scolded, reaching for a jug on the table in front of her. "Give the boy a moment, won't you," she snapped, too used to such blunt overbearing displays by her husband.

Isaac simply ignored her, though, and asked his question again with even more urgency, eager to know the details of Nathan's impromptu journey of the mind before its memory sank irretrievably into the oblivion of his subconscious. "Where were you exactly? I could tell that it was dark and enclosed, yeah?"

Nathan grasped for the glass being offered and took a gulp of water to quench the dryness still choking at his throat. He hadn't expected to slip embarrassingly into a Trance state in the middle of the polite chatter over Barbara's perfectly laid-out tea and biscuits in the main house. It had been months since those slips into Trance had happened so spontaneously. In fact, ever since he'd begun sitting in meditation under the controlled conditions of Isaac's instruction, he had felt completely free of the psychic instability that had led him to seek out The Sanctuary in the first place.

"I was in some kind of underground crawl space... It felt so real," Nathan answered, not in the least surprised that Isaac had shared in the vision.

"It *was* real," Isaac said, emphatically. He'd been watching Nathan closely throughout, tuning in, and intuitively knew the experience had been a clairvoyant episode transporting Nathan to some future moment. The fear had been palpable to Isaac. Barbara and Mia, on the other hand, hadn't noticed anything other than Nathan initially beginning to slur his words mid-conversation before closing his eyes and quietly slipping into a seemingly distant uncommunicative state.

"Could we have a moment, ladies?"

Isaac's request hung in silence. Barbara knew only too well how long Isaac's 'moments' could be. "Are you sure that you're OK?" she asked. "I'd hate to leave you alone with this unfeeling brute if you didn't feel up to it."

Nathan responded with a broad smile, indicating that he'd now fully recovered from his fleeting slip through time. "I'm fine, Barbara. Really. Just a little tired, that's all," he reassured.

With that, Barbara linked arms with Mia. "Well, let's

you and I drive into the village, my lovely. There are some wonderful shops there," she suggested. "The *menfolk* apparently need some time," she added, with a roll of her eyes.

Mia gave Nathan an uncomfortable look, concerned over finally witnessing one of the disturbing psychic episodes that Nathan had previously alluded to and also conscious of the fact that they'd only just left Annie's funeral. A fun shopping trip into the village hardly seemed appropriate under the circumstances.

Nathan reassured her with a smile. "I'm fine… Buy me something pretty," he joked, answering Mia's questioning gaze and indicating that he really was OK.

Now that the painful ritual of the funeral was over, she knew that Nathan was keen for life to get back to normal as quickly as possible. So, with a sideways look at Barbara, Mia grinned and resolutely nodded her acceptance of the invitation. And still linked arm in arm, the pair headed out – Mia assuming the role of the daughter Barbara had never had and Barbara that of the mother Mia had lost.

"I'm worried," Isaac whispered, as soon as the door had closed. He was sensitive to Nathan's emotional state on this day of all days, but he could no longer ignore the feeling he'd been having for some time that he and Nathan were in danger. Being potentially open to all manner of negative and positive thoughts and emotions while succumbing to feelings of paranoia was something every sensitive had to be constantly vigilant about. It was an occupational hazard. But it was becoming increasingly impossible to shake the feeling of being watched and followed. And Nathan's inadvertent clairvoyant Trance state, tainted with fear and the need to escape, only added to that worrying sense, finally forcing

Isaac's hand. "Remember the warning of danger that the drunk gave you in A&E?"

Nathan didn't need to answer. The predicament he faced was constantly on his mind. Since learning of the horrific murder of Alex while in Trance, he had struggled with not being able to report what he knew to the police at the risk of being arrested as a suspect. The only evidence he had to offer involved intimate details of a crime he shouldn't have known anything about. Yet he could only avoid suspicion falling on himself by proving that others had been responsible. While those previous spontaneous slips into Trance were largely under control, his now frequent forays into that Void of the mind under Isaac's guidance only seemed to leave him with even more fragmented visions of sickening violence that he had to keep to himself. But he had no choice. Confiding in Isaac too soon and involving his contacts in the police would be useless. Aside from implicating him even further, conventional police procedure would not have uncovered any of the critical evidence found only in the Void – the Void held the answers. If he could just attain enough control of those mental states, he was sure that he'd be able to piece enough solid evidence together to nail Caleb and Bedlam for Alex's murder. For the time being, his only option was to keep as low a profile as possible and wait. Confronting her killers, or even simply being spotted in the vicinity of the Ashton Arms or the Carousel Club, would be suicidal.

"We have to be careful," Isaac said, interrupting Nathan's thoughts. "I've got a bad feeling. I can't put my finger on it, but there are forces building. Negative forces."

Isaac's demeanour was as serious as Nathan had ever seen.

"It's time I show you something…"

Isaac motioned Nathan into the Library at the far end of The Sanctuary's corridor. It was identical to the séance room in size and décor except that two of its four walls were lined with shelves stacked with all manner of books and leather-bound volumes – some modern, but most archaic-looking – that reached almost to the ceiling. Occupying the centre of the room was a solid wooden table, large enough to seat eight, that could well have been crafted from the same timber as the hefty séance chair in the séance room next door, and against the wall, positioned under a window that looked out onto the dense woodland to the rear of The Sanctuary, was a glass-topped display cabinet.

Isaac strode over to an old Victorian-looking antique safe positioned inside the now redundant original fireplace nestled in what would structurally have been the far gable end wall of The Sanctuary. While Nathan looked on, the contents of the safe were carefully laid out in piles across the expansive tabletop by a stern-looking Isaac.

"This represents the entire history of The Sanctuary since its inception back in 1863," Isaac finally announced, surveying what must have amounted to several hundred documents spread across the table. "And the display cabinet over there contains every apport ever to have materialised during the séances… Passing down such records to the future has been vital for the Circle's continued survival," he explained. "Trusting word of mouth alone would have been unreliable at best and dangerous at worst. So each successive Medium at The Sanctuary has been entrusted as Guardian of the historical records while they themselves added to the body of work in each of their tenures."

"And which is your particular contribution?" Nathan asked, not quite sure why he was being shown the collection.

Isaac responded with a wry look. "I'm afraid, as Guardians go, I've been found lacking," he admitted. "I've just never found the time to go through all of the documents that thoroughly, to be honest. The old guard here at The Sanctuary have been hassling me about my 'duties' since day one... You might have noticed that there's the odd pain in the butt within the Circle," he added with a wink. "They do mean well. And without them, there'd be no Circle to speak of."

Nathan knew for sure from his now regular visits to The Sanctuary that Isaac was referring to Mike and Doreen and a couple of their sour cronies. They had been Circle members long before Isaac's tenure and seemed to hold a tight-lipped resentment for his casual approach to running the Circle, and their obvious invested sense of ownership of The Sanctuary's long history often saw them openly reminiscing with each other about 'the good old days' in blatant attempts to undermine Isaac's authority. Nathan simply found them unfriendly and would have avoided all contact with the clique whenever their paths crossed, if not for him being pre-emptively shunned and ignored by them first.

"Feel free to glance through anything you want," Isaac suggested, "but I'd particularly like you to take a look at these." He placed his hand on top of a large envelope that was thick with content. "Take your time. I'll leave you to it."

Isaac walked off, closing the Library door behind him, leaving Nathan alone to peruse through the documents, folders, notebooks, diaries and unsealed envelopes of varying sizes strewn across the table.

Nathan hesitated before reaching out to browse through the collection, conscious of the trust that had seen the works passed down through the generations. At a glance, the earliest were ink-written in the most exquisite of hands, while many of the later ones had been typed out, and there being so much material to choose from, Nathan simply opted to grab a couple of the closest piles and begin idly flicking through them. The passing seconds soon turned into passing minutes as the gravity of intriguing entry after intriguing entry slowly began pulling him deeper into the history.

In some of the documents, the progression of protocols that had been adopted over the decades was recorded. In others, every word ever uttered by the sitting Medium while in Trance had been committed to paper. One even ventured at predictions for the future, with nineteenth-century talk of '*the first of two Great Wars in Europe*' breaking out in 1914, '*explosions of light and fire*' that would wipe out cities in a flash, '*sky-travel*' to the Americas, and one almost apologetic suggestion of future machines with '*artificial brains*' possessing humanity's entire knowledge base. The odd single leaf would simply offer a greeting from across the ages, a funny quip, an amusing poem or some commentary on world events of the day along with the occasional ageing newspaper clipping. There was even a document titled *Genealogies* amongst the papers, consisting of several A4 sheets stapled together, identifying the family histories of some of the Circle's past Mediums. Nathan picked up a stray Tarot card – *THE MAGICIAN* – that was lying loose amongst the countless leaves of paper and admired the incredibly detailed artwork of the image before sliding it carefully back where he'd found it amongst the prediction of a Great War that *had* actually eventuated.

After flicking through a number of the piles, Nathan's attention turned to the large old yellowing envelope that Isaac had suggested he should take a look at. The remnant of sealing wax on the reverse side was incredibly brittle and spoke of its age, and sliding the papers out onto the table, he was immediately surprised to see four separate lengths of tightly coiled rope also fall from the envelope. Nathan examined the ropes before setting them aside.

The pages of the documents themselves were handwritten in a scrawling but legible script, and Nathan was struck by how quick-witted this particular author had been. Every page was crammed with countless additions and diagrams in the margins, headers and footers. The odd passage, however, had been penned beautifully and precisely, indicating that enthusiasm was the main reason for the bulk of the scrawl. It had obviously been more important to capture every thought as it occurred rather than worry about the aesthetic appeal for future readers.

Nathan's idle browsing was brought to a sharp focus when he flicked to one particular page showing a precise scaled diagram of The Sanctuary's séance room. Dimensions were given to mere fractions of an inch and pinpointed the exact location of where the nominated carved wooden séance chair should be placed. Also clearly indicated on the plans were the four small scorch marks on the floorboards of the séance room that the author, according to the accompanying text, had burned into the wood himself. There was even mention of the lengths of rope he'd provided from across the decades, which were the same ropes that had been used to restrain him to the chair during his séances. The envelope's contents, Nathan had by now realised, belonged to the quantum physicist Hugh Wells, whom he'd encountered in the séance, and these were his notes from the 1920s on an experimental séance being planned. The words were written with such flair that Nathan became completely absorbed as he read on in more depth: 'The likes of Isaac Newton did not develop the mathematics of Differential Calculus, as is often quoted,' Hugh opened. 'Such mathematicians can only be said to have cleverly noticed what the human brain does so naturally when observing Reality.'

The odd and forthright statement grabbed Nathan's attention.

'...The brain of even a young child performs the mathematics of Calculus at lightning speed when catching a ball,' Hugh explained, 'with the brain effortlessly calculating the constantly changing speed and trajectory of the ball until it is safely caught in the child's hands. The mathematics of Differential Calculus, therefore, must be thought of as an innate building block of every functioning human mind, rather than just some unfathomable tedious subject to be endured in the school curriculum... The "genius" of early mathematicians was in becoming aware of that innate feature of the mind and externalising it for observation; their "accomplishment" was in committing the observations to paper in penning their equations so that it could be utilised as a tool. Their "failing", however, was in not realising that their initial observations ultimately held more significance than their actual accomplishments.'

Mathematics exists innately within the very framework of consciousness was scribbled down the adjacent left-hand margin and underlined several times, and at the top of the page was written *Mathematics is the language of consciousness* – Hugh's side notes seemingly emphasising the salient points for the reader's benefit as thoughts had crossed through his mind while he wrote.

Mathematics explained as an outwardly projected study of what actually occurs naturally within our minds as we observe our world and Cosmos struck Nathan as fascinating and *did* instantly make the otherwise tedious subject far more interesting.

Bridging the years, Hugh's thoughts continued to scrawl from the nib of his pen. 'In the same way, the individual illuminations of Eudoxus, Euclid and Archimedes, 2,300 years ago, that led to the realisation that the Area of a Circle $= \pi r^2$, were not just mathematical inventions created so that school students could henceforth inanely calculate the area (A) of a circle,' Hugh pointed out dryly. 'Like Newton, those ancients had, by their clever observations, stumbled upon the inner workings of our perception at a consciousness level. And the formula πr^2 scribbled down by countless generations of school children since, can be seen as yet another external projection of something innate within us all... Put simply, πr^2 is just another building block of human awareness that has been exposed – a building block involved in the very mechanism in which our minds psychically construct our world of shapes and objects.'

Geometry is simply consciousness defining the illusion of Space and Mathematical constants such as 'π' are the mental struts of consciousness on which our perceived Reality hangs filled the header and footer of a new page in yet more enthusiastic scrawl.

Nathan was captivated by Hugh's thoughts and how they echoed the words Hugh himself had uttered through Isaac in Trance at that first séance: '*Consciousness* is not a mere observer of Nature's laws in action; it is the *Creator* of those very laws.' It became immediately obvious to Nathan how the character and mannerisms of Hugh portrayed at the séance, via Isaac, mirrored perfectly the character and mannerisms portrayed in these words written in Hugh's own hand. They were evidently recognisable as the same voice. Nathan read on, eager to learn more.

'Our psyche at its most primal level is ruled by symbols. Is it any surprise, then, that such scribblings as $+$, $-$, $\div$, $\times$, $=$, Δ, ∞, $\geq$ or even $y' - 4y = x^2 - 3x + 4$ should eventually spew out onto paper. Because, in truth, the entirety of mathematics – known and unknown – stems from every sentient being's functioning mind,' Hugh reiterated. 'And every mathematical formula and equation ever penned is no less than an external description of one facet of human consciousness itself – but they are not just an insight into the mechanisms of consciousness; they are an actual exposed "fragment" of that very consciousness.'

Nathan felt a profound sense of realisation stirring within. His mind was spinning. The words resonated and made complete sense with their simplicity and insight and were enough to assault his whole view of the 'mind' he'd been studying and doctoring for years. His eyes flitted across to read yet another note scrawled vertically down the right-hand margin of the page: *The entirety of scientific knowledge merely represents humankind's pitiful and limited attempts to describe consciousness.* Hugh's point only became clearer. 'Mathematical equations have little to do with the intellectual wrangling of the individual scientists who write them but are instead born out of a fleeting transcendental moment exposing that intrinsic building block of consciousness. Scientists over the centuries, without realising it, have been gradually mapping out human consciousness with their equations under the mistaken impression they were describing an external natural world and Cosmos...' Nathan's pace of thinking quickened as he was led along a pathway of logic and reason. He wasn't quite prepared, though, for the consequences of the next step he was about to take.

'...It follows, then, that *ANY* observation made of *ANY* physical phenomena in this Cosmos, describable with a mathematical equation, must also represent an externalised innate fragment of our consciousness...'

Nathan reeled inside. The statement was colossal in its implications.

'...A moving object's *MOMENTUM* can be described mathematically in terms of its mass and velocity by an equation. Therefore, a moving object's *MOMENTUM is* a fragment of *CONSCIOUSNESS*; and that same moving object's *ENERGY OF MOTION* can also be described by mathematical symbols scrawled upon paper. Therefore, every moving object's *KINETIC ENERGY is* a fragment of *CONSCIOUSNESS*; even physical *FORCE*, that very palpable instigator we rely on in this world, being mathematically describable, *is* a fragment of *CONSCIOUSNESS*. And so on, ad nauseam, for every physical phenomenon in the Cosmos that can be observed – including *GRAVITY*. For Gravity *is* a fragment of *CONSCIOUSNESS*. And if the amount of *ENERGY* contained in physical Matter can be described in terms of its mass and the speed of light by that infamous equation $E = mc^2$, it follows that the amount of *ENERGY* contained in the entirety of cosmic physical *MATTER* is a fragment of our *CONSCIOUSNESS*. And since *TIME* is a term in the equation that describes the speed of light, *TIME* – along with *SPACETIME* – itself *is* a fragment of *CONSCIOUSNESS*. Therein lies the illusion of Matter and Time in our Reality.'

Everything Nathan had been learning about since first arriving at The Sanctuary suddenly converged into a single moment of enlightenment. The text began to merge. His eyes scanned the lines without the need to read any more as the relentless flow of words burgeoned into a cascade that swamped his visual cortex and overflowed out through countless neurones and synaptic connections until both cerebral hemispheres were sodden. Nathan recognised this feeling all too well, and he fought slipping into Trance. His very being was drowning in Hugh's thoughts and reasoning.

The illusion of physicality had been laid bare through such simple concepts that it was hard to conceive how something so obvious could be missed. Nathan's hold on concrete reality had finally been lost in the most profound way. There were no more doubts or questions. His being soared with euphoria in an utter surrender inspired by the words, and his efforts to fight a slip into Trance waned. The *suspension of disbelief* he had craved had finally been delivered. The idea of mental control of physical matter – that had seemed so hard for him to accept through its challenge to an objectivity born out of reason and logic – had just been proven by reason and logic itself.

'This is the true state of Reality,' Hugh summed up in closing his preamble. 'The very subatomic particles constituting Matter that we are now studying in Quantum Mechanics can be described mathematically. They too are fragments of consciousness – quantum particles of *CONSCIOUSNESS*, born of the Mind, that transcend into the *PHYSICAL*. Subatomic particles are the Mind's precursors to the fabric of Reality and all that makes up the Cosmos, both seen and unseen. And being of – and inseparable from – the Mind, they can be ultimately manipulated by the Mind to dematerialise and materialise across Time. Every child ever born has materialised into a co-ordinate of Spacetime, with quantum particles fed through an umbilical cord gradually coalescing and organising into a physical form. The Physical Medium's umbilical light cord during phenomena is just the visible quantum template of the same physicalised cord that feeds a foetus. In short, the Mind is a time machine.'

A silence hung in the air.

The door to the library opened and Isaac glanced in. "Nathan?" he called out, scanning the empty room. "Nathan?"

Isaac closed the door behind him again, assuming that his young protégé had already left, and made his way to the main house.

Nathan had vanished.

35

....
....
....
....
.... *BLUE* ....
....
....
....
..... *SUSPENDED IN LUMINOUS ELECTRIC BLUE* ......
....
....
....
....
....

Nathan's awareness had again been lost to an electric blue plasma of nothingness. A *nothingness* that contained the sheer totality of *everything*. An infinity of ultimate contradiction.

A place where the polarities of perceived Reality collapse so that such notions as *positive* and *negative*; *light* and *dark*; *right* and *wrong*; *good* and *evil*; *love* and *hate*; *them* and *us*; *up* and *down*; *north* and *south*; *near* and *far*; *known* and *unknown*, *matter* and *antimatter* are all rendered meaningless – their collisions cancelling each other out to equal zero, revealing the true nature of physical Reality and its source. A place of creation and annihilation. A place where nothing need have come before, because nothing can truly be said to have come after. A Zero Point Void of Consciousness. An interface between physical *existence* and *nonexistence*. A place of perfect balance mirrored in the language of the psyche by the symbols = and *0*.

Nathan's awareness began to kick in again as the plasma of *BLUE* dissipated to a familiar wall-less prison cell of endless *WHITE*. But the blank Void abided only for a moment before the emptiness was disturbed by another of those singularities of sound burgeoning into the deafening crescendo of a spine-chilling scream – *Aaaaagh!* The contorted face of Alex launched into his vision. She was gagged and tears streamed down her face and neck to join thin rivulets of blood running down from multiple needles that had punctured and defaced the once flawless skin of her naked breasts. He heard her give a muffled pleading whimper before her body jerked again with agony – *Aaaaaagh!* Nathan was sickened and overwhelmed. Witnessing that torture was more than he could stand. The perpetrators were close, standing around her, and he knew Caleb must be amongst them. He wanted to scream in anger but had no voice that would be heard. He wanted to rip out his brother's heart but had no hands with which to claw and tear. He wanted to weep but had no physical tears to shed. Most of all, he wanted to escape what he was seeing and escape his inability to save Alex but was trapped by whatever unknowable force was holding him in this place.

That dizzying sense of vertigo hit again as the scene suddenly fragmented and crumbled, leaving him in a superluminal freefall that defied his wildest imaginings and surpassed any sensation he had experienced before. All flashes of imagery fell away in his descent until all that was left was the white void. He was nothingness falling through nothingness. A white ghost invisibly transiting a realm of pure white. And without any external parameters to relate to, other than the passing of Time, he felt once more as if he was momentarily suspended – hanging motionless – despite his unimaginable speed.

A sudden jolt. A sideways slip. He was out of control and aware of falling once again. Some gravity that had spontaneously emerged was pulling on him…

"Nathan…"

He recognised the girl's voice and those same repeated words…

"Nathan…"

She called to him like she had done so many times before, and somewhere ahead in the oblivion, she was begging him to follow…

"NATHAN!"

The girl's abrupt insistence focused his attention, and yet more imagery began to swamp the Void. Nathan had no idea as to where or when he had been thrown but felt unnerved in the dimly lit confined space in which he now found himself. On scanning the scene, he saw the figure of the girl he'd encountered at his apartment come into view over by the far stone wall. The swirling translucence of the girl's light body appeared denser and more physical than before – her presence was, this time, almost palpable. She now mouthed inaudible words and pointed to something at floor level over by the wall, but Nathan couldn't make out what he was being shown. And in her frustration at not being heard or understood, the figure swept rapidly away across the low-ceilinged room only to drift back to approach Nathan more closely. Her features were clear. A young and pretty face. A lithe athletic physique. *Who was she? What did she want?* The phantom reached out and beckoned to him to take her hand. The gesture was compelling but Nathan resisted. For all he knew, the consequences of contact in such an ethereal state could be catastrophic. It had taken weeks for the abdominal burn he'd received to heal following their last encounter, and in this seemingly inescapable dimension in which he was trapped, he just couldn't take that risk. He craved physicality again – a physicality that he now understood was no more than a thought away. An intention. A purposeful mental step of faith into the unknown. But this location felt dangerous, and he feared that he might never escape from it.

The girl fleetingly found a voice. *"Please help me... I can't live through this anymore..."* Her pleading words ebbed and flowed through Nathan's thought field in her struggle to communicate, before becoming inaudible again and then resounding back as if caught and propelled by the wind.

"...You're the last Guardian across Time, Nathan... HELP ME...! Before it's too late!"

With that final plea, the girl's light body shot towards him, exploding again into his being and fragmenting all the imagery into nothing but whiteness. This time, Nathan managed to absorb the seismic onslaught that was her pain, and as the impact of her energy subsided, he finally understood her pleas. She had somehow become trapped in a formless existence with no way out.

The terrifying thought that he, too, may already be irretrievably trapped in a looping moment of Time gripped him again for a second before the words of Isaac suddenly echoed out of nowhere... *"The Void can be a frightening place unless you remain fearless..."* Isaac's instruction had not let him down. *"All manner of memories will force themselves upon you in that realm... That's why it's crucial to remain on your guard at all times and maintain control with a concerted mental effort."* Survival depended on regaining control, so Nathan set about surrendering all thought from his mind, concentrating single-pointedly on the emptiness and resisting all intrusion into the stillness in which he was existing. Again, he found himself on that sheer precipice that was the portal to the physicality of his own Here and Now. And the fall back began.

Pullen stared at the monitor on his desk. The surveillance images he had been scanning through with the click of a mouse now revealed a shot of Nathan Carter talking with an older man at the cemetery – a man who was instantly recognisable. Pullen clicked back and forth between the surveillance shot and the image of the previously unidentified unconscious male that Fitzpatrick had managed to snap surreptitiously on his phone, through a protective ring of distracted medics, when he had been the first officer to respond to the incident at St Mary's A&E. Fitzpatrick had known that the photo procured would never be admissible, but he had worked with Pullen long enough to have learnt to throw the net wide and take chances in an investigation. Legalities could always be worked through later in building a case once a suspect had been identified from amongst even the most innocuous or outwardly irrelevant of information amassed.

Pullen clicked between the images. Fitzpatrick had done well. By the time he'd seen fit to call him in to St Mary's on account of the incident being anything but routine, the naked man had already been stabilised and transferred to Radiology for brain scans. And since the unconscious patient had mysteriously disappeared from ICU shortly afterwards, but for that image on the resourceful detective's phone, this potential co-conspirator – resurfacing as one of the mourners at the funeral of Carter's aunt – would probably have never been identified as being the very same man that went missing from A&E. Tracing the registration number of the vehicle he'd been photographed getting into when leaving the cemetery had taken just moments.

Pullen clicked back to the scant police reports he had pulled up on Isaac McKinnon. The records showed surprisingly little contact with the law, but what dealings he did have were highly relevant. Alex Stanton had been brutally assaulted both physically and sexually. And McKinnon had been arrested as a young man for fracturing someone's skull in a brawl and then questioned years later over allegations of sexual assault. The matter of the violent assault had been referred to the military justice system as he was a private in the Army at the time, and he had been released without charge on Part 4 Bail concerning the sexual assault allegations. But Part 4 always smelt to Pullen. The guilty were inevitably amongst the innocent walking out of the station doors when, frustratingly, there wasn't quite enough evidence to hold them any longer. Pullen had also learnt from bitter experience that computer records of events prior to the late 1980s were notoriously unreliable. In that man-intensive period of inanely transferring paper records to computer hard drives, inevitable human error meant that omissions and blatant inaccuracies were common, leaving Truth and Fact the unfortunate casualties of the new electronic era. Pullen suspected there could be more to Isaac McKinnon than what those few scant computer entries were showing.

Pullen clicked back to the shot of Isaac McKinnon on the hospital bed and stared at the image, unsure of what was troubling him. With another click, a close-up headshot of Nathan Carter filled the screen. Outwardly, the young doctor looked an unlikely suspect, but the experienced detective knew full well that the most dangerous of murderous psychopaths do not present foaming at the mouth with glazed staring eyes. They are more often than not intelligent and seemingly personable individuals possessing the ability to draw their victims in with a charming smile and friendly demeanour that belies their depraved motives.

Pullen mulled over the facts as he stared at the photo: Carter was known to the victim, Alex Stanton, and by all accounts they'd had a casual ongoing sexual relationship, which phone records did tend to substantiate – a fact that a shaven-headed Carter had played down at the time, Pullen recalled. Carter's inner-city apartment was also not too far away from the canal where the victim had been found dumped, and the group of early-morning joggers that had come across the body had reported seeing at least one shaven-headed individual fleeing the scene as they'd unexpectedly rounded the bend in the tow path. Most damning of all, though, was Nathan Carter's blatant lying over McKinnon's suspicious admission into hospital. Throw in a sniff of McKinnon's potential for violence and sexual abuse and the foundations of a case could be made against the pair.

The dilemma facing Pullen was the usual one when any investigation begins to pick up pace. He had enough suspicion to want to bring Carter and McKinnon in for questioning, but in cold stark policing terms, any lawyer would rightly argue that he possessed little more than the fact that Carter had simply *known* Alex Stanton and that McKinnon had apparently *chosen* to discharge himself from hospital care following a cardiac arrest. Even the grainy CCTV footage from the park was such poor quality that it would likely be more useful to a defence team. That just left professional misconduct on Carter's part in that spurious hospital admission, which was a matter for the health authorities and didn't amount to anything he could use. If picked up, they would undoubtedly be out in a few hours. Pullen's instincts alone weren't enough to gain a warrant to search both of the suspects' properties to look for any incriminating evidence, and any such contact with the police would do little more than alert the pair, allowing them to cover their tracks by destroying evidence. On the other hand, sitting and waiting for another victim to go missing and turn up mutilated and dead was not an acceptable option.

Pullen suddenly clicked back to the police reports, his actions possessed by some glimmer of realisation surfacing rapidly from his subconscious before it sank back into the depths. He stared at the screen for a second or two with a keen focus before decisively clicking back onto that singular image of McKinnon's unconscious frame lying on the bed. "What's wrong with this picture?" he muttered to himself, unable to grasp what had been subliminally troubling him. Pullen snatched at the phone receiver. "Get me everything you can on Isaac McKinnon," he barked at Fitzpatrick. "I want everything from his favourite pizza topping to how he could afford that damn house... And find out who the girl is with Carter at the cemetery. She could be in danger."

Pullen pressed *PRINT* before standing to grab his jacket as the first of two sheets of paper edged their way slowly from the mouth of the printer. The words 'IDENTIFYING CHARACTERISTICS: *Large tattoos of eagles on both forearms.*' could be seen emerging on the copy of the old police report that had caught Pullen's eye; the second sheet edged out of the printer, slowly revealing the image of an unconscious McKinnon lying in hospital – his exposed arms possessing no such identifying marks.

The synapses in Nathan's cerebral cortex began to fire and reconnect, leaving the pleas for help uttered by the girl still echoing within the auditory centres of his brain. Opening his eyes in confusion, he found himself lying naked next to a pile of his own clothes on the floor and flailing aimlessly in his attempts to stand. The girl's voice continued to reverberate through his mindstream... *"Please help me. I can't live through this anymore!"* He grabbed for the edge of the wooden table to heave himself unsteadily to his feet. And with a final surge of awakening, the echo of those pleas faded into subconsciousness along with those visions of Alex's fate.

"Good God!" Isaac exclaimed in shock, on entering the Library again and rushing over to Nathan, whose nakedness left no doubt in Isaac's mind as to what had occurred in his absence.

36

The pair sat at the table in the Library talking for some time after Nathan had sufficiently recovered. He was not in the mood now for anything but definitive answers, and since Isaac had just invited him to view The Sanctuary's archives, it was likely that the enigma of a man was finally ready to provide them.

"So the burn you suffered that day you turned up unconscious at A&E involved an experimental séance with Hugh that went wrong?" Nathan asked.

"It wasn't the experiment that went wrong," Isaac replied. "Something else was at play. Something unforeseen and more powerful than I've encountered before. Unfortunately, I've had no communication with Hugh since and have no idea how he was affected. The last entry in his notes is from the day before the experimental séance in 1929. After that, the trail goes cold."

Nathan was beginning to piece things together. Even in those hours following the cardiac arrest in the car park of St

Mary's – and his subsequent disappearance from Intensive Care – Isaac had remained guarded about disclosing the full extent of what he'd been involved in, despite being pushed for critical information so that urgent medical care could be given. Nathan had recognised the ectoplasmic burn as being similar to the one he himself had suffered in his apartment, but it had been Barbara's concerned bedside interjections that had forced Isaac's hand. Even then, his perfunctory explanations had been limited to some feverish gibberish about 'quantum vacuums' and 'genetic resonances' that had made no sense whatsoever and seemed of little relevance to the pressing medical emergency being faced at the time.

Nathan thought for a moment. "Mia mentioned something about the séances here at The Sanctuary being suspended in the early 1930s. Do you think that Hugh purposely chose to break contact with you after what happened in the experiment?"

"Quite possibly. But we know from Births, Deaths and Marriage records that not long after the experiment Hugh fathered a daughter before succumbing to an aggressive cancer in 1931. Other than that, we know nothing about the intervening period. It's as though all trace of him had been wiped clean."

Nathan took another moment in an attempt to reconcile everything that he'd learnt. But his thoughts were suddenly distracted by something registering in his peripheral vision as Isaac reached over the table to flick through a pile of papers. Isaac seemed somehow different – then it dawned. Both of the impressive eagle tattoos on Isaac's arms had vanished.

Isaac noticed Nathan's gazing confusion and stopped mid-reach to present both of his forearms in response. "I'm surprised that you didn't notice when you were examining me in A&E," he said with a smile. "Those bad boys are hard to miss."

"You're telling me that they've been missing since you dematerialised?"

"I'm afraid so. The pigments aren't a part of our essential being, so they just drop out of the air as dust. I even had to have three filled molars removed as a precautionary measure when I first started here. That's commitment for you."

Nathan reached for the sleeve of his T-shirt and tugged it back to reveal the skin of his right upper arm. The black and grey wolf tattoo that had adorned his shoulder since he was eighteen had vanished, too.

"It seems that on rematerialising, new quantum particles are only ever drawn to the template of our true energy body," Isaac continued, "while any substance produced by our cells or hydrated through our bodies tends to reconstitute along with us... Which is fortunate. It'd be a life-threatening prospect resulting in messy floors covered in faeces, stomach contents and blood otherwise!"

Nathan was left still staring at his shoulder in disbelief.

"Why some matter doesn't reconstitute we just don't know yet. That's Anne-Marie's main line of research." Isaac gave a final resigned look. "It's a great way of removing tattoos, though... A pity. I'd grown quite attached to them."

The reality of what had happened in the Library finally struck home. In coming around to find himself naked, no amount of reasoning would lead to the conclusion that he had actually lost physicality. On the contrary, reasoning would only suggest that he had simply undressed while in an oblivious altered state of mind – an act that the delusional, the diabetic and the hypothermic in crisis are regularly caught doing. But the absence of the tattoo proved otherwise. This time, in the journeyings of his mind, he had undoubtedly dematerialised and slipped through Time in a discarnate state, devoid of his physical self.

"I knew from the very outset that you were a natural," Isaac said, "but this is very powerful. If you can dematerialise and rematerialise here, then it's only a mental step for you to actually physicalise in whatever spacetime coordinate your consciousness has traversed to. Hugh and I had to prepare for years to achieve what you've just come close to accomplishing on your own. It's incredible. Perhaps you have some degree of genetic resonance with someone in The Sanctuary's bloodline. After all, the whole of humanity is genetically connected one way or another."

Nathan frowned, remembering the last time he'd heard Isaac utter the words *genetic resonance*, and his attention darted back to the papers still spread out on the table, his eyes scanning across the array of sheets for the document headed *Genealogies* that he'd flicked through earlier.

Seeing that his protégé had already made the connection, Isaac saved Nathan the effort and reached over for the document and, after turning to the relevant page, tossed it over to him.

Nathan studied the typed schematic of the family history presenting in front of him. "Isaac… This means you're related to Hugh!"

Isaac nodded. "Hugh's my grandfather. This shows the Cavendish Line back to the 1860s when the Circle first began."

"So Hugh was an outsider who married into The Sanctuary's bloodline?"

"Well, not all of The Sanctuary's sitting Mediums have descended from the Cavendish family. The traits predisposing to Mediumship often skip a generation or two before showing up again. It just wouldn't be viable to rely on family members alone. It was just coincidental that Charles Cavendish's daughter, Marjorie, happened to fall in love with and marry Hugh, the Circle's Medium of the day." Isaac paused for a second. "But take a look at the previous page," he suggested, with more than a hint of intrigue in his voice.

Nathan immediately flicked back a page to find an almost identical handwritten schematic drafted out showing the later years of the Cavendish family line from around the 1920s. He recognised it as the same scrawling handwriting that had filled the pages of Hugh's notes. And while the entries in both the handwritten fragment and the typed history were largely the same, there were some notable discrepancies.

Nathan looked back at Isaac with a confused shrug.

"The first printed history I showed you is a conventional one, compiled from records of Births, Deaths and Marriages. The second handwritten one was Hugh's attempt to predict a family history in a Trance state, by clairvoyantly perceiving what the future would hold."

"A predicted genealogy?"

"Not a bad effort on Hugh's part." Isaac smiled proudly, visibly in awe of his forbear's psychic prowess. "That's how Hugh first tracked me down across time in choosing a future genetically resonant descendent to work with. But he was by no means the first to attempt such a feat," Isaac quickly added. "The other genealogies you have there were all prepared in Trance in attempts to identify future Mediums who would sit in the Circle in years to come. Hugh simply adapted the protocol to his own needs, directing his efforts solely towards his quantum research."

Nathan rapidly thumbed through the other sheets to reveal countless similar scrawling efforts in various hands from over the years. He shook his head while studying the similarities and discrepancies between the predicted and actual genealogies, his mental faculties in overdrive, grasping for the countless questions now formulating deep within his mind. "These incorrect entries," he finally asked, pointing at Hugh's scrawling version, "are they blatant mistakes or do the names appear somewhere else in the family line?"

"Interesting question," Isaac replied. Nathan was not disappointing him. "When psychically reaching out over many decades into the future, there's inevitably going to be errors – the odd omission, a misspelt but recognisable name or a misplaced aunt misrepresented as a sister, and so on. And, of course, frank mistakes too. But we have to wonder whether or not Hugh was, in fact, correct at the time of penning the entry," Isaac added with emphasis. "It opens up the whole question of free will versus preordained destiny. Perhaps some unexpected event or accident prevented a particular marriage that Hugh had initially and correctly foreseen and that would have otherwise led to a particular birth – history would then have suddenly taken a different path. That's where the parallels with Heisenberg's work and Schrödinger's quantum mechanical work on Probability Waves become interesting," he added. "Everything exists in a flux of virtual possibility until just one of the possibilities eventuates and all the others collapse. But it would be wrong to assume that all possibilities constituting a Probability Wave are equally as likely in actual terms. Otherwise, there'd be nothing but Chaos in this universe and physical existence would never have eventuated."

Nathan fell silent and flicked back to the typed historically correct version of Hugh's family tree. Something else was troubling him and he found himself studying the page for several seconds, the printed entry of Isaac's name holding his focus: 'Isaac Aaron McKinnon,' it read, and Nathan mouthed out the words to himself slowly as he considered them.

He did a double take before looking up at Isaac. "I, A, M!"

"Yes," Isaac confirmed, having been watching Nathan's mind ticking over. "My full initials are I. A. M."

The cryptic proclamation of 'I AM' that was scratched into the séance room floor finally held a meaning.

"One of Hugh's protocols to confirm my physical presence in 1929 was being instructed to scratch my initials in the floor for posterity. Hugh actually scratched the first set of initials himself in the séance-room floor in his preparations for the experiment. He needed to know if the flooring would scratch readily and what tool was sufficient and whether the implement could be found easily enough by me in the blackout conditions… Seems my writing was as skewed as his in the darkness," Isaac said with a laugh. "It has certainly been amusing how many people over the years have attached lofty spiritual meanings to our careless uneven scrawls. Several have been entirely convinced that 'I AM, I AM' was a sign that the Almighty Himself had paid a visit in one of the séances." Isaac grinned broadly. "Exodus 3:14! *Ehyeh asher Ehyeh*; *I am I AM*. It's the biblical name that God used to identify Himself to Moses in the Old Testament."

Nathan was by now too fascinated to respond to Isaac's

show of irreverence. "Didn't you ever recall having carved out those initials when you very first came to The Sanctuary?" he asked, eager to make sense of the incredible revelation.

"Not at all. I was just as intrigued by the markings as anyone else when I first arrived. The subconscious mind reclaims many of the memories of our experiences in Trance. Even on reading Hugh's experimental notes and instructions passed down to me across Time, I'd simply assumed that the two sets of I AMs had been scratched in by Hugh himself in his preparations. Little did I know that I'd been responsible for one of them myself back in 1929. But the existence of lettering carved out by me eighty-five years in the past, before my future-self found cause to traverse back to carve out that very lettering, certainly opens up a mind-bending philosophical can of worms," he admitted. "Such are the paradoxes thrown up when meddling with Time."

Nathan's mind was still spinning with all that he'd had to take in. "Thanks for letting me see the records, Isaac. It means a lot," he said, well aware of the trust that had been extended to him.

"Well, the time had to be right. As I said, I haven't been the best of Guardians." Isaac became momentarily pensive, realising that he'd just been provided with the opening he'd long been waiting for. The moment had finally come. "Perhaps you will do a better job in your tenure?" he added, in a questioning tone.

Nathan returned Isaac's gaze as the subtle instant of transition passed seamlessly in the silence between them. Although he had initially been under Isaac's guidance out of a need to quell and control the psychic instability that had plagued him, the fact he was being groomed to take over the Circle had never been spoken of. Ever since he'd learnt from Mia how new sitting Mediums had been chosen at The Sanctuary, it had been obvious to Nathan that Isaac had all along seen him as a successor. The scrawled entry he'd viewed in Isaac's journal predicting the date of his first visit was evidence enough of that. But up until the last hour or so, he'd considered Isaac's unspoken notion far-fetched. Now all that had changed. Having the free will to either refuse or accept the tenure presented the greatest dilemma he'd ever faced along his life's path. In truth, he didn't know how he could avoid accepting the tenure. Nor could he know the consequences if he refused.

Isaac smiled. Nathan's silent response was enough of a tentative acceptance not to have to discuss the matter any further, at least for the time being. The Circle would be in good hands. But in his final act as sitting Medium, Isaac knew that he must now confront whatever negative forces seemed to be gathering to threaten them and The Sanctuary. It wasn't the first time over its history that The Sanctuary and its followers had come under attack, and it probably wouldn't be the last. Isaac just hoped that he was up to the task.

"Think back, Nathan. Is there anything else you can remember from your Trance states? Anything about the time or location you just travelled to? Anything at all. No matter how trivial or cryptic."

The whole experience had already faded like a dream on waking, and Nathan thought hard, desperately trying to grab wisps of memory from his subconscious.

"There was a girl!" he suddenly blurted, doubting its relevance and thinking twice before sharing it with Isaac.

"In Trance?"

"Yeah, I've seen her before. She said something strange about me being *the last Guardian across time.*" Nathan shrugged, at a loss to drag out any more of the memory and fully aware of how nonsensical it sounded. With all the talk of The Sanctuary's Guardians over the last hour, he even wondered if his mind was playing tricks on him.

All colour drained from Isaac's face. "What did you just say?"

Nathan answered with a questioning glance.

"Tell me how you know those words!" Isaac snapped aggressively.

Nathan was unsure how to respond. "Well, like I said, I vaguely remember a girl speaking to me when I was in Trance and—"

"Did you look inside the cabinet after I'd left?" Isaac snapped again, cutting him off and pointing in the direction of the display cabinet nestled under the window.

Nathan was at a loss to even guess at what transgression was supposed to have occurred. "No. Of course not!"

Isaac darted over to the glass-covered display cabinet and rattled the lid firmly to check that it was still locked. "Has anyone at The Sanctuary ever spoken to you about what's in here?" he demanded abruptly. "Think! Is there anyone?"

Nathan drew a blank. "Absolutely not. What's wrong?"

Isaac failed to answer and uncharacteristically fumbled with a set of keys from out of his trouser pocket before finally inserting a small brass key into the cabinet's lock. Lifting the lid to retrieve a small envelope, he carefully opened the sealed flap to check inside. His being slumped at seeing the contents still there and realising that Nathan had been telling the truth. Pulling out the small piece of paper secreted inside and raising it to within just a few inches of his face, Isaac began to read, squinting in order to make out the miniscule lettering cryptically prophesying the destruction of The Sanctuary to *rubble and dust* when the *last Guardian across Time* became known.

"What the hell's going on?" Isaac's obvious alarm was now beginning to infect him, too.

Isaac stared into space, his expression one of a man being forced to accept the inevitability of an impending defeat against superior forces. "We have to leave here immediately," he finally barked. "Everything must come with us. Everything!" he added, motioning to the contents of the cabinets and the documents covering the table.

Nathan looked on, none the wiser, perplexed at what could have inspired such a reaction in a man of Isaac's strength.

When Mia and Barbara eventually returned to The Sanctuary from their trip to the village, giggling to each other and girlishly swinging logo-emblazoned bags that announced their newly acquired designer garments, it was as if all hell had broken loose in their absence. Every cupboard and drawer in the usually immaculately kept house had been left open, with piles of contents left on the floor ready for packing.

"I've been trying to call you," Isaac snapped brusquely without a word of explanation as he continued busying himself.

"We had no reception," Barbara replied, glancing around the room, a frown creeping into her expression, trying to process the entirely unexpected scene. "Isaac! What on earth are you doing?"

At that moment, Nathan entered from the rear of the house carrying a suitcase in each hand and two large jewellery boxes wedged under each arm.

"My jewellery...?" she exclaimed, eyeing them with increasing confusion.

Isaac glanced across at her. "We needed something to transport the apports in." A solemn pause followed while he stared at her with the gravest expression she had ever seen on his face. "It ends here, Barbara," he uttered, a finality punctuating his delivery. "It's over... The Prophecy has been spoken," he added, glancing in Nathan's direction.

Barbara grabbed onto the back of an armchair to steady herself.

"Will someone tell me what the hell's going on?" Mia shouted, losing her usual composure before heading over to Nathan, who'd already placed his awkward load down next to a couple of half-filled packing boxes. A silence hung in the atmosphere, just as it had a couple of hours before when Isaac had asked for a moment's privacy while he and Nathan talked, and from where Mia was standing, a lot seemed to have happened in that moment.

Barbara stared disbelievingly into space, tears welling in her eyes, needing no further explanation. Isaac walked over and placed a sympathetic hand on his wife's shoulder while motioning for Mia to take a seat.

"We haven't much time," Isaac said, reaching inside his pocket and pulling out the small envelope that contained the ominous prophecy by way of explanation. "We must leave here immediately."

37

Hugh's hand again rested on a sheet of foolscap – the slowly expanding tell-tale blot of blue Indian ink from the nib of the pen in contact with the paper marring the otherwise blank pristine page – and several minutes elapsed before there was any sign of movement. With eyes closed, he finally drew in the deepest of breaths. And as if fuelled by the prolonged subdued sigh of exhalation that followed, the pen he was holding in his now dithering hand began to move eerily across the page, its wanderings recorded by the wavering blue line issuing from the nib. The traverse would stop and start erratically, only to shoot back across to the left margin and continue again in a broken line as the nib repeatedly lost contact with the paper's surface, leaving short stabbing ink marks in its wake, and with yet another sigh from Hugh, the nib began scratching at the surface of the paper once more. A letter began to form out of the trail of ink… N… The nib stopped momentarily, as if the effort had been too much, before the dithering hand continued on, leaving more short stabbing ink marks on the surface of the paper between the letters... I... CHO... LAS... MO... SLEY...

After some time, Hugh roused and opened his eyes. He centred himself and gathered his focus from out of the rapidly dissipating ethereal haze that was clouding his mind, and looking down, he gazed upon the fruits of his efforts – always a moment filled with intrigue and anticipation. This time, his involuntary scrawling in Trance had revealed something entirely unexpected. The fragmented genealogy before him opened again with the roughly scribbled yet decipherable name of *Nicholas Mosley*, but the centre of the page also offered up the name *Oswald Mosley*, with the indication of a future illegitimate son of his by the name of *Fredrick*. What Hugh saw next filled him with dread. Orphaned on its own to the bottom left of the page was the name *Nathan*, while over to the right margin the genealogical scrawling of the Mosley line ended with the name *Caleb*. And written in between both the names, as if in someone else's hand, was the word *KILL*. The existence of a future Mosley bloodline could only mean that the Dark Circle at the Hall would not be overcome in his own lifetime, whatever efforts were made. He would have to look to the future if he was to stop them. *But which one to kill?*

Hugh dropped the pen and took a few moments to recover his senses fully, unaware that behind him the last translucent flicker of the discarnate light body that had guided his hand to write *KILL* had just vanished back into the Void.

"The road is long... this white line's my friend... that I'm foll-ow-in'..."

Jim Cooke reached forwards to pump the volume on the dashboard radio, his strained enharmonic rendition of the latest favourite drivetime song being almost drowned out in the sonic onslaught issuing from the self-installed speakers rattling in the vehicle's door upholstery. "*From where I've come, the sun has sunk… be-hind two lanes. Yeah!*"

His right hand slapped out a heavy straight four on the steering wheel in time with the blaring music, leaving him momentarily transported out of his pitiful mediocre existence into that of a spotlighted frontman in an arena full of dazzled adoring fans. The lyrics would've truly told his life's story had he been cruising endless desert highways, armed with a six-string, instead of being the delivery driver he was. Still, a man needs to dream.

"*In the dance of a narrow beam, I got no sense of who I've been… or where I'm go-iiiin'*," he howled in a crescendo, his wavering hanging note craving resolution in the next power chord crash of the first beat of the chorus. But he was to be denied all resolution. He suddenly grasped onto the wheel tightly with both hands as an electrocuting paralysis gripped him. He strained for breath, his jaws clenched in an agonising spasm. The cacophony of sound inside the driver's cab now pounded inside his skull. *How could it end like this?* His eyes widened in terror as his vehicle began veering to the right into oncoming traffic, a flash of sapphire blue being picked up in the beam of his headlights a split second before his truck collided sickeningly with the Ford Sierra carrying a young family travelling on the opposite carriageway.

All was quiet. The red lamp was flicked on, throwing long threatening shadows across the floorboards and walls. The

Circle members, hollow-eyed in the dim miserly light, turned to one another expectantly as they let go of each other's hands. The words *A DIOCESE FOR TRUTH* could just be made out, carved across the back of the heavy wooden séance chair, the silhouette of a motionless figure sitting in the chair partially obscuring the ornately carved lettering.

"God forgive me," Hugh whispered to himself, having no way of knowing if his murderous attempt across time had been successful. They were the last words he would ever utter as The Sanctuary's sitting Medium – a prayer that there *was* a greater power that could offer him absolution.

38

Dear Isaac,

Rapidly failing health leaves me far too weak to communicate with you through our once usual means. Ironically, I am left with no other choice but to put pen to paper, rather archaically, and trust that you find this letter amongst the other documents I left for you. I say 'trust' as I am now bedridden and must rely on others for everything. A matter of great irritation for me. This damn cancer ravages me more each day, and the only relief from pain that I can occasionally find is within that stillness of Mind I have worked so hard to cultivate. My heart is heavy, though, as I near my end. I fear for what I have set in motion and feel only guilt for imposing myself across the century that separates us. I must inform you that our work has been usurped by individuals with motives that can only be described as evil. And what I have done in my attempts to stop them is just as evil.

Since our mutual experiment has already been performed between our times, it is obviously too late for me to prevent you from reading my experimental notes, so I can only pray that, in some future moment, after you accept the tenure and review The Sanctuary's archives, these words will serve to prevent you from ever embarking on our journey of the Mind across time. What I have glimpsed of a potential future leaves me fearing for the fate of humanity. And we are both to blame. The dark séances at the Hall and the Guardians of the Mosley bloodline are a threat to our very existence. They must be extinguished before they kill countless others. If I have failed in that, Isaac, you must not. The ones named Caleb and Nathan must die...

39

The two patrol officers scanned the empty apartment. Despite an overturned chair in the lounge area, a table lamp lying on the floor and the front door having been found ajar, the concerned neighbour's report of muffled screams amidst some kind of brief physical altercation didn't inspire so much as a raised eyebrow from either of the beat-hardened cops. This was the third domestic they'd responded to that night, and the half-packed suitcase abandoned on the bed surrounded by piles of hurriedly folded clothes said it all. The young professional woman, Mia Kerr, who according to neighbours had lived at the apartment block for a couple of years, could easily have forgotten to shut her front door amidst the heightened emotion of rushing out after a scorned love interest in some heated lover's squabble. Packing to leave, after all, is the oldest gesture in the book when it comes to domestics.

NATHAN. Early thirties/athletic build/dark hair. Silver Audi TT, one of the officers jotted down in his notebook from the information he had gleaned from the worried neighbour. 'Find the boyfriend and you'll more than likely find the missing girl cuddled up in his arms' was the immediate conclusion. But the scene would be preserved in any case and a report logged, with routine follow-up intended to track down the missing girl if she didn't show up. But show up they usually did.

> *... Isolates of Dimethyltryptamine (DMT) are known to break down rapidly due to the effects of the enzyme Tyramine Oxidase in the gut, so oral administration to subjects is ineffective. It is of note, though, that the DMT-rich Ayahuasca infusion traditionally used by Amazonian Indians in their shamanic rituals does remain psychoactive when imbibed, suggesting that some chemical inhibitor to the gut enzyme is naturally present in the ingredients which limits the rapid breakdown of DMT on ingestion – this would account for uptake into the bloodstream at levels adequate enough to induce mind-altered states. In order to extend those mind-altered states in duration through intravenous administration, further research is necessary to isolate the chemical inhibitor present in Ayahuasca and determine the extent to which the enzyme Tyramine Oxidase suffuses the entire body. No Jew, as yet, has exhibited any observable side effects from the administration of DMT. It is suggested that doses be increased to determine fatal levels while administration directly into the cerebrospinal fluid via lumbar puncture will be investigated...*

Sitting on the treatment table in a forwards lean, Caleb took several slow breaths and sank deeper into a relaxed state with each exhalation. He could feel the spinal needle puncturing the skin and advancing between the lumbar vertebrae but registered no pain or discomfort. The need for preparing the site with local anaesthetic had been dispensed with months before; such was his mental control now. He sensed the surgical steel being pushed even deeper through the tough ligamentous tissue until there came a familiar 'pop' as the tip of the 6-centimetre-long needle broke through into the fluid-filled space at the base of the spinal canal. The most delicate part of the procedure now complete, he was finally able to surrender and relax fully into a deepening self-induced meditative state.

Anne-Marie removed the long central stylet from the core of the main needle and collected four vials of the cerebrospinal fluid dripping slowly from the needle's hub projecting out of the lumbar spine of her subject. Setting the collection tubes aside for later testing, she then temporarily re-inserted the stylet back into the main needle while she loaded two separate syringes from a vial of DMT isolate. Caleb's blood levels of Moclobemide were optimal – the Monoamine Oxidase Inhibitor having proven the most effective of the commonly prescribed antidepressant medications trialled. Holzer's experimental notes appropriated from concentration camps had proven invaluable. The enzyme Tyramine Oxidase had been renamed Monoamine Oxidase in 1939, and Anne-Marie had instantly realised on first reading the notes that the mystery inhibitor Holzer had been searching for in Ayahuasca was now a pharmaceutical all too readily available in tablet form to control the angst of millions. She had also realised that the effects of Moclobemide would ensure adequate durations of the altered states produced by DMT in her experimentation.

Anne-Marie slowly depressed the plunger of the syringe, gradually forcing the psychogenic drug directly into the spinal fluid. It would soon bathe every nerve root emerging from the entire length of the spinal cord, and as it diffused around the cerebrum and on into the communicating network of cavernous ventricle cavities within the brain, no part of the central and peripheral nervous system would be immune from the drug's effect.

Anne-Marie carefully removed the spinal needle and applied a small dressing.

"Relax. Breathe and relax," she whispered, as Caleb, who was well versed in the procedure, deepened his meditative state. "Just breathe and relax."

Picking up a second syringe of DMT, Anne-Marie extended his right arm to expose the veins in the cubital fossa. She injected the second load of DMT directly into Caleb's bloodstream…

The aqueous suspension jetted out of the needle tip nestled in the lumen of the vessel and was propelled away with a beat of the heart. At first, the pulsing venous blood sluggishly ascended the arm like a rollercoaster car making the slow ascent to the top of a treacherous summit. But when the blood finally rounded the arc of the subclavian vein and plummeted downwards through the superior vena cava and on into the right atrium of the heart, the next contraction saw the molecules of DMT rapidly coursing through the vessels of Caleb's chest cavity. Seconds later, the drug-contaminated oxygenated blood returning from the lungs spurted into the heart chambers once again, and with another powerful contraction of the left ventricle, the blood was ejected through the aorta and up into the vessels feeding the brain. The Trojan molecules crossed the blood-brain barrier as if it didn't exist, and on storming out into the neural tissues, the ensuing attack on the brain cells was met only with total surrender. With a spark of synaptic activity, the hypothalamus was finally breached and Growth Hormone flooded into the bloodstream to be delivered to every cell in every extremity of the body. And, all the while, a slowly progressing pincer movement of DMT molecules diffused throughout the spinal fluid to infiltrate the entire central nervous system from both within and without.

All sense of his physical being was now lost. In a hallucinogenic maelstrom, Caleb saw himself plummeting through the centre of his own trachea, the seemingly endless descent becoming tortuous with sharp twists left and right, until he was eventually ejected out into a freefall through a cavern of darkness. A Void. But without any parameters of dimensional Space or Time with which to refer to, his superluminal trajectory was rendered nothing more than a motionless hang. Caleb, in his Trance state, had lost all connection with physicality.

After only a cursory verbal warning to satisfy due procedure, Pullen gave the nod for the door to be forced open with a single swing of the ram, and a posse of armed police swarmed in to secure the apartment, which was found to be empty.

"Tear it apart!" were his only instructions as he strode into the modern open-plan apartment belonging to Nathan Carter. It was so immaculate that Pullen could be forgiven for thinking that he'd just walked through the looking glass into the cover shot of a lifestyle magazine, just as it had looked when he'd routinely questioned Carter there after Alex Stanton's body had been found dumped. Anything incriminating was likely going to be well hidden. Finding the latest girl to go missing still alive, albeit restrained and tortured half to death, would have been too much to hope for, but the mere possibility had been enough to obtain the search warrants he'd needed, given the circumstances. Pullen glanced at his watch. Units would already have executed warrants at St Mary's to search Carter's personal effects and apprehend him should he be found there, and by now, Fitzpatrick should also have gained access to Isaac McKinnon's residence a few kilometres away in the carefully synchronised operation. But the fact that Pullen hadn't heard anything yet meant that neither Carter nor the missing girl, Mia Kerr, had been found at either location. He only hoped that some evidence would be unearthed. It had been a long night of rushed operational preparations following Fitzpatrick routinely keying in the name *Mia Kerr* that previous evening – the name having been identified from a list of tenants living at the address to which he'd tailed Carter and the girl during surveillance. Pullen hadn't believed his luck when Fitzpatrick called him at home with news of a match with a missing persons report lodged only hours before – a report that had triggered a whirlwind of planning to secure the warrants and organise the raids.

Pullen paced around the apartment, overseeing his team of officers setting to work, expecting to be in for the long haul. But he didn't have to wait more than a few minutes before the issuing of the warrants became justified.

"Sir, I think you should take a look at this."

He walked over to the officer standing next to an open kitchen cupboard where the waste and recycling bins were kept. The usual array of cleaning fluids and spray cans had been removed one by one in the search, revealing a pile of glossy magazines secreted at the back of the cupboard and hidden from view by the water pipes and drains. Pullen shone the beam of a small pocket torch into the recess and illuminated the obscenity depicted on a partially visible front cover. "Sick Son of a Bitch," he uttered under his breath, with visions of Alex Stanton's mutilated body on the morgue slab immediately coming to mind.

With the evidence having been photographed in situ and processed, he pulled on a pair of gloves and braced himself to take a closer look. As disturbing a prospect as it was, his investigation left him with no choice but to look through the pages of graphic images showing such sickening torture. But even decades of hardcore police work could not have prepared him for what he would be faced with inside the covers. These were no magazines. They were pictorial catalogues of currently available girls, each conveniently identified by a number at the bottom right-hand corner of the page – to be ordered from to feed the depravity of sadists. Only a few leaves in, a series of photos over several pages recorded the systematic gang rape by masked men of a young woman whom he recognised all too well. A girl whose photo had been stuck to the whiteboard in his office for over six months. Jessica Mahr. The headshot of beaming prettiness had been placed in Pullen's hand by the grandmother, her arthritic trembling hand having reluctantly surrendered the snapshot. He could still feel the warmth of the old woman's skin as she'd clasped his hand in both of hers with a tearful plea to find her granddaughter – the twenty-year-old university student having been the seventh girl to be reported missing. And, like in all of those other cases, the disappearance had been so complete and clinical there had not been one single lead to follow up on, until her amputated limbs had started to show up at the refuse tip.

Pullen continued to search through the magazine with greater urgency, feeling nothing but guilt as he dismissively flicked past countless agonised faces equally deserving of pity, despite him not recognising them. He did recognise the centrefold, though. Staring up from the pages, her eyes pleading for mercy, was yet another of the abducted girls he had been investigating – the twenty-two-year-old, the third to go missing, was pictured with a red-hot branding iron hovering over her abdomen as she helplessly lay tied to a tabletop, spread-eagled and naked.

A grim-faced Pullen had his thoughts redirected by a second officer holding yet another evidence bag.

"Sir," he cautiously interrupted, offering the bag to the senior detective. Inside was a full-face leather zip mask identical to those worn in the obscene photos. Finally, Pullen had the proof he needed that the cases of all the missing girls were linked. And that link was Nathan Carter. He had to be the mastermind behind all of those vicious crimes. The fact that Carter had thrown all caution to the wind and risked bringing attention to himself by a second girlfriend of his going missing was undoubtedly a sign that his depravity was escalating, and it was a matter of urgency that he be found.

Pullen carefully placed the catalogues inside an evidence bag, having seen enough and frankly too sickened to look anymore. The thought that images of Alex Stanton's agonising torture and even death had also been published and distributed for promotional purposes in some unholy commercial enterprise nauseated him. He could only pray that Mia Kerr was unharmed and still alive and that Nathan Carter would be tracked down quickly and arrested.

40

"The place is swarming with cops, Nathan. And they're looking for you. Your face is all over the TV, for Christ's Sake!" Adam's voice was hushed yet full of alarm. He'd had to pick his moment in slipping out of the hospital to call and warn his friend. "They're talking to everyone. And your locker's been searched." Adam was torn as to whether he'd done the right thing in keeping tight-lipped about Nathan's whereabouts; keeping tight-lipped in the face of police questioning was another one of those knee-jerk social conventions stemming from his roots that he would always be hard-pressed to break. "What the hell's going on? They asked me about your relationship with Alex and wanted to know about Mia. Is she OK?"

Nathan was confused and didn't respond. The phone call had woken him from a dead sleep, and he was still groggy and trying to get his bearings in the unfamiliar surrounds of the farmhouse while Adam's voice ranted in his ear. He stifled a groan as he attempted to straighten his stiff neck and back, courtesy of spending too many hours in the armchair that he'd passed out in the night before. The emotion of the past week, along with several sleepless nights, had caught up with him at the most inopportune time. Mention of Mia, though, suddenly brought him to his senses, and he glanced over at the lounge room clock – 8 am. "Shit!" Nathan snapped, an uneasiness descending upon him. "Keep your phone with you, Adam. I'll call when I know what's going on."

Nathan hung up and leapt out of the chair before Adam even had a chance to reply. Mia was supposed to have arrived at the farmhouse at around 8 pm the night before, and he just couldn't believe that she wouldn't have woken him when she'd arrived. "Mia! Mia!" he shouted, racing through the house and glancing into the kitchen before heading up the steep narrow staircase two steps at a time. The beds in all the rooms were still made and had obviously not been slept in, and peering out of the bedroom window through the undrawn curtains, Nathan could see his car alone, parked in the driveway below.

He immediately dialled Mia's number and ran downstairs, but the call went straight through to her message bank. Becoming increasingly concerned, he tried both Isaac's and Barbara's phones, only to be faced with the same automated response. Nathan had suggested the farmhouse as a safe place they could head to in their haste to escape from The Sanctuary – a grateful Barbara and Isaac having said that they would arrive shortly after Mia, at closer to 9.30 pm, after packing up as much of their life as was feasible in the little time they had. It seemed the planned relaxing time away with Mia wasn't going to pan out, but it was the least he could have done considering Isaac and Barbara's obvious distress in their whirlwind decision to abandon their much-loved home.

Nathan tried Mia's home phone. No answer. Already having a case full of clothes packed into the trunk of the Audi in anticipation of their road trip, along with two jewellery boxes filled with apports and a couple of suitcases crammed full of the Library's documents taking up the front and rear seats of the compact sports model, Mia had insisted that she would finish packing at her apartment and then take her own car down to the farmhouse. But if she was still at home, it didn't make sense that she would ignore his call and let it go through to yet another answering service.

Bearing in mind Adam's warning about the police looking for him, Nathan hung up the very second he heard the first syllable of Mia's recorded message. Perhaps they were questioning her, too. He glanced over at the piles of documents from The Sanctuary's archives that were strewn across the coffee table and floor. He had been poring through them for hours that previous evening before falling into an unconscious sleep in his chair. Nathan also eyed the pile of folders that Mia had handed to him with a parting kiss through the open car window just as he was about to pull away from The Sanctuary. The most disturbing of the documents taken from AXIS was still perched on top of the pile where he'd left it, and he quickly grabbed the printout, holding out the hope that he had just woken from some nightmarish dream. The document was all too real. Nathan stared again in disbelief at the clinical report he had discovered displaying a full DNA profile and Blood Typing. It bore the name *Nathan Carter* and was dated the same day he had visited AXIS. His thoughts went back to Anne-Marie's inappropriate advances in her office that day and the deep scratches she'd inflicted to his back – her talons had collected as much testable material as any rape victim's fingernails ever had.

The same chill that had struck him the night before ran the full length of his spine on recalling the contents in the other disturbing AXIS folders spread across the coffee table. To have procured a testable sample could only mean that Anne-Marie had been covertly setting him up for something, and since he was now being hunted as a serial killer, the last thing he needed was a DNA sample out there that could be used against him in some way. Being framed for whatever unfathomable reason would only put Caleb and Bedlam in the clear, but any possible connection between them and Anne-Marie seemed implausible. Still, she was definitely involved in something. Her deceptiveness to Isaac, *The Quantum Energy Template of Physicality* paper and the experimental notes from Nazi concentration camps on the use of DMT were evidence enough of that.

Fear for Mia's safety was now setting in, and he had no choice but to head back to her place to see if she was OK. It was only a forty-five-minute drive, the southern limits of the city giving way quite abruptly to the rural setting Nathan had woken up to. But simply turning up there and knocking on her apartment door was no longer an option. Hearing that the police had raided the hospital in some dragnet operation could only mean that his worst fears had finally caught up with him. He was now a suspect in the murders of both Alex and the girl in the park.

It was obvious that he couldn't take the Audi now that the police were looking for him, so he grabbed the keys to Adam's old VW Kombi from the key rack by the back door.

Adam kept the vehicle at the farmhouse for the occasional off-road fishing trip and camping expedition. It looked like a heap but was as reliable as hell, and knowing that Nathan liked to keep the bodywork of his Audi sport pristine, Adam had freely offered them the use of the van during the planned vacation. Despite relishing the thought of driving the orange Kombi even less than the prospect of driving Mia's Fiat Panda, Nathan resigned himself to the fact that his own car would be a liability.

In case Isaac and Barbara had been delayed for some reason and turned up at the farmhouse, he scribbled out a note to leave on the front door explaining as much as he could and that he'd returned to the city in search of Mia. He then gathered together the AXIS folders, deciding that his mentor should take a look as soon as it was possible to meet, especially considering what had been gleaned in delving through The Sanctuary's archives and Anne-Marie's dossiers. Nathan also collected together the array of Tarot cards he'd found secreted throughout the eclectic cache of records that stretched a century and a half across time, fleetingly captivated again by the incredible artistry of the images. The curiosities wouldn't have inspired so much as a second thought if it hadn't been for the creased scrap of paper he had noticed when emptying the display cabinet of apports at The Sanctuary the day before. At some point in time, the small paper provenance label had obviously become separated to be left wedged and forgotten between the green felt lining of the base and the display cabinet's wooden sides. *THE LOVERS. Apported Tarot Card, Inaugural Séance, 4th November 1863. Sitting Medium, Spencer Cavendish*, Nathan had read, having teased it out of the gap with his fingers. Since no such corresponding Tarot card had been evident inside the cabinet, it had become immediately clear that not all of the apports had been on display, contrary to Isaac's belief. So when Nathan happened to stumble upon three other Tarot cards from the same deck – *DEATH, THE DEVIL* and *THE HIGH PRIESTESS* – secreted in the AXIS folders, some intrigue perpetrated by Anne-Marie had become apparent. And remembering also previously seeing *THE MAGICIAN* card secreted amongst the pages of the archives in The Sanctuary's Library, his unrelenting search for the missing card amongst the records to prove Anne-Marie's deception in not informing Isaac had begun. The search had taken several hours, and five other Tarot cards, along with one other provenance label, had been located before the AXIS records gave up *THE LOVERS*, making nine cards in all.

Nathan placed the two small provenance labels he'd found in his shirt pocket so he wouldn't lose them amongst all the papers and put the Tarot cards and relevant documents – along with the dossiers compiled on both him and Isaac – into one of the folders then headed for the shed where the Kombi was kept. It was time that he confided in Isaac to try and make sense of all the physical and psychic evidence that he had collected concerning Alex's murder. Perhaps Isaac could provide the missing link and now finally use his contacts in the police to nail Caleb and Bedlam, and even nail Anne-Marie if her involvement in framing him could be proven. Whatever covert work she was involved in at The Sanctuary likely held some vital clue.

The Kombi's engine spluttered into life, and as he pulled away from the farmhouse to make his way back to the city, his feeling of unease was only growing.

*

Even at a distance, the skin of Fitzpatrick's face felt as if it was burning in a mask of intense heat. He and his team stood and watched on impotently as smoke billowed from the roof of the historic building. The vicious flames eating at the fabric of the house danced threateningly some twenty metres into the air as multiple fire crews struggled to bring the fire under control. The blaze in the long separate annexe over to the left had already been extinguished, its roof having completely collapsed into the interior of the structure, freeing up crews to tackle the fire in the main building.

Still holding the warrant he'd intended executing at The Sanctuary, Fitzpatrick wondered if anyone had been trapped inside – McKinnon himself perhaps or the missing Mia Kerr. Torching the property might have even been an attempt to destroy evidence and cover tracks. And while that would make any further investigation all the more difficult, Forensics might still be able to salvage some threads of useful clues. He could only hope that his boss had met with more luck at Nathan Carter's city centre apartment. Pullen wasn't going to be pleased, and Fitzpatrick was dreading placing the *bad news* call, knowing full well that he would be hung up on after having been made to feel as though he had struck the match himself.

"DI Pullen…"

"Bad news, boss," Fitzpatrick opened, bracing himself for the onslaught.

Nathan frowned as he slowed in his approach to Mia's street and jolted to a stop midturn with a stab of the Kombi's brakes. Her apartment block up ahead was now a crime scene, with a small deployment of officers patrolling out front and a team of masked and suited Forensics officers meticulously combing the premises inside and out. Mia hadn't answered her phone for over an hour, and now he was faced with the shocking sight of police vehicles parked outside of the building with the pavement taped off. Whatever had occurred was serious. A cascade of unthinkable scenarios passed through his mind, and the blood drained from his face as nausea hit. Mia was either injured or missing or dead, and he knew full well that he would now be a suspect in that crime, too. Trembling as much with anger as fear, Nathan floored the Kombi to make his escape from the immediate vicinity. He needed to gather his thoughts as to what he should do next and had to force all that he knew about Alex's torture and murder out of his mind so he could focus. But those words uttered by Caleb – *I like your taste in women* – made that impossible. He switched off his phone as a precaution to prevent him from being tracked and flicked on the dash radio in case there were any news reports being broadcast as to what had happened. He just had to hold onto the hope that Mia was still alive and safe. Whatever her fate, he now knew that he had no other option but to hunt down Caleb and Bedlam.

41

9th November 1989, The Sanctuary

In darkness heavy with ominous cloud, a lightning flash lit the sky with fleeting clarity. But with it came a shattering thunderbolt from nowhere. A destroyer of all sanctuary. The illumining fingers of destruction struck the building with devastating effect, and though sure in its foundations for centuries, in a cruel instant, its fabric exploded into flames. *THE TOWER* – the eighth card to apport. It undoubtedly predicted a future catastrophe at The Sanctuary, and it could be no coincidence that countless souls that same day had come together and chosen freedom. The *Wall in Berlin*, according to the nonstop news reports, had just fallen.

An old woman's arthritic hand held the card as reverently as any Guardian that had come before. This time, however, she was removing the card and its provenance label from the display cabinet, along with the other cards that had apported in more recent years: *THE MOON* – its pale illumination hinting at the collective unconscious where nothing is as it seems, its gravitation threatening to draw anyone orbiting too close into a hellish long dark night of the soul; *THE DEVIL* – the shadow self, the beast within projected onto others in our own shame, and the card of *DEATH* – despised for being such an ever-present reminder of our impermanence.

It was clear to the old woman that two remaining cards had yet to materialise at The Sanctuary – the collection of cards when brought together were intended to form a traditional ten-card Celtic Cross Tarot spread, and there being only eight cards known to have apported to date, the spread was still incomplete. And it was imperative that it remained that way.

Her bent expiring frame shuffled across the Library floor and over to the antique safe that had been, in more recent times, relocated inside the recess of the long since redundant fireplace. Marjorie had just one last thing left to do before she left The Sanctuary for good.

42

11th October 1905, The Sanctuary

Lodge took his seat in the séance Circle. That he had a keen interest in psychic research was well known, and since being granted a professorship in Physics, it was common for him to be invited to any number of séances held by Mediums around the country who were vying for his endorsement as to their authenticity. This particular invite, however, promised to be a much more worthwhile affair. He had often heard talk about the work at The Sanctuary, and given that the eminent Parisian physician Charles Richet, known for his research into the workings of the Mind, was also an invited guest, it presented a real opportunity to further his understanding of Physical phenomena. Moreover, it was to be a séance distinct from any other he had attended before – an experimental séance the likes of which had never been attempted, and both he and Richet were acting as esteemed independent observers throughout the proceedings being held that evening.

Richet disagreed strongly with Lodge as far as a Life after Death was concerned: "All psychic phenomena can be explained by a physiological process, Oliver! A sixth sense that, despite its elusiveness, is no different to our other five," the Frenchman would constantly assert in their discussions that on the occasions they met would extend throughout an entire night until daybreak. "The light phenomena and apparitions we observe in these séances *must* have a substance and physicality. And I am convinced that the luminescent ectoplasm generated by the Medium is some key transitional substrate – halfway between Matter and pure Energy – that is worthy of the most intense scientific research."

Lodge respected the man greatly, despite their differing opinions, and could also not fathom why the scientific establishment – in knowing that Energy and Matter are equivalent, through Einstein's equation $E = mc^2$ – would not bother to consider what transitional substrate might be involved in that conversion to *physicality*. Richet had been the one to coin the term *ectoplasm* to describe what was undoubtedly being observed in the experimentally controlled séances. And although Lodge agreed that there was definitely an explainable physical basis to the phenomena, the Frenchman's unwavering pragmatic line of scientific reasoning frustrated Lodge in its failure to explain the manifestations of deceased individuals they had both observed and that were recognisable to multiple witnesses.

Richet nodded a polite acknowledgment to Lodge from across the candlelit room as he too took his seat to complete the Circle. And from out of the gathered intelligentsia present, the Circle Leader, a severe-looking man in his fifties wearing eyeglasses and formally dressed in jacket and waistcoat, stood and approached a low wooden table set in the centre of the ring of chairs, a table that Lodge had earlier examined himself after also having inspected the bindings of the Medium sitting over in the elaborately carved séance chair. Charles Cavendish, who had taken over the tenure from his father, was without doubt impossibly restrained, discounting any possibility of fraud on his part. The solid construction of the small table, too, in Lodge's estimation, was unremarkable except for the odd array of rectangular markings etched across the surface of its polished top.

The Circle Leader raised his left arm rather overdramatically in the air and showed everyone a small pile of Tarot cards held in the palm of his hand. Lodge and Richet had both already examined the cards that had been selected from a Tarot deck by Charles himself just prior to him being bound to the chair. Two of the cards making up the pile, however, had been retrieved earlier from out of the safe housed in the Library next door – Lodge having been advised that *THE LOVERS* had apported over forty years before in Spencer Cavendish's tenure, during the first séance ever held at The Sanctuary, while the *THREE OF SWORDS* had apported just weeks before in a séance held by Charles. A séance that had been the inspiration for the extraordinary experiment about to be attempted.

Satisfied that everyone had seen the cards in full view, the Circle Leader began slowly dealing them face up onto the table, carefully placing each individual card sequentially within the confines of the etched rectangular cells on the tabletop so that the vibrant images were clearly visible to everyone, despite the dim light conditions: first was *THE LOVERS*, placed just left of centre... the *THREE OF*

SWORDS was then laid horizontally across the face of *THE LOVERS*, partially obscuring it... Above that was placed *THE MAGICIAN*... Below, *THE HERMIT*... to the left, *THE HIGH PRIESTESS* and to the right, *THE DEVIL*. The first six cards now formed a small cross within a cross.

The Circle Leader paused for a moment and raised the remaining four cards he was still holding into the air once again, as if to confirm to the onlookers that there had been no sleight of hand in any of his actions. He then completed his task by dealing out the remaining cards in a single vertical row to the right of the double cross array, from the bottom upwards. *DEATH*, *THE MOON* and *THE TOWER* took their allotted places. And with a final 360-degree show of the last card, *THE HANGED MAN* was laid down and adjusted so it fit exactly within the lines of the topmost etched cell, completing the traditional Celtic Cross Tarot spread.

The objective related to Lodge was clear: *to communicate across Time*. In a deep Trance state, the Medium Charles Cavendish would attempt to warp the illusory fabric of Time and Space. And if the hypothesis was correct, the physical substance of the cards would first transmute into ectoplasm and then into pure energy – energy that constituted the mere potential for physicality. Then, through the ethereal wanderings of the Medium's mind across the hypothesised Zero Point Void of Consciousness, the energy templates of the dematerialised array of cards, seen to have apported away, would rematerialise in a future moment at The Sanctuary during a second séance to be held by Charles in just a few days time. At that point, a bridge across Time itself would be shown to exist – a portal connecting two points in Time through which anything might be possible. By including

THE LOVERS and the *THREE OF SWORDS*, both having apported previously, it was believed that those cards might in some way 'seed' the process. After all, apports had been known to dematerialise and vanish again spontaneously, so the atomic fabric of those cards could well retain some inherent instability in their physicality.

The Circle Leader prepared to return to his seat. His last task was to blow out the candles in a small candelabra hanging centrally over the table, plunging the séance room into darkness. There could be no question of impropriety or suggestion that he might spirit the cards away into some hidden pocket when the darkness ensued, so the onlookers had been instructed to hold hands in an impenetrable ring while the Circle Leader prepared to blow out the last flickering flame. Leaning forwards with both arms stretched behind him, his hands were grasped tightly by those sitting either side of his vacant chair, and through his pursed lips, a bellow of air extinguished the last vestige of light as he was guided backwards into his seat.

The atmosphere was oppressive and suffocating, and the lightless conditions were only made worse by the all-consuming silence enforced throughout the prolonged and interminable wait for something to happen. A wave of weak electrical charge finally crackled though the stagnant air, and a luminescence could clearly be seen emanating from the Medium's abdomen. The demarcated area of light expanded inexorably to engulf the table and cards and threatened to fill the entire room. But with a sudden crack of intense lightning, the luminescence imploded back towards Charles Cavendish, who began to scream as if burning to death inside some invisible flame.

Lodge could not afford to be distracted by everyone else's panic. Not even the sound of a man being burnt alive would distract his enquiring scientific mind once it was fully engaged on its objective. His intense gaze had not been averted from the table for even a split second. And in that final flash of ectoplasmic light before darkness ensued again, he witnessed that the tabletop was now empty. There had been no trickery involved. The cards *had* vanished through Time.

The withered fingers of Marjorie's dithering hands had somehow managed to negotiate the safe's door, and although it had taken her some time to retrieve the documents from inside, piles of The Sanctuary's historical cache were now spread across the top of the Library's large oak table. For a moment, sentimentality took hold as she reminisced over all those years, with her thoughts lingering on her darling Hugh, who'd passed away so many years before. She had always blamed his cancer on the emotional stress that he'd suffered after having turned his gift towards stopping what he had started in an attempt to avoid a catastrophic change across Time. More than anything, though, she blamed herself for ever telling Hugh about her father's experimental séances. Charles, too, had realised the terrible enormity of what he had set in motion and had done his best to erase the episode from history. But when Marjorie had unthinkingly shown Hugh the contents of the secret compartment in the base of the safe that she'd known of from being a child, with a click of the lever hidden in the roof of the vault, a Pandora's box of horrific consequence had been unleashed once again.

The fact that Hugh had been responsible for killing in the process was something that he had never recovered from. She knew it had tormented his every living second, thereafter, and their marriage nearly hadn't survived as a result. Hugh had been adamant that the truck driver – according to those clairvoyant wanderings in his Trance states – was fated to die anyway, by colliding with a tree a few kilometres further along the road. But in his attempts to prevent what he had glimpsed of the future, by reaching across time to kill off the dark bloodline, hapless innocents in that car had died, too. And even Marjorie, at eighty-nine years of age, still wasn't in a position to know if Hugh had ultimately succeeded. Only time would tell.

Marjorie's thoughts came back to the task at hand. She had to secrete the Tarot cards so they would not be found. The four cards that had materialised earlier in the history of The Sanctuary had been removed from display many decades before in the 1930s. Hugh, like Charles before him, had come to the conclusion that no one in any future Circle could know of the existence of the Tarot cards. Fearful of the unknowable consequences of destroying such apports from across the fabric of Space and Time, the decision had been made to secrete them away so that they would never be found while still preserving them. As a result of all the well-meaning duplicity, later Circles at The Sanctuary had mistakenly believed that the first card ever to apport had been *THE DEVIL* in 1939, but there were always those who would whisper of some veiled intrigue across the years. Simply destroying all record of Hugh's experimental notes would be just as futile, if not dangerous. The fact that Isaac had made contact in the séances from across the years meant he was already in possession of the work in some future time, and any attempt to avert that fact would create a whole new set of unknowable consequences. The safe's secret compartment was no longer an option. She couldn't take the chance that the entire collection of apported cards might be found again by others.

Marjorie eyed the letter Hugh had written to the future, which she had secreted in the safe's hidden drawer compartment all those years before as he lay on his deathbed. Her love for him remained unending, but the letter was a curse that she wanted no part of – the consequences to the fabric of Time in any attempt by her to destroy the letter were just as unknown. Promising Hugh that she would place the letter in with his experimental notes for Isaac to find was the only time she had ever lied to her husband. His scientific work had caused enough problems, and his inability to leave well alone, even in death, by writing the letter, could only make matters worse. That Isaac must never receive the misguided directive to kill again was clear to her, and this would be her last-ever opportunity to act. Marjorie set about concealing the Tarot cards throughout the thousands of historical pages and scoured the records again to double check that her prior efforts at removing any archival reference to the cursed apports had been thorough enough. And when her task was completed, she laboriously returned the vast body of documents back into the safe's interior.

Leaning on her cane, she glanced around the room, accepting that she would never set foot within these four walls again. Her long-held position as Circle Leader had, disappointingly, come to an end with no new Medium having been named to continue The Sanctuary's work. And now she had no choice but to leave the house she loved. She was growing weaker by the day and such a large house was beyond her, so its management was to be transferred to a Trust. It was her gift to the future. A new Circle would soon rise again at The Sanctuary, and those new Guardians, whoever they might be, would thankfully be oblivious to what was held in the records.

A tear rolled down her cheek, and with one last glance around, she slowly shuffled out of the room, closing the Library door behind her for the very last time. Her failing memory, though, and fatigue through all the exertion, had led her to forget to retrieve Hugh's letter from within the safe's secret compartment.

43

Mia's awareness returned with searing pain in her arms and wrists. It felt as if both her shoulders were on the verge of dislocation as she hung, spread-eagled, her limbs lashed to the thick diagonal members of a wooden cross. She fought the choking dryness in her mouth and throat and gasped for breath in the stale air of the surrounds. Light had been denied her by a blindfold bound tightly around her head that pulled painfully at the roots of a clump of her hair twisted in with the blindfold's vicious knot. Other than pain, the only parameter left for her to make sense of the nightmare she now found herself in was *sound*, and the only sound she could hear was that of her own panicked breaths as she struggled to come to terms with her plight – a hand placed across her mouth and an arm around her neck in a terrifying chokehold had been the last thing she'd remembered after realising someone had entered her apartment. She had screamed and tried to fight back but hadn't stood a chance.

Mia called out with a tremble in her voice. "Is there anyone there…? Please!"

Only silence answered.

Gritting her teeth through the pain, she kicked and writhed against her tethers, managing only to release an indignant scream of frustration on realising that her efforts were pointless. Whatever energy she had left, she had to conserve. At least in engaging her legs, she had been able to find a position that relieved some of the agonising tension on her shoulder joints, and she let out a weak relieved sigh.

The relief was fleeting. With the sound of a single *click*, her retinas suddenly burned with a barrage of light that penetrated through both the blindfold and her closed eyelids, her head unable to find a single pose that would allow her to evade the visual assault. She was not alone, after all.

Moments passed before she screamed out again into the pervading silence. "Who are you? What do you want?" she pleaded, the futility of her questions only heightened. No answer came.

Mia took a long inhalation and held her breath momentarily in an attempt to calm herself and regain control. She resolved not to play the game and wouldn't give whoever was there the satisfaction of seeing her helplessly squirm and sob. But her intentions dissolved in a stream of silent tears when she felt the cold steel of a blade against her right cheek. She froze, her eyes screwed up tightly behind the blindfold. The flat surface of the knife trailed slowly and sensually down her face and across her lips, where it lingered before continuing on to her left cheek and down over her jawline. There it was turned onto its cutting edge as it threateningly traversed her throat, moving with all the tenderness of a caring lover, the sharp tip depressing into her skin and pricking teasingly as it lost contact under the angle of her jaw. The terror of anticipation over those next few moments forced a gasp from Mia as she felt the tip of the knife make contact with her throat again before it slid rapidly downwards across her décolletage and under the collar of her T-shirt where it began violently ripping and sawing with increasing frenzy until the thick ribbing on the garment's neckband gave way. It felt as if another's hand was now holding the blade as it slashed through the remainder of the material, tearing it away to expose her waif-like upper frame. In the torturing silence that returned, Mia had to surrender to the thought of her assailant now surveying her exposed body, but any attempt to block out the demeaning physical and psychological assault on her person ended when the slow loving caress of steel gently resumed its journey across her abdomen. Fingers slid down the top of her shorts to grasp the waistband in a fist, the knuckles lingering for a moment against her stomach beneath her navel. Then the frenzied slashing and ripping started again.

Mia screamed, unable to control her reactions any longer. "No! Please stop!" she pleaded.

The remnants of her shorts fell away, leaving her hanging in just her bra and panties, and she began to cry uncontrollably, unable to bear the thought of her imminent fate.

"Well, just look at you, darlin'," uttered a man's voice approvingly, as Mia felt the knife being stroked gently up her inner thigh and across the material of her underwear.

The tension was broken by a second voice. "She'll keep. Let the little slut hang for a while," spat a female voice venomously.

Mia's confused thoughts had little chance to process

that Anne-Marie was one of the two attackers sharing the knife before Bedlam's powerful hand suddenly grabbed and squeezed at her tethered left arm in a tourniquet grip. She felt a painful hypodermic stab into her vein before the nightmare she was living through faded rapidly away from her awareness, along with the dawning consequences of having entered Anne-Marie's office simply to pick up those document boxes bound for The Sanctuary.

Nathan parked up within sight of Brophy's gym but far enough away that he wouldn't be noticed. Being a Sunday morning, the gym didn't open until 10 am, and the road up ahead was deserted except for some eleven-year-old boy on a BMX bike – no doubt stolen – cruising back and forth across the road in a decidedly unconcerned figure-of-eight circuit, nonchalantly flailing a cricket bat in one hand – no doubt procured from the same place as the bike – while using the wing mirrors of several parked cars for target practice as he rode around. No one would have dared approach him. A passing police patrol would probably think better of it themselves. Nathan knew from countless media reports that the area was a powder keg. It had been the scene of a number of riots in recent times that had shown the thin blue line to be lacking, despite the public spin police command had tried to put on the disorder. Several officers had been seriously injured recently when their snatch squads had been strategically outmanoeuvred, leaving them exposed and savagely kicked and stomped on. Only the bravery of their comrades and a threatening rush from mounted units had saved their lives. The kicks and stomps had been fully intended to kill or paralyse; either would have sufficed. What hadn't been reported in the media was that the volleys of petrol bombs regularly raining down on police shields were made and stored conveniently at hand days in advance of a riot, and any sense of the authorities taking back control of the streets was only ever sheer delusion. The streets cleared when, and only when, Brophy decided that his boys had had enough fun and needed to regroup in a nearby pub for a few well-earned beers on the house. The only rioters ever likely to be arrested in the carefully orchestrated events would be those outsiders left on the streets that had been successfully manipulated and whipped up into a frenzy. As for those of his associates that had political motivations for civil unrest, the skirmishes kept them satisfied and keen. For Brophy's own purposes, though, distracting the police and tying up their limited resources was all about timing when he had a warehouse to rob or a few truckloads of illicit cigarettes to hijack off some Eastern European gang he'd caught wind of. The streets were Brophy's. And the smartest of police knew better than to interfere.

Nathan watched on from a distance. Fortunately, the prepubescent delinquent's circuit stopped well short of where the Kombi was parked, so there was little chance of being seen. It was likely to be a long wait. Possibly even a wait of several days. But he had no other choice. The reports of Mia's abduction were now all over the radio, and this was the only location he knew for certain that either Caleb or Bedlam would at some point make an appearance. Nathan was gambling on Mia's safety that the pair had been involved in her abduction and would show up at the fight gym sooner rather than later. The only thing he could think to do was ambush Caleb when he was on his own and beat the information out of him as to Mia's whereabouts. He would be ready for him this time. In the alleyway behind the Ashton Arms, he'd been blindsided by his brother's cowardly attack.

After only twenty minutes, though, Nathan saw the squat figure of Paulie exit the gym and make his way over to the Ashton Arms. Years of blows to the head were starting to manifest in a tell-tale shuffling gait. Any coaching Paulie did these days was obviously confined to verbal directions outside of the ropes as to how a particular opponent might best be decimated. But Nathan was under no illusion that the barrel-chested man wasn't still capable of inflicting more damage with one jab than most fighters would achieve in a flurry of combinations.

The Ashton was still a couple of hours from lunchtime opening, and Paulie disappeared down a side street to let himself in through the back entrance, and although everything went quiet again, the sight of Paulie meant that others would almost certainly be around.

It was only a couple of minutes later that the doors to the gym opened again, and Nathan's pulse instantly spiked as Bedlam exited with a bodyguard, the accompanying hulk of a man surveying the street in all directions before walking ahead. And as ironic as that at first seemed, Nathan guessed that a fighter like Bedlam had undoubtedly made just as many bloodthirsty enemies as he had fans. The bragging rights of king-hitting a figure like Bedlam and taking him down unawares in the street would elevate any assailant brave enough, or stupid enough, to the status of legend. The presence of security did complicate matters, and the only thing Nathan could do was watch them from a distance until such time as Caleb made an appearance.

The bristling oversized minder swaggering along in a black leather jacket, V-neck knit and jeans checked both ways down the street before heading across the road to a new white BMW parked directly in front of the pub, the luxury executive sedan being amongst the small number of vehicles that had been carefully avoided by the bat-wielding youth. More relaxed and unconcerned in his demeanour, Bedlam sauntered a few steps behind. But as the champ reached the median line in the centre of the road, the kid who'd been scooting around sped directly at him and cockily skidded the bike with a screech of rear tyre, coming to an abrupt stop just centimetres short of scuffing the Italian leather of Bedlam's shoes. The minder glanced sneeringly over his shoulder as he opened the driver's door. Countless hours of bag and ring work were no preparation in how to deal with a brash eleven-year-old on a pushbike.

"Forgetting something, Mister?"

Letting slip a dry smile, Bedlam put his hand in his pocket to retrieve the rest of the promised vehicle protection money but inadvertently pulled out a fifty along with the intended ten-pound note. And with a lightning right that impressed even Bedlam, the youngster snatched both of the notes and powered off out of his saddle and down the street before the off-duty fighter even had a chance to react.

"Thanks for the tip, Mister!" Nathan heard the kid yell as he sped past the driver's side window, while the pair up ahead could be seen shaking their heads in laughter as they got into the car.

Moments later, the BMW pulled off. He thought it unlikely that Bedlam would recognise him with the regrowth of hair since they last met at the Carousel Club, even if he did manage to catch a glimpse into the Kombi, but just in case, Nathan grabbed an old floppy fishing hat that Adam had left on the passenger seat. And, for good measure, he slipped on a pair of Adam's less-than-fashionable sunglasses that had been thrown onto the dash.

"Dear God, Adam," Nathan muttered as he checked out the quickly improvised disguise in his rear-view mirror, the comical-looking reflection breaking the tension for a second. It was certainly a change from his last masquerade when he had first checked out Brophy's gym. It served its purpose, though, as Bedlam's vehicle glided inconsequentially by. Sitting low and sinking into the backrest, Nathan glanced to his right as the car passed, his world suddenly slowing to a frame-by-frame flash on catching sight of the driver. The chiselled minder sitting in the driver's seat, with his glare fixed firmly on the road ahead, was Caleb.

Nathan's world returned to real time with a staggering realisation. Caleb was almost unrecognisable. Only those skeletal features of his facial anatomy that were fixed and unchangeable made it possible to identify him. Whatever bizarre metamorphosis had been taking place was now complete, and since last seeing his brother in the alleyway behind the Ashton Arms, it was obvious that Bedlam and Paulie had been training Caleb up as a formidable fighting machine.

Nathan was suddenly paralysed by his own thoughts as the image flashed into his mind of when he had walked in on Caleb standing bare-chested next to his bed at Annie's house: the faint bruising to his lower back... the puncture wound to the cubital fossa of his arm... the inconceivable transformation... Anne-Marie's 'Quantum Template of

Physicality'… dematerialisation of human tissue… DMT… lumbar punctures… intravenous administration… the hypothalamus… secretion of Growth Hormone. The cascading realisation was startling. Everything he had witnessed in Caleb's transformation could be explained in what he had read at the farmhouse concerning Anne-Marie's scientific research and her extensions of the experiments originally carried out in the Nazi concentration camps. If Caleb had repeatedly been taken to a point of dematerialisation, then rematerialisation into the quantum template of his true energy body would account for his healing. And the use of DMT had somehow been key. *But how had Caleb become involved with Bedlam and Anne-Marie?* And had his initial assumption been wrong? Was Bedlam, in fact, Caleb's bodyguard?

Looking in his wing mirror, Nathan saw the BMW make a right turn, so he quickly ripped off his makeshift disguise and reached for the Kombi's ignition, making a swift U-turn to tail them. Fortunately, Bedlam and Caleb seemed to be in no rush. Even in the Kombi, he was confident that he could keep up with them at a safe distance. But an all-consuming desire to catch up to their vehicle and ram them off the road in the hope they would be fatally injured kept seeing his right foot pressing too heavily on the accelerator. He eased on the brakes. Killing the pair wouldn't help him find Mia, and his bright orange chase vehicle couldn't have been more conspicuous – it simply hadn't occurred to him that he'd be engaged in tailing a couple of killers when he'd grabbed the Kombi's keys at the farmhouse. He eased back even more. The traffic was still sparse and he'd have to keep more of a distance than he felt comfortable with if he wasn't going to be spotted.

Nathan had no idea where all this was leading or what his next move would be. Whatever eventuated, he knew it was going to be dangerous. He would never have relished the prospect of taking on Bedlam alone. But the combined firepower of the two men he was following now made any potential confrontation with them nothing less than suicidal.

Mia came around again to the familiar excruciating pain in her shoulders and arms, her legs and core immediately engaging in an automatic response to gain some relief. The cloud of drug-induced unconsciousness had now cruelly lifted, leaving her facing the stark reality of her hopeless situation once again. She shuddered, remembering how she'd been stripped of her clothes. In some warped way, the thought of the male assailant teasing her exposed flesh with the knife seemed less horrific than the thought of a woman violently tearing off another woman's clothes in order to aid a sexual attack. Mia retched, nauseated at the thought of the perverse mental, physical and emotional abuse she'd already been subjected to at the hands of Anne-Marie and her accomplice and was panic-ridden at what fate awaited her when the light was next turned on. Her returning senses registered the smell of urine. She must have been held for hours, and in her drug-induced stupor she had soiled herself where she hung. She began to weep and mouthed Nathan's name over and over again. But praying that he would somehow come bursting in through the door to save her wasn't going to help. In truth, Nathan would have no idea of where she was or even that she'd been abducted.

In the minutes that passed, Mia tried again to control

her emotions by channelling anger instead of fear. Whatever happened the next time she faced her attackers, she was determined not to falter in her resolve. If they cut at her body, she would not react, no matter what pain she suffered; if they raped her, she would not react, no matter what indignity she was forced to endure; and even if they chose to end her life, she would not react, no matter how much her being wanted to grasp onto life.

Was that a sound? Mia thought she heard a weak tortured moan from somewhere in the surrounding darkness and cocked her head to listen. She didn't dare call out and bring attention to herself in case her captors were still there watching, and while she wouldn't wish her worst enemy to be in the same predicament as she was, the mere fact that there was someone else there inspired in her a glimmer of hope.

44

Subject 49322/CX had been taken as far as she could go experimentally. The word 'she' and any reference to gender, however, now only held relevance at a cellular DNA level with the presence of two X chromosomes in the genetic code. The genitals, uterus, ovaries and breast tissue had been surgically removed not long after the amputation of the arms and legs – the absence of a vulva having at least saved her from the repeated rape and abuse at the hands of Brophy's clients who were willing to pay big money to satiate their depravity. It was an arrangement that had proven immensely profitable in the inevitable downtime between dissections while the subject's physiology was being allowed time to recover from the post-operative shock of the amputations.

The redundant pelvis, sacrum and lower lumbar vertebrae had been discarded next, with care being taken to ligate and preserve the protective dural sheath surrounding the length of remaining spinal cord. That way, the normal flow of cerebral spinal fluid within could be maintained upwards to the brain as the spine was being shortened vertebra by vertebra; a catheter inserted into the ureters exiting the kidneys sufficed for a while on dissecting out the bladder and urethra, but once both kidneys had also been removed, the subject had been totally reliant on dialysis; drips now fed nutrients and regulatory hormones directly into a bloodstream being replenished from a bank of processed and frozen blood collected from the subject in the months prior to the start of the experiment; and a modified heart-lung machine, connected to remnants of the aorta and vena cava, had even taken over the function of those two vital missing organs, its output pressure monitored and ingeniously geared down as necessary. Yet all the while, the eyes – reduced to mere stalks projecting from the brain – had remained intact and functioning throughout.

The only visible evidence left of subject 49322/CX now was a pouch of scalp and facial skin that had once adorned a feminine jawline. Fed by a perfusion medium of serum, glucose, electrolytes and other nutrients to maintain tissue vitality, the remnant flesh enveloped a bony crucible formed from the base of the skull, which supported an inner pouch of meningeal membrane containing a small mass of vital cerebral neural tissue bathed in merely a few millilitres of remaining cerebral spinal fluid. The limit had been reached. There was nothing more that could be removed.

Anne-Marie eyed the mound of flesh inside the incubator that had been connected to a barrage of equipment, her hand hovering over the master power switch. The experiment had finally come to a conclusion and 'life support' to maintain the subject's conscious awareness was about to be turned off. Such moments were always a reason to pause: The euphoria of the incipient idea. The months of planning to realise the experimental potential. The disappointment of failure after failure. The endless nights alone scribbling out solutions that were doomed to fail again. Then the breakthrough. An unexpected spike in the graph. Some aberrant piece of data so fleeting that it might have almost been missed. The Holy Grail that no one else had believed in.

Subject 49322/CX had survived far longer than any other experimental subject. The functional MRI scans had allowed for pinpoint accuracy in systematically obliterating any redundant neuronal tissue in the brain associated with each body part removed. Those parts of the brain still active in any particular targeted bodily function would light up on the scans like cities and towns across a continent at night in some geostationary satellite's snapshot of the world. Those neural beacons of light would then be surgically extinguished. A great improvement on the original hit and miss experiments by Holzer in the concentration camps of the 1940s. His hypothesis had been simple: dissect away everything superfluous to *Awareness* and you would be left with the neural seat of human consciousness in a Petri dish. His resources were primitive. But the limitations in the medical technology of the time were more than compensated for in his endeavours by an endless supply of subjects to experiment on in the camps. While he had no choice, in his day, other than to retain the major organs such as the heart, lungs and kidneys, his warped genius did stretch to proposing the design of a simple electrical pump that might bypass the heart. A suggestion that most mocked as simply fanciful at the time. Anne-Marie's contribution to the continued research lay in the realisation that she had the technology at her disposal to complete Holzer's work. And she, too, had an adequate supply of subjects, courtesy of Brophy's sex trafficking ring. It was her study of Isaac's work, though, that had impacted her research the most. Keeping those experimental subjects alive over an extended period of time, while systematically erasing their physicality, effectively allowed her to target her analysis of the dematerialisation process in controlled laboratory conditions, in what had become an obsessive search for the quantum energy template of *physicality* itself that Holzer had started back in the 1930s.

Anne-Marie fleetingly wondered what subject 49322/CX might be thinking of at this very moment. Maintaining some degree of communication throughout the procedure had been key to the success of the experiment, and at first, that communication had remained verbal. The distressed subjects, pleading for death rather than life, had been fully aware of what was being perpetrated against them – a fact that Anne-Marie had used to her advantage in promising that the life-supporting equipment would be turned off if only they'd cooperate just a little longer. Once the lungs, trachea and larynx had been removed and the facial muscles of expression dissected out, the functional MRI scans had become even more crucial in assessing the degree of Awareness. Showing the subjects photos of their past that had been posted on social media and playing recordings of a parent's distraught pleas in police press conferences never failed to elicit a real-time radiographic light show that marked neural areas to be left untouched. Finally removing the eyeballs from the orbits of 49322/CX and then severing the auditory nerves from the auditory cortex had been pivotal moments. They had provided Anne-Marie with a definitive result. The unexpected spike. The Holy Grail of Grails. Despite no longer being able to see or hear, subject 49322/CX had still responded with bright flashes of neural activity both to recordings of her grandmother's voice and recent photos posted of her boyfriend, who was now finding solace and healing in a new relationship.

The findings had stunned Anne-Marie. Neural activity was being registered in the radiographic light shows, despite the absence of sensory organs. Little of the brain was left, except for the sensory relay bodies of the thalamus that had by now no neural connections to any other structure and the choroid plexus of vessels responsible for the secretion of cerebral spinal fluid – the CSF. That carefully preserved fluid was contained inside the still intact, yet now fragile, ventricular cavity system that once occupied the central interior of the brain like some symmetrical subterranean system of descending interconnected caverns. Its cavity walls were by now so incredibly thin and only structurally maintained by the remnants of redundant grey matter that once bordered it. The system of four fluid-filled internal caverns would normally communicate with the space surrounding both the brain and entire spinal cord through foramina – small openings in the cavernous cavity walls that allow the CSF to flow through in a continuous stream, with the brain and attached spinal cord floating within the very CSF produced by its own interior. Following all of the obliteration, the fluid now contained inside the still-intact ventricular cavities merely bathed the surface of the scant brain tissue remaining. And, to Anne-Marie's utter amazement, she'd had no choice but to conclude that the seat of consciousness within the pouch of flesh, so aggressively sought after at the expense of so many lives, lay not in any 'last-standing' master neural cell but actually within that seemingly innocuous fluid-filled space. Or, at least, was somehow tethered to the *physical* through that fluid-filled space.

Holzer himself had noted that maintaining the cerebral spinal fluid surrounding the brain seemed essential if the very life force of a subject's conscious mind was to be preserved throughout the progressive and controlled elimination of physicality. He also dared to suggest that it was no coincidence that the CSF flowed from the top of the crown right down to the root of the spine, and hypothesised a link between the anatomical extent of CSF flow and the supposed spiritual flow of life force from crown to root described for many thousands of years by Eastern mystics.

Anne-Marie's hand continued to hover over the master power switch to the incubator. The act of terminating a perfectly good experimental sample just because the objectives had been met was almost a crime. There had been too many abortive attempts in procuring a viable experimental sample, especially if more questions needed to be answered.

After a moment of hesitation, Anne-Marie's hand pulled away from the switch and she walked off, closing the lab door behind her. Subject 49322/CX, Jessica Mahr, screamed to the core of her discarnate being. *'I can't live through this anymore!'* She had been left trapped within the Void – a Void in which she could see everything that was happening across the span of Space and Time but was powerless to do anything about it.

45

"Where are you, Nathan?" Isaac asked with urgency, his voice rasping over the speakerphone. "Barbara and I finally made it to the farmhouse this morning and we saw your note. We've been trying to call for hours but we had no signal."

Nathan had left his phone off as a precaution, deciding to turn it on just for a few moments every now and then when he was on the move. The police already had his phone number from their investigation into Alex's murder, and he didn't want to risk them being able to track his location. Considering that he had been mostly on the move when briefly checking the phone and the police would be searching for an Audi TT – not a Kombi – within the grid-less maze of the city's haphazardly laid-out streets and laneways, Nathan was as sure as he could be that his whereabouts were still unknown. But he'd had to weigh the risk of being found against even the remotest possibility that Mia had somehow managed to get to a phone to contact him.

"Is everything OK? Why didn't you show up last night?"

"The Sanctuary has burnt down. Completely destroyed," Isaac blurted before breaking into a fit of coughing, obviously having been affected by smoke inhalation.

"*What?*" Nathan was shocked by the news. His thoughts rested for a second on the dire warning of what would happen should anyone remain at The Sanctuary once the prophecy had begun to run its inevitable course. Since The Sanctuary had now already been '*reduced to rubble and dust*', it seemed that the predictions had, once again, fully resolved and been proven correct.

"Is Barbara OK?"

"Yes, yes. We're fine. There's too much to explain over the phone." Isaac managed another rattling cough to clear his airway. "I'll fill you in when I see you. We have to meet."

"Mia's gone missing. Just like Alex!" Nathan interrupted. "Caleb has got her. I just know it. He and a group of guys he's been hanging out with were involved in Alex's murder!"

"My God! Your brother…? Tell me where you are. I'll come straight away."

Nathan craned his neck to keep an eye on the vehicle up ahead. "I'm tailing him and one of the guys, heading south out of the city. They went into a block of warehouse apartments down a side street off Sackville for a couple of minutes before heading off again… Mia could be in there for all I know, but following them was my only option." Nathan slapped hard on the steering wheel of the Kombi, the gesture pitifully insufficient at releasing even the smallest fraction of the anxiety pent up inside of him.

Isaac could hear Nathan's growing anger and distress over the phone. "Keep calm. We need to think this through.

It'll be too dangerous for you to confront anyone on your own."

"I can't stay on the phone for too long... Hold on, they're turning..." The line fell silent while Nathan prepared to manhandle the Kombi around the corner, praying with heart in throat that he would make the traffic light's green filter arrow before one of the five vehicles in front of him stopped dutifully behind the thick white line of the road junction on an imminent flash of amber. "...We're heading west past the cemetery, now," Nathan finally added, breathing again and updating his rolling commentary. But the line remained silent. "Isaac? Are you still there?"

"They're heading for the Hall," Isaac eventually answered, his words ominous, knowing that the road led directly to the abandoned building. "*A Diocese of a Lie*," he added in a whisper to himself. "The Dark Circle. This is unbelievable... They must be holding séances again. But why is your brother there?"

Nathan was as confused as Isaac. He'd learnt of the Hall and its supposed past links to a Dark Circle through Isaac's very occasional talk of it. But it had been Barbara's visible shudders at the mere mention of the Hall's name that had first alerted him to its more negative associations. "We'll speak no more of that place. Not here!" would be her adamant response in cutting Isaac off before he would have a chance to elaborate much further. When on his own, Isaac had been far more forthcoming. The Hall had been built in the 1500s by Sir Nicholas Mosley, and the association with that family name, albeit a negative one, had always stuck with the Hall, even to the present day, despite it having been sold on to another equally powerful family way back in the mid-1700s.

Perhaps it was because the original ancestral home of the city's First Family would always remain a potent symbol of their power, regardless of whose name happened to be on the Deed. More likely, though, it had been the sheer infamy of Oswald Mosley that had rekindled the Mosley family's continued negative association within the collective psyche of the local community. Oswald – the leader of the British Fascist Party in the 1930s who had seen allying himself with Hitler and Mussolini as the quickest and surest way to seize power in Britain at the time – came to be understandably despised, causing the Hall and the name of Mosley to be even more impossibly entangled. And from what Nathan had read in the Library's archived cache of documents, the association with Mosley stretched even to The Sanctuary's Circle itself. There was anecdotal evidence that back in Hugh's tenure, during the 1920s and early '30s, a series of disputes regarding protocol had seen the sudden stormy exit of Circle Leader Henry Mathieson, with Hugh's 'disrespectful larrikin attitude' and 'unyielding obstinacy' being cited as the reason. According to the reports, animosity between the two had been simmering for some time, so Hugh was more than happy when his wife, Marjorie, had taken over the position as Circle Leader.

It also wasn't long before rumours were rife that Mathieson was attempting to set up his own Circle, blatantly plagiarising the protocols he had learnt in his time at The Sanctuary, especially those particular to Hugh's work. The Hall was amongst the supposed venues where Mathieson would hold those initially, by all accounts, abortive séances. The pretender's political ambitions and associations were dubious, too, his leanings being sympathetic to Oswald

Mosley, who happened to be a second cousin of his. Mathieson openly moved in such social circles, likely in the hope that Mosley's Master Plan would one day see him also installed in a position of power in the New Order. Hugh had been glad to be rid of the man from The Sanctuary. But talk of Mathieson seeing himself as a sworn enemy of Hugh and his Circle had also surfaced. A rumour that Hugh hadn't taken lightly.

Nathan was left asking the same question that Isaac had just posed. *What the hell were Caleb and Bedlam doing at the Hall? And what link did they have to this Dark Circle that would cause Isaac to be so worried?*

"Look, it's vital that you don't do anything until I get there."

Isaac's voice over the phone brought Nathan's thoughts back to the moment.

"If you're right about them killing Alex, who knows what they're capable of. I'll meet you there in twenty minutes. But don't attempt to follow them into the car park. You'd be asking to get ambushed. There's only one way in and out through the office precinct so we can't lose them once they've entered."

Nathan was just relieved that Isaac was on his way. Alone, he didn't stand a chance. Isaac was a powerfully built man who had proven that he was more than capable of handling himself both physically and mentally when faced with difficult and dangerous situations. Isaac was right. Clear thinking was going to be imperative if they were going to find Mia. Be that alive or dead.

"There's a park across the road from the precinct. Wait for me there. But first, give me the address of those warehouse apartments they went into. I'll make a call and have the police check them out."

Isaac's contacts in the force could at last prove useful, and the offer was a huge relief for Nathan. Carrying on tailing the BMW had been his only option, but the thought that Mia, or even some evidence of her whereabouts, might have only been metres away from him inside one of the inner-city apartments had made it hard to drive away.

"I'll be there in twenty. Do nothing until then," Isaac commanded again through another rasping cough.

Nathan immediately switched off his phone. The BMW was still in sight up ahead but was slowing, and he had to adjust his speed to almost a roll so as not to get too close as their vehicle indicated and turned right into a narrow approach road that led into the precinct of offices Isaac had described. Nestled amongst the surrounding buildings, the Hall came into view as the Kombi cruised slowly past the entranceway and pulled up at the kerbside a few metres further on.

Nathan glanced to his left as he wrenched the handbrake on. He now found himself looking directly at the park gates that he had entered through on the night the young woman had been brutally raped and murdered. All the leads he'd been following had now disturbingly led him back to this place where his nightmares had begun.

Surveying the scene of devastation where The Sanctuary and main house had once stood, Pullen kicked at the ash beneath his feet while being briefed.

"I can't confirm arson, at this stage. We'll have a team

walk through when it's safe. There's still some mopping-up to do and that could take a while." The lead firefighter had found himself caught up in one of Pullen's looping interrogations. "Both buildings undoubtedly went up at the same time, and it is strange that the scorch patterns at the two sites don't seem to match. Accelerant was likely used in the main house, whereas the fire in the outbuilding seems to have been electrical and more like what is seen with a lightning strike… But don't quote me. It's certainly out of the norm."

"You're sure there was no one in there?"

"That I can't guarantee," the firefighter answered adamantly from over his shoulder, already on the move in his eagerness to get back to his duties.

Pullen's brow remained furrowed as he turned abruptly to Fitzpatrick. "Anything on their location?" he snapped.

"Nothing definite, boss. A couple of brief signals from Carter's phone were picked up to the south. It looks like he may be heading back into the city."

"Keep on it. It's our only lead at this stage."

Undeterred by a blunt directive to stay clear of the smoking shell, Pullen made his way over to what used to be The Sanctuary, leaving Fitzpatrick glancing nervously up at the unsecured walls and then back over to the fire crews, who were busily distracted in the remains of the main building.

Pullen peered in through the window spaces as he walked along. The charred remnants of book spines littering the debris inside caught his attention in the ruins of what must have been a substantial Library only a few hours before. "You said McKinnon used this place for fortune telling?" he shouted over to Fitzpatrick with a cynical snort as he scanned the interior, the vestiges of the roof now covering most of the floor area.

"A psychic centre of some sort."

Pullen shook his head in derision and was just about to turn to leave when he noticed something over by the gable end wall, partially covered with the roof debris.

"Get the fire chief back here," Pullen barked. "I want to know what's inside that safe!"

Nathan studied the reflection of the street in the Kombi's oversized wing mirror as Isaac exited his vehicle on parking up a couple of car lengths behind. The man seemed out of sorts and at a loss as he glanced up and down the street, but it only took a moment for Nathan to realise that he'd completely failed to mention the Kombi when they'd spoken on the phone earlier. Shouldering open the driver's door, he swung out and waved to catch Isaac's attention.

"Nathan," Isaac wheezed, slamming the passenger door shut, clearly short of breath. "I can't believe Caleb has taken Mia. But we *have* to believe she's OK."

Isaac was undoubtedly suffering from smoke inhalation and Nathan became immediately concerned. "Did you discharge yourself?" he asked sternly, failing to believe that any medical officer would have released him so soon from care. "There can be serious complications, you know."

Isaac waved away Nathan's concerns. "That doesn't matter right now," he replied. "You mentioned in the note at the farmhouse that you'd come across some things in The Sanctuary's documents. Several apports were missing from The Sanctuary, is that right?"

Nathan was on edge and eager to act. Mia's safety was his only priority, and talk of The Sanctuary's apports could wait.

"I think we should be making a move. Who knows what they might be—"

"It's understandable that you want to rush over there and kick the doors open, all guns blazing. But we don't even know if Mia's there for sure," Isaac counselled. "The Dark Circle is undoubtedly involved in all this somehow, so anything you found might be important. If we are going to save Mia, information is the best weapon we have at this stage," he urged through another round of coughing.

Nathan let out a relenting sigh, and reaching into his top pocket, he pulled out the label describing the provenance of *THE LOVERS* card that had been missing from the collection of apports on display. "Recognise this?"

"I can't say that I do. Not in my tenure, at least. Where did you find it?"

"It was out of sight, wedged down beneath the felt lining and the wood of the display cabinet," Nathan answered, replacing the piece of paper back into his pocket for safekeeping. "Last night, I started searching the records for any mention of that missing apport, and I couldn't believe my luck when I ended up actually finding it, along with several other Tarot cards. But there was never a mention of the cards anywhere... It just doesn't make any sense, Isaac. The Sanctuary's records are so detailed. If someone had so much as fallen asleep in the middle of a séance in 1899, the event would have been recorded somewhere by someone. So it's unlikely they'd fail to document something as significant as an object materialising. And things also don't ring true with the records themselves. Gaps appear before the chronology picks up again. Entire sections have been removed, and it seems that the missing cards from those periods had been purposely hidden throughout the rest of the cache."

"How many cards did you find?" Isaac asked, intrigued.

"Nine in all. All of them are apports. I'm sure of it. And someone went to great lengths to make sure all mention of them was erased from the entries across history." Nathan reached over the back of his seat to pick up the folders he'd grabbed from the farmhouse. "I don't think you're going to like this," he warned. "Anne-Marie's been secretly raiding The Sanctuary's records and—"

"No, Nathan," Isaac countered in Anne-Marie's defence. "She was given permission to borrow some of the material for research purposes. You're mistaken."

"Then why were these locked away in her office?" Nathan pulled out a pile of papers he'd retrieved from The Sanctuary's own records and those from the AXIS folder labelled *The Sanctuary* and laid them out on the upholstery of the Kombi's custom front bench seat.

"I found *THE LOVERS* card that was missing secreted amongst The Sanctuary's documents from the 1860s period, during Spencer Cavendish's tenure. The provenance label I just showed you, identifying it as an apport, must've simply been misplaced, preventing the evidence of the card's existence from being completely erased. But I also found these."

Nathan flicked through the papers and retrieved two other Tarot cards. "All of the cards are from the same deck. Both *THE DEVIL* and *DEATH* cards were in a folder labelled *The Sanctuary* that Mia discovered in Anne-Marie's office at AXIS. Surely Anne-Marie would've told you about something as significant as the existence of previously unknown apports, unless she was up to something underhand!"

"But what makes you so sure that they're all apports?"

Nathan reached inside the AXIS folder and produced *THE HIGH PRIESTESS* along with another small provenance label he retrieved from his shirt pocket: *THE HIGH PRIESTESS. Physical Séance. Apported Tarot Card, 7th October 1936. Sitting Medium, Henry Mathieson.* "Since both of the cards identified with the labels are apports, it seems likely that the other cards from the same deck secreted away are also apports, especially as all evidence of their manifestation had been removed along with the provenances, too... But the really significant thing according to the records is that Henry Mathieson had parted company with The Sanctuary years before 1936. So the physical séance referred to here must be one carried out at some other place. Perhaps the Hall. And the fact remains that Anne-Marie has been in possession of apports that even *you* didn't know existed, not to mention some horrific human experimentation research papers I found in her files. Perhaps you don't know her as well as you think."

Isaac paused for a moment in thought. "I trust Anne-Marie, Nathan. There has to be some innocent explanation. Do we know when these other cards apported exactly?"

"Pretty much to the day," Nathan replied emphatically, before glancing over his shoulder in the direction of the Hall again.

Isaac sensed Nathan's growing unrest. "It's important. Trust me," he reassured, "I need to know everything if we are going to help Mia."

Nathan relented again and reached for a sheet of paper he'd scribbled notes on the night before in his exhaustive research. "Whoever originally hid the cards wanted to make sure that there was little chance of them ever being found, without actually destroying them. It seems that many saw the apports as spiritual relics that were sacrosanct, whereas others had a more scientific view. The records contain long theoretical discussions about Causality and the potential consequences to history and current Reality when apport portals are opened and how Spacetime might be altered if such materialised physical Matter from a different Spacetime coordinate is destroyed or tampered with. Either way, whoever hid them wanted them preserved."

Isaac raised his eyebrows. "This is incredible."

Nathan handed the sheet of notes to Isaac. "The provenance on the label I showed you was dated 4th November 1863 in Spencer Cavendish's tenure. That was the day of The Sanctuary's inaugural séance. It's inconceivable that an apport manifesting on that day, of all days, wouldn't have been recorded. Likewise, on the 9th November 1989. A séance due to be held was mentioned months before, but there was no record of the actual event itself. Yet I found *THE TOWER* secreted amongst the documents of that tenure."

Isaac studied the chronology scribbled on the page of notes:

THE LOVERS 1863, *THE THREE OF SWORDS* 1905, *THE MAGICIAN* 1914, *THE HERMIT* 1929, *THE HIGH PRIESTESS* 1936, *THE DEVIL* 1939, *DEATH* 1945, *THE MOON* 1969, *THE TOWER* 1989.

Nathan collected together the remainder of the cards he had found. "It seems that the cards were simply preserved by hiding them amongst the years of documents related to each tenure, *after* removing any evidence of the cards actually being apports. It was the perfect hiding place. Without the provenance attached to it, they were just another curiosity amongst the eclectic collection of archive material. No one ever had reason to look for such small needles in so many haystacks of documents, until now."

Isaac reached over and picked up an old yellowing newspaper clipping he'd noticed amongst the papers with *THE HIGH PRIESTESS*. It reported on the political implications over the staging of the 1936 Berlin Olympics – the 'Nazi Games' – in light of British parliamentarian Oswald Mosley's scandalous visit to Germany. Such day-to-day commentaries were commonplace inclusions throughout the historical records, and the clipping only served to further confirm the timing of Mathieson's séance.

"There's something else I found out that you should know, Isaac." Nathan had been torn as to whether he should share the information he had found out about his friend and mentor, but he finally resolved to tell him. "Anne-Marie has compiled dossiers on both of us, and you—"

"Enough!" Isaac snapped with a glaring scowl, his expression now one of pure hatred.

The sudden change in demeanour took Nathan by surprise, and before he could react, Isaac had lunged and grabbed his throat in a choking grip, forcing him back into the corner between the driver's door and the seat's backrest. A flash of movement in the street registered in Nathan's peripheral vision as a procession of vehicles cornering at speed headed towards the Hall. A black panel van was following at the rear, and for a second, he helplessly wondered if Mia could be inside. Struggling for breath and rapidly losing consciousness, he had no way to resist Isaac's superior strength and the control being exerted over him. Any resistance was futile. All faded to dark.

Moments later, uniformed security guards descended on the Kombi from down the tarmac access road and helped manhandle Nathan's unconscious body out across the front passenger seat before throwing him unceremoniously into the back of the Kombi through the sliding side panel door. One of the guards climbed into the driver's seat, and with the engine spluttering into life, the van lurched off towards the Hall.

46

Pullen waved Fitzpatrick into his office.

"The safe door had been left open with nothing obvious inside, boss," he reported. "It must've been cleared out before the fire. But these were in a hidden drawer compartment in the base," he added, handing Pullen three plastic evidence bags, each containing fragments of water-damaged and charred paper. "We'd have missed them completely if it hadn't been for the metal warping in the intense heat."

Some of the ink on the paper had run and partially obscured the writing, but the fragments of a handwritten letter meant for the sole attention of Isaac McKinnon were clearly readable through the plastic: ... *The dark séances at the Hall and... the Mosley bloodline are a threat... They must be extinguished before they kill countless others. If I have failed in that, Isaac, you must not. The ones named Caleb and Nathan must die...*

Pullen was left momentarily speechless on reading the

distinctly old-fashioned script, realising the obviousness of the connection. The Hall. It was now the third time the place had cropped up in his investigations. The proximity of the abandoned premises had been of note but only due to it being within one of the supposed hunting grounds of the serial killer. On routinely checking the building in the course of the investigation, it was found to be securely boarded up, and the 24-hour security patrols in the surrounding precinct had reported nothing suspicious.

The neurones in Pullen's brain fired and misfired in attempts to make a connection: *Who is Hugh Wells and why did he write the letter? Does all this have links to some kind of cult? Does some criminal network stretch further than just these two suspects? And why is Isaac McKinnon being directed to kill Nathan Carter?*

Pullen's attention was drawn back to the fragments of paper in the evidence bags, his eye catching sight of the name *Mosley* – a name that he thought he recognised from somewhere.

"Get on to Special Ops," Pullen barked. "I want every available officer in here within the next hour. I want plans of the interior of this Hall. Now!"

Pullen could not afford for his next raid to fail.

There was nothing unusual in seeing a groom – on this his wedding day – pacing nervously around awaiting the arrival of his bride. Oswald Mosley, however, suitably attired in his wedding suit, was pacing nervously around awaiting the arrival of the Führer. Oswald was all about social and political advancement, and such things as matrimonial ceremonies were merely a necessary formality. His wife-to-be, Diana, had been just another one of his many mistresses throughout his first marriage. But it was Diana's contacts in the highest echelons of the Reich, now so obviously in the ascendency, that had more recently spurred his proposal of marriage. That Hitler himself would be present as a guest at his imminent wedding was more than he could ever have hoped for.

"Relax, my friend. The Führer is looking forward to meeting you," Goebbels reassured with a patronising smile, not in the least mistaking Mosley's nervousness for prenuptial jitters. As Minister of Public Enlightenment and Propaganda, Joseph Goebbels had the uncanny ability to read minds, albeit in order that he could control them. "I hope my humble residence is not a disappointment, considering the venue of your first marriage."

Oswald looked approvingly around the plush surrounds of Goebbels' Berlin home. It was the perfect setting for a marriage of relative secrecy. His friendship with King Edward was enough of a talking point in the corridors of Parliament back home without running the risk of further exposing the King of England's Nazi sympathies. But as fine as the venue was, it certainly didn't compare to the Royal Chapel at St James's Palace where he'd married his first wife, heiress Cynthia Curzon. Back then, European royalty were amongst those on the guest list, including Edward's parents, King George V and Queen Mary. Oswald prided himself that he could successfully manipulate himself into the highest of circles. Though, at the time of that first marriage, Cynthia's father, the British Foreign Secretary, Lord Curzon, had adamantly opposed the union, having rightly suspected Oswald's motives. Curzon might have wished that he'd not relented – Oswald started married life by promptly seducing Cynthia's younger sister before going on to screw the old man's second wife.

"We're honoured to be considered as welcome guests in the home of such an esteemed member of the National Socialists," Oswald replied, more than a touch too sycophantically. "That will be reason enough for us to remember our wedding day."

Goebbels had the measure of Mosley. But he did like the man, the pair having a great deal in common. They were both eloquent public speakers, formidable politicians, adept social climbers and prolific womanisers; he did seriously doubt, though, whether Mosley ultimately had the charisma or the necessary authoritarian ruthlessness to succeed in his aims of seizing power in Britain and forming an unconquerable Fascist axis with Germany and Italy. Having a sympathiser in the British Parliament who had the ear of the King, however, could only be helpful to the Reich. An alliance between Germany and Italy was about to be ratified in the next few days. And since Mosley was already forging a relationship with Benito Mussolini, Goebbels thought it wise to nurture the friendship. In truth, it was Oswald Mosley's paramilitary Blackshirts that interested Goebbels the most. Having access to an army of loyal fascist thugs on the streets of Britain would be priceless in destabilising the democratic fabric of that country, if and when circumstances demanded it.

Goebbels forced another smile. "I think I hear a car," he suddenly announced.

Mosley tensed at the thought of finally coming face to face with the Führer.

"I believe it is your bride," Goebbels quickly added,

enjoying the subtle control he'd just exerted over Mosley's heartbeat. "Come!" he ushered. "I will not allow such a beautiful lady to be kept waiting by her groom."

Hitler was not as Oswald had imagined. Not that Mosley expected any of the firebrand rhetoric that he'd seen on the newsreels. But just how quietly spoken and affable the man seemed to be, sitting relaxed and cross-legged in a luxuriant armchair within the comfortable surrounds of Goebbels' home, still came as a surprise. The softness of the Führer's words at times became lost behind an animated hand, the fingers of which would periodically come to rest on his lips before the understated diatribe would begin again. For, despite all the cordiality fitting for the occasion of a marriage, this was no polite conversation that the translator was relating. The politicking was inevitable, even amidst a pleasant post-wedding soirée – something that Diana, sitting dutifully next to her new husband, fully understood. And whenever or wherever Hitler chose to speak, those present were expected to listen. Only Goebbels dared interrupt.

"So you see, Oswald, the Führer is keen to strengthen the ties between our two countries. It would be a formidable alliance. And while the Jew in Britain is possibly less of an overt scourge than in Germany, they need to be eradicated from all quarters."

Oswald was able to follow the German well enough. The constant commentary of the translator was for Hitler's benefit solely and served only to ensure that the Führer was never at a disadvantage or seen to be in any way of inferior intellect in his inability to speak English.

Oswald played the part required of him by waiting for the translator to finish before smiling his understanding and agreement with a nod. He was familiar with all of Hitler's speeches, even those given to his most loyal followers behind closed doors back in the early days. *Why hate the Jew? ...Because through that hatred we will climb to power!* Such insight into the psyche of the masses. Such mastery of oration. Yet the master was now courting him, Oswald, as the next dictator that would rise and seize power in Britain. Mosley's chest puffed with supercilious pride, unaware that the members of the High Command present saw him as nothing more than a weak but possibly useful pawn in their long-term strategy. Mosley had nothing against the Jews himself. But if realising his ambitions meant eradicating them from every seat of political and economic power, then so be it.

As awestruck by the Führer as he was, and despite holding the hand of his new wife, Oswald was far from oblivious to one particular distraction in the room, his frequent glances having been directed throughout to a pretty young girl of no more than eighteen who was standing behind Hitler's right shoulder. Oswald's weakness. Her coyly averted eyes, avoiding his obvious attention, only heightened her allure.

Goebbels motioned for the girl to step forwards. "The future!" he announced.

Hitler smiled adoringly at the young poster girl he'd hand-picked himself out of tens of thousands, stroking her arm as she stepped past.

"The world will soon be populated by such Aryan perfection," Goebbels asserted, admiring the girl, who was now standing statuesquely and gazing forwards as if into the glorious future she had been fed. "And she will soon be honoured by bearing the ultimate gift to the Reich."

Hitler smiled, imagining the Reich's future dynasty.

But Oswald was no longer listening. He desired the girl. He needed to have her on this night of all nights – whatever the danger. And Oswald, as his past indiscretions had proved, always got what he wanted.

47

Nathan surfaced into a dazed awareness, unable to move. He had been stripped naked and his wrists and ankles securely tied to a chair. A faint charred smell permeating through the air now hit his olfactory senses, and looking down, he steadied his blurring focus on the solid wooden armrests to which he was tethered. He instantly recognised the ropes. They were the ones kept amongst Hugh's research notes – the very same bindings that were used simultaneously across time in Hugh and Isaac's reckless experimental séance to warp the Spacetime-Matter continuum. Above his head hung makeshift lighting in the form of a glaring incandescent bulb bayoneted to cabling slung roughly around pipework that ran across the ceiling of an expansive cellar space. And while the unshaded bulb cast its overly bright light in a narrow cone around his immediate vicinity, the room he now found himself in was large enough that its far walls, corners and recesses were almost lost in shadow. Positioned directly opposite him, some two to three metres away, was a sturdy-looking chair. The words *A DIOCESE FOR TRUTH*, carved unmistakeably across the backrest, grounded him back into full awareness.

Nathan kicked and tugged at his bindings in an involuntary response, but it was futile. The ropes were tight enough to have almost compromised the blood flow to his hands and feet, and the chair he was tied to was as heavy and solidly constructed as the séance chair opposite. Still trying to make sense of his predicament, Nathan began to realise the source of that charred aroma of burnt wood. The timber under his immobilised forearms was scorched. He was tied to the fire-damaged séance chair that had occupied The Sanctuary's séance room for over 150 years, and that could only mean that the chair opposite was a replica – two separate séance chairs must have existed. One for each Circle... *Why would Isaac have risked retrieving a burning chair from the blaze at The Sanctuary?* Nothing made sense, but the thought of Isaac finally triggered that all-too-recent memory of sitting in the Kombi with the man he'd once considered his friend and mentor. His mind raced.

"Na-than...Na-than..."

He immediately looked over to his right to be faced with the horrific sight of Mia's naked body strung up on a diagonal cross fixed to the closest wall. She was cut and bruised and barely able to lift her head. Panic hit at the thought of what she had already suffered. But at least she was alive. "Mia!" he called out in his abject helplessness, anger rather than blood now coursing through his veins.

"Just listen to the love birds," mocked a derisory voice from behind, footsteps signalling someone's approach. A heavy backhand blow connected with the left side of Nathan's cheek, the force causing the vertebrae in his neck to crack audibly with the whiplash. "Hey, Bro."

"Caleb!" warned a commanding voice.

Caleb immediately relented in the physical assault and stepped back behind the séance chair again.

Nathan had never hated so much. No amount of Anne-Marie's experimental manipulation of the quantum energy template of Physicality could account for Caleb's transformation into the monster he now was. He must have always been that way inclined, and if it hadn't been for the loving and caring environment his parents had provided, those inherent sadistic traits would surely have surfaced much earlier in his life.

"*Nathan…*"

A feeble male voice called out from somewhere in the far reaches of light, and Nathan peered confusedly into the dimness. At the far side of the cellar space, an inverted cross constructed from timber as thick as railway sleepers came into focus, its horizontal beam only a few feet from the floor. And in a blatant spectacle clearly meant to disturb the soul, a man's body hung upside down, suspended from the vertical beam by his left ankle, his arms outstretched with both wrists tied to the low cross member, his right ankle lashed behind his left knee in an obscure pose.

"*Nathan. Don't… let… them…*" The man faltered in his attempt to speak.

"Isaac?"

A shock-induced skip in Nathan's heart rhythm was instantly followed by a sharp intake of his own breath – he was still struggling to process the scene as Barbara's lifeless body came into focus lying on the floor near the cross.

"No... No! *Bastards!*" He finally erupted, tears beginning to flow freely down his face, his heart centre constricting in pain at seeing the head of that beautiful and kind woman twisted unnaturally over to one side. His mind was a maelstrom of disbelief, rage and realisation. Again, he kicked and tugged and strained violently at his bindings in vain.

"See. I told you he doesn't like being restrained!" Caleb called out. "Gets him *real* angry."

Nathan immediately felt even more vulnerable at Caleb's taunt. His brother obviously still remembered that day on the riverbanks all too well – an incident never spoken of since.

"Enough," the commanding male voice from moments before calmly asserted.

The man emerged from the shadows and approached to check that the restraints were still secure following the outburst. "All starting to make sense now?" he asked.

The solidly built figure standing in full view was the same man who had sat in the front seat of the Kombi earlier. Nathan seethed, suddenly caught up in the rapid flow of his own mindstream as it surged over an edge in a waterfall drop that left him being sucked helplessly down a torrent of white-water thoughts, while the current of the rapids threw him mercilessly against jagged realisation after realisation: in the reflection of the Kombi's wing mirror, he'd mistaken the imposter's different gait and body language for that of an Isaac out of sorts, on account of the inferno he'd just escaped from; and the voice, both over the phone and in person, had sounded different and hoarse in an attempt to disguise it, not because it was affected by smoke inhalation. Nathan had been tricked by his own expectations in a suspension of disbelief of his own making. The doppelgänger had obviously abducted Barbara, Isaac and Mia sometime after he'd left them, and to have known about the note he had written, the imposter must have tracked him to the farmhouse.

Nathan looked tearfully back over to Barbara's lifeless body, wondering if her neck had been snapped so callously before or after the whereabouts of the farmhouse had finally been given up. The final twist and turn before the tumbling white waters of confusion gave way to the still waters of full realisation was linked to something that Nathan had already discovered. Before being rendered unconscious in the Kombi, he had just been about to reveal the most surprising fact that he had found in the document cache. *Isaac had not been an only child*. Nathan had come across a page that had been removed from the main *Genealogies* document and secreted in the main cache in such a way that stumbling across it without knowing of its existence would truly have been like finding a needle in a field full of haystacks. In that Trance attempt to predict the future, the partial family tree generated had prophesied male twins in the Mosley line – Isaac and Lanus – to an unspecified mother. The handwriting of the document had been Hugh's and was dated shortly after the experimental séance had taken place. It was the only record relating to Hugh that could be found in the vacuum of information around that entire period before he had died, and Nathan couldn't help but think that if Hugh or Isaac had known of the existence of another identical resonant such as Lanus, who was involved in the Dark Circle, they wouldn't have taken such a cavalier approach to their intended experiments.

The sudden spike in anger and outflow of emotion had sapped Nathan of energy. Of the three people left in his life that he loved, one lay dead and the other two hung close to death at the mercy of a group of sadistic killers whose motives were beyond any kind of sense or reasoning. The situation seemed hopeless, but if they were all to survive, he knew he had to calm himself and at least control the one thing he could – his own Mind. "What do you want, Lanus?" he demanded, attempting to grab back at least some power by letting his captor know he knew exactly who he was.

Lanus showed no surprise. "Want?" he replied. "My dear boy, you've already provided us with what we want."

Caleb's laughter boomed around the cellar space, and Lanus leant in close to Nathan's face.

"You see, Nathan, you're going to help us with an experiment of our own."

A uniformed security guard marched in and dutifully placed a small square wooden table midway between the séance chairs. It had been scorched by flames, too, and Nathan immediately recognised it as the one from The Sanctuary that had been nestled between the armchairs when he'd first met Isaac all those months before. He also recognised the security guard, now looking every bit the paramilitary recruit he was, as being the same man who had led him up to the Neuropsychological Research lab on the day he'd visited AXIS. That alone proved his suspicions that Anne-Marie was somehow involved with the killings and abductions.

Nathan just could not comprehend why lives had obviously been risked to retrieve items from a fire that was advanced enough to begin consuming everything inside. He glanced across towards Mia again, who seemed to have fallen into unconsciousness or was at least now so weak as to be unable to communicate any longer. He was beside himself with his powerlessness.

"It's time!" Lanus barked, nodding in Caleb's direction. And with that short command, a door behind Nathan opened and the sound of countless footsteps could be heard marching across the stone floor towards him.

The upper hierarchy of the Hall's Dark Circle now streamed into the room. Brophy's mountainous frame headed the procession, followed immediately by Paulie and then Mike and Doreen from The Sanctuary – Isaac had been duped. Mike had obviously been complicit in helping raid the Library's cache.

"Join hands!" ordered Lanus with an expression of granite, momentarily sending the room into a frenzy of activity as everyone took their places, forming a standing ring around the two séance chairs and table.

Nathan scanned the other faces without recognising anyone else. Bedlam was conspicuously absent, but he knew that it would only be a matter of time before Anne-Marie made an appearance. And, right on cue, she appeared. But instead of dutifully joining the others, she approached Nathan and came to a halt directly in front of him. It became instantly clear that she was more than just a rank-and-file member of the Dark Circle and held some degree of authority.

Nathan looked up at her smirking expression. She held his gaze for a few seconds before her eyes slowly tracked down his body to take in all of his nakedness, and reaching over to grab his hair firmly, she moved in close.

"Such a shame, Nathan," she whispered breathily before glancing down again. "We could have had so much fun." With a sneer that revealed the ugliness behind her mask of beauty, she threw Nathan's head violently back against the chair's backrest, the sharp edges and ridges of the elaborate carved lettering cutting into his scalp.

"I don't think you're his type," Caleb jibed with a grin, nodding in Mia's direction as he joined Anne-Marie.

Now in full view, Caleb was barefoot and wearing a black hooded silk robe, as if he was making ready to take the long walk to the Cage through one of the Carousel Club's chanting bloodthirsty crowds. Anne-Marie seemed distinctly unimpressed when he put an arm around her shoulder and squeezed her tightly in a mock embrace. "Besides, if you did fuck him, you'd be fucking your own brother, Sis. That's perverse, even for you."

"Half-brother, you half-wit," Anne-Marie responded, pulling away and walking over to Lanus standing by the table.

Caleb leant in close to Nathan's face. "Welcome to the family, brother. And say hi to your real dad," he added venomously, pointing towards Lanus, all trace of the sardonic grin having fallen away.

Nathan was left speechless. *What was Caleb talking about?* His parents were John and Jen Carter. But before he could connect any further thoughts, Caleb landed another backhand across his face. It broke the skin, drawing blood from his lip and leaving him dazed for a moment.

Regaining his senses, he saw Anne-Marie handing Lanus the pile of Tarot cards he'd recovered from the cache of documents the night before at the farmhouse. Whatever their importance, it now became clear that Nathan himself had been duped into placing the cards directly into the hands of the Dark Circle, so undoing a century and a half of efforts to conceal them.

Anne-Marie walked back over to Caleb and disrobed

him. He was naked under the gown, and sauntering unashamedly over to the other séance chair, he took his seat and waited calmly while she tethered him by the wrists and ankles. Caleb's demeanour had changed, and with a few deep breaths, he began slipping into a deep meditative state while Anne-Marie, masking her actions from Nathan's view, slipped a syringe out of her pocket and administered an induction dose of DMT.

Over by the table, Lanus was slowly dealing out the cards in the exact order that Nathan's research had uncovered, taking his time to ensure that the cards were placed perfectly in position within each of the cells etched into the surface of the polished wood. After the ninth card had been duly laid down, a nervous-looking Mike stepped forwards from his place in the Circle and handed Lanus one final card that obviously belonged to the same deck. Lanus revealed the card to those gathered, inciting a collective murmuring of anticipation. The Celtic Cross could now be completed, and the Tarot spread that in 1905 had apported away, to be scattered throughout time, would finally be brought back together as one – as initially intended in the experimental séance by Charles Cavendish. That portal across time would be opened once more. But now usurped by the Dark Circle at the Hall.

The SS officer paced slowly and silently around the civilian being manhandled by two guards in a thorough search of his person. If the man had anything to hide, Rattenhuber would find it. The Death's Head skull adorning his cap and double-lettered insignia on the collar tabs of the black-jacketed uniform were tailored to incite fear. And Rattenhuber could taste a man's fear. But it was the inconspicuous diamond emblem on the lower left sleeve of the uniform's jacket that should have instilled real terror in the subject under scrutiny.

The search complete, Rattenhuber approached closely and stared coldly into the man's eyes for a long moment before shifting his attention to the minutiae of the facial musculature in an attempt to detect the slightest of tell-tale flickers. Still there was nothing. "Strip him!" he ordered in an instant, and the two guards quickly moved in again.

"Hans!" Hitler voiced. "That won't be necessary."

The guards ceased immediately and snapped back to attention, leaving SS General Gruppenführer Johann 'Hans' Rattenhuber, Chief of the RSD, Hitler's crack bodyguard unit, dutifully relenting with a click of his heels.

Rattenhuber was far from happy with the arrangements thrust upon him, though. The Führer's interest in the occult had never before stretched to being locked in a room in total blackout with foreign individuals that were unknown to him, all in the name of some *experiment*. The frequent séances and ritual goings-on at Heinrich Himmler's Wewelsburg Castle in Büren, 400 kilometres to the east, were easy to secure. Security there was so tight that no one but the elite higher echelons of the SS ever got within a kilometre of the place. But here in Goebbels' Berlin home, there was no possible way of providing the usual level of protection, and his order for the armed contingent of guards to march out of the room had to be forced out through gritted teeth. The door was finally locked behind them by Goebbels, who then made his way to his own seat in the circle of chairs.

Still standing in the centre of the room, Henry Mathieson

breathed a sigh of relief at surviving the search, and being keen to get on with the proceedings, he immediately walked over to the séance chair to take his seat. Two members of the gathered dignitaries had been charged with tying him to the chair, while Rattenhuber insisted that he, at least, be the one to check and verify that the Englishman was secured by the ropes without any chance of escape. Mathieson had come a long way since those days at The Sanctuary under Hugh's tenure. With everything he had learnt there, he'd since become a formidable Physical Medium in his own right. And, thanks to Oswald, he was about to demonstrate his prowess to the Führer.

Oswald, though, was absent from amongst the esteemed gathering. Having excused himself with the onset of a migraine that might only have been exacerbated by the red lighting conditions in the séance, he left his new wife, Diana, to represent him in the Circle. With everyone of note locked inside the makeshift séance room, and the guards preoccupied and focused on what might be happening behind that closed door, Oswald – being the trusted fascist leader that he was – had free rein to wander through Goebbels' home unchallenged in his search for the young object of his desire.

48

The relentless Sun scorched the barren scene, a distant escarpment along the horizon providing the only visual relief to the endless desert sands. This place was devoid of all but the most resilient of life that would survive mostly on the carcasses of the parched unfortunates who had wandered too far and finally succumbed. Three vultures circled above, their fleeting eclipses of the Sun tormenting a man below with his imminent fate. Torturously suspended by just his left ankle, the man hung upside down on an inverted wooden cross, his arms outstretched and bound tightly to the horizontal beam positioned only a few feet above the unbearably radiating heat of the sand. His right ankle was lashed behind his left knee in an obscure pose. *THE HANGED MAN.* The Christ and Antichrist. As if his predicament wasn't dire enough, on the ground lay a small dagger that had been maliciously used to pierce his abdomen with a single stab wound. Having been abandoned by every God and Saviour, he could only pray to the Universe that he would have already bled out by the time those aerial scavengers descended to tear him apart.

Another séance having finished, the Circle members slowly streamed out of The Sanctuary to utter vaporous cordial good nights into the cold night air. Inside, Mike, ever-dutiful, had already fetched a brush and pan with which to sweep up the broken glass from the photo frame that had earlier flung itself across the room at the beginning of the séance. His thoughts, as he knelt down to pick up the larger fragments of glass, were focused on nothing more than the need to reframe the sepia-tone photographic portrait of Charles Cavendish that had graced the mantelpiece for over a century. But Mike found himself momentarily shocked at what he then saw, prompting a venomous rejection of the helping hand being offered by the young newcomer, Nathan, who was still talking with Anne-Marie in the séance room. Mike turned his back to any prying eyes and palmed the apport he had just found underneath the broken photo frame and secreted it in his pocket. *THE HANGED MAN*. The tenth card of the Major Arcana and the last card that would ever materialise.

"*Bitte. Kan ich mein Baby sehen?*"

The exhausted teenage girl's pleas went unheard as her newborn child was hurriedly cleansed and swaddled in readiness for being spirited away.

"*Bitte! Bitte!*"

It was hard to know if those busying themselves around the metal-framed bed in the dingy room were purposefully ignoring her or were just so preoccupied with their newly arrived charge that they couldn't hear the young girl's weak, fatigued cries. The answer came when the man who'd been standing quietly in the corner of the room throughout the delivery stepped forwards, raised his Walther PP.32 Automatic and coldly fired three bullets into the girl's forehead just as the infant was being carried away into an adjacent room. Her child was never meant to make it through to full term. The summary execution of 'the ungrateful whore' chosen to bear the bloodline of Aryan perfection had been ordered by Hitler himself as soon as the affront of that unexpected pregnancy had been realised. But there were those in Mosley's Blackshirts who were more than just street thugs bent on mindless violence, and their influence extended beyond the shores of England. The pregnant girl needed to be kept alive just long enough for her to give birth and so had been kidnapped and hidden away before that initial order of execution could be carried out.

Everyone present at the delivery knew the peril that their conspiracy had put them in, and the quicker the infant was spirited away and the young teenage mother's body disposed of, the better. To the Germans, the bastard child was an abomination – a humiliating affront to the Führer; to the fanatical supporters of Mosley, the child was everything. The Mosley bloodline had been forever melded with Aryan blood in a womb chosen by the Führer himself as the chalice for the Reich's future dynasty. A dynasty that now belonged to Mosley.

The newborn was handed to a nurse who was ushered outside by a guard of three armed men. They climbed into a waiting vehicle to begin the long and dangerous journey back to England. The child would be placed with an adoptive family sympathetic to Mosley's cause until the time was right, and they would dedicate their lives to protecting the bloodline and ensuring its survival into the future at any cost – and by *any* means. Not that the conniving, womanising traits hidden within the genetic coils of Oswald's newborn bastard son, Fredrick, would need any help in unwinding. He would prove quite capable of forcing himself upon and inseminating any woman that he or the line of Guardians chose to target in order to propagate the bloodline.

49

Lanus sauntered back over and knelt down. He held *THE HANGED MAN* card directly in front of Nathan's face and waved it tauntingly side to side. "I really do have to thank you for providing us with all the other cards in the spread. We might never have been able to recover them all without your efforts."

Nathan stared at the image on the card, sickened by how it mirrored the way Isaac had been trussed up and suspended.

Lanus glanced at the card in his hand. "Oh! We do seem to have forgotten something," he said, turning his head and giving a single nod.

One of the uniformed paramilitary henchmen present immediately responded by pulling out a small dagger from a sheath on his belt before walking over to the inverted cross. He thrust it to the hilt into Isaac's abdomen and tossed the bloodied blade onto the floor.

Isaac barely made a sound as the single wound was inflicted; such was the lightning speed of strike.

Lanus glanced at the card again. "Yes, I think that does it," he said, comparing the image against Isaac's tortured silhouette.

Nathan was too shocked to respond. His senses were struggling to process the enormity of what had just happened. He wanted to lash out. He wanted to do harm. He wanted to kill. But any connection with the anger that should've been erupting from inside somehow eluded him. Instead, the helplessness that his restraints imparted only served to direct an ever-increasing amplitude of pulsating rage into his solar plexus. A faint musty sulphurous odour began to develop in the air.

"Now, down to business, Nathan," Lanus continued matter-of-factly. "Firstly, it is true that you are my son, and Caleb and Anne-Marie are indeed your siblings by different mothers." Lanus looked over at Caleb. "It was just so inconvenient that the long search for my firstborn male heir led me to such a brain-damaged imbecile."

Lanus looked coldly over to his son.

"Thanks to Anne-Marie's efforts, he does now possess all the traits I could wish for in a son… Except for the powerful natural gift that you seem to have inherited from the family line."

"You're lying, you murdering bastard!" Nathan spat, finally finding words.

Without breaking eye contact, Lanus responded by summoning Anne-Marie, who immediately strode over to hand her father a thin wad of papers.

"DNA doesn't lie," Lanus said. "We intended placing Caleb with a surrogate family until he was of age. But in an attempt to deny me my firstborn heir, those at The Sanctuary had taken it upon themselves to kidnap the girl I'd inseminated before his birth. When he was eventually found with your aunt, after thirty years of searching, Anne-Marie thought it was too much of a coincidence that his adoptive brother just so happened to turn up at The Sanctuary around the same time. So she did some digging."

Lanus thrust the pages in front of Nathan's face.

"Hugh Wells wasn't the only one searching out future *resonants* of the bloodlines across time," he said, holding the genealogy so that Nathan had no choice but to look. "These days, though, thanks to my lovely daughter, we can profile the DNA to confirm the predictions," he added smugly, turning his head to smile at Anne-Marie.

Nathan didn't recognise the handwriting, but the scribbled ink filling the page undoubtedly identified someone in Trance – Henry Mathieson most likely – as being the author. This was a fragment of a genealogy he'd never seen before. The left side of the page was blank except for the name 'Leonie Wells' set beneath the names 'Hugh and Marjorie Wells'. The right-hand side, however, was filled with a scrawling ancestry that stretched from Oswald Mosley, through his illegitimate son Fredrick, to Lanus and finally to Caleb. The Mosley bloodline of the Hall's Dark Circle and the Cavendish bloodline of The Sanctuary had become one inside the womb of Hugh and Marjorie's daughter Leonie with the birth of twin boys.

"Leonie, my birth mother, was a whore, Nathan. Plain and simple. My father, Fredrick, seduced her into rejecting The Sanctuary and everything it stood for. She'd do anything that he said, by all accounts. And here we are."

"What's that got to do with me? And what's it got to do with her, for God's Sake?" Nathan shot a troubled glance towards Mia. "Just let her go!"

Lanus slowly pulled away the top sheet of the genealogy to confront Nathan with another sheet of predictive scrawl. In the centre of the page was the name Jen Carter embedded within a Trance prophecy naming her as *'the mother of the new heir'*.

"Turns out that the wording of the prophecy was misinterpreted," Lanus said with a shrug. "After being stolen, Caleb had been moved in those attempts to hide him from us and ended up being adopted by your parents. Jen Carter was eventually tracked down, but those searching for Caleb didn't realise that her adopted child was the very heir they had been searching for all along. They assumed instead that they were being directed to give up the search and, in time-honoured fashion, propagate the bloodline again to produce a 'new' heir. Jen Carter had been correctly identified but wrongly targeted. I had no idea who she was, at the time. I was just instructed to inseminate her, so I did… I raped your mother, Nathan. Needlessly, it seems…"

Nathan screamed inside, his pent-up rage growing exponentially. No words could possibly vent the anger now pulsating within his being.

"Being a good Catholic girl, she was never going to give you up," Lanus continued in his nonchalance. "We'd just intended that she feed and clothe you until it was time to steal our own flesh and blood back. But, following the car crash, we lost track of your whereabouts again," Lanus added. "The Sanctuary used their influence to make it seem that you hadn't survived, which threw us for a while… Who knew that we'd find both you and Caleb together so many years later with your aunt, hidden in plain sight."

Lanus paused and leant in close to Nathan. "You're more

of a Cavendish than a Mosley. You haven't got what it takes to be a son of mine. That's why we put so much effort into Caleb's recovery."

In a simultaneous moment across Time, Marjorie lovingly stroked her daughter Leonie's cheek before the attending physician pulled the sheet over her head with such clinical detachedness. A homebirth of twins for a thirty-two-year-old expectant mother was always going to have its risks.

Wiping the tears from her eyes, Marjorie walked over to the bassinet in which both healthily crying newborns lay. She had to choose. Fredrick Mosley knew nothing of the second child, and even though Marjorie despised the slick interloper who had split the family apart and temporarily stolen her daughter's mind, she had no choice but to give one of the children up to him. While Leonie had finally come to her senses with the sobering prospects of motherhood, and would have done anything to prevent Fredrick having access to either child, Marjorie had no option. He was their legal father – albeit an absent one, after abandoning Leonie as soon as he had learnt of the successful insemination.

Marjorie stared at both newborns for some time before reaching in and picking up the child on the left, her intuition guiding her actions. "*Shh*, Isaac," she whispered, in an attempt to quieten the sound of two cries. Hugh's trance predictions of their daughter bearing twins *had* resolved but in the most heartbreaking of ways. 'Isaac' would undoubtedly be the name eventually chosen by his new family, whoever they may be. "Take the other bastard child to him. I don't care to speak to the man."

A nurse carried the baby out of the main house and over to The Sanctuary's Library, where Fredrick and his posse of minders were impatiently waiting – with the insemination, the Mosley bloodline had not only been preserved but strengthened with Cavendish blood.

Back in the main house, the other infant was reluctantly handed over to another nurse. Marjorie knew that she would not lay eyes on Isaac again. Having already caught a fleeting glimpse of him as an adult in that experimental séance thirty years *before* his birth, she had no other choice but to let events run their course.

Marjorie cradled the newborn in her arms in a chilling repeat of twenty years prior. The stakes this time were much higher. If only she had known then what she knew now, Isaac's twin brother – Lanus – would never have been handed over to Fredrick so readily. She deeply regretted that her actions had drawn those Guardians and high-ranking government officials amongst the supporters at The Sanctuary into an inconceivable web that stretched to abduction, falsifying Birth Certificates and what amounted to human trafficking of babies. But fighting fire with fire was the only option. There was no accounting for where the most resonant of those supposed Aryan genes for targeting by the Dark Circle would ultimately be located for insemination. The pregnant teenager from a near-destitute family who had been raped by Lanus was rescued just before she'd come to full term and spirited away to The Sanctuary for safety. This time, the Dark Circle had to be denied the firstborn son and heir. Lanus must never find the child. The girl had been extended the best care possible from doctors loyal to Marjorie and The Sanctuary's Circle and had also been promised an extraordinary amount of money to set her up in a new life with a new identity if she surrendered the child for adoption. And on learning of her imminent fate when the rapist came back to claim his child, the girl readily agreed.

Marjorie would never know if Hugh's attempts across time to kill off the future bloodline would succeed. And she had hidden Hugh's letter to prevent Isaac from being inspired to kill, too. She'd been forced to be a spectator, only ever able to let the events over the decades run their course. But this was now a new chapter in Time. Resolving to hide the newborn away, in the same way that she'd hidden the cards, Marjorie handed the 7 lb baby boy over to one of her most trusted members of The Sanctuary's Circle. Childless Annie Davenport smiled and kissed the newborn on the head. "Hello, Caleb," she said.

50

18th November 1929, The Sanctuary

Lodge looked long and hard at Hugh, weighing up whether or not he should accept the invitation to act as observer in the experiment. He was torn. He had witnessed the Celtic Cross Tarot spread vanish in Charles Cavendish's experimental séance at The Sanctuary all those years before, and that an equally audacious experiment was imminently being proposed in the same location could not be a coincidence. Hugh obviously knew about Cavendish's work but was unaware that both he and Richet had been invited to act as observers in that séance, too. But Lodge wasn't in a position to inform Hugh of the fact, at the risk of causally affecting the overall experimental result across time should he lose the internal struggle with his dilemma and accept the invitation. Lodge was acutely aware that he could already be acting as 'observer' to the experiment across time, without anyone else being aware of the fact. The initial objective back in 1905 had been for the entire Celtic Cross to apport to a designated future coordinate of Time in a planned future séance – the hypothesis being that at the instant the spread of cards materialised at The Sanctuary in the future, in its specific arrangement on the etched table, a portal of communication would exist between that Medium holding both future and past séances, separated only by the illusion of Time. The materialisation of the Celtic Cross would be proof that such an open portal in a séance could allow for the transfer of not only clairvoyant information but for the transfer of Matter as well. Hugh's intention now, however, was to use the four apported cards that had so far come into his possession as *seeds* to rematerialise the entire Celtic Cross from across Time – as Charles had initially planned – but also further intended to utilise that open portal in the perpetual *Here* and *Now* of events in an even more audacious experiment to switch coordinates and physically manifest *himself* eighty-five years into the future, in an ungodly piggyback effect across time, while the Medium Isaac McKinnon, in a simultaneous future séance, would materialise eighty-five years into the past.

Lodge, still deeply torn, leant forwards and picked up THE HERMIT once more. Having witnessed both its materialisation in Hugh's séance the evening before *and* its dematerialisation twenty-five years prior in Charles Cavendish's experimental séance back in 1905, it had now become obvious to him that when Charles Cavendish had aborted the second of his planned séances, the cards of the spread, no longer having a location to apport to, had become scattered across Time rather than maintaining their arrangement through to a single future coordinate as initially intended. Most of the cards had been thrown *forwards* through Time like a handful of stones cast into the ocean, with several still yet to manifest. But Lodge now knew for certain that *THE LOVERS* card he had witnessed dematerialising from Charles Cavendish's experimental séance in 1905 had actually travelled *back* in Time to rematerialise in the inaugural séance of 1863 held by Spencer Cavendish, who had been oblivious as to the future source of that singular apport. Moreover, Lodge now realised that the second card ever to have materialised – the *THREE OF SWORDS* – had also apported back in time to one of the routinely scheduled séances held just weeks earlier in 1905 by an equally oblivious Charles himself.

A terrifying mind-bending truth was becoming all too clear to Lodge. The experimental séance he had attended in 1905 was the source of all the cards materialising forwards and backwards in time – with the materialisation of the *THREE OF SWORDS* in the earlier routine séance having paradoxically inspired an unwitting Charles Cavendish to organise the very experimental séance that would be the source of that errant card. And the ramifications of that were truly horrifying. An eddying loop in the Spacetime-Matter continuum must have been created by the experimental séance. An eddying loop in which both reality and history in that 'local' area of the continuum had been changed without anyone realising it – other than for Lodge himself observing from a unique perspective thrust upon him across the years.

The young scientist Hugh Wells sitting in front of him waiting for a reply was undoubtedly correct. While the reasoning behind current scientific knowledge might well hold relevance to our mere perceptions of physical Reality, Lodge now agreed that any such reasoning was rendered worthless when it came to understanding whatever incredible quantum mechanisms lay behind both Physicality and Reality or the Past and the Future. A whole new language of mathematics, as yet unknown, would be required to understand that. And the fact remained that when Charles had performed his bold experimental séance in 1905, the Spacetime-Matter continuum – along with Reality, along with History – had changed in an instant. What *was*, was no more. And what *would be* had simultaneously changed, too. And no one in the Past or in the Future, other than Lodge himself, was any the wiser. *Future* action had changed the *Past*, rather than *Past* action shaping the *Future*.

The ripple effects throughout the flux of Reality, with all its infinite subtle interconnections, Lodge resolved, needed to be investigated further. Heisenberg's, Schrödinger's and Bohr's recent groundbreaking research was all undoubtedly relevant. It opened up the possibility for Lodge finally to present a paper unifying his own theories with the mainstream of current quantum mechanical understanding that would quieten his many detractors in the scientific community. And being able to attest that he had witnessed simultaneous contact with future and past moments across time would indeed be the pinnacle of his scientific career. A Nobel Prize in Physics would be an inevitability.

For a fleeting moment, Charles Cavendish's soul-disturbing screams as he had appeared to be burning to death in Hell's fire during that first experimental séance echoed with Lodge. But the old man put the thought out of his mind. He tossed the card depicting *THE HERMIT* back onto the table.

"I accept your invitation, Wells," he finally replied.

*

Judging by the hatred in his captive's eyes, Lanus knew that the time was near and snatched THE HANGED MAN away from Nathan's view and swiftly stood. The tell-tale odour of ectoplasm building was now obvious.

Nathan was still mentally reeling over the confession about the rape of his mother, and triggered by the restraints leaving him powerless to protect the ones he loved, those childhood wounds inflicted on him by that gang of youths on the riverbank were once again exposed and opened up by flashback blades cutting into his psyche. The barely contained rage centred in his solar plexus was now excruciating.

Lanus handed the genealogy papers to a security guard who marched out, leaving only two other guards with him in the centre of the standing Circle. He then struck Nathan across the face one more time for good measure, the pungent odour of ectoplasm becoming instantly stronger.

Satisfied that they were close, Lanus took his position next to the table of cards and ritualistically held the final card once again high in the air while Anne-Marie remained by his side, staring at Nathan without any readable expression.

"You'll go into Trance now, Nathan. And you will open up a portal across Time that will unleash our own intentions for the past. And when we control the past, we will also be able to control the future… *Heil Mosley!*"

The room echoed with an incessant terrifying mass reply that repeated and repeated and repeated in an unholy mantra. Nathan was instantly unnerved by the escalation in the group display of madness. Their psychotic role-playing had ended in murder, and there seemed no boundaries to their cultish crazed delusions. The sounds of the countless voices continued to reflect and echo and re-echo back on themselves in the low-ceilinged space, amplifying into a thunderous assault on Nathan's being. He felt the axes of Space and Time and Matter stretching away to infinity...

"Everyone into the safe room. NOW!" Lanus ordered with an urgent bellowing command above the noise, as he prepared to place *THE HANGED MAN* in position.

Amidst the clamour of the rapidly retreating Dark Circle members, Nathan's slip in consciousness was momentarily halted when he saw Lanus nod to the two remaining security guards and then motion towards Mia.

"Do what you want with the girl. Show him what we do with whores like her!"

Anne-Marie was already on the move towards Nathan as the two henchmen drew blades and lunged at Mia, viciously cutting at the ropes tethering her. But before Nathan could open his mouth to yell out, he felt the stab of the needle being wielded by Anne-Marie piercing his exposed arm, just as Lanus placed the last card down in its appointed place – the pair themselves then running for the door to evacuate from the room.

DMT began to course through Nathan's veins as he helplessly witnessed the first horrifying moments of what was to be Mia's fate. A shock wave exploded through the room as a rage beyond rage finally erupted from him. The room was instantly filled with a blinding flash of light as the atoms and molecules of the surrounding atmosphere were stripped of electrons. *How calm he suddenly felt... How tranquil... Serenity... Dissipation...*

The Dark Circle's plan had worked. Nathan had been forced against his will into an explosive Trance state through those carefully orchestrated tactics of 'Shock and Awe'. That gem of information provided by Caleb, as to Nathan's darkest childhood secret, and forcing him to watch the murders and assaults of the ones he loved just could not have failed to provoke such a cataclysmic reaction. The Celtic Cross was again complete. The portal had opened. And both Nathan and Caleb had vanished into the Void.

51

The pristine white quantum Void of Consciousness became marred by flashes of imagery. Nathan had no sense of how long he had been suspended in the endless zero-point vacuum before his awareness began to flood back instant by instant: there was noise; there was clamour; there was shouting, and as the blankness gave way to a 360-degree panorama of activity, he could see teams of men digging and dragging and hauling. He was again discarnate, trapped in some corner of the Void.

The sound of a horse snorting through its bridle caught his attention, and he looked confusedly upwards to his right where a formidable-looking man in period clothing was surveying the scene from his saddle. Nathan followed the man's downwards gaze across the deep foundations of the excavation site to where several men were busying themselves installing a fire grate. His own gaze then focused on the surrounding stone flooring and the masonry walls lining the exposed subterranean space being constructed by other teams of men – he was still in that same cellar space at the Hall. In being forced into Trance, his awareness had traversed through the Void to a different coordinate of Time but had not moved in location. He had been thrown into the past to the very place where the nightmare had first begun within the scheming mind of Nicholas Mosley, over four hundred years before.

Memories of the horrendous events that had transported him there came flooding back into Nathan's mindstream. Terror struck at the thought of what was happening to Mia at this very moment, close enough to reach out in space yet too far to reach out across centuries of time. But before he could turn his mind to how he was going to get back to rescue her, a flickering distortion in the fabric of the scene at a point in space in front of him sent waves of disturbance through his energy field. Nicholas Mosley above had seen the aberrant flicker, too, and whipped at his spooked horse, shouting out authoritatively in an attempt to regain control of the normally trusted animal as it circled uneasily and grunted its objections to his master's commands. Transfixed, Nathan continued to stare into the distorting space ahead, captivated by the phenomenal display, and with a sudden crack of electrical energy, the light body of his half-brother flashed into view. For a moment, Caleb seemed just as disorientated and confused as Nathan had been but quickly settled on recognising his surroundings, realising that he was exactly where he was supposed to be. The horse reared, it taking all of Mosley's skill and brute strength to exert control. The Lord of the Manor swore out loud on seeing the ghostly spectre, and several of the builders looked on in utter shock, too, as they caught sight of the apparition within the cellar space they were constructing.

While Nathan remained invisibly discarnate, Caleb was obviously on the verge of physicalising, and the significance of the last heil to a new Führer that Lanus and the Dark Circle had been chanting now chillingly made sense: *THE MAGICIAN 1914* – the first of '*two Great Wars in Europe*' breaking out; *THE DEVIL 1939* – the outbreak of '*the second war*'; *DEATH 1945* – nuclear '*explosions of light and fire*' that will wipe out entire cities in a flash, and *THE TOWER 1989* – the '*Wall in Berlin will fall*'. Using the portal opened in Isaac and Hugh's experimental séance, the Dark Circle intended changing the course of history by sending Caleb back in time, and they were close to achieving everything that they wanted to succeed in. Caleb was using the séances across time to seek out the energy fields of every genetically resonant member of the two bloodlines accessing the Void in Trance until – through the seed card of *THE HIGH PRIESTESS* – he could locate the traitorous Mathieson in a dark séance being held in 1936.

Nathan's hatred and uncontainable anger seethed through the ether, and his brother was quick to register it. Caleb at first seemed shocked at Nathan's presence, and they were left staring at each other, mirroring that instant in the corridor at the Carousel Club. And in a twisted repeat of his vanishing act to escape, Caleb bolted back into the Void through ancestor Nicholas Mosley's solar plexus. But this time Nathan was ready for him and lunged into the tail of Caleb's energy field as his own genetic resonance locked him onto that fleeing malevolent expression of ego intent on inflicting a catastrophic change to the past. He now knew that the collective illusion of current Reality in his own Time's frame of reference was about to come to an end, unless the

Dark Circle's plans could be stopped. If Caleb was allowed to succeed, the consequences for the freedom and destiny of billions of souls across time would be devastating.

Nicholas Mosley felt a cataclysmic lightning bolt from nowhere strike him and he was thrown from his mount. He lay writhing on the ground as if burning in the invisible fires of Hell, and no one dared approach. A single horseman urgently galloped away to bring back a clergyman to exorcise the malign spirit. Everyone else stepped back, fearing the phantom that had possessed their master. An abandonment of duty that would cost several of his men their lives once Sir Nicholas had recovered from the large burn that the 'Devil' had left across his abdomen.

Nathan searched the darkness. The last time he had experienced such an all-encompassing absence of light within the Void was during his struggle to free himself from that underground grave he'd seen himself in. But there was no sense of that suffocating dank air in the surrounds presenting to him now. Here, there was only silence. Caleb was somewhere close, so he had to be on his guard. His brother could be watching and waiting to ambush him at any moment.

Instant relief from the suspense came with a small sphere of light that ignited in front of him, providing a sensory parameter he desperately needed. It illuminated the face and torso of a man sitting tied to a chair with his eyes closed, and as the light grew in luminosity and expanded across the room, it engulfed a small table covered in an array of Tarot cards. Nathan immediately recognised the ambience and décor of The Sanctuary's séance room, if not the antiquated garb of those now becoming visible around the Circle. He also immediately realised the significance of the cards. But before he could think of how to warn them not to proceed with the experiment, a flash of light that was Caleb shot across the room and penetrated the umbilical plasma of energy emanating from the Medium with a lightning crack that exploded blindingly. A terrifying instantaneous implosion of ectoplasm sucked Nathan's energy field along with it through the Medium's solar plexus and back into oblivion – Charles Cavendish was left screaming and fighting for life. Burning alive. Burning alive in the Here and Now, along with every genetically resonant Guardian of the bloodlines across the centuries who had ever dared to reach out in that eternal moment and touch the zero-point quantum oblivion of creation itself. Those flames of energy flashed through Time to ignite the fabric of The Sanctuary where Isaac, blocked in his escape by the arrival of Lanus and his men, had been forced to remain too long to avert resolution of the fateful prophecy predicting that The Sanctuary would be *'reduced to rubble and dust'*, while whoever remained would *'perish at the hands of a new bloodline'*.

The traverse through the Void was superluminal. The journey unbearable. Nathan was *nothing*, yet at one with *everything*. He felt the pain of a trillion deaths and the sacred joy of every single birth that had ever given rise to life, all speeding through him in every instant. Each myriad angst was countered by an equal ecstasy, leaving him in an eternal peace while simultaneously suffering an insufferable pain that had no end and no beginning… A sideways jolt. His deceleration to physical Reality again was beyond phenomenal as dilated Time reversed and his potential for physicality transformed into an infinite mass that rapidly lightened again to more earthly proportions. Awareness kicked in just as Nathan's head struck masonry on colliding with the opposite wall in the back alleyway of the Carousel Club, his scalp glancing off a metal stud fixed into the brickwork before he crashed to the ground. Landing heavily on his back, he was still shaking the cloudiness from his head when he saw Caleb in the half-light walking slowly towards him. A wave of rapidly intensifying paralysis swept over his body while a breath-denying crushing sensation against his chest pinned him to the ground, and the grip he was under only intensified as Caleb came closer and knelt over him. Nathan was perplexed by the replaying events: *Am I reliving a past moment? Have I possessed my own body from a future Time? Has concussion played tricks on my mind about a future that never happened?* The answer came when Caleb pounced, forging a new outcome in the fabric of Space and Time and Matter. The pair had all but physicalised, and Caleb began mercilessly pounding heavy blows on his brother's face, head and throat in flurries of punches meant to kill. Nathan was losing consciousness as the back of his physicalising cranium was smashed repeatedly into the hard cobblestones by the sheer force of each blow – lethal blows that were wreaking havoc on the still-fragile rematerialising tissues of his skull. Defenceless and still paralysed, he had to react or his life this time would not be spared in that back alley. Having no other course of action open to him, he surrendered himself completely in a last-chance attempt to dissolve his physical self back into the Void.

Caleb's physicality and uncontrolled rage now worked against him. The momentum of his vicious intent left his arms flailing in a muscle memory-fuelled flurry of punches into nothing but thin air. Nathan, fuelled by instinct alone, finally seized the moment to lunge into Caleb's quantum energy field with equal vicious intent. Caleb fell to the ground, instantly immobilised by the burgeoning force now being exerted by the partially visible phantom on top of him. His physicalised brain was being starved of oxygen and he had slipped too far out of the Void to fight back. Their energies were locked in a battle to the death, and it seemed that Nathan, despite being weakened, would at last get the ultimate revenge.

"Shh-ouldn't you be... g-getting back to Mia!" Caleb stuttered in choked words. "Time means... nothing, here. Maybe she's not been raped yet!"

Nathan was distracted long enough for Caleb to break the hold, the dagger glares of the warring brothers meeting for a second. The DMT was still energetically active, and with one concerted deep rasping breath, Caleb's existence in that illusory timeframe of consciousness ceased. He vanished, as did Nathan, already knowing that he'd reacted too late to lock on... Caleb had escaped.

The dimly lit back alley behind the Carousel Club was again quiet and deserted, as if nothing had happened. And inside the club, the fights on the night's bill continued on seemingly as before. But outside, the scene had been subtly yet irrevocably changed, signalling a rift in the historical imprint of Spacetime and Matter. Nothing would ever be the same. The Akashic Field – that infinite Cosmic record of the Past, Present and Future – had started to be rewritten.

The Führer's eyes were wide with awe and disbelief. The diffuse luminescence generated by the Medium that had sparked into existence and ripped through the pervading darkness had now taken the form of a discernible light body still connected by an umbilical cord of radiating energy. *Through what otherworldly invocation had the Englishman Mathieson summoned this Spirit? Had it descended from Heaven or arisen from Hell?* At a loss for answers, the Führer felt incredibly small and insignificant. For once, he was faced with something far greater than his own estimation of himself – a phenomenon that was immeasurably more powerful than all the legions of troops and countless squadrons of tanks and bombers at his disposal. He craved this power. Without it, there would be others who might conquer the Reich; with it, he would control more than just the world.

To Rattenhuber's alarm, the body of light drifted in the Führer's direction. The expression on Hitler's face, now illuminated by the phantom light, remained totally unperturbed and even peacefully spellbound by what he was witnessing, prompting the head of personal security to remain seated in fear of the consequences of intervening.

The light emanating from the body gradually became less intense, but before it faded completely, the physical form of a young man standing in front of the Führer became increasingly more discernible the dimmer the light became. And just before darkness again ensued in the room, the silhouette of the naked blond Aryan Adonis before them had seemed all but palpable.

The darkness was complete, and no one knew how to react except for continuing to sit in an awestruck silence. A silence that was broken by the young man's voice.

"My Führer, I come with warnings from the future and a gift from the past," Caleb began in a scripted greeting.

"*Mein Führer. Ich komme mit einer Warnung aus der Zukunft, und einem Geschenk aus der Vergangenheit,*" repeated the translator dutifully in a subdued whisper.

"There is much you should know about the forces that will oppose you. And there is much you should know about future technological advances that can be within your grasp, now."

The translator's voice again hissed quietly through the air.

"This physical display was necessary so that you can be in no doubt as to the sincerity of the descendants of Oswald Mosley who sent me. You may turn on the lights… But just one at first, please."

Rattenhuber didn't hesitate. He snatched the army issue torch from his belt and immediately shone it towards Hitler's seat, its broad divergent beam cutting through the darkness to reveal a naked man on his knees holding out a card in a gesture of subservience to the Führer. *THE HIGH PRIESTESS* from the Celtic Cross – usurped in the Void – had also apported.

"*Nathan!*"

As awareness again returned, the whiteness of the Void that he seemed so hopelessly trapped in was momentarily indistinguishable from the sterile white walls and ceiling of the surroundings in which he now found himself. It was as if he was waking from a sleep that had lasted for centuries.

"*Help me!*"

The sound of a girl's voice was reverberating uncomfortably through his being, jarring with his nascent senses.

"*Nathan! Nathan!*"

In his confusion as to where he was, he looked down at an array of equipment, tubes and cords and realised that the focus of his awakening was centred in mid-air with a bird's-eye view of the scene below – gravity, once more, holding no place in his mass-less discarnate state.

"*NATHAN!*"

Finally, he registered the girl's familiar voice, and the outline of a suspended light body came into view in front of him, just as it had done before in the Void and again in her ghostly visitation in the study of his apartment. If there was ever any proof of an eternal Here and Now of events in simultaneous moments of existence, then this was surely it. It was as though he was living three moments at the same time through a clairvoyant insight that had rendered his future unnervingly superimposed onto his past. His sense of Reality and his sense of location in illusory Space and Time shook and vibrated disturbingly as he fought to stay centred in just the one place.

"*Please help me. I can't live through this anymore… I'm trapped. She cut away my body until there was nothing left… They did the same to other girls, too… I just want to die!*"

Captured by the girl's thoughts imprinted into the ether, Nathan looked down at the array of equipment below that he recognised all too well – a neonatal incubator… a heart-lung machine… dialysis… an MRI scanner… This place was the laboratory at AXIS. And the '*She*' referred to was undoubtedly Anne-Marie.

Housed inside the incubator below was a small mass of human tissue, and revulsion hit as the full enormity of Anne-Marie's depravity sank in. He was inside the out-of-bounds, electronically-guarded imaging suite he'd walked past on his visit there months before – Caleb's transformation had come at a cost, and the thought of the suffering those girls must have endured in proving Holzer's warped theories correct was sickening. And now knowing that it had been the tortured soul of one of the girls calling out for help as he'd left the lab that day was agonising for him.

"I've seen everything... You've got to stop them... You're the last Guardian in Time, Nathan. The only hope... HELP ME!"

Before Nathan could process those words, the girl's cloud of light shot through the illusion of Space and collided with his own thought field. The explosive impact instantly shattered the Reality that had been presenting before him into an energetic cloud of quantum particulate consciousness. Nathan had been flung into empty eternity. A mere potential. A nothingness. He was again at one with the Void.

52

The rising potential difference either side of the zero-point interface had reached critical. On one side, an expansive still silence of nothingness. On the other, a blazing maelstrom of erupting primordial energetic activity. The breach would come through the smallest of fissures. A single pair of subatomic particles appeared suddenly in the vacuous stillness, only to vanish again – created and annihilated in an instant. Then another pair appeared and then another. The balance had shifted and the expansive stillness was now being swamped through the barrier that had separated the two polar opposite domains so impenetrably. *Consciousness and Physicality*. Those miniscule unleashed particles *collided* explosively and *split* and *collided* and *fused* and *collided* in what seemed violent random confusion. But some subtle overall intent was exerting control – Consciousness. The entirety of the particles was being swept into collections of more slowly revolving vortices, and the physical precursors of atoms and molecules within were beginning to aggregate closer and closer together under their own gravity and electrical forces. Another fall to physicality had begun.

Nathan opened his eyes and shivered in his nakedness. He was once again back in the cellars of the Hall. Isaac still hung on the inverted cross, but Mia now lay on the stone floor, not too far from Barbara's body. Otherwise, the cellar was deserted. Lanus and the Dark Circle were nowhere to be seen, obviously not expecting their victims to survive.

Nathan stood unsteadily and staggered over to Mia. She was breathing, albeit shallowly. To add to her injuries, the skin of her face and arms had been badly burnt when the portal had opened and she needed urgent medical attention, but the most he could do for now was attempt to revive her if she went into arrest.

The sound of a faint sighing exhalation came from Isaac's suspended body.

"Hold on, Isaac!"

Anxiously scanning around the room, Nathan noticed the dagger lying in the centre of a pool of Isaac's blood on the floor in front of the inverted cross, and he hurried over to grab it.

The bindings proved difficult to hack through in Nathan's depleted state, and it was even harder to manhandle Isaac's body onto the ground without injuring him further. With the blood already lost from the deep abdominal wound, it was obvious he wasn't going to make it. His skin, too, looked as if it had been burnt in a flash of nuclear radiation.

Isaac attempted to speak in such a whisper that Nathan

had to move in closer to be able to hear. "I love you, Nathan… Like the son I never had."

There wasn't the time for Nathan to explain that they truly were family. All he could do at that moment was hold his uncle and comfort him while he passed.

Isaac, though, was intent on summoning his last breaths to speak. "Lanus and the Circle… They locked themselves down in one of the stone-lined priest holes for protection from the portal opening… I heard Lanus asking if everyone's syringe of DMT had been prepared… They're holding an induced trance séance, waiting for the birth of their New Order. You've got to get Mia help while there's still time… but, Nathan…" Isaac's hand scrambled weakly for the dagger on the floor that Nathan had placed down after cutting him from the cross. He picked it up and forced it into Nathan's hand. "As soon as she's safe… you must use this on yourself. Dying is the only way you can stop their madness. They are using your energy within the Void, as we speak. And, believe me… if I had the strength at this moment… I would kill you myself."

Nathan threw away the knife as if it was cursed, just as Isaac slumped lifelessly in his arms. It seemed that he hadn't even been safe from those he had loved the most – a betrayal that he had no time to process.

He checked Mia's condition again before rushing towards the heavy wooden door of the cellar space in an attempt to find an escape route. It was ajar. In the corridor outside lay the burnt bodies of the two henchmen that had attacked Mia. They had obviously taken the brunt of the explosion of energy and had succumbed in their panicked attempts to flee.

Nathan ran further along the dimly lit corridor and tried a couple of doors that opened into empty rooms disturbingly furnished with shackles attached to the walls. Behind the third door he tried, the shackles were attached to the ankles and wrists of two young girls left to rot in the makeshift cell, the stench emanating from the room making Nathan heave. One of the girls was obviously dead.

After checking that the younger of the girls was still alive but unconscious, Nathan ran further down the corridor, only to be faced with the dead end of a stone wall. The Dark Circle had entered the cellar through the same corridor earlier, so it couldn't just lead nowhere. The wall was likely false and part of the elaborate centuries-old priest-hole system common to manors of this era, but it was anyone's guess how it opened.

Running back into the cellar, Nathan found his clothes, which had been thrown on the floor when he'd first been tied naked to the séance chair. He pulled on his jeans and slipped his oversized shirt onto Mia's exposed body in an attempt to provide her with some warmth. Mia and the imprisoned girl needed help urgently, so he had to find a way out. He raced over to retrieve the dagger in the vain hope that he could use it to pry open the hidden locking mechanism between the masonry work at the end of the corridor but couldn't immediately see where the knife had landed after he had thrown it away. Scanning around again in desperation, he finally caught sight of the bloodstained metal over by the wall near where Barbara was lying and hesitated before reverently stepping over her body to pick up the knife. But as his hand touched the hilt, a musty smell that was somehow recognisable struck his senses. Nathan stared into the gloom. Built into the wall was a small square opening framed by the ornate stonework of a fire grate, and from its mouth came that familiar stench of damp rotting earth.

Nathan instantly felt as though he was again vibrating and beating in enharmonic resonance between simultaneous moments of existence: the dark confined crawlspace he'd been trapped in while in Trance; the construction site of the Hall; the light body of the girl in the low-ceilinged room who'd been pointing towards a wall as if showing him something… He tentatively climbed inside the opening. The smell was unmistakeable. If the fabric of the seventeenth-century Hall was fenestrated with secret priest holes and impenetrable hidden cellars, then it was conceivable that they had built an escape tunnel, too. He had found a way out.

Nathan carefully moved Barbara's body before carrying Mia over to the tunnel's opening. The subterraneous escape would be hell, but there was no other choice. He simply had to trust his clairvoyant insight from the *past* that was now resolving in the *present* of this predicted *future* moment. The partially collapsed crawlspace would become narrower, but at least the cellar's faux fire grate opening was wide enough for him to position Mia inside, and scrambling to manoeuvre himself ahead, he clutched her limp body.

A powerful hand suddenly grabbed hold of Nathan's ankle and yanked him out of the tunnel's opening and back into the cellar.

Bedlam was standing over him, smiling. "Where do you think you're taking the girl, Nathan? I figured I might just have her to myself one last time before she expires. Hell of a way to go, don't *ya* think… Maybe you can watch this time."

Bedlam pounced on him as if he was one of his victims in the Cage, delivering a combination of punches that left

Nathan senseless. The fighter knew exactly which of his strikes would stun and which would kill.

Nathan came to his senses slumped in the charred séance chair just as Bedlam was starting to lash one of the ropes around his wrist to tie him down. Being rendered helpless yet again while someone he loved was about to be assaulted in front of him was not an option, and summoning all his strength, he swung his free arm in a wide arcing right hook to the temple of a distracted Bedlam. The fighter fell to his knees, unaccustomed to the mental struggle of grasping for the temporarily disconnected neural connections that would allow him to stand. Nathan released his partially tied wrist and lunged out of the chair, following up with a solid kick to Bedlam's head that sent the already dazed fighter flat onto the ground. He was just about to open up with more vicious blows that were entirely intended to kill when he felt someone grab him around his neck and place the blade of the dagger to his throat – Isaac's powerful frame staggered backwards a few steps, trying to stay on his feet.

"Isaac, no!"

"There's no time left, Nathan! I've got to do this!" Isaac was sobbing as he began to increase the pressure against Nathan's throat. Even the slightest of movements would have meant certain death.

"No, Isaac!" Nathan pleaded again.

Bedlam finally got to his feet and began laughing at the unexpected spectacle playing out in front of him. "Now this *is* funny," he mocked, walking slowly towards the pair. "Kill him if you want. Don't think for a second that I believe all this shit about Reality going to end. Lanus and those crazy fucks are holding a séance locked inside a hidden room lined with two-metre-thick granite blocks… and I've disengaged the locking mechanism." Bedlam smirked. "Lousy bastards tried to keep me in the dark about what they had planned. Now they'll die a slow death in there and I'll take over everything. The whole fucking empire. So save me the effort. KILL THE FUCKER!" he screamed venomously at Isaac, motioning threateningly towards them.

Isaac momentarily lost his footing, allowing Nathan to break his grip on the knife. And in a lightning strike, he thrust the blade into Bedlam's throat, just as Isaac dropped to the floor.

53

Nathan clambered along on his stomach in the darkness, knowing that survival depended on him keeping moving. The putrid stagnant air lacked oxygen for his lungs, and it seemed that every muscle in his body seared with pain as he clawed along with his free arm, dragging the dead weight of Mia's body. He couldn't be sure if the partially collapsed tunnel led to safety or if it led to an impenetrable dead end, just like every locked door and corridor leading from the cellar that had frustrated all other efforts to escape. He just had to trust in that clairvoyant memory imprinted across Time – that memory of a gentle waft of air on his face as he would finally break through to safety. Doubts began to set in, though, when the walls, roof and floor of the centuries-old crawlspace became gradually more and more constricted as he struggled along. It was obvious that there was no way back. If the tunnel ended or had become blocked, then they would die together in that unseemly grave. But with his next clawing reach, his hand suddenly felt a change in the texture of the dirt. It was grittier and stonier to the touch, and he definitely sensed that he was now moving on a shallow upwards incline. His fingers were being cut and grazed by pieces of rubble and broken half-bricks, so he turned awkwardly onto his back, hauling Mia's limp body on top of him to protect her. The jagged edges of masonry that had once framed the exit to the tunnel ripped at the skin of his back as he slid along the ever-increasing gradient. Gaining a foothold and holding his breath in a concerted effort, he strained and pushed towards the hope of safety. *Resolution*. A waft of breeze caressed his face. And with a final thrust he broke out into the night air.

The steeply sloping terrain and sound of gently babbling water could only mean that the tunnel had opened out amidst the long grass of what must have been the bank of a stream. Nathan pulled Mia out of the tunnel exit and laid her down for a few seconds while he caught his breath. He had been drugged, nearly beaten to death in a battle across centuries of time, and the forced one-hundred-and-fifty-metre subterranean crawl had taken him beyond the point of exhaustion. But he had to keep going. Mia was unresponsive and her pulse was at best weak, and getting her medical help without delay was his only thought. Lifting her up into his arms, he unsteadily negotiated his way up to the top of the shadowy bank, only to find his bare feet stepping onto the cool grass of a close-cropped lawn area stretching between neatly manicured flower beds. The presenting scene was illuminated by the orange blanket glow of street lighting running along the park boundary, not far from where he had parked the Kombi earlier. A shiver went through his partially clothed body. Not with cold. This was the same park he had walked to in a Trance state on the night of the murder. He had thought he'd been the killer. When, in truth, he'd been unconsciously drawn to the park in an automaton attempt to avert the horrific fate suffered by that girl at the hands of the Dark Circle. Now in his arms was their latest victim.

Ahead, a path led to the nearby park gate, but before he had even taken a few staggering steps towards it, Mia's already limp body slumped in his arms. All tone had been lost in her musculature. Nathan reacted immediately, realising that she was in cardiac arrest, and placed her flat on her back on the path. He checked for a carotid pulse before thumping her sternum hard in a precordial strike with his closed fist, not knowing if he had the physical strength left to resuscitate her. There was still no pulse, and leaning over her, he had no choice but to attempt compressions rendered so weak that they were unlikely to be effective. *Twenty-eight... Twenty-nine... Thirty.* He sealed his mouth over hers and forced whatever life giving breath he had left into her starved lungs before hopelessly starting compressions again. *One... Two...* Mia's chest rose slightly in a shallow breath. She was back. But before he could inhale a breath of his own and exhale his relief, he suddenly caught sight of a boot approaching his face at speed. Nathan fell to the ground, unconscious – the apparent spectacle of a bare-chested male manhandling, striking and forcing himself upon a defenceless half-naked girl, at the very location of a recent rape and murder, had inspired a man passing by the entrance to the dimly lit park to take matters into his own hands before making an emergency call to the police.

Pullen tossed the clear polythene evidence bags containing the catalogue of depraved images and the leather mask retrieved from Nathan's apartment onto the table of the interview room. "You're done, Carter," he calmly stated. "Just tell me what you and McKinnon have done with the girls."

Dressed in a one-piece evidence suit, Nathan sat at the table and held his head in his hands in both frustration and despair. "Mia… The girl. Tell me if she's OK!" he asked for the third time, desperate to know her condition.

Pullen remained silent and turned to Fitzpatrick sitting next to him, giving an unimpressed look. The detective sergeant responded with an equally sceptical expression.

"The rest of the girls!" Pullen persisted, raising his voice. "Are they alive?"

It was immediately obvious to Nathan that he was more than just a suspect in the park murder and Alex's death. Pullen was now linking those two murders with the spate of abductions that had been all over the news.

"Where's McKinnon? And who is Hugh Wells?"

Nathan was shocked at Pullen's mention of the name. The incessant questioning and constant switching in the line of interrogation intended to break him down was working, and the detective's knowledge of Hugh only confused him even more.

Pullen pushed another clear plastic evidence bag containing the letter written by Hugh across the table.

Nathan recognised the handwriting immediately but couldn't conceive where the letter had come from. He read the words and shook his head in disbelief. The Circle had reached out to Isaac across the years. Hugh had wanted him dead, too.

"Anything to say?" Pullen hoped that the growing body of evidence that had been presented throughout the interrogation would make Carter realise that holding out was useless. And letting slip that Isaac McKinnon was being urged to kill him might just make him think twice about protecting his accomplice's whereabouts.

Nathan was in no state to assure the detectives that his continued silence was not based on guilt. He had been weakened and depleted by being thrown repeatedly across the Void; he was concussed from the kick to the head he had suffered in the park, not to mention the blows endured from both Bedlam and Caleb. He was also trying to come to terms with the fact that Barbara and Isaac had been murdered, and his worry over Mia's condition was all-consuming. In the Trance states of the Void, everything had been clear. Now that he had physicalised, so much had sunk frustratingly out of his grasp and into his subconscious.

Pullen slammed one last plastic evidence bag down in front of Nathan. "What's this about?" he snapped.

Nathan looked through the clear plastic at a small scrap of paper that read, *THE HIGH PRIESTESS. Physical Séance. Apported Tarot Card, 7th October 1936. Sitting Medium, Henry Mathieson.* It had obviously been found in the pocket of the shirt in which he'd wrapped Mia.

A flood of memory instantly resurfaced at the sight of the small provenance label. "The cellars…" Nathan said to himself, piecing things back together.

Pullen and Fitzpatrick threw each other a glance, surprised by the apparent abrupt turnaround in the suspect's willingness to talk.

"Where?" Pullen demanded, jumping on the opportunity to finally force a confession. "Where!"

"The old Hall," Nathan replied. "There's a series of

hidden cellars that were used as safe rooms and escape routes centuries ago." His delivery was now becoming full of urgency. "There's a young girl in there that needs immediate medical attention. You've got to find her."

The detectives looked at each other again, even more perplexed at the eagerness with which Carter now seemed to want to cooperate. Pullen gave Fitzpatrick a simple nod, prompting the DS to make an exit to follow up on the new information.

"Interview suspended at 23.31 hours," Pullen said for the benefit of procedure, before pressing *STOP* on the recording device.

"The girl. Mia," Nathan pleaded. "Please tell me if she's OK."

Pullen stood silently and headed for the door, unwilling to relinquish any leverage that he had. "You've got a lot more talking to do yet," he said, before exiting the interview room and calling to an officer out in the corridor. "Take him back to the holding cells."

It only took a matter of seconds for the canine unit searching inside the Hall to lock onto the scent of human activity, and the highly trained Belgian Shepherd – an asset that the Queen's men didn't possess all those centuries before – was now barking and lunging excitedly at a point along a seemingly impregnable stretch of masonry in the expansive cellars. Pullen's influence during the formative years of DS Fitzpatrick's police career became immediately evident. "Tear it down," he commanded. "One of the girls is in there. We need an engineer. Get a compressor and pneumatic drills if you have to!"

There was one room in the network of hidden cellars that would never be found and penetrated, no matter what tools were employed or how many dogs insistently barked at the meticulously engineered masonry walls. Trapped inside the elaborately designed priest hole, those members of the Dark Circle, having ended their séance hours before, were beginning to realise that they had been betrayed by one of their own.

54

Nathan was led back into the interview room some hours later to face a stern-looking Pullen sitting silently next to a second detective whom Nathan recognised from the routine questioning he had been subjected to at his apartment at the time Alex had been killed.

"Interview recommenced at 09.20 hours," Pullen uttered into the microphone before again falling into a silence that lasted twenty uncomfortable seconds or more.

Nathan finally returned Pullen's intense stare with an equally expressionless gaze.

"The girl… Mia Kerr. She's dead," Pullen finally announced, carefully watching for the slightest change in his suspect's demeanour on hearing the news.

Nathan continued to stare without any trace of reaction. He was numb. His world had ended, and there was no expression of emotion that could possibly convey what he was feeling inside.

"You'll be going down for multiple life sentences without

a prayer of ever being released, Nathan." Pullen's voice was deliberately quiet and uncharacteristically soft. "Nothing you can say will change that. So why don't you just tell us where the other girls are and end this. Or at least let us know if they're still alive."

Pullen fell silent again for a few moments before turning over a crime scene photograph from a pile in front of him. He pushed it across the table in a gesture that suggested the game really was up.

Nathan gazed upon the image of Isaac and Barbara lying on the stone floor beside the inverted cross in the Hall's cellar and watched on as Pullen turned over a second surveillance photo taken of the funeral guests at the cemetery only a couple of days prior, clearly showing him in conversation with the latest victims.

"You're the only common link in all the killings, Carter. Now tell me. The rest of the girls. Are they still alive?"

Nathan remained expressionless and uncommunicative.

Pullen suddenly exploded, his aggressive manner entirely premeditated, as he slammed down photo after photo from the pile in an ever-growing line across the table, recreating the array of innocent youthful smiles he'd had to look at each passing day in his office. "Look at their faces, Carter!" He slowly turned over one final picture and tossed it over to Nathan. "We found this one rotting in one of the cellars at the Hall, along with another girl chained to the wall."

Nathan finally reacted on seeing the image of the decaying corpse. "The younger girl... Is she still alive?" he asked anxiously, with apparent concern.

"Barely," Pullen answered, sensing that the unrelenting psychological breakdown strategies he'd employed in his interrogation had done their job. Carter had already spectacularly caved in, spilling the location of the hidden cellar at the Hall, and the fatigued suspect seemed on the verge of giving up everything he knew. "Would you be willing to take us to where the other missing girls are? Or at least show us where you disposed of the bodies," he asked again, in a softer tone.

Nathan thought for a moment before answering. "OK. I'll take you," he replied, with a resignation in his voice that Pullen would entirely misinterpret.

Being granted a warrant to search the Neuropsychological Research lab at AXIS had presented no problems for Pullen, on account of it being the workplace of the murder victim Mia Kerr and a place of interest according to the prime suspect in custody. The main lab had already been cleared of its bewildered personnel, and they were being held in a conference room on the ground floor for questioning while the search was being completed.

The building seemed devoid of security staff, despite its high-tech nerve centre, and finding someone amongst the skeleton staff to open the electronically-locked door to the imaging suite Nathan Carter had led them to had proven frustrating. But override codes had at last been accessed and Pullen escorted Nathan – now handcuffed and garbed in a remand-issue jumpsuit – into the room.

Pullen looked around the equipment-filled space. There was nothing in there that he wouldn't have expected to see in any laboratory environment, and there was certainly no sign of any of the victims he had hoped to find. "What are you playing at, Carter?" he snapped brusquely.

"Over there," Nathan motioned with a nod of his head, slowly walking over to the incubator containing the dissected remains he had seen in the Void.

Pullen followed, keeping a safe distance, his reactions on a hair-trigger, despite the detainee being securely manacled with his arms behind his back. The suspect seemed distracted, constantly glancing around the room as if hopelessly looking for an opportunity to escape.

"The dismembering of the girls was only the beginning," Nathan offered in a preoccupied monotone delivery. "They were systematically dissected away. That's all that's left of one of them."

Pullen couldn't believe what he was hearing. Nor could he believe the calmness with which this sadistic killer was describing his depravity. He took a couple of careful steps closer to peer inside the incubator and was shocked to be confronted by the sight of a small mass of what seemed to be living tissue. The detective shook his head, struggling to process what he was seeing with what he was being told.

"Dr Anne-Marie Burns, the head of research here, has been experimenting with the control of Reality itself at a quantum level. And so were Isaac McKinnon and Hugh Wells. That's why they vanished from the hospital and the ambulance. They dematerialised in one of their experimental séances."

Pullen stared back at Nathan in disbelief. He knew he'd been dealing with a psychopath but hadn't been prepared for the delusional babbling issuing from the prisoner's lips.

"The kidnapped girls were being systematically dissected away in experiments to isolate the quantum template of Physicality and their body parts disposed of. This is all that is left of the last girl to be experimented on."

Pullen was at a loss as to how such a warped fantasy and flight of thoughts could ultimately have led to such horrific crimes.

"I have to ask you something before I tell you any more, though," Nathan said. He had stalled for long enough but needed just a few more seconds.

The detective wasn't one to negotiate.

"What was the girl Mia's cause of death?"

The last thing Pullen wanted to do was engage in any form of dialogue that would indulge Carter and allow him to gloat over the perversions that had been committed. On the other hand, appeasing this crazed mind was a small price to pay if he could finally bring the case to a successful closure.

"Cardiac arrest brought on by internal bleeding due to the rape and repeated violent beatings she'd been subjected to," he answered, without emotion. "She was dead by the time the ambulance arrived at the park."

A pungent sulphurous odour tainted the sterile air. Nathan remained still for a second then took a deep breath, inhaling the devastating truth of Mia's fate. That he had revived her only for her life to have been extinguished and lost again with that knock-out kick to his head was unbearable. His eyes rolled upwards at the ceiling in an attempt to contain, for just a few seconds longer, the intense rage held inside of him, a flicker of light high above the incubator signalling what he had been waiting for. With a savage reaching kick, he smashed the frontage of the incubator and darted towards it, ripping the still-vital human tissue out of its life support with his cuffed hands. He finally let out a scream, releasing all of his anguish, pain and torment. And in a blinding flash of light, his dematerialising form shot towards the remnant flickering light above that had been Jessica Mahr – his being resonating with those repeated encounters with that pleading discarnate girl in the Void's simultaneous moments across time. The explosive impact flung him once again into the empty eternity of *nothingness*. Jessica Mahr had been set free; she could finally die and be at peace.

Too shocked to react, Pullen was rendered paralysed. The last thing that he would ever witness was the locked handcuffs and jumpsuit dropping to the floor as his prime suspect vanished in a flash of light. And Nathan Carter's physical form was momentarily replaced by the naked figure of a startled and frightened young boy.

55

Jen Carter studied her reflection in the vanity mirror of the passenger-side sun visor as she was fixing her hair and checking her make-up. They were only ten minutes away from her parents' house and she was determined this time not to give her mother any chance to criticise her appearance as soon as she walked through the door. Jen stared through the make-up. *"What happened?"* she thought to herself, cupping her face with both hands and gently pulling the skin around her eyes taut. She was still beautiful; she could see that. Just not in the girlish way that she once was. Her blue eyes still glinted like jewels. Her straight black hair still shone much like it did when she was a teenager. Even her small dainty nose was recognisable as the same nose that she'd always had. *It's just my skin*, she told herself. For a moment, she remembered herself with a fresh complexion, wearing a flowing hippy skirt, strumming protest songs on the grassy quadrangle of her faculty. *Where did that girl go?* It's not that she wasn't more than content with her lot, but she did wonder on odd occasions like this if she could have done something a little less predictable with her life other than meeting a guy at uni and marrying immediately after graduating with a first in Journalism. Behind her serene appearance there used to be a part-time screaming banshee, full of liberal good intent, who would frequently be dragged by police from the ranks of a student protest picketing whatever it was they were picketing that day. The young banshee was probably still somewhere inside, but frankly, she had stopped looking for her long ago, realising that she couldn't recall even one single cause that she'd so vehemently screamed and writhed about while being carted away. Mortgages, bills and the responsibility of raising a family will do that to a person, she had decided – point-blank refusing to accept that the sexual assault she had suffered eight years before had anything to do with it. *Why give the bastard the satisfaction?*

She looked across at her husband, his focus on the road as he drove. John was a saint. He had unquestioningly accepted Nathan as his own when her own moral dilemmas wouldn't let her abort following the rape, and since doctors had told her years before that it would be unlikely that she could bear children, she saw Nathan as a miracle gift that healed all of the trauma. She sometimes secretly regretted having adopted Caleb. There just wasn't the connection she had hoped for. Not that she wasn't a doting parent to him. But after she'd fallen pregnant and given birth to Nathan, she finally understood what it was to be a mother, despite the horrendous circumstances surrounding the assault. If it had not been for her sister, Annie, the adoption of Caleb would never have happened in the first place. Annie had been in the process of adopting the abandoned baby herself, but when her husband, Frank, fell seriously ill, making it impossible, it was decided that she and John would take Caleb on instead to fill the childless hole in their lives.

Jen flicked the sun visor back up and looked across at John again, his eyes still fixed reliably on the road ahead. He was even more handsome now than when they'd first met. She half turned in her seat towards him and smiled contentedly, completely letting go of all those self-conscious thoughts she'd been having over those last few moments. She truly was a lucky woman. *I couldn't have wished for a better—*

Suddenly she saw John's hands tighten on the steering wheel, his jaw dropping and face contorting. Quickly turning to look ahead to follow his stare, she screamed at the glare of oncoming headlights and in an automatic maternal response motioned to position her body across the gap between the front seats in a futile attempt to protect her children. Time decelerated to a frame-by-frame view of events, the imminent peril warping her perceptions. And in the drawn-out seconds before the truck hit, she found herself dumbstruck and looking at the figure of a naked man sitting in the seat where young Nathan should have been. Their eyes locked. She somehow recognised the piercing blue eyes, the unblemished skin and the straight jet-black hair. The man looked calmly back into her eyes, his left hand reaching across to the buckle of Caleb's seat belt… The flow of Time resumed. And with a flick of his wrist, the belt began recoiling back into its mounting. Jen blinked away her disbelief, and on opening her eyes again, young Nathan was back in the rear seat, staring at her, wide-eyed and naked. Both brothers were now unsecured inside the vehicle and at the mercy of the terrifying forces about to hit.

*

In simultaneous moments of the Here and Now, Hugh drew a deep breath and gathered his focus from out of the rapidly dissipating ethereal haze that was clouding his mind, and looking down, he gazed upon the fruits of his latest efforts. The genealogical scrawling towards the bottom of the page again ended with the names *Nathan* and *Caleb* with the word *KILL* written in between: *Nathan... KILL... Caleb*.

Hugh dropped the pen. Behind him, the translucent flicker of the discarnate light body of Sir Oliver Lodge had once again guided his hand before vanishing back into the Void.

At the zero-point interface of consciousness, the once blazing maelstrom of erupting primordial energetic activity had been reduced to a mere spattering of subatomic particles that lingered, in a final vestige moment, before vanishing in an instant of annihilation, along with Time itself, leaving only an expansive silent vacuum of nothingness. *The Void...* Hugh and Isaac had been vindicated. In Nathan offering his very existence as sacrifice and ending Caleb's life, both of their potential histories had been erased. It was the only way to save the ones he loved from the rape, torture and murder that awaited if he were to have survived the car crash and lived. Current Reality – the one he had mistakenly thought of as so *real* – had been altered just enough that a catastrophic change to the destiny and freedom of countless souls could be averted.

56

Dr Nathan Carter was sitting at a desk in a side office gazing intently at the open wallet in his hand, his piercing blue eyes fixed on a small photograph of himself and his parents in a staged pose of happy family smiles, when a familiar voice from the doorway redirected his attention.

"You still here, you crazy bastard? It's already gone nine. Shouldn't you have finished by now?"

Adam was leaning leisurely against the doorjamb.

"I'd seriously be thinking of getting outta here before the shit hits the fan. It's way too quiet for my liking!"

Nathan closed his wallet and gave a friendly nod. "Hey, Adam. I'm almost done," he replied. "A patient's just been shown into 3. I thought I'd just check it out before I go."

"*Aaaah*, yes, the little cutie in Cubicle 3." Adam gave a closed-mouth smile. "I'll admit that I couldn't help but check out *her* chart as I walked past. I'm on it. Get outta here, Nathan. I'll catch you tomorrow."

"It's OK, Adam. I'll do it. The rain's torrential. I figured I'd hang around until it stops anyway."

"Your call," Adam answered, as he walked off down the corridor. "Don't say that I didn't warn you!"

Nathan made his way over to the main treatment area and grabbed the paperwork hanging outside the cubicle as he swished the curtains aside. '*Mia Kerr*', it read. The twenty-something Eurasian girl with fresh-faced good looks sitting on the edge of the mattress was possibly the prettiest girl he'd ever laid eyes on. Adam hadn't been wrong.

"Hi, I'm Dr Nathan Carter. I'll be taking care of you this evening. You've twisted your left ankle quite badly, I believe," he opened with his well-versed professional banter.

"Yes. I can be a little clumsy at times," Mia replied. "I've always got some scrape or bruise. This time, I tripped down the stairs at my apartment complex. It's so swollen. I'm worried I might have broken it."

Nathan knelt down to take an initial look. "Can you put any weight on it?"

"Not really."

"If you can hitch yourself further onto the bed and lie back, I'll—"

Mia had already started to comply before Nathan had fully finished his sentence, and her right foot connected squarely with his face.

"Oh! I'm so sorry," she apologised, sitting forwards. "See what I mean about being clumsy."

Nathan held his face, checking the bony margins of his nose with the tips of his fingers. "It's OK. I'm fine… Accidents happen," he replied in a muffled tone from behind his hands.

Mia moved closer. "What on earth did you do there?" she asked on noticing the long faint scar across his right cheek, instinctively reaching out.

Nathan had never felt such a soft caress as the girl unexpectedly touched his face. Their eyes met in a moment filled with tension before both of them remembered themselves and where they were.

"Car crash when I was a child," Nathan answered, summarising a lifetime of hurt in a sentence.

"I hope everyone else was OK?"

Nathan gave a forced smile but didn't answer.

"Let's examine your ankle. I'll organise some radiographs considering the extent of the swelling. But I'm pretty sure with a bandage and some pain relievers you'll be on your way."

Outside of the cubicle, behind the curtaining, A&E suddenly came alive with activity, and Adam's commanding voice could be heard barking out orders as a naked middle-aged man in cardiac arrest was wheeled in with burns to his torso.

And across the city, outside an old derelict Hall, another naked man with identical burns had just been found lying unconscious in a car park. But this time it was not Hugh Wells crossing the Void… Caleb was seeking revenge.

This book is printed on paper from sustainable sources managed under the Forest Stewardship Council (FSC) scheme.

It has been printed in the UK to reduce transportation miles and their impact upon the environment.

For every new title that Troubador publishes, we plant a tree to offset CO_2, partnering with the More Trees scheme.

MORE TREES
LET'S PLANT A BILLION TREES

For more about how Troubador offsets its environmental impact, see www.troubador.co.uk/sustainability-and-community